PRAISE FOR GIVE US THIS DAY:

"The go-to guy for pure thriller reading pleasure, Tom Avitabile delivers with every word."
– *New York Times* bestselling author John Lescroart

"Tom Avitabile writes with verve and velocity in his terrific thriller. *Give Us This Day* presents FBI female vet Brooke Burrell, who's kind of a post-modern though equally jaded Clarice Starling. Little does she know that her cushy, quasi-retirement is about to be interrupted by a villain as fiendish as Hannibal Lecter, though on a global level. Give yourself only this day to read it, because that's all you're going to need."
– Jon Land, *USA Today* bestselling author of the Caitlin Strong series

"Avitabile masterfully navigates one killer of a thrill ride within a cautionary tale of global proportions . . . and in Brooke Burrell exhibits a remarkable grasp of the female psyche."
– Olivia Rupprecht, bestselling author of *There Will Be Killing*

"In *Give Us This Day*, Tom Avitabile has created another action-packed thriller that offers a diverse and likable cast of characters, a diabolical villain, and a remarkable doomsday scenario that will both frighten and amaze the reader. Avitabile is a master storyteller who keeps getting better and better.
– Joseph Badal, Tony Hillerman Award Winner of *Ultimate Betrayal*

FORGIVE US OUR TRESPASSES

TOM AVITABILE

This is a work of fiction. Names, characters, places, and incidents either are the product of the author's imagination or are used fictitiously. Any resemblance to actual events, locales, organizations, or persons living or dead is entirely coincidental and beyond the intent of either the author or the publisher.

Studio Digital CT, LLC
P.O. Box 4331
Stamford, CT 06907

Story Plant Paperback ISBN-13: 978-1-61188-322-0
Fiction Studio Books E-book ISBN-13: 978-1-945839-62-7

Visit our website at www.TheStoryPlant.com
Visit the author's website at www.TomAvitabile.com

First Story Plant paperback printing: February 2022
Printed in the United States of America

To my brother Joe Campo, the first "character" I ever met, who is now, I am sure, cracking up every angel he meets.

To my niece, Sue Campo, who left us too soon.

To Anthony Lombardo, Retired First Grade Detective NYPD, a dear friend and contributor to my work, whose entire life and career redefined "meritorious." You'll see Anthony standing next to Saint Peter staring down the wise guys and letting them know he'll be watching them.

And to the 13 members of our U.S. armed services who joined a long list of men and women dating back to the Revolutionary War, who have become the currency by which the cost of freedom is paid.

PROLOGUE

One year ago ...

Federal Agent Brooke Burrell was out for blood. Crouched low, with her sidearm in both hands, hunting her prey as she darted between the maze of cars stalled on the city-bound lanes of the Manhattan Bridge. Her bruised ribs, under her nearly perforated Kevlar vest, complained with almost every footfall.

All the while her eyes were locked on the blue-and-white ambulance commandeered by the son of a bitch who shot her. He had killed so many while almost destroying New York City in a terrorist attack. The murderous bastard wasn't going to escape this time.

f

In the driver's seat of the ambulance, Paul Grundig was frustrated with the traffic. Then he heard something over the unit's police band scanner that made him rethink his plan to get to the Wall Street heliport, which was his back-up escape point. There, he had a helicopter waiting to take him to Teterboro Airport and his chartered jet standing by to fly him to Turks and Cacaos and a new identity.

The radio squawked, "All units, the federal authorities have closed the Manhattan Bridge in pursuit of an ambulance believed to have suspects fleeing the attack on Big Allis. All non-assigned units are ordered to converge on the bridge."

Paul looked around. So far, no cops were charging the ambulance, but that wouldn't last long. He looked in the back at Girbram. He was lying on a gurney, having taken a slug in the leg. He would only slow Paul down.

"What are we going to do?" Girbram asked.

"We?" Paul said as he put the barrel of his gun on the sheet over Girbram's heart and fired.

Paul went out the driver's side of the rig and looked for a way off the bridge.

f

Brooke saw him get out. She was hidden from his view by the back of the ambulance. She stepped lightly with her gun pointed straight up. People in the cars around her ducked, some mesmerized. Some idiot beeped his horn.

f

Paul instinctively turned in the direction of the beep and caught a glimpse of someone moving between the cars to his rear. He ran towards the middle of the span.

f

Keeping low, Brooke followed him from the far side of the cars. When she peeked over the hood of a car, Paul had disappeared. She stood and scanned the area but saw no sign of him among the people who got out of their cars to see why the traffic was at a standstill. She ran over to the edge of the roadway and up ahead saw Paul climbing down the slanted girders of the bridge. Smaller lattice-like straps of steel across the girders made for a simple ladder of sorts.

Brooke closed her eyes. For a second, she considered just calling it in and letting the cops handle this, but a sociopathic killer like Paul would not give up, and he'd use the people in the cars as human shields at some point, and maybe get away. Then she thought about all the death and pain this son of a bitch had caused, and before she had a chance to stop herself, she had holstered her gun and was over the side and climbing down, fitting her foot into the latticework while holding onto the grimy girders.

f

Paul jumped the last few feet from the girder down onto the pedestrian walkway. The M train rumbled down the middle of the bridge that carried the subway line, as well as cars, between Brooklyn and Manhattan. Paul looked back and, seeing the woman's arms and hands holding onto the steel cross-girders as she descended, took a shot at her.

f

The bullet hit the beam and shattered in front of Brooke. She slipped and fell the last five feet to the ground. It knocked the wind out of her for a moment. Her vest took the brunt of the red-hot, scattered lead, but a fragment pierced the fleshy part of her left arm. Her sleeve became wet with blood, but it wasn't too deep. She groaned as she shook away the pain and unsteadily got herself up. A runner who was jogging by stopped to help her.

"Thank you. But take cover. Get everybody down." She pulled her US Treasury windbreaker aside, flashing her tin clipped to her belt. "I'm a cop, and there's a guy with a gun up ahead. Get everyone down."

Another shot rang out and skidded across the concrete of the walkway. There were only a few pedestrians on the walkway. The jogger crouched low and yelled at those who were walking to get down.

The wide-open walkway provided no cover for Brooke. The cyclone fence that separated the walkway from the train tracks had many pad locked service gates, one was a few feet from her. She took out her gun, aimed, turned her head and fired three times at the lock.

With great pain shooting through her, she kicked the gate, and the perforated and mangled lock gave way. The gate swung open and she got out of Paul's line of fire as a bullet whipped by where she had been standing a split second before. The long chain-linked fence between her and Paul offered a small amount of cover. He couldn't get off a clean shot through the chain link from an angle.

f

From the cockpit of his news and traffic helicopter directly above the bridge, pilot and traffic reporter, Tom Colletti, called out over the NYPD radio frequency. "The woman, er ..." He tried to remember the code name she identified herself with. "... Stiletto! Stiletto is pinned down in a gun fight right below me, in the middle of the Manhattan Bridge. She needs help." He didn't notice the red indicator light still flashing above the "recording" button of the copter's high-resolution gimbal-ball-mounted camera.

f

Paul couldn't get a clear shot through the wire of the fencing at the shallow angle, so at the next gate he also shot the lock off. Once inside the subway's right-of-way he advanced along the trackside towards Brooke's position.

Brooke was taking cover behind a tool shed alongside the tracks. As she peeked around the corner, a shot ricocheted off the edge of the structure. Instinctively, she groaned and fell against the shed as if she were hit.

f

Paul saw her get hit and stepped up his pace. With his gun stretched out in both hands, he carefully approached the shed that Brooke had used for cover. He was four feet from the side of it when she suddenly rolled out on the floor and fired as soon as she cleared the shed. Paul couldn't drop his weapon fast enough to take a good bead on her on the ground and his bullet angled over Brooke's head. But Brooke's shot was also a little off the mark. Instead of being dead from a solid hit, center mass, Paul grabbed his side.

"Drop the gun!" Brooke yelled over the loud buffeting sound of the helicopter directly overhead. "Drop the gun or I will drop you where you stand." She struggled to her feet in three separate painful moves, while keeping the gun shakily trained on his heart.

"Okay ... Okay." He dropped the gun. "You know, we can still make a deal."

Brooke's blood began to boil. "How much? A million?" She fired into his leg, and he fell back onto the tracks. "A million for Nigel? Or two million for Charlene Logan?" She fired into his other leg. "Make it three million for Cynthia." She fired again into his thigh. "Or make it five"—she fired again into his other thigh—"for my staff—the nineteen people, mothers and fathers that will never go home again."

She saw Paul was in agony. But couldn't see the small .32 caliber pistol he was hiding under his body which was aimed at her, from the hip, so to speak.

With the chopper above, neither heard it, but she caught it out of the corner of her eye. It was a silver blur for a split second, then the speeding M train slammed into Paul just as he got a shot off. Brooke averted her eyes from the moment of impact. When she opened them a second later, she said, "And that was for Joe Garrison." The man that Paul had pushed to his death under the wheels of the Lexington Avenue subway train, starting this whole nightmare.

Then, as though she had just seen something she couldn't make out, she tilted her head sideways. The look on her face was one of someone trying to remember what she had just been thinking. Then she coughed. Blood trickled down from her lips. Her last conscious thought was of her husband and the child she was hoping they'd have but would now never hold.

A cry escaped her lips and she collapsed.

Three days later ...

At New York Presbyterian Hospital, Nurse Phyllis Pasquarella was holding up her iPhone and showing her day-shift replacement the most impressive selfie that she'd ever taken. It was of her and the president of the United States standing right next to her at her station on the fifteenth floor. Both women's eyes were wide in excitement as the very man she had stood next to in the picture was now on the TV addressing the nation.

A tall navy officer interrupted, "Excuse me ..."

One look and Phyllis said, "Room 1501, first room on your right."

f

He didn't expect the trepidation and fear that hit him the moment he saw her, in this room, in the bed, hooked up to all manner of machines. His eyes moistened. She was sleeping. There were IVs in her arm and a soft plastic oxygen cannula under her nose.

The navy man looked down to see the Medal of Freedom pinned to her blanket. It had been awarded to her personally by his and her "boss," president of the United States, James Mitchell, who'd been there an hour earlier. He was sorry he'd missed the moment, but his thirteen-hour flight from Diego Garcia had fought head winds over the Pacific. He was also delayed by a Pacific squall that prevented him from leaving his submarine for the first twenty-four hours after he found out his wife was wounded leading the counterattack against the terrorists.

Now, with just the two of them in the room, Commander Brett "Mush" Morton, captain of the USS *Nebraska*, leaned over and kissed his wife's forehead, smoothing back her hair gently with the tips of his trembling fingers, trying not to disturb her.

The doctors had told him over the phone that she wasn't even aware of the bullet that nicked her femoral artery in the gunfight on the bridge. *Adrenaline*, he thought. Then he thanked God that the first SWAT cop on the scene was a former military medic and immediately stemmed the rapidly fatal loss of blood that a femoral injury normally brings about.

The beeping of the respiratory monitors punctuated the low sound of the TV as the president, now speaking at the memorial service for those who died in the attack on New York, continued on his theme about courage ... about her.

He put his hand on hers. He felt the surgical tape from the PICC IV needle in her arm under his fingers. The president finished his remarks and a lone bugle played "Taps." Even with the TV behind him, Mush could hear it echoing off the buildings across the way from City Hall.

Her lips were dry and parched. He poured some water into a cup and, with his finger, lightly moistened her lips. She stirred. Brooke's eyebrows raised, then her eyes half opened.

He smiled and said softly, "Hi, babe. You had us all worried here."

It took a second for her eyes to focus, but then she closed them again as a broad grin covered her sleepy face. "Mush, you're home!" she managed through a breathy sigh.

"For good. I'm going to take care of you. Be there for you. Be there for our family."

She hitched her head in a gesture for him to come closer.

He leaned in, kissing her on her cheek.

She swallowed dryly then said in a weak voice, "We'll have ... have to work on that ..."

CHAPTER 1

EVERY PASSENGER fumbled to grab their armrests as the giant, hi-tech Boeing 787 Dreamliner, cruising at 33,000 feet over the Pacific, suddenly made a gut-wrenching lurch to the left. Everyone screamed and was terrorized. Everyone except the man in 33A who already had a grip on his open laptop ... and a smile on his face.

f

Six miles below, the plane was a mere dot in the cobalt-blue Oahu, Hawaii sky as Brooke Burrell-Morton looked at her watch then blew her whistle. "Good go-round! Okay, hit the showers. Remember, everybody's here at 1 p.m. tomorrow to drill before the game."

Her girls collected the soccer balls and brought them to the team's equipment manager, Jenny Kupalli, who stuffed the duffle bag and dragged it behind her as she walked off the field, slump shouldered.

Outside the locker room, Brooke waited for the teenage girl to head to class. "Jenny, may I have a word with you?"

"Yes, coach?"

Brooke didn't like this new bruise over her left cheek. She decided not to comment on it but instead asked, "Do you have a dog?"

That confused the high school junior. "Uh, no."

"I just wanted to make sure because you've been moping around school and practice today like somebody ran over your puppy."

Brooke tilted her head down and to the left to catch Jenny's averted eyes. Even though she ended the question with a lilt and smile, the girl seemed to shrink and said in a weak tone, "Sorry, coach," and walked away.

Brooke's coaxing smile dissolved to tight-lipped concern as she watched the young woman fade into the packed hallway of students returning to afternoon classes after the Friday break period. Her phone vibrated.

Brooke waited until she was in her office in the athletic department before she even looked at the phone. Long ago she had decided to be a quiet example to the device-addicted students by not being tied to her smartphone. She consciously avoided using it in the hallways or classrooms of Pearl Harbor High. Besides, it was probably her husband, Mush, just letting her know he'd be home *regular time today*. Just like most every other day since he got promoted to rear admiral.

f

Brent "Mush" Morton did his best to let his wife, Brooke, know he was okay with driving a regulation navy desk rather than the 5.7 billion-dollar USS *Nebraska*, a fleet missile boat, in which he had been tooling around in, and under, the Indian Ocean, when he first "picked her up"... literally.

She didn't have to try as hard to show him that she was good with their new married life together, embracing the vastly spun-down pace of *not* being a lead agent or director of a federal law enforcement agency. For Brooke this wasn't hard. She was so ready for married life.

The bump pushing at the waistline of the PHHS tracksuit that she wore when she coached was proof that she was on her way. She looked down at the phone, expecting to see "Mush" listed as the last call. "Uh oh," was all that escaped her lips.

Brooke had faced down terrorists, been shot by bad guys, and outwitted homicidal maniacs, but a message from her baby doctor sent fear rippling through her body. That was because she half expected the universe to play a trick on her.

After all, it had been her job. She had vowed to protect and defend the constitution. In the line of duty, she was called on, or forced, to do things that contradicted her beliefs. She had the "warriors dilemma." The contradiction that killing the enemy was still violating the ten commandments. There was no "But!" addendum to "Thou shall not kill." No asterisk denoting: "* *except for enemies of your country*." Yet she, and everyone else who ever took a life in the name of the greater good, hoped there was that special exemption for "bad dudes" who would kill millions if not stopped. But she figured there wasn't, that her duty to her country put a black mark on her eternal soul. Therefore, her pregnancy had an evil specter over it. It was foreboding, and she was half-expecting her "bad" karma to be returned to her in some horrible event preventing her from bringing her baby to term.

Then she relaxed and said, "Hello, hormones. You've had your fun, now go away."

f

Brooke was relieved. The call from her OBGYN was just to let her know her iron levels were a little lower than they'd like. Her obstetrician recommended an over-the-counter iron supplement to boost the levels.

CHAPTER 2

THE OPULENT, all-glass, I.M. Pei-inspired UniDynamics main office in Oahu was the posterchild of garage-born digital startups—gone monster. The parking lot was full of higher-end vehicles. There wasn't an expensive ride that was over three years old in the entire lot. It made her wonder, *Does the janitor park out back or is that his Mercedes 300 on the end?*

One thing was certain: the Rolls-Royce Sweeptail parked nearest the main entrance in a spot separated from the others had to be the personal transportation of the twenty-eight-year-old surfer dude, Brian "Duke" Sterling, who came up with algorithms. Algorithms for everything from phone companies, to military radar, to aerospace.

Right alongside the multimillion-dollar set of British wheels sat a pristine 1930s Ford wagon, with actual wood along the sides. It had no back seat, and three brightly colored surfboards stuck out from where the rear window should be. It was the "escape pod" for the billionaire who was so addicted to surfing that he celebrated making his first one hundred million by moving his company, lock, stock and barrel, to the land of Diamond Head. Ostensibly, so that he could catch a wave between billion-dollar contracts.

At 5 p.m. Brooke waited outside by the vinyl wrapped to a satin-blue, BMW 850 in the spot with the name T. Kupalli on the concrete parking baluster. She had learned that Jenny's father, Tua Kupalli, was a superstar programmer for the company. She had also learned, through her old buddies at the FBI, that he had a minor criminal record, mostly for bar fights and, in one case, killing a neighbor's cat. But that kind of rap sheet was almost normal for most Hawaiian males who grew up in the coffee plantations of Kona. It was a hard life in this otherwise paradisiacal environment, and this breed of islanders lived by "survival-of-the-fittest" rules. The fact that he had an unusually high level of computer skills was his ticket out of that life.

Brooke knew she was sticking her nose in where it didn't belong, but Jenny's bruises and recalcitrance were sure signs of abuse. Maybe she could help her father if he noticed it too—or at least that was her "good angels" rationale as she saw him approach his car. He was shorter than she expected. Jenny was already five-nine. *Must be the mother*, she thought.

As he got closer, he removed his sunglasses and recognized her. "You're from Jenny's school?" He put his briefcase in the car.

That surprised Brooke. She had never seen him before. "Yes, I'm Jenny's soccer coach. I was wondering if I could have a word with you?"

"About Jenny?"

"Yes. You see, I'm concerned."

He banged the top of his car. "Is there something she's screwing up at school?"

Brooke was thrown by his sudden rage. "No, no, not at all. But she has been somewhat despondent lately. I was wondering if you knew of any reason, pressures or issues at home?"

He looked her up and down, judging her. "What are you getting at, Miss ...?"

"Brooke, Mrs. Brooke Burrell-Morton."

"You're married? To a guy? Usually you phys-ed girls ..."

Brooke stepped in. "Usually what?"

He looked her up and down again. "Nothing. So what's your point?"

Brooke's years of police and investigative procedure kicked in and she reverted back to the persona she had when she carried a federal badge. "Look, Mr. Kupalli, by Hawaii state law, I am duty bound to report any suspicions to the authorities. But I know how that can destroy lives and careers." She looked over at the sleek edifice of UniDynamics main office.

"Are you threatening me?" Now he stepped in.

She modified her instinct to physically stiff-arm him and, instead, put her hand up in a "stop" gesture. "Hey, back off. I'm trying to give you a chance to fix this. Before ..."

"Before what, you skinny dyke?"

She put both her hands up, rather than putting her fist in his face. "Whoa, you are out of control. I can see this was a mistake." She shook it off and turned to walk away.

He called after her, "Your big mistake, girly. You forget all about this, you hear me?"

Brooke stopped, took a deep breath, and started towards her car. Then she thought about Jenny. Brooke had training, could floor this guy in seven different ways and slap the cuffs on him before he took his next breath—if she still had cuffs—but Jenny could only put up her hands to cover her face and take it. She about-faced, marched up and got into his. "Are you beating your daughter? Does that make you feel like you're in charge? Things suck at work? Taking it out on Jenny?"

"Fuck you, cunt!" He punched the side of his BMW and actually dented the door. "You stay away from me and Jenny or ..."

Brooke decided to dip into her past life and training. She got big. It was how she was trained to confront and *not* run from threats. "Or what? Are you threatening me? You giving me a reason to get a restraining order against you? You know what? Forget you. I'm going to report you to the school board, child services, and, I'm sure, your probation officer."

All 260 pounds of Tau Kupalli lunged at her. Brooke deftly deflected him, and he fell, smashing his head into the side of his already dented door. He fell onto the ground, down and out for the count.

A crowd of UD employees had formed, attracted by the yelling and the altercation. Most of them were in shock. Brooke used her command voice. "Someone call the police. I'll need some of you who saw this as witnesses."

A six-foot-four bald-headed man threaded through the crowd. "I'm Lawson, head of UniDynamics' security. Ma'am, please step away from Mr. Kupalli."

In a plain and declarative voice, free from excitement or exertion, she informed him that, "He attacked me. And then he fell."

"Please step away," he said as he helped a groggy Kupalli to his feet. "You okay, Mr. K? Do you want to press charges?"

"Him press charges? He attacked me." She looked up. The crowd was walking away. Quickly the reality hit her: they were all afraid for their jobs. This creep, Kupalli, must be a big kahuna here in the surfer's kingdom. Then she flashed on who *she* was now. An admiral's wife, in an altercation with a "kanaka maoli" ... A *white* admiral's wife at that. This could not end well. She turned to the corporate cop. "Do you care to take my name?"

"He's not pressing charges, so why don't you just leave the property."

Against everything she believed, all she had been in her previous life, and the justice she fought for all her career, Brooke surprised herself and decided to just walk away. Her rationale was that this Kupalli thug wasn't long for civilized society. He'd bring attention to himself again. She just hoped it wouldn't be by murdering his daughter.

f

The usual, *"So how was your day, dear?"* dinner conversation at the Burrell-Morton home was decidedly more colorful than most nights. She told him of her suspicions and confrontation with Kupalli.

Mush put down his fork. "No! He went for you?"

"The idiot was off balance and too low."

He shook his head as he chuckled. "A guy twice your weight comes at you, and all you can do is critique his attack posture?"

"Mush, this guy is a classic enraged male. He wasn't acting, just reacting."

"Still, I think I'd like to have a chat with this tub of lard," Mush said, setting his jaw.

She reached across the table and grabbed his hand. "Oh, that's sweet, Admiral, but as much as I love you for wanting to defend me, save it for something that's a real threat. Anyone could see this jerk coming a mile away. Besides, I think Mr. Kupalli and I are never going to cross paths again."

"I don't know. That sounds pretty ominous. I mean, coming from you, an ex-operator with three service stars, three gunshot scars and secret commendations that no one will see for seventy-five years."

Brooke frowned. She knew Mush loved her for who she was now, and not for her exploits working for the president of the United States and the Quarterback Operations Group. She looked him in his eyes. "Honey, focus on the 'ex' part of ex-operator. I'm now very happy to be Mrs. Admiral Lady."

"Fair enough." He gently caressed her hand. "So how was the rest of your day, dear?" he said as he placed smile "number 3" on his face.

"Well, after that brief encounter, I went to Ewa Beach and sat and looked at the water and put everything into perspective. And it worked. I've decided that if I see any further signs of abuse, I'll go through proper channels. But between you and me, I'd like to think that just by me confronting him, I'm letting him know that someone was watching him, and that might just alter his behavior."

"Let's hope so."

"Want dessert?"

"What do we got?"

"Fresh strawberries, and I think there's some vanilla ice cream left over from the weekend."

"Great, let's have it out on the lanai."

"Perfect," she said as they collected the plates and went into the kitchen.

Out on the lanai, Brooke set out the strawberries, ice cream and Brussels sprouts. Mush demurred from any mention of oddity, having already acceded to her new cravings. Instead he said, "I still think I want to go have a chat with Mr. Kupalli."

"That's sweet, but really, it was nothing. He's just out of control, and maybe I shouldn't have confronted him. It's just that when I saw Jenny ..."

"Your maternal instincts kicked in?"

"More and more lately." She worked the spoon into the frozen rock-hard ice cream.

"Here, let me ..." Mush took the spoon and the container.

"My hero!" she said with a sigh.

CHAPTER 3

THE NEXT morning as Brooke had the girls doing warmup drills before the game, she kept an eye out for Jenny. She forced herself to focus on the game. During time-outs she'd look over to the sidelines, but no Jenny.

Having coached the girls to a narrow win, Brooke's elation was tempered because she couldn't help worrying about Jenny. *Had the big slob taken out his anger with her on his daughter? Is the poor thing cowered in her room, or, worse, in an emergency room?* Her mind was full of guilt. She saw Gladys Goldstein in the stands. She was the school guidance counselor, and, as a great supporter of the school, always came to the games to cheer the girls on, even on a Saturday.

As they were leaving, Brooke made a point to catch up with her. "Gladys, got a minute?"

"Sure, Brooke. Nice game. It was touch and go there for a second."

Brooke nodded her head and added, "But that Shelly girl, she's got a sixth sense for where the ball is."

"I guess it's all about the goalie."

"Certainly, for defense ..." Brooke stopped walking.

Gladys noticed and also stopped. She walked back. She tilted her head.

"Gladys, Jenny Kupalli didn't show today. I'm concerned," Brooke said.

Gladys looked both ways and spoke in a lower voice. "Are you talking about what concerns me as well?"

"The bruises?" Brooke said.

"Yes."

"I confronted her dad and ..."

"Hold it. You did what? Brooke, we're just educators. That's the job of Child Services or the police."

"I know, but I thought I could reason with him, so I went to his work ..."

"What! You shouldn't do anything like that off of school property, Brooke. The union's jurisdiction, the school's insurance coverage and the state's legal coverage only applies to school grounds. You took a big risk, Brooke."

"Yes, I guess I'm new to all this."

"Look, abused kids are an epidemic around here. Too many drugs, too much sun. Hell, too much coffee. Whatever it is ... If we put our careers on the line for every child that is a victim of something, there wouldn't be enough teachers left for the rest of them. We have to let the authorities do their job and we'll do ours. If you want to fill out a TO-250 form, come to my office on Monday. I'm a notary, and we can get it processed the next day. Then you'll be out of it, Brooke."

At that moment, an Oahu police cruiser pulled up to them as they stood in the parking lot. Two female officers got out. They approached the two ladies.

Brooke had an immediate fear. *Oh my God, Jenny is dead!*

One of the cops checked her phone. She held it up. On it was a picture that somebody who had witnessed the entire altercation had taken of Brooke standing over Kupalli in the parking lot the day before. "Is this you?"

"Yes."

"Would you come with us, please?"

"What's this all about?"

"You are a person of interest in the murder of Tau Kupalli."

Gladys put her hands over her mouth.

"Is his daughter Jenny alright?" Brooke said.

"Please come with us, ma'am." The other cop opened the back door to the police car.

Brooke looked around. She was worried about how this looked, but because she and Gladys had stopped to talk, everyone else was already in the parking lot. As she was getting in, the cop put her hand above her head to guide her into the back cage of the cop car. Brooke turned to Gladys. "Call Jenny. Text me that she's okay."

Gladys nodded and hurried back to her office to pull Jenny's records.

f

On the way over, Brooke knew that trying to talk to these cops who were sent to get her was fruitless, so she just watched the Hawaiian landscape pass by as she tried to get her head around, *Kupalli murdered.* The cop didn't say the murder of Kupalli and his daughter, so that was a good sign. Then her cop mind went to the dark side. *Did Jenny do it? Finally lashing out? Was his fast-trigger temper to blame?* One thing she knew for sure: Jenny's life was changed forever.

She looked at her phone, hoping to get a message from Gladys that Jenny was alright. Then an odd notion came to her. It was her first time in the back of a police car. This unit was rigged for prisoner transport. It had a caged-in back seat, like a taxi, but with a hard plastic, one-piece back seat bench. *Easier to hose down vomit, blood, lice or spit,* she thought. She ran her finger along the rail used to cuff a prisoner to, and, given that she was just being driven to an interview, thought, *Like an Uber, only with restraint bars.*

CHAPTER 4

BROOKE WAS escorted to the lobby of a government building where a tall man, wearing a sharp-cut suit and perfect tan, extended his hand as he introduced himself. "Mrs. Morton? Kyle Simms, head of 5-0."

"Pleasure, Simms. Let's get to it," Brooke said as if she had been the one to call this meeting. It made him raise an eyebrow.

He extended his arm in the direction of the elevator. "Please." The well-mannered Simms let her enter first. He pressed the button for the top floor. She noticed the manicured hand. *Buffed, not polished.* She detected the faint smell of cigars. *Must have caught him coming back from a smoke break*, she imagined.

"To the right," he said as the elevator door opened. He pointed to the glass doors of a sunlit corner office. When they entered, he gestured to a small conference table opposite his very impressive desk. She noticed his "Love Me Wall." It was de rigueur for military officers. His was filled with photos and newspaper headlines in wood frames. There was a plaque on the wall: Operation Desert Storm. A framed picture showed a platoon of Rangers. From across the room, she couldn't make out which one of the younger men was Simms. A Ranger beret with a silver bar pinned to it was resting on the credenza. It told Brooke he had been a first lieutenant. Brooke took a seat.

"Coffee?" Simms said.

Brooke considered it, then her overactive bladder of late. "No thanks. Is Jenny Kupalli alright?"

"The daughter? Yes, she's with child services right now."

"Thank God. I was so worried when she didn't show for the game this morning."

"Mrs. Morton, you are here as a courtesy. I have an inkling of your former service to our country. So I wanted to give you every chance to tell me your side of the story."

"Courtesy? You send a unit, a cage unit? To my school! You could have just called me. I would have driven right over."

"I'm sorry, you know how this goes. I ask them to drive you over as a courtesy, and somehow they assign an RMP, not a detective's car. Sorry. Wasn't intentional."

Brooke wasn't buying it. She had used this technique to soften persons of interest the same way by putting a little police procedural fear into them before their conversation. "Are you considering me as a suspect?"

"Again, right now you are a POI. Nothing more."

"Let me ask you, are you recording, transcribing or in any way preserving our conversation today, Saturday at 2:03 p.m. at 5-0 headquarters?"

Simms smiled. If they were, and they weren't, she just made the whole practice inadmissible in court. "No. Kyle Simms, Deputy Director of Law Enforcement, HPD state police department," he said, clarifying his rank just to match her pseudo-official disclaimer.

His official response told Brooke that she didn't need a lawyer. Over the next ten minutes she read him in on her total encounter with Mr. Kupalli and her suspicions about Jenny's abuse.

He listened intently, scratching notes. When she paused, he waited. But she was not falling for the "fill-the-silence" ploy. So, he sat back, looked at her for a few seconds. She just looked back. It was a standoff.

He broke the stalemate. "And you had never met him before?"

"I don't believe he ever came to a game. Seems like the kind of guy who wouldn't cheer on an equipment manager."

Simms nodded. Then, as if he made a hard left turn, said, "Do you own a 9-mm handgun?"

Brooke sighed. Simms was going to go strictly by the book. "Yes. Glock 26."

"Do you know where it is now?"

"In the fingerprint safe by my bed."

"Would you be willing to voluntarily surrender the weapon for ballistic elimination?"

"For my protection, and yours, you'll need a warrant, hopefully limited in scope, Deputy Director. As I'm sure you're aware, my husband is a high-ranking naval officer. Poking around our home might violate his Fourth Amendment rights and no less than three national security protocols."

"Fair enough. Off record?"

Brooke shot him a look. Her defenses reared up. "Wasn't this all off record?"

"True, but this is more personal than professional."

"Okay. Shoot."

"That's what I'm asking you. Did you shoot this model citizen?"

That was an odd question to ask off the record, Brooke thought. "Nope. In fact, just the opposite. I had hoped that I put the fear of God into him. I believed he'd have second thoughts about smacking around his daughter now that he knew I had eyes on him. But a Skel like him, he must've pissed in someone's Cheerios somewhere along the way, and that's what probably contributed to him achieving room temperature last night."

f

Simms had to stop himself from smiling. Not because of Brooke's cop-bravado-laced answer, but because of meeting his objective. He drilled down for his most professional tone. "You're not planning to leave the island anytime soon, are you?"

"Not at all. It's the state semi-playoffs."

He closed his folder and slid his gold pen in his jacket pocket. "Got a good goalie there. Sticky hands," Simms said, referring to the secret weapon of Pearl Harbor High School's girls' soccer team, Shelly Bran, and her intuitive defensive skills.

"That we do, Deputy Director Simms."

f

The next morning, Brooke had just gotten over a mild case of morning sickness and decided to retrieve the mail from the end of her driveway. She wrapped a robe around herself and walked out barefoot. As she approached the mailbox, a base security jeep pulled up to her house, with an HPD unmarked car in tow. She immediately wished she had gotten dressed. She clutched the robe a little tighter.

Two HPD detectives, a man and a woman, had pulled the routine duty of serving a search warrant. "Are you Brooke Burrell-Morton?"

"Yes."

"Is this your primary place of residence?"

"Yes, it is."

The taller one showed the document to Brooke. She looked around, a little perturbed that they did this right here on the street, neighbors and all.

They walked by her to enter, but she turned and said, "Hold it, Detectives. Just give me a minute." She read the warrant carefully.

The two detectives looked at one another. The woman shrugged. "This is a new one, somebody actually reading the thing," she said in a low tone. Not that they had to, but they waited, mostly out of curiosity.

Brooke finished and looked up at the two of them. "My understanding from Simms was that this was a narrow writ concerning firearms. But this says weapons."

"That's what they handed me. You've already granted us access. You agreed with DD Simms to open your gun safe," the male detective said. "You can always challenge it in court if anything comes out of this. But for now, I'm going to have to ask you to stay outside the premises until we're done here."

"Look, guys, ya kinda caught me getting the mail here." She pointed out her robe, pajamas and bare feet. "I need to change if I'm going to be out of the house." She said that to the lady cop.

"Of course," he said, as he turned to his partner. "Jessica, will you escort Miss Burrell-Morton into the house and stay with her while she changes, and verify the contents of her safe."

Brooke knew they wouldn't let her back in the house alone until they searched it. Although she knew the search was coming, in fact insisted on it to clear her name, she expected it later in the day. As she led the lady cop to her bedroom and opened the safe, she couldn't help feeling out of place. Being the subject of a search and not the agent in charge of one. Still, with all her training and knowledge of police procedures, she had the nagging thought in the back of her head that she was missing something.

CHAPTER 5

THE PASSENGER who was in 33A, Waleed, who carried out the first successful test of the avionic systems hack on the Boeing 787, was now meeting with the rest of his cell in Penang, "the pearl of the orient," a geo-political aberration run by the Chinese in the otherwise Muslim country of Malaysia. Due to the nature of the cell structure, neither he nor any of the members of his immediate group knew who they were working for, much less where the control of their cell resided. All they knew was they were picked for the "great cause" because of their sworn-to-death adherence to its tenets and beliefs. For his part, Waleed was grateful to have been chosen for this. He had watched from the sidelines as many others valiantly fought for the cause. Now fate and God had placed him in this group, led by his sister's husband, Hassam.

His brother-in-law, Hassam, knew of Waleed's devout calling and his hatred of the infidels. Waleed had undergone military training as an insurgent operative to be dropped behind enemy lines and inflict death and destruction. After his service, he took a job as a policeman—only to be fired from the ranks for being too violent. That made him the perfect weapon for The Cause. Perfect because, despite his skills and abilities, at five foot three and of diminutive stature, he was an unimposing figure. A slip of a person that no one would suspect of having the balls to swat a fly, much less an airliner out of the air. That allowed him to board many flights, pass many check points, and avoid much scrutiny as he test flew each version of the software, for each type of aircraft that he was tasked to test over the months.

Hassam gave him the credit that he was due in front of the entire cell. "Brother Waleed, your successful proof of concept for the last manufacturer has allowed us to move on to the next phase."

Waleed nodded. This was the end of months' worth of him flying to nowhere and back, just to activate a successful hack of different airliners in flight from the computer he was given. His flights were chosen by aircraft type, not destination. He was ordered to always choose a seat above the baggage compartment below, which was different in each type of plane.

In the other room, outside where they were meeting, was the "nursery," as he thought of it. There, a thousand laptops, all in shipping boxes, awaited their one-way journey. These machines were the tentacles by which the great creature of revenge would reach up to the skies and pluck their targets out of the air.

It had been a long road to get to this point, but now their moment of victory was close at hand.

The first part of the attack was the successful hack of Caravan.com, the new behemoth worldwide retail web site whose prices were guaranteed to beat their American super-site competitor. The middle-eastern startup grabbed global market share almost overnight with the ad campaign: "That's Amazin' ... No, that's Caravan!"

That hack of the massive Caravan site was a tremendous feat in and of itself. Now it was his cell that would activate the final part of the plan. The dissemination of the laptop shipping boxes with the "hacked" Caravan.com labels that, once scanned, would have them on a thousand planes at once next Thursday.

At exactly 1327 hours and 32 seconds Greenwich mean time, the auto programs would commence and automatically hack into the plane's guidance and control systems wherever they were over the earth. Part of the genius of the plan was finding the sweet spot in airline schedules where the one thousand planes, on which the laptops were shipped, would be at altitude at the same time. As a further requirement, none of the planes that would be over "Muslim" countries at that time were targeted.

The only thing that could stop them now was a leak, or discovery by some other means, of their operation. For that reason, the coder who managed to crack into the systems of Boeing, Airbus, and McDonnell Douglas, was recently eliminated. He was a non-believer, a digital mercenary who was only interested in money. Someone like that could easily betray them for more money, so he had applied a pressure no man who loved his family could resist. But still, even with this insurance policy, the Hawaiian man was not "of the cause" and had outlived his usefulness, and so did the "leverage" they used to insure his obedience. Waleed was honored to personally have severed those loose threads. It was the one time over these last months when he got on a plane and actually had a place to go and a mission that was more than scaring the living daylights out of airline passengers.

CHAPTER 6

BROOKE'S MONDAY morning routine was to post the practice schedules for the week, and arrange for busses and cheerleader squad logistics. Since she started at the school, she used her experience as the head of investigations as well as organizer of personnel and resources to "tighten up the ship," as Mush would say. To make the soccer team, and to a lesser extent the entire Phys. Ed. Department by extension, into a smoother-running operation. She had won the support of Mr. Garofalo, the department head. He was all too happy to let this "eager beaver" have a shot at more efficiency.

Brooke looked around her "new" office. She had a chuckle to herself when she realized that she too had a "Love Me Wall." Only hers wasn't filled with mementos of military postings or missions she had survived. Instead, there were a few keepsakes from her own high school sports and academic career.

Back then she was the "tomboy" who was out to prove she could whip any boy—and often did. Until she realized, at a certain age, that the boys "brawned up" enough to overpower her. From that point on she decided that since she couldn't outrun, out-jump or outplay them, she'd simply *outsmart* them.

Later, her big moment of epiphany came once she realized that it wasn't a competition at all, but a partnership, with each bringing their own unique strengths to the mix. That was the beginning of her "Plays Well with Others" demeanor that shot her up to the top ranks of the FBI and then the president's top-secret operations cluster out of the White House and, most recently, a directorship of a government agency. *A field promotion,* she mused to herself, recalling the unique way that she was hired. Harold Barnes, the director of FinCEN, landed in a helicopter right on the soccer field to cajole her into coming back to government service. He flew in from his Washington office at the US Treasury and then by chopper because the matter was so urgent. She held out until she got the same salary and power as he had. That negotiation only worked because she didn't want to go back in the first place. That was until he made an offer that *she* couldn't refuse ... especially the money, which would be a big help with the family she was in Hawaii to start.

f

This Monday she went through her routine while still a little queasy from an intense bout with morning sickness, and without Jenny, who was excused from school over the death of her father. Brooke needed to appoint a new equipment manager. Brooke was about to head to Susan Marsh's home room to ask her if she'd like to be the new EM for the team, when the principal, Rona Epstein, walked through the door with two detectives.

"Brooke, I'm so sorry," Rona said as she stepped aside, letting the officers pass her.

"Brooke Burrell-Morton?" one of them said.

"Yes."

"You are under arrest for the murder of Tau Kupalli."

"Rona, call my husband." She asked the cops, "Where am I being booked?"

"Main HPD."

"Rona, tell Brett now please."

"Of course. This is horrible." She left.

When she was sure Rona was out of earshot, Brooke turned to the cops. "Hey, fellas, a little professional courtesy here. Cuff me in front and let me put my team jacket over the bracelets. You know, the kids and all ... because when this is all found to be some kind of screw up, I need to come back here and still be their coach."

"You were on the job?" one of them asked.

"Navy JAG, FBI, then SAC New York, then special assignment White House, then Director CinFen US Treasury, my last posting ... in New York ... last year."

"Shit! You in the middle of the attack?"

"I was lead agent for all agencies. My team thwarted the brunt of it."

The two cops looked at one another. This was way above their paygrade.

"Guys, I understand you got a job to do. I'm just asking for a little blue consideration."

"Tell you what, just walk out with us. We'll cuff you and Mirandize you in the car."

"Thanks, fellas, I appreciate that."

"Sorry we got to do this, ma'am."

"No problem."

In the car they read her her rights. She of course knew the Miranda warning by heart, but the third line was where she mentally dropped out of the proceedings. *You have the right to an attorney* ... She wouldn't be needing that. She was a JAG in the navy and, because of her law degree, an FBI agent. This whole thing was obviously a misunderstanding.

f

Mush left his office as soon as he got the call from Brooke's principal. He dismissed his driver and drove his official vehicle himself. On the way, his mind reeled with what his wife must be going through. She had a stellar career as a law enforcement officer. Her file overflowed with commendations and notation for conspicuous bravery. She held the esteem of presidents and some of the biggest people in government, and now she was under arrest. Charged with murder! The thought forced him to put a death grip on the steering wheel. He made it to the police station as Brooke and the detectives pulled up. He ran over to the car. "Brooke, what's going on?"

"Brett, get out of here in that uniform. Come back in civvies."

"I don't care. What's this all about?"

"Admiral, sir. Please step back. We need to process the prisoner."

"That's my wife. A patriot and a law enforcement icon. She's not a prisoner."

f

Brooke had been in interrogation rooms a thousand times before, but this was the first time she'd sat on the other side of the table with her cuffs secured to a bar in the middle through a longer loop of chain.

The door opened and a young man in a suit entered. "Mrs. Morton?"

"Burrell-Morton," she said, correcting her name for the hundredth time.

"Yes, of course, apologies. I'm a public defender. James Chu. I've been reviewing the charges." He referred to the folder he had been given ten minutes prior.

She held up her hand. The chain rattled against the metal table. "I did not request, nor do I qualify for, a PD. I am *pro se* on this."

"Actually, I'm your standby attorney, by order of the judge."

"*Judicas protegens asinum*," she said, using a Latin term she didn't learn at Harvard Law.

"Wait, is that Latin? *Judicas protegens asinum* ... Judge covering his ass?"

"Protecting ..." Brooke corrected the "piggish" Latin she just employed.

"Yes. He has an aversion to reversible error," James said.

"There's only one error here. I didn't shoot anybody."

"Yes. That's obvious. But why would you say that? No one was shot."

"Wait." Brooke was confused. "Let me see those." She snatched the folder from his hand and read the charges in the complaint. She banged the table. "That sneaky son of a bitch!"

"Who?"

"Simms. He never told me Kupalli had his throat slashed. He led me to believe the vic was shot. Do you have the original warrant?"

"Er ... yes. Right ..." He pulled the file back towards him, but she snatched away the entire folder again.

She flipped through the pages referring to each as she recognized them: "302s. Motion for decreased bail ... Here it is. See. See right here." She underlined the sentence with her finger. "Weapons, not firearms! I knew there was something fishy."

"Excuse me, are you a lawyer?"

"Was. JAG Corps."

"Okay, all of what you said aside, they found a K-Bar knife in your garage."

"But forensics had to come up clean on it. A, I didn't kill anyone with it and, B, after gutting a fish, my husband usually soaks it in Clorox.

"Are you saying you are innocent of these charges?"

"How long have you been practicing?"

"A year."

"I'm innocent until proven guilty. You have heard of the Sixth Amendment. They still teach that in law school, right? But, more importantly, there's no proof here."

The door opened and Mush came in. Brooke was glad she convinced him to not wear his uniform to her arraignment.

She stood, as best she could with the chain, as he came to her and hugged her. "Are you okay?"

"I'm pissed, but I'm fine. This is crazy." She turned to Chu. "Could you give us the room?"

"Certainly. I'll knock when they come to get us," he said and left.

"Thank you." She looked into Mush's eyes.

"You're welcome. For what?" he said, his eyes locked in on hers.

"For not asking me if I killed him."

He hugged her again. "I know you. I know your heart. And right now, you're about creating life, not taking it."

"Since I was a kid, I always felt I was alone. Sure, I had close friends, family ... But I was always separate and apart from them. Never wanting to burden them with my fears, my nightmares or my hopes. But you, you've become part of me. It's such a great feeling to truly have a partner here inside ..." She held her manacled hand over her heart.

"A soulmate?"

"You know, I never liked that term. Thought it was all 'schoolgirl crush' speak. But yes, yes, you are part of my soul. God, I'm so lucky you asked me to marry you." She placed her hands on his chest and kissed him a long, long time.

There was knock at the door. They separated.

"Are you ready?" He wiped a tear from her cheek and kissed it off his finger.

"As long as you are with me, I'm ready for anything, my love." She collected herself and straightened her clothes.

She tuned to James Chu. "You know, James, maybe me appearing *pro se* was a little too aggressive. Can you find a 'notice of appearance' form?"

f

Ten minutes later, Brooke was standing at the defendant's table addressing the judge in her bail hearing. "Your Honor, I'm handing up a notice of appearance, signed by both myself and Mr. Chu, that I will not be acting as sole counsel, *pro se*, and that Mr. Chu will now serve as co-counsel."

The bailiff handed the judge the document. He placed on his cheaters and perused them for a few seconds, then removed the glasses. "Notice of appearance is accepted. I'm really happy, Mrs. Burrell-Morton, that you are exercising better judgment by not solely representing yourself in a capital murder case and giving Mr. Chu here a more active role."

Brooke then gestured to Chu to start. He cleared his throat. "Your Honor, Mrs. Burrell-Morton has a clean record plus a record of service to this nation beyond exemplary. Her husband is an admiral stationed here. She is not a flight risk. We ask that bail be waived."

The judge turned to the prosecutor. "Mr. Jensen, are you in agreement?"

"No, Your Honor. The people request the defendant be held without bail and remanded to custody. This was a brutal, vicious and cold-blooded murder. We have witnesses—"

"Save it for the trial, Counselor. I agree she is not a flight risk, and I also agree it's a grievous crime, so I'm going to set bail at $250,000." He banged the gavel.

Brooke was thrown by what the prosecutor was saying when the judge cut him off. *They have witnesses ... To what?*

f

Mush was able to cash in some of the savings bonds that he had received like clockwork from his father's savings plan through Navy Federal Credit while he was growing up. He only needed $25,000 or

10% to secure Brooke's bail from a bail bondsman across the street from the court. That was relatively easier than his next task.

f

The next morning, Mush sat across from the commander in chief, Pacific, and asked CINCPAC for a leave of absence.

His superior officer was sympathetic. "Mush, I understand. Take all the time you need. Off-load your duties to Steve and Graham."

"Thank you, sir. That's very accommodating of you."

The moment hung. CINCPAC's demeanor shifted, softened. "In the short time I've known your wife, I really admire her. This is a horrible miscarriage of justice."

Mush couldn't help feeling there was a "but" coming. He let the silence ask for him.

"Mush, this is delicate. Your career is stellar. Flag officers exist in a bubble ..."

Mush shut him down. "Sir, I'm fully prepared to resign my position as SUBCOMPAC and my commission if you feel I will bring disrespect to the flag."

The CINCPAC pushed back from the desk, he looked out the window. The USS *Enterprise* was steaming out with two carrier escorts abeam. He spoke without looking at Mush, "Been married 35 years, and to this day, I would sacrifice everything to defend and support my Phyllis." He took a deep breath and looked back to the Admiral, 20 years his junior, "Brett, we are, first, officers and gentlemen. And a gentleman never abandons a lady. You go. I'll deflect any flak."

With his boss's blessing, Mush knew his next confrontation wouldn't be as smooth.

f

"No way! Are you kidding? Mush, we're pregnant! With this hanging over my head, I'm on suspension from school. If you take leave, we won't have any money for when the baby comes!"

"Honey, it's not like the FBI. I'll keep getting paid. I already have over sixty days built up from my time being deployed on the

Nebraska. Plus, I get six weeks paid vacay. By then I'm sure this will all be straightened out." He placed his arms on her shoulders.

She looked up at him and felt the same tingle of command voltage coming from him as she did when he was the nuke sub skipper that plucked her out of the shark-infested Indian Ocean. It reassured her that he had this charted out, had set his course, and was all ahead flank. She found a warm comfort in that. She hugged him.

f

The next day it was Brooke giving the "orders" to James Chu. "Look, if you really want to help me, you'll get me all the disclosure and reports, forensics and eyewitness accounts today! Especially who these so-called witnesses are. And what exactly they witnessed."

"I was going to do that once I found pro-bono experts to review the evidence."

"James, I have been in law enforcement for fifteen years. JAG, FBI, CINFEN. I'm pretty much an expert myself. Just get me everything as soon as you can. You want to get experts? Knock yourself out, but I need to see everything. I have some favors I could tap."

Chu still hadn't figured out how to deal with this woman. She seemed to have a skillset that made his efforts moot.

CHAPTER 7

HIS ALTIMETER watch read 8,000 feet. The result of catching a pretty decent updraft. He banked left. The only sound was the rustle of the Poly-Fiber wing above as the wind rushed by his ears. The Shenandoah Valley stretched out before him as he glided like an eagle above the green canopy. He'd have to clear that outcropping of trees because you could really get hurt banging off branches and limbs on the way down. But 8K feet gave him lots of glide path. Looking straight down, he saw a deer at full gallop. The bucolic Disney-like vision of a running, frolicking deer quickly turned to a horror film as the bob cat pounced on the doe and started dinner. He turned away, focused on the horizon. His other watch lit up. On the screen of the Apple watch was Brooke's picture. He hadn't seen her for almost a year. He took one hand off the bar and pressed the watch. He yelled over the jetstream, "Brooke, nice to hear from you. Look, I'm hang-gliding right now ... Can I call you after I land?"

f

For some reason, Brooke yelled back as if it mattered. "Please. Be safe, Kronos."

Mush overheard her loud response. He entered the den. "Was that Kronos?"

"Yes. He's such a big kid. Close to forty and he's hang-gliding. Yet he answered his phone. He'll call back."

"You called him?"

"Yes. Maybe he knows Kupalli."

"One super geek to another?"

"Something like that. Besides, my best defense is to find out why Kupalli was killed, and Kronos can find your kindergarten picture on your Aunt Mary's Facebook page from fifteen years ago."

"Who else from your old gang could help us?"

"The Quarterback Operations Group is probably packed up and out of the White House already."

"So, you don't think the new president, Pearson, will keep it going?"

"Doubtful. President Mitchell was an independent. My guess is Pearson will adopt the shell of the idea but will fill it with his own people."

"I was going to make a smoothie. Want a strawberry sprout greenie?"

"Maybe later," Brooke said as she dabbed the cell phone on her cheek, deep in thought ...

It was back in her NY office at the FBI when her former boss, Joey Palumbo, approached her about joining Bill Hiccock's Special Operations Group down in the White House. He was all boy about it, beaming at the name—Quarterback Operations Group—because Hiccock had been a Heisman trophy-winning quarterback in college. That decision to join lead to her nearly being killed in the Indian Ocean, blown off a smuggler's ship only to be saved from being shark food by Mush in his submarine. He saved her life. And now she had a new life—together with him.

It also was where she first met Kronos, the eccentric technosapien, who had pulled digital miracles out of his sleeve over and over again. If there was anything nefarious that the computer genius, Kupalli, was up to, Kronos would find it.

f

Vincent "Kronos" DeMayo, former hacker for the mob and now the reigning US techno-warrior, called Brooke back as soon as he had his hang glider stowed in the bed of his Ram pickup. He had been with Brooke since the Quarterback Operations Group began. He had always liked her, not because she was a fox or really hot, but because she was cool. A cool professional, unphased by circumstances ... just like him. Brooke was cool with guns and people shooting at her and shit. His cool under fire was when the digits all had to make sense and the code ... the code had to be perfect the first time out. She was a natural and so was he.

When he heard her pick up the call on her end, he said, "Yo, Brooke, how's it going?"

"Thanks for calling back, Kronos. I got a situation here and I was wondering if you could help me."

"Not a question you ever have to ask, Brooke. Shoot."

Brooke brought Kronos up to speed on her plight.

When she finished, Kronos said, "Off the top of my head, I ain't heard of the guy. But let me do a little digging and I'll get back to ya."

Brooke knew that Kronos doing a "little digging" was really Kronos digging, and keeping on digging down, down, down, until he smelled Chinese food from a Beijing kitchen.

f

Mush was trying to adjust to being home three days a week. Which was a big adjustment from the five days at the office, which in itself was the biggest adjustment of all, from the eight-week, blue and gold crew rotation of the USS *Nebraska*'s nuclear deterrent patrol under fathoms of ocean. Being in command of a fleet ballistic submarine was the love of his life—until he met the actual love of his life. Now their love was making a baby. So he needed to ratchet down the thrills and adventure aspect of hiding under the frigid water, avoiding instant death by a Russian hunter-killer sub, for the more mundane duties of being captain of the house. Keeping it shipshape was now the order of the day, so he was looking for things to do around it. He decided to finally change one of the lights in the fixture above the foyer by the front door.

There was a knock on the door. He came down off the ladder and answered it. "Admiral Morton? I'm Detective Russell, HPD."

"Afternoon. What can I do for you?"

"Is your wife home?"

"ID?"

"Sure." He flashed his tin and creds.

"What's this about, Detective?"

"Actually, this is an unofficial visit. Mention James Mitchell to your wife. I'm sure she'll want to see me."

"That name also works with me. Come in. Can I get you something? We just made lemonade."

"Sound's great, thanks."

"She's out on the lanai. Through that door. I'll bring it out to you."

Russell found her on the chaise reading from her laptop. He noticed the strawberries and Brussels sprouts on the table and the slight baby bump. *Preggers,* he thought, *just like my daughter.* He introduced himself.

"Did the devious Deputy Director Simms send you?" Brooke said.

Devious? he noted to himself. "No, actually someone way above his pay grade."

"Bill Hiccock?" she asked the six-foot, fifty-something detective with grey-blue eyes beneath a forest of salt-and-pepper hair and a barely middle-aged-spread beltline.

"Don't know who that is."

Brooke took a wild guess, going for the top of the pay grade. "Did President Mitchell send you?"

"Not directly. The president and I were fighter jockeys in Iraq. He was my wingman, actually. If I knew Lt. Jimmy Mitchell would be the commander in chief one day, I would have re-upped. Anyway, when you relocated here, he called me—from the Oval Office. He asked me to keep an eye on you. And to be there if you ever needed anything."

f

Lately, being eighteen weeks pregnant, Brooke found herself more emotional than usual. She held back a rising cry that was erupting in her chest. She took a deep breath. Her emotions were now in check and she could speak without choking up. "Sometimes the president and his wife forget they didn't give birth to me."

"Well, if you ever decide to be adopted, you could do worse than Jim and Delores."

"Amen." She motioned for him to take a seat. She noticed he did it without the expected mild grunt from an older man.

"My daughter craves asparagus and peanut butter." He jutted his chin to the sprouts.

"How far along is she?"

"Ending her first trimester."

"Well, we'll probably meet each other at kindergarten registration in a few years."

That made him smile, but Russell just had to ask, "Devious? Simms?"

"He a friend of yours?"

"We're both vets on the force. We got a little social group of the guys on the job who served."

"Well, he's a real sweetheart."

"I know he held back all the details of Kupalli's murder from the press."

"Ya think? All I heard was Kupalli was murdered, then Simms plays a little bait and switch and leaves me wide open on the warrant, and that's how I'm currently enjoying the scarlet letter of attempted murderess."

"For what it's worth, that ain't Simms's MO. That's definitely a DA move. We're in an election year. A Haole mainlander killing a Kamaaina is a great way to get press."

Brooke knew Haole was an ethnic term for a white non-islander but tried to remember what the other word meant. "Kama'aina? Wait, I remember that ... Child of the island?"

"Close: 'child of the land.' Although Kupalli's not a Hawaiian, a Kanaka Maoli, he was born here. His family came here way back when to work the plantations."

"So, Simms was just following orders and I'm just a political prop?"

"One could read the situation like that and not be terribly wrong."

Mush came out and placed a lemonade in front of Russell. "Here ya go." He looked at Brooke. "Honey, want more?"

"No, I'm good. Wanna join us?"

"In a minute. I got to call the base. Graham called. Told him I'd call him right back." He turned to Russell. "Detective, did I overhear that you served with James Mitchell?"

"Two tours Iraqi Freedom. F/A 18 Death Rattlers."

"Legendary squadron. I'd love to talk to you about that."

"Any time, Admiral," Russell said.

Mush went back inside.

Brooke just noticed. "Weren't you a little tall for a fighter jockey?" She remembered that James Mitchell was the more classic height of 5'9".

"I did the 'Hard Ride.'"

"The what now?"

He held up his hand and spaced his thumb and forefinger roughly three inches apart. "I had my crew chief remove about three inches of foam from my seat. Made even a smooth landing a bit like jumping a horse in a steel saddle. Amazingly, there was no regulation on the books calling for a cushy tushy."

Brooke laughed. "I heard of flying by the seat of your pants, but never that one."

"Speaking of which, I hear you are going *pro se*."

"Not to worry. Plenty of cushion where I need it most,"

"You seem slim."

"Legal cushion. Got nearly fifteen years in as a lawyer in one form or another. Been in enough murder trials to bring back Perry Mason."

Russell got serious. "I looked at the murder charges and the reports. Now, I can't do anything against 'the job,' but if there's anything you need, here's my card. I'm off duty more than I'm on these days."

Brooke took his card. "Have you ever run into Kupalli?"

"Years back, when I was on patrol. He was known to not handle his liquor too well."

"Any idea who would want him dead?"

"Aside from his anger issues of late, the guy was a computer nerd as far as I can tell. He certainly wasn't the Casanova type, so I think we can rule out jealous husbands. His wife disappeared two years ago and was declared dead last year. So she's not a suspect. That leaves, wrong place wrong time?"

"That's usually the cause of death in New York, or Chicago, but here in paradise?" She raised her arms. "It doesn't seem to fit the palm trees and warm breezes."

"Don't let the travel brochures fool you. We get our share of nasty on a daily basis. Can I ask, purely unofficially, why you confronted him?"

"His daughter is on my soccer team at school. She showed signs of abuse. I confronted him to let him know I was watching. To think twice before he raised a hand to her again."

"That's when you hit him?"

"No. He disparaged parts of my female anatomy then lunged at me. I just deflected him."

"Into the side of his car, leaving a dent?"

"Actually, he made that depression in the door first when he punched the car trying to intimidate me."

"Son of a bitch."

"Yes, he was." Brooke leaned forward. "Wanna help me? Can you get me a copy of his LUDS and bank accounts?"

"Phone and bank records? I don't think so. That kind of crosses the line."

"Got it. And I respect that. So, I guess I'll call you if I need to get the neighbor's kid, Tommy, to stop playing drums past ten." She smiled to take the edge off the "thanks for nothing" offer.

"I'm sorry, got my pension and all. I'm in my pad years. I don't need to bring a departmental action on myself."

"Totally get it. How come you never went into commercial air?"

"Developed a faulty ticker. Not too serious, but enough to ground me, so I walked a beat and pin-balled up the ranks."

"How many years in?"

"The dirty thirty."

f

The following day was all quiet at the Burrell-Morton ponderosa. Mush was reading the paper when there was a rhythmic knock on the door. He identified the beat as the "Let's Go" rhythm they play at ball parks. Mush answered it. "Whoa, Kronos! How are you doing? What are you doing here?" They bro hugged.

"I haven't been to Hawaii in years and Brooke always said, 'anytime I wanted to come.'"

Mush wasn't buying it, but he was glad her old team member went active on Brooke's behalf.

"Well, come in, man. Let's get you some grub."

Kronos turned around and waved to the driver of his town car SUV. Soon there were three suitcases and two equipment roadie cases in the foyer.

Brooke came in and gave him a hug to beat all hugs. "What are you doing here?"

"I need to work on my bottom turn into the barrel."

Brooke was momentarily thrown, then remembered. "Oh yeah. Where's your surfboard, dude?"

"Did I forget that? I guess I'll have to borrow Mush's."

Her eyes sparkled. "It's good to see you, and thank you for coming. You're a true friend. Knowing you, you must be starved." She pecked him on the cheek and went to kitchen.

Kronos was in mild shock at the rare show of affection.

Mush picked up on his surprise and offered in a reassuring but low tone, "She's pregnant and feeling her emotions more."

"Cool. I can't wait to meet the superhuman-hero-baby you guys make."

Kronos looked around the two-story historic home nestled in the Hale Alii section of the base. It was a lovely old home, impeccably upkept, reflective of Mush's 08 rank. It featured a truly open living room with a dining area off to one side that seamlessly flowed into a lush green and flowery-edged lanai. The backyard beyond looked out over the water. A cozy bench stood on the grass at the threshold to the sands of the beach. Not enough waves for surfing, he noticed, but picturesque nonetheless. There were three bedrooms upstairs. He didn't know if they found the house appointed with all the touches that made it look like a family home, or whether it was Brooke's touch that elevated it above an officer's billet.

Although he would have been happy crashing in the little half bedroom and attached bath on the first floor, Brooke had given him a cozy bedroom with private bath on the opposite end of the house from her and Mush's. It was the classic American home for these two super-patriots to have the classic American baby.

Three hours and two extension cords later, Kronos was squared away and had transformed the dining room into computer central.

Brooke brought him an Arnold Palmer. "Here ya go. Half iced tea, half lemonade, Kronos." The luggage tag on the suitcase caught her eye. "First class! Swanky."

"I hack, remember."

"I don't think I want to know this."

"No, I guess you don't, so then I guess you'll really hate this. I just hacked into UniDynamics. So far, Kupalli wasn't working on anything that could invite death. I'll keep digging. Also, I hacked into the email of Brian Sterling, the CEO. I'm going to meet him and his friends at Diamond Head tomorrow morning."

"He agreed to that? Did you know him?"

"No, and he doesn't know I'll be there, yet."

Brooke just smiled.

CHAPTER 8

WALEED HAD been working part time at Caravan ever since he was selected for this operation last year. The failure of the attack on New York created a dire need to inflict harm on the great Satan and the evils of capitalism. This blow would rock their foundation. Destroy the very core of their worldwide nervous system.

In a short time, he became a trusted driver with a part-time route. More importantly, he was able to locate the favorite bar of Mo, the foreman at the distribution center.

An imam gave Waleed special dispensation to drink alcohol in fulfilling his mission. He actually hated it, so he made a practice of tipping the regular bartender very well to water down his glass. The man happily did so because Waleed would always buy rounds, ingratiating himself to the foreman and anyone else from the distribution center.

Also, in a trick his brother-in-law, Hassam, taught him, he would occasionally show up with rare perfumes or coats or jewelry and offer the foreman these items at a fraction of their price. He justified this discount by explaining that these items were from other truckers who claimed these items magically "fell off" their trucks. Of course, there were no other truckers. Waleed used the cell's money to purchase the expensive items.

The foreman liked the way his wife "thanked" him on those nights when he bore Waleed's presents.

Waleed genuinely grew to like Mo. He hoped that in the end their comradery would result in the foreman not being too nosey when the day came, otherwise Waleed would have to slit his throat.

His familiarity with the workers at the distribution center would make it easier to execute the simplest part of the plan. At twenty-eight hours before the attack, he would simply load the one thousand laptops in his Caravan box truck and drop them off at the processing center, the center being the main portal through which the hacked shipping labels and phony accounts would enter the distribution delivery system. The barcoded phony labels guaranteed that each package would be routed to a separate commercial flight in accordance with, and fulfilling, the vaunted RUSH—NEXT PLANE OUT DELIVERY promise to Caravan's elite customers.

They named this service Sultan's Express. It was an accommodation not available to the general public, but only to the high-net-worth individual customers of the gigantic global superstore. Caravan's chief investors being Dubai and the Emirates, this extravagant service was part of their culture. In a very short time, this immediate delivery service was a saving grace for movie stars, politicians, millionaires, and billionaires, who were the cream of the crop in society and needed whatever they ordered in a matter of hours, not days.

The real corporate reason for the existence of this on-demand Sultan's Express service was that those grateful influencers, having been given this perk, would surely become an asset of the company, and could be counted upon for support in government halls and public opinion whenever a company as large as Caravan needed damage control or to influence legislation.

To Waleed it was the sweetest of all ironies: that wealthy Arab sheiks fed the bourgeois needs of the super-rich and powerful, and that had become the key to The Cause's plan to destroy the very capitalist system that the infidels coveted.

Waleed's training was instrumental in controlling and ultimately disposing of their hacking programmer, who first was able to hack into Caravan itself, then the avionic control systems of the major aircraft manufacturers. His killing this genius was a necessity, for a leak or weakness on Kupalli's part could stop the extermination of up to 350,000 capitalists in midair, and countless thousands on the ground as the planes fell.

Despite his training, he eased his conscious over his personally snuffing out this life with the notion that since hundreds of thousands would die, one more life was of little or no consequence.

CHAPTER 9

"OH MY GOD! Oh my God." Brooke's voice carried throughout the house.

Mush ran into the living room to find Brooke sitting on the cushion in the bay window with tears in her eyes. "What's wrong, what's wrong?"

She looked up at him. "Butterflies."

"Huh?"

"It's a little butterfly ... I just felt it. There, there it is again." She grabbed his hand and placed it on her belly. Then whispered, "Feel it? There. Right now. That's her, him ... ours."

Mush thought he felt it, a slight fluttering. But he was sure it was more pronounced in her body than the slight sensation that made it to the surface and to his gently placed hand. Still, the emotions of the moment were overwhelming. They both now had tears of joy in their eyes.

"Honey, that's wonderful. I love you so much." He hugged her, suddenly aware and contorting his body so as not to put pressure on the, on the ... "baby." *Oh God, a baby, our baby. Saying hello to us.* He kissed his wife again and again.

Kronos stood in the doorway to the room in his Hawaiian shirt, swim trunks and sandals as he cleared his throat. "Er ... sorry to interrupt." When they both turned with tears in their eyes he was suddenly concerned. "Gosh, everything okay?"

Brooke wiped a tear from her eye. "Couldn't be better. How did crashing the surf party go?"

After surfing with and befriending Duke Sterling, Kupalli's boss, Kronos gleaned no inkling of anything the company was working on that could be suspicious. As it came up in conversation between two surfers, Kronos jumped on the news story of the last few days when Sterling identified himself by answering the "So what do you do, Duke?" question. When he said he owned UniDynamics, Kronos naturally asked, "Is that the place where that guy in the news worked?"

After a little more conversation, he learned that Kupalli had always been a little rough around the edges, but brilliant at his craft. Kronos could relate.

He had already breached behind the UniDynamics' firewall and found nothing on Kupalli's work computer that was outside the corporation's usual business, nor could he find anything damning on UD's servers. The security protocols and team sharing would not allow the privacy any nefarious hacking, or nasty dark-web activity, demanded. That left the probability that anything illegal or extracurricular that Kupalli may have been involved with was on his home computer.

Brooke didn't like this, but Kronos had reached the end of his intrusion into the professional life of Kupalli. "So where does that leave us?" Brooke said.

"I need physical access to Kupalli's home computer, laptop and iPad to dig further," Kronos said like it was obvious.

So it came to be that a pregnant, former goody-two-shoes and her nerdy, cyber cowboy proceeded to hatch a plan that any second-story man thief would be proud of.

CHAPTER 10

As Gladys walked into the Starbucks, Brooke got up from the table that she had commandeered and handed over the mocha latte, with one shot, that she had ordered for her workmate. Kronos's and her whole plan rested on this guidance counselor at PHHS.

"Gladys, thank you for coming."

She spoke in a conspiratorial tone. "Brooke, I can't believe what they're saying."

"Gladys, I swear to you on my unborn baby, I had nothing to do with Kupalli's death.

Gladys was torn. "I want to believe you, but the TV, the papers ..."

"You can't go by that. They don't know the facts."

"But Brooke, but you ... You told me, the other day, with Kupalli, you ... you ..."

Brooke put her hand across the table on to hers. "I'm innocent, Gladys. All I did was talk to him, to let him know someone was watching him. Gladys, I swear that's all that happened ... except him lunging at me and falling."

Gladys took in a deep breath.

Brooke zeroed in on her. "I need your help, and it would be better if you didn't ask me any more questions about what I'm about to ask you. And Gladys, I'm literally fighting for my life here, or I wouldn't think of asking you to do this."

She pulled back from the table. "You're scaring me. What is it?"

"All I'm asking is for you to call Jenny in to your office for a chat. See how's she doing, how she's handling the terrible situation. Is she planning on returning? That kind of thing."

"Brooke, you know I couldn't divulge what she tells me. It would be unethical."

"And I respect that. All I would ask is that if she should mention another person, a friend or associate of her father, or relative, anyone who might have done this horrible thing, please just give me that name."

Gladys considered her request. It was the look of need on Brooke's face that convinced her to add, "If anything like that comes up."

Brooke relaxed. "Of course. I hope she's alright, poor kid. First her mom, then her dad. I know you'll do all you can to help her, Gladys."

"I'm just a high school guidance counselor. This kind of emotional trauma is beyond my training. But I'll ask to see her."

"I need to ask, when will you call Jenny in?"

"Tomorrow?"

"Thanks, because it's important."

f

The next morning, Kronos and Brooke were sitting in a parked car down the street from Jenny's house. The girl and her court-appointed guardian left through the front door off the modest home at 9:30 a.m. The guardian drove. The guardian was armed under her jacket and was probably a plain-clothed policewoman or US Marshal.

Brooke gave it five minutes before they both got out of the car. They went around the back, donned blue latex gloves, and Brooke picked the lock. They were through the patio door in under half a minute. Kronos went right to the desktop computer and plugged in his gizmo. Brooke went through the house searching for Kupalli's laptop. She found two laptops along with an iPad. Kronos had only two more gizmos with him, but as soon as he turned on the iPad, he saw it was Jenny's and connected the remaining device to the other laptop. "Twenty-two minutes," he said, then sat on the floor so as not to leave impressions in the cushions.

f

When Jenny and the guardian got to the school, they went immediately to Gladys's office, but she wasn't there. A teacher's aide said hello. "Jenny, Miss Goldstein was called to the principal's office to address the needs of another student. She asked me if it was okay to meet with her tomorrow."

Jenny looked at her guardian who nodded.

"Jenny, how are you doing?"

"I'm okay, Mrs. Haskell. Thank you for asking."

They headed out of the school and drove back home.

f

"Two more minutes," Kronos said.

Brooke was checking drawers and shelves, looking for any clues. In the bedroom, she suppressed the immediate need to start picking up around the bed. On the nightstand she found a pill bottle. She popped a shot of the prescription and took one of the pills. She was replacing the cap when she heard a car pull up. She ran to the window and peeked through the blinds. "Kronos, they're home. We got to get out."

"I can't unplug now. We'll lose everything."

"How much longer?"

"Minute fifteen on the desktop. The others are done."

Brooke ran to the patio door. She ran across the neighbor's backyard, around the house next door, and slowed as she crossed the front lawn next to Jenny's house.

Jenny was getting out the car when Brooke approached. "Jenny. Jenny, how are you doing?"

The guardian, a plain clothed, HPD policewoman, interceded. "Ma'am, you have to back away. You may not talk to this girl."

Jenny froze.

"I just want to tell her I care about her, and I hope she's being strong."

"Ma'am, you must step away or I'll call the police. Inside, Jenny."

The girl started walking into the house.

Brooke looked between the houses. No sign of Kronos.

"No, wait!" She composed herself and spoke to the woman. "Look, I need Jenny to know I would never do anything to hurt her." She called out over the guardian. "Jenny. Jenny, I would never hurt your father." Jenny opened the door but stopped and turned back towards Brooke.

f

Kronos looked at the front door, now ajar, as the daylight and Jenny's shadow streamed in.

f

Brooke stepped closer and spoke directly to Jenny, who started walking back towards Brooke, her eyes filling with tears. "Jenny, honey, I needed you to know this. When this is over, I want you to know that I'll be there for you." She looked to the space between the two houses. Still no Kronos.

The guardian got between Brooke and Jenny and put her hand over her service weapon. "That's it. Jenny, get in the house now," the guardian ordered.

"Look, I understand you got a job to do, but I'm being wrongly accused. I need Jenny to understand that."

Unfazed, she had already keyed her radio. "Dispatch. This is badge 2843 mobile, court appointed guardian at 342 Magnolia. I need a unit to respond. I have a female in violation of a court order." The woman didn't wait for an acknowledgement, she grabbed Jenny and marched her towards the house.

Brooke took a deep breath. She hadn't lied. She really felt all those things. She tensed as she watched them go into the house and disappear behind the closing door. Waiting to hear a scream or gunshot.

Brooke breathed a sigh of relief when a few seconds later she saw Kronos come around between the two houses. She signaled for him to go around the neighbor's house.

f

In the car, Kronos said, "That was cutting it close."

"Just because I have to ask, did you get to shut down the computer?" Brooke said as she pulled out of the spot.

"Hopefully. I saw the screen go black as they came into the living room. I don't think they saw me slip out the patio door."

Just then a police car came speeding down the block, lights and siren going.

"Maybe they did see me!" Kronos said, turning his head to follow the passing police cruiser.

"No, she called the cops to get me out of there."

Kronos relaxed. Then after a minute he said, "Hey, I want to apologize."

"For what?"

"The other day, when I barged in. It seemed a sensitive moment."

"No, Kronos, it was a great moment. I felt the baby move for the first time." The smile on her face gave her voice the lilt of a young girl.

"That is soooo cool!"

CHAPTER 11

IN THE Manhattan headquarters of MBN News, it was turning into a routine day. Reporters were out on the streets of New York and in towns across America, filing stories and doing "packages" for broadcast that made up the on-air content of any news network. To support the million-dollar on-camera talent, who were literally the faces of the emerging network, hundreds of behind-the-scenes people kept the place running with split-second timing and efficiency.

In Edit Bay 2, on the fifth floor, news editor Dave Temple was just finishing up a two-minute-twelve-second piece for the twelve-noon show. Although he would load it up on the broadcast server, he had a good reason to make a personal copy on a memory card. He turned to his assistant. "Joe, grab me an SD card." He pointed to a box with recycled cards in it.

Joe plucked one out and handed it over.

Dave slid it into the reader and clicked "export" on his editor screen.

"Why are you doing this?"

"I'm off-loading the interviews and B-roll from the women's shelter story. I'm going to use it for class tomorrow morning."

Joe was aware of Dave's Brooklyn College, Electronic Journalism class that he taught twice a week. In fact, Dave hired Joe from that very class two years before.

Dave's intention was to show his students how raw news footage comes in from the field, and how it becomes a finished news story ready for air.

Dave looked at his work sheet. They had forty-five minutes till a producer had them booked for a Wall Street story. "Hey, Joe, let's grab a bite now while we can." He stood up, took the SD card from the reader, closed the edit file and put the card in his shirt pocket, and then headed for the third-floor cafeteria.

f

"Just a minute, Detective," Mush said to the man at the front door, as he turned and called upstairs. "Brooke, it's detective Russell." He stepped aside. "Come in. She'll be right down."

Russell waited by the foot of the stairs.

Brooke came bouncing down. "Detective, to what do I owe the pleasure of this visit."

"Well, you know what they say: one good visit deserves another."

That took the bounce out of Brooke's step. "Oh, I guess you heard."

"Heard? Brooke, there's a bench warrant out for your arrest for violating the separation order. It was all I could do to convince them to let me bring you in, rather than a damn SWAT team."

Mush whipped his head towards his wife and winked. "What the hell? Brooke, what's he talking about?"

She sighed. "I went to see Jenny. I couldn't take the fact that everyone believes I killed her father. You have to understand, I was her coach. She trusted me. I couldn't let her go on believing I took her dad from her. All I kept thinking was, what if she were my daughter?" Unconsciously, Brooke placed her hand on her rounded belly.

Mush jumped in. "Russell, my wife is pregnant. Her emotions sometimes get the better of her lately. Can you cut her some slack?"

Russell didn't hear him. His eyes were glued on the guy sitting in front of more computers than NASA's mission control. "Who's he? What's he doing?"

"He's a friend, and he's helping me with my case."

"How are computers helping your case?"

Kronos called out from the dining room as he switched screens from Kupalli's hard drive to a few legal research sites. "Case law. Searching for precedent. Maybe even an Amicus brief in support."

"Isn't that your lawyer's job?"

"Public defender? Tell me another one." Brooke dismissed his question.

"True. Look, let's go. You're going to get yelled at by a judge and, if you're lucky, he won't revoke your bail and you'll be back here in a few hours."

"Let me get my bag." She turned to Mush. "Honey, call James Chu. Ask him to meet us there."

f

Mush drove down to the court a few minutes behind Russell, who was delivering Brooke to the judge in his detective's car. She had told her husband to expect this since she and Kronos did their little "field trip" to Kupalli's house. They say cops and crooks are two sides of the same protein. There was a little bit of truth to that in Brooke. Normally the merit-badged girl scout, she wasn't above bending little rules to catch the bigger crook. But in her entire career, she only got written up once at the FBI; for shooting a guy in the leg to get the location of a bomb set to go off and kill millions.

Twenty minutes into the court appearance, Brooke hated that Chu played the female card, but he was on a roll. "Your Honor, my co-counsel regrets her impetuous act. Once again, she is pregnant and, as I can attest, more emotional than usual. She has a prior relationship based on trust with the victim's daughter. She has admitted to this court that she was in the wrong in her attempt to speak with the child, and she has vowed never to violate that stipulation again. Your Honor, she has no previous criminal record, her record of service in law enforcement to this country is beyond exemplary and reproach. We ask for your indulgence in finding favorably for my client in this matter."

"The defendant will approach." The judge took off his glasses and cleaned them, coughed and replaced them. "Mrs. Burrell-Morton, someone of your background should certainly understand the rationale and power of the court. You have shown reckless disregard for the terms of your bail."

James Chu closed his eyes. *Here it comes.*

"However, your counsel asks for forbearance due to your condition. I will excuse this breach, just this one time. But don't misconstrue. I'm not one to countenance lawlessness casually. You so much as sneeze the wrong way and your bail will be revoked, and you'll await your trial from a detention cell at the woman's facility in Kailua. Do I make myself clear?"

"Yes, Your Honor. Thank you. I promise it won't happen again."

"No, it won't, because you'll sacrifice your freedom."

"Yes, Your Honor."

f

On the ride home, Brooke remembered something. "Mush, I need to stop by the pharmacy."

"Everything okay?"

"Yes, I forgot, with all this going on, that the doctor says I need an iron supplement."

Mush waited in the car as she went in.

She found the iron pills then walked to the pharmacy desk.

Her pharmacist, David, was happy to see her. "Hi, Brooke, how are you doing with the pregnancy?"

She held up the jar of pills. "Doc says I need a little more iron."

"Those are a good brand, high efficacy."

"Do you have a minute?"

"Sure."

She nodded over to the consultation area, separated from the pharmacy, where customers could have sensitive discussions with their pharmacist.

"What can I do for you?"

She reached into her pocket, took out her phone and dug for the pill she had taken from Kupalli's nightstand.

"Can you tell me what this is for?" She took care to zoom in on the picture of the bottle on her phone to exclude Kupalli's name on the label.

"Hydrocodone! It's a narcotic analgesic indicated for the relief of moderate-to-severe cancer-related pain. Not too widely prescribed here."

"Why not?"

"In sunny climates it can cause violent rage in some people predisposed to bi-polar disorder."

"Rage, huh?" She showed him the tablet. "Is this the pill?"

"Hold on." He walked over to his computer. He pulled up the online version of the Physician's Desk Reference. He came back over to her. "Yes, the PDR has this as being the generic form."

"Thank you," Brooke said, her mind racing with the possibilities that Kupalli was under the influence when he hit his daughter. And came at her!

"Brooke, you don't have to answer this, but is this the admiral's? Is Brett okay?"

Brooke snapped out of her thoughts. "What? Oh, no, no, he's fine. This is something I'm looking into. Thanks for your help. See ya next month."

"Take two iron tablets for the first few days, ramp up your blood, then one a day should do it."

"Mahalo," she said as she left.

f

When Brooke and Mush came home, Kronos was chomping at the bit to show them what he had found. "Kupalli started out looking clean as a whistle. Then, buried way down deep in his hard drive, was a one-kilobyte file. Something that small is usually machine generated for use by the system. But then it would have been in a utility directory of some sort. Instead this was right out in the open. And whammo, one single string of code. Which led me to this."

He hit the return key. The screen blinked and came back looking the same.

"Kronos your 'this' looks the same as your 'that.' It's still a hard-drive directory."

"Yes, but not the same one. This hard drive is in a dark cloud."

"You mean the dark web?" Mush said.

"Yes, but then in a cloud where his other drive is stored."

"Okay, so what did you find?" Brooke said.

"This guy is good."

"Coming from you that must mean he's almost as good as you."

"Almost! He's a dark hat alright. Here, this is some of his recent work. He hacked into Caravan."

"The new retail company?"

"He's been a busy boy."

"What did he do to Caravan.com?" she asked.

"He hooked into their routing programs and logistics."

"What did he do, get a new TV or a first-class ticket?" she said, nudging him.

"Make fun. I'm here, ain't I?"

"What else?"

"He clicked the mouse and a new set of pages came onto the screen. Looks like corporate espionage. Big ticket stuff. Downloaded software. Machine code, actually."

"Is there a difference?"

"Machine code is already compiled and easier to duplicate and rebuild without any resemblance to the original program."

"And why did he do that?"

"Well, here he was into the airplane manufacturers. Avionics and control."

"Wait. Military?"

"No, seems like commercial."

"Okay, so not a spy. Still, why then?"

"My guess, he's working for Bombardier or some other competitor of the new high-tech planes."

"So, would stealing code like this get him dead?"

"Not likely, but there are still a few strings left that are really tough to crack. But I'll crack 'em, then they may give us something."

"Okay, thanks. Keep at it."

f

That evening, Mush had drawn Brooke a bath, lit some scented candles and dropped some oils in the tub. He turned on the heater in the bathroom. He poured a glass of non-alcoholic wine. It was like grape juice, but it went with the mood. She had been through a lot lately. Nothing like her old life—getting blown off a ship or blasted out of a building, or outsmarting the most dangerous terrorist on earth—but she'd done none of those things while pregnant. He hit the dimmer and turned on the blue tooth speaker. The soft jazz set the perfect mood.

Mush, proud of his stage setting, made one final check then said to himself, "All that's missing is the girl." Then, out loud, "Honey!" He walked into the bedroom, but she wasn't there.

He found her on the banquette in the bay window, looking out at the moon slicing a shimmering path through the deep-blue Pacific.

He approached cautiously and in a soft voice said, "Honey, did you hear me?"

She reached up and grabbed his hand tight. "Oh Mush, what if I'm bad at being a mother? What if this little person, who will be dependent on me for everything, what if I can't or don't know how? I never played with dolls. I hardly ever changed a diaper. Why did I want this so badly?"

Mush held her tight, smoothed her hair. "Brooke, I believe in you. One of the most important roles of parenting is protecting your baby. You're the world's best at that. You know why you wanted this?"

She pulled away from the wet spot she was creating on his sweater. "Why?"

"Love. Love brought you to this point, babe. You got to trust that love will see you through it. I think you're going to be the world's best mom. The fact you're worried about all this proves it. And you know the other great thing about this?"

"What?"

"I'll be your executive officer for this deployment. And I got some pretty decent daddy skills I've been honing for a while."

They found each other's lips and kissed.

"Now, where was I when I came in. Oh yeah, take off all your clothes."

f

Brooke slipped into the warm scented bath. Mush handed her the faux wine. They toasted. "To the mother of my child. I love you more and more every day."

After they took a sip, Brooke said, "Just remember that, when I can't see my toes, Romeo."

"Seems to me you may have always had an issue with seeing them."

"Right ... boob man."

He leaned over and kissed her. He almost fell into the tub.

f

Mush left the bathroom and met Kronos in the hall.

"Mush, I need to see Brooke."

"Trust me, you ain't seeing her now."

"Oh. This is big. I think I unraveled Kupalli's rat's nest. But we have to do something quick to save his wife."

"Slow up. Brooke told me Jenny's mother died two years ago."

"Not so much. I really need to speak with Brooke."

f

Brooke was in a robe, toweling off her hair as Kronos showed her what he had found. It was a classic kidnap proof-of-life photo. A woman, ostensibly Mrs. Kupalli, was shackled to a chair with a newspaper held up so that the date was readable. There was one picture per week in Kupalli's dark email folder. The newspaper in the last photo was just two days ago, the day Kupalli was killed. The length of hair and general increasing paleness in the pictures proved this was legit.

"Brooke, we got to call the cops," Mush said.

"And tell them what? Guess what we found while we were looking through Kupalli's drive, which we purloined through illegal entry and theft? I don't want my baby in prison diapers."

"Kronos, do you know where they're keeping her?" Mush asked.

"Aside from it being an Oahu paper, no. The metadata was stripped out of the pic. It's a copy. She's in front of a brick wall with no identifying aspects."

"Kronos, is there any way to search for the original picture?" Brooke said.

She could see the switch go on in his head. He turned inside himself and trotted off to the computers.

She looked at Mush. "This could change everything."

"If she were being held captive, then Kupalli was being blackmailed and forced into hacking?"

"Yes, so that means that whatever Kronos discovered he was hacking is now something worth kidnapping and maybe murdering for," she said.

"Why am I suddenly thinking that I'm going to be worried about you?" Mush put his arm around her.

"Let's see what Kronos finds first. If he can't locate her, then we'll figure out how to use this in my defense."

"And if he locates her, are you going to call it in?"

"That, I gotta think about." Brooke's eyes started moving as if she could see before her the plan she was mapping out.

"And there it is, exactly what I was worried about!" Mush said.

f

The key to Kronos's search was the date on the paper. He used that first as a filter. Then he geofenced his search on the dark web to the island of Oahu only. He further refined his search by file size and type, which included all the various extensions that indicated photo or image file.

This blind search resulted in 106 similar smartphone picture files. He simply dropped them all into preview and looked at twenty at a time. In the third set, there it was. This version of the original photo of the bedraggled and emaciated woman had the metadata intact.

He Google mapped it. Turned out it was taken sixteen miles away, in a ground ammunition storage area that made up the Lualualei Naval Magazine. His guess was it was abandoned, as were many World War II former military bunkers, pillboxes and observation posts that still dotted the island. This one seemed to be in the thick forest of the Ewa reserve.

f

Twenty-three minutes later, with Brooke holding the flashlight, Mush and Kronos put their backs into the crowbar, and the chain and lock holding the rusted, steel blast door shut, gave way. The door groaned and squeaked as they pushed it open. Brooke went in low, leading with Mush's service .45 cal. sidearm in one hand and a flashlight in her other. The smell was horrendous. The light flashed on a shape, a human shape in the middle of the round concrete structure. As she approached it, she could make out the withered body of a woman, bound in a chair. She was wrapped in a blanket, her hair matted and scraggly long. Her skin was pale white. Brooke placed her fingers on her neck. There was a faint pulse. Mush used his nail clipper to nibble away at the nylon restraints and freed her right arm and both legs.

One hand was left free for her to feed herself from a dirty bowl of what looked like croutons, nuts and raisins. Open bottles of water were also on the box next to the chair. Empty syringes littered the floor. They had to be careful not to be stuck by them.

Was she being drugged? Brooke wondered. It was obvious the person keeping her alive had no compassion for a female, in that her clothes were the clothes she was kidnapped in. Yellowed and stained from sweat and dead skin. Her legs were deep purple, a sign of atrophy. She was light as a feather to lift. Mush and Kronos got under her arms and gently carried her to fresh air. The seat of her chair was cut out and fashioned as a toilet with a bucket below. A similar bucket was at the entrance. Obviously, the last thing her captor did was empty the bucket outside after he switched it out.

She was still unconscious as Brooke called Russell first.

f

Russell was very cool and followed Brooke's plan. She told Kronos to make his call. He dialed 911 from his cell phone and, acting like he just found her, asked for an ambulance. Russell intercepted the radio call for any HPD unit to assist the ambulance dispatched to the Lualualei Naval Magazine and answered to the dispatch that he'd cover it.

When he got there, he dutifully took a statement from Kronos, who told him he was visiting from the mainland and was coming back from a late hike to see the Lani Kai at sunset, then fell asleep. He went on to tell him that he woke up in the dark and got lost, and when he passed this pillbox, he heard moans and crying coming from behind the metal door. He said the chain and lock were already broken.

Russell knew every word was bullshit, but he unquestioningly wrote it down. He added the notation that the man he interviewed was just a "Good Samaritan." Then he walked over to Brooke, who was fifty feet away, leaning on Mush's pick up.

"Why didn't you call this in, instead of coming here yourself?" Russell asked.

"I didn't know if she was alive or not."

"What the hell difference would that make?"

"If she was dead, like her daughter believes, then she could have stayed dead a little longer. Until I figured out what it meant."

"You figured out? Lady, you ain't on the job anymore."

"No, I'm just being accused of murder. Railroaded if you ask me."

"Are you saying that if she were dead, you wouldn't have called it in?"

"Maybe anonymously. But that's all academic. She's alive and I did call it in. I called you."

"Why did you have to come to Hawaii?" Russell said, shaking his head.

"Maybe to save her life. If you believe in destiny ..."

He looked at Brooke. He was caught up in what she just said. She could see him consider the fatalism of all this. He started nodding. "Providence or not, that's a version of your story which neatly and conveniently could exonerate you."

Brooke took a deep breath. "Spoken like a good cop, Russell, but I ain't your perp. Look, either way there's a crime scene in there that needs to be processed. We touched nothing in there. I placed three fingers on her neck. The guys carried her out. But I'm sure there are no prints. Can't vouch for any footprints, though."

Russell was rapidly trying to catch up to the events he was suddenly in the middle of. "So, let me get this straight. HPD finds nothing in Kupalli's past to point to any killer other than you, and you somehow dig up that he was being blackmailed and his wife was the leverage?"

"Yup. I'm sure once Kupalli was killed, the bastards just left her here ... to die."

"And I'm going out on a limb here to guess you came across this evidence in a less than legal way?" Russell's eyebrows rose halfway to his hairline.

"In the main, no. The result of perfectly legal digital diligence."

"In the main ..."

"Yeah, in the main ..."

"But on the side, maybe a little illegal trespassing, or B & E?"

"Oh, was there a reported breaking and entry as it relates to this case?" Brooke's wide-eyed look was precious.

Russell just smiled. "Look, however this happened, you may have saved this woman's life. That will count when you get to the sentencing phase of your trial."

"Thanks, now I feel all comfy. How you going to write this up?"

"Against all my instincts, anonymous lead?" He didn't know why, but Russell asked that as if to get her approval. *This woman is an alpha dog. She's got me trying to please her*, he thought, then shook that thought out of his head.

"Can you make that stick?"

"I got some juice after thirty years, although I may not have a pension after this."

"For what it's worth, there may be more here than a kidnap/blackmail rap."

"Look, Brooke, your cop instincts aside, this is the limit of my cover and my promise to President Mitchell. After this I can't cover, protect or shield you any longer."

"I understand, but at least maybe Jenny won't be an orphan."

Russell looked at her. His posture relaxed, and the soon-to-be grandfather in him said, "When you put it that way, good job, lady."

CHAPTER 12

EJ 304 was a fun course. Electronic journalism was cool and forced students to think both visually and with an ear towards composing a reporting narrative. It was an extra added dimension to newspaper reporting, where you did it all with words and maybe one image. And, of course, if a picture was worth a thousand words, video was thirty pictures per second. So, the whole approach to creating a news story around all this torrent of video information coming at the viewer was a skill Dave Hampel was there to impart. Which images to pick over what words was the heart and soul of modern broadcast news.

Journalism majors, here at Brooklyn College, rushed to sign up for Dave's class on EJ, simply because he had access to today's news. That made his class assignments and his lectures as close as a student could get to an actual newsroom experience.

Today was no different. He was taking them through the steps of post-production on a news story, a two-minute-twelve-second package that ran on the network yesterday. Complete with all the raw footage, interviews, B-Roll and reporter takes and reverses.

Over the bi-weekly two-hour classes, students were able to observe how to select and combine all the elements of a story as it comes in from the field. The fact that Adjunct Professor Hampel had several Emmy's for news editing/producing made each minute of the class pure gold.

He ran yesterday's raw footage for his Electronic Journalism class. It was shot to tell the story of a women's shelter and a sewage pipe overflow which forced the women into the streets and to other shelters. The footage started with "B-Roll" of the outside of the shelter. This is usually at the head or tail of the footage, depending on whether the cameraperson rolls up to a non-breaking story, where he has time to shoot the exterior because there's no rush. Or at the end of the footage if it's a breaking story where there was no time until the end of the shoot to take the routine necessary shot of the place where it all happened.

Next on the "roll," an old term for when news used to be shot on a roll of film, an angle on the street signs in the corner, followed by a shot of the city workers digging up the street. Then an interview with an administrator shot over the shoulder of the reporter asking the questions, then "reverses" of that reporter re-asking the same questions but on a straight-on camera angle, that, when cut together, made it look like two cameras were there.

The SD card footage ended with the reporter's master take of her intros and outros as she was looking into the camera. The pre-roll caught her primping her hair, quickly looking down at her notes, mouthing the name of the shelter, then looking up and counting down from, "3, 2, 1. The terrible smell and unsanitary condition which suddenly erupted at the Saint Joseph's Women's Shelter was not the most disturbing part of the sewer pipe break in this eighty-year-old structure. The crisis— Shit! Eighty-five-year-old! Let's go again. In ... 3,2,1. The terrible smell and unsanitary condition ..."

She did a second take ...

As the footage ran on the monitor behind him, Dave started pointing out how six minutes of raw footage was then edited down to a two-minute-twelve story that ran yesterday on the 6 and 11 p.m. news.

The class wasn't listening. They were glued to the screen.

Dave, with his back to the screen, didn't notice the shelter footage end and and the next recent video file show up in "date created" order. It was a raw video from over a year ago that must have been on the SD card before he added the new video files to bring to class.

Then they reacted. "Oh shit. Look!"

"Damn."

"Oh my God!"

He turned to the monitor and was as riveted as the class. Especially when the train hit the bullet-riddled body.

f

Having immediately dismissed his class, Dave was in the TV station's conference room an hour later. They cleared out a sales department meeting and were watching the footage. The die-hard news people had the same reaction of shock and disbelief at what they were seeing as Dave's class.

It was obviously helicopter footage shot from above the Manhattan Bridge. A blonde woman was firing a handgun into the body of a man who fell back on the tracks. His body jolted with every penetration. She kept firing, without mercy. Suddenly, a silver subway train swept into the shot and ran over the body as the woman collapsed. After the train rumbled by, there was a bloody mess on the tracks and she was lying beside the rails, bleeding from her upper leg and barely moving. The footage then showed the view downward as the helicopter turned away and flew up the river to the heliport. Soon the fast-approaching yellow lines that marked the helipad's landing zone filled the screen. That final close-up image of the painted tarmac filled the screen and stayed there for a few seconds until the helicopter's power was shut down.

Everyone looked at Tom Colletti, the news chopper pilot for the station.

He shook his head. "This was the day the terrorists attacked the generator in Queens and the water mains in Westchester. I was tasked by the FBI, through New York control center, to be on the lookout and advise the location of a blue-and-white ambulance."

"Who is she, Tom?"

"All I know was her radio call sign was Stiletto."

"So, Tom, let me ask you, at one point earlier that day, you med evac'ed a cop from Teterboro Airport. Did you manage to get any news done that day?" Mel asked.

"I went live many times, but there was lots of news copters and army and federal aviation up there, and NOT fouling the air intake of an airliner with my chopper was high on my list." Tom raised his hand as Mel was about to speak. "And before you bring it up again, Mel, I also became part of the story when I landed on the approach of the Manhattan Bridge, at the request of the FBI, to stop a terrorist suspect from escaping. Once the cops reinforced the roadblock, I took off again and went to see what was happening on the bridge. That's when this footage must have been recorded."

"How come you didn't go live with this while you wereover the bridge? How come we never saw any of this on the fucking air?" Mel was rabid.

"The FBI ordered me not to report anything further so as to not give the terrorists any tactical overview of the situation on the bridge. I didn't even know the camera was rolling. I guess I missed the flashing record light on the DVR panel. It was kind of an unusually busy day."

"Christ, Tom, we're the fourth estate. We don't take orders from government agencies," Mel Teason whined.

"Hey, Mel, the city was under attack. We had the eye-in-the-sky overview. I sure as hell wasn't about to aid and abet a terrorist group in the name of journalistic ethics."

"Oh right! You're not a journalist, you're a traffic reporter."

Tom answered Mel's condescending tone in turn. "Oh right, you didn't serve in Iraq and Afghanistan, you're just a friggin' academic."

Cheryl Addison, owner of the station, had had enough and took control. "Gentlemen, save this for the schoolyard. The question before us now is what do we do with this footage?"

Mel jumped right in. "Is there any question? We have an exclusive on the biggest story since 911 to hit this city. Obviously. What happened on that bridge was squelched by the government. The public has a right to know."

Cheryl turned to the corporate counsel. "What's our exposure here, Rod?"

"Well, according to Tom, the FBI's order was specific to not airing anything contemporaneously of any footage that would give the terrorists a real-time strategic advantage. What we have here is an unintentional recording, but we are now after the fact. Therefore, unless we have agreed to a government request to suppress, and I personally know that such a form did not cross my desk, in my opinion we are good."

Cheryl looked at Diane Price, her ace reporter and rising star in local news. "Diane, what's your angle?"

The forty-six-year-old veteran journalist who was suddenly dropped from her national network anchor spot without fanfare or explanation was momentarily shocked and was deep in thought.

After she was dismissed from her Washington DC anchor post, Diane sought out her friend and Wesleyan University buddy, Cheryl Addison, who hired Diane on the bounce, no questions asked.

Aside from helping out her friend, Cheryl was enjoying increased viewership and ad dollars due to the polish and style of a national talent on her local New York station. Plus, the three local Emmys Diane had won so far gave her a leg up on the males who occupied Cheryl's executive position at the rival stations.

"Diane. Diane? What's your angle?" Cheryl again said, then commented, "Oh, I can tell this is going to be good!" reading the look on Diane's face.

The room nervously laughed but cut the news diva some slack.

Diane took a considered breath and deliberately stated her position. "What we have here is an execution, cold, brutal and illegal. This woman, obviously an agent of some kind in the federal government, denied this victim his rights and his life."

"Do we know that for sure?" Cheryl said.

"I think Tom made that clear. This federal agent took the life of a man with his hands up. He was down. She didn't have to fire. In fact, she should have helped him off the tracks. Instead, the government delivered the death penalty, without a trial, jury or sentence. This is the ultimate abuse of power."

All the journalists in the room immediately knew that this meme was ratings gold. Exclusive, bloody footage of a government out of control was another guaranteed local Emmy. Hell, maybe even a Peabody.

All in the room, that is, except for Tom. "Come on. You're going to crucify this woman based on thirty seconds of footage?"

"The video doesn't lie," Diane said.

"Ever hear of the sin of omission?" Tom said.

"There's no room for religious zealotry in a newsroom," Diane snapped back.

"What? It's, it's a turn of phrase, Miss Collegiate!" *God! Are you people all that stupid?* "You, we, don't know the context of this video," Tom said.

"Tom, thanks for your input, but this is a news department decision. Your opinion is duly noted," Cheryl said with the tone of finality.

Knowing when he was being dismissed, Tom couldn't help but add, "Bullshit. This is a continuation of the sales meeting we pushed out of here. All you care about is ratings and another Emmy in the display case."

CHAPTER 13

THE HEADLINE on the front page of the Honolulu Star-Advertiser's website proclaimed, "Back from the Dead! Girl Loses Dad, Gets Mom Back in Same Week!"

The story went on to explain the mysterious circumstances of a Hawaiian woman who was held hostage by kidnappers for over two years. Her side of the family, believing her dead, had her legally declared so. It spelled out in the article how, on Tuesday, her husband, Tau Kupalli, forty-two of Oahu, was found dead under suspicious circumstances. The story identified a local woman, an admiral's wife, Mrs. Brooke Burrell-Morton, as being arrested and charged with the murder. The story then went on to quote persons "close to the case" as saying that, although Hawaiian authorities were investigating, no connection at this time could be made between the killing, the suspect and the kidnap victim.

Waleed closed the newspaper's website. He was told by Lelani, the Hawaiian deviant they hired to keep the Kupalli woman alive, that police had stumbled across her, and, most disturbingly, that she was alive. They were in this predicament because that simpleton Lelani didn't finish her off. Instead the damned fool was just going to let her starve to death. *The incompetent idiot.*

Waleed then opened Malaysia Airlines' site and bought a first-class seat to Honolulu.

f

A craving for Chinese food hit Brooke, so at the dinner table, she, Mush and Kronos were discussing where they were and what should be their next move over containers of Moo Shoo Pork and Buddha's Delight.

"Individually, each of Kupalli's hacks are within normal targets for corporate hackers," Kronos said.

"Wait. So that is actually a thing? There are corporate hackers?" Mush asked.

"Yeah, they're split between activists and mercenaries," Kronos said.

"Are you saying these are separate events? That they don't necessarily add up to one picture?" Brooke made a circle in the air with her chopsticks.

"Could be, except ..." Kronos began.

"Except for the kidnapping and attempted murder," Brooke said. "Is there anything else we're missing? I mean, if I'm hacking for someone else, do I have to deliver anything? Is there a digital receipt kind of thing for delivering this back to whoever's paying?" Brooke asked.

Kronos went on to explain that some hacks are for hack's sake, to deny service or damage a site or system. Others are for ransom, locking up systems or threatening to erase all storage, usually paid in non-traceable Bitcoin. If Kupalli was engaged in industrial espionage, then the code itself would be the product. In that case, the code could be delivered by lots of digital means, including old school where the code is loaded on a memory stick, then a standard dead drop is performed or even simply mailed to whoever is paying.

"Kronos, will we ever know what Kupalli was up to that would justify kidnapping his wife?" Mush asked.

"Now comes the hard part. There's over one hundred gigabytes of generated code on his dark drive. It all has to be gone through to see what he was up to. Imagine a bookshelf packed with books that is ten yards long."

"That's a lot of books," Mush said

"No, that's just 'one' gigabyte of information ..."

"So, wait, then, 100 gigabytes is ... a thousand yards of books on a shelf?" Mush reasoned.

"And we could only be looking for maybe one page or one word that has been replaced, and is indistinguishable from all the other published pages. That change could give away the ending or have a secret message that only somebody who knew it was there would understand."

"How are you going to do that?" Mush asked.

"Book one, page one," Kronos said as he motioned as if he was turning a page in a book with his thumb and forefinger.

CHAPTER 14

THERE ARE few things as spectacular as a field of Red Lehua wildflowers. The preponderance of these spiny, crimson flowers, so ubiquitous on the island, made it an obvious choice as the official Hawaiian state flower.

A soft breeze from the east created an undulating blanket of red, which made the brown-stained, rusted-out trailer standout as the eyesore that it was nestled in the plush landscape of this relatively remote part of Oahu.

When he entered to check it out, Waleed discovered that the inside made the outside look like a million dollars. As expected, he found and removed a small .32-caliber pistol from a panel over the wheel well.

He went outside and waited until nightfall behind an old, tireless van that was propped up on its rims on cinder blocks. His cautious logic being that the cover of night made him less conspicuous and lessened the chance of witnesses. Although there was no one near this desolate spot so far off the main highway.

He heard it off in the distance. A single light beamed through the warm Hawaiian night as the road curved and twisted through the lowlands. The light bounced as Lelani rode his motorbike off the highway and rumbled over the rough terrain, right up to the rotted hulk that he called home. He swung his leg, got off the bike and wrestled with the sticky door to the camper.

Lelani dumped a can of pork and beans in a crusted pot sitting atop one burner of the small propane stove next to an even smaller sink. As soon as Waleed entered the trailer, Lelani went for the wheel well.

"Looking for this?" Waleed said, pointing the pistol at his head.

Lelani froze. "Who are you. What do you want?"

"I want you to get high. Take the works out of the drawer—the one right next to you—and go for the sleigh ride."

"I don't feel like it right now."

Waleed pulled back the hammer on the .32. "Feel like dying?"

Lelani put his hands up. "Okay. Okay." He grabbed his works from the drawer and tied off his arm with one end of the rubber strap in his teeth. Then he started slapping his arm to bring up a vein. He lit a benzene torch and cooked his hit in an old teaspoon. Waleed watched as he injected himself. Within a minute Lelani was falling out of reality. Waleed shut the burner under the beans, then opened both gas jets on the two-burner stove but stopped before the igniter clicked. He relit the benzene torch five feet away and simply left the trailer.

He was walking back to his car which he had parked a half a mile away when an explosion rocked the ground. He turned and saw the fireball as it rose in the sky, followed by black smoke. He watched the smoke rise and had an odd thought. *He* is *getting high.*

Responding fire companies didn't try to fight the fire. It was burning out on its own, and all of the trailer was already destroyed. The pumper truck used its reserve tank to hose down the patch of vegetation fifty feet from the burnt hulk, lest a spark or ember find fuel in the dried grass. One of the firemen used a hook tool to drag a motorbike away, so its gas tank wouldn't boil off.

Given the single fatality, odds being he was the resident of the trailer, HPD detectives quickly concluded, given the lack of fresh tire tracks in the dirt around the camper and the drug paraphernalia, most of which survived the fire, that it was a drug addict not practicing the use of his brain.

At some point, someone from the county would notify the owner of the land, if it wasn't the state itself, that the victim was squatting on, that there was a death on the property and a clean-up needed. The detectives took the requisite number of photographs which would go in the official file on the fatal fire of the mobile structure 2.2 miles off Route 750, Kunia Road near the quarry.

CHAPTER 15

"WANT SOME Cheerios?" Mush asked as Brooke came down to the kitchen in her robe.

She walked over to him and wiped the drop of milk from his chin, then kissed him good morning. "Thanks for letting me sleep."

He got up to get her a bowl. "You went out like a light. Banana or Brussels sprouts?"

"I think I'm starting to get over that. Let's go traditional."

"Banana it is." Mush delivered a sharp salute.

"Are you finished with this?" She took the local section of the newspaper, as she saw Mush had moved on to the sports pages.

She quickly scanned the front page. "You know, I never thought that a good day would be one where my name isn't in the paper."

"Here ya go." Mush put the bowl down in front of her.

"Oooo, blueberries too."

"Enjoy."

As she spooned in the cereal, she perused the Honolulu paper. One item caught her eye. It was a photo taken from a helicopter of a burning trailer in a desolate part of the island. But it was what was in the picture that drew her brain out of her wakey-shaky morning mode. "Where's my phone?" She patted her pockets and found it. "Kronos!"

f

"Russell ..." He had the phone under chin as he was making his morning coffee in the break room.

"It's Brooke. Did your department take plaster casts of the tire tracks outside the pillbox where we found Mrs. Kupalli?"

"Why do you ask?"

"Because that night I noticed a single tire track consistent with a motorcycle but narrower."

"And ..."

"In today's paper there's a picture of a fire scene, and outside the burnt-out trailer is a motorbike."

"Again, and ..."

"My guy Kronos can't find any social media presence on Mr. Lelani, the man who was identified as the victim of the fire. But we found he does have a record."

"I see where you're going. I'll get back to you."

f

Russell hung up and shook his head. There was a reason Brooke worked for the president of the United States. She was as sharp as a well-stropped razor. He picked up the paper from Randall's desk and walked down to forensics.

"Judy, what did we find with the tire cast taken from the Kupalli rescue?"

"Hold on." She banged a few keystrokes into her keyboard, and an evidence sheet came out of the laser printer. The sheet pictured a plaster cast of a tire tread. Judy paraphrased what she noted on the sheet. "It's a pretty generic tire used on motorbikes and small motorcycles. It's not original equipment, so there's no tying it to a make or model of bike."

"Could it be the type of tire on a bike like this?" He showed her the bike in the newspaper picture that accompanied the article.

"A definite possibility. Bring me the bike and I'll see if it's a match for wear and tread depth."

f

Rather than getting into a pissing contest with the detectives who caught the trailer fire death, or get some uniforms to retrieve the bike, Russell signed out an HPD van himself. He did marshal a uniform to drive while he read the report. He learned that Akoni Lelani, who was positively identified by dental records, was a discard from society, a straggler from low-end job to job. Arrested a few times, each for petty theft, public nuisance and drunkenness. He attended a court-ordered outpatient rehab clinic. To all appearances, he was practically indigent. Yet he had made steady deposits of six hundred dollars a week for the last two years. Russell thought and then muttered under his breath, "Son of a bitch!" *That certainly bodes well for him being paid by someone to keep Mrs. Kupalli alive.*

f

When they pulled up, Russell realized how totally consumed by the fire the trailer where Lelani lived was. If it was an accident, it was the perfect storm of accelerant and opportunity. Of course, if it wasn't ...

f

Within an hour of delivering Lelani's bike to the police vehicle lock up, Judy from forensics called him. "Russell? It's a match. There's a 98.9 % certainty that that motorbike was at the pillbox."

"Thanks, Judy, good work."

"Can I ask how you even thought to try to match this bike to the kidnapping?"

"A little bird told me."

"Okay, fine. Be that way."

"Later, Judy."

"Later, Russ."

f

That afternoon, Russell was back at the Morton's. Brooke, her lawyer, James Chu, and Mush met out on the lanai. The conversation was grim.

"Your intuition was correct. Lelani was the kidnapper. Although it's hard to establish a motive or that Kupalli was paying him a ransom to keep her alive."

"So, the deposits were cash?" Brooke said.

"Totally untraceable," Russell said.

"Can we find a way to connect Kupalli to Lelani, working in the same place, school, neighbors, a traffic accident? Any way to prove their paths ever crossed?" Chu asked.

"We're looking into that, but that's not a healthy line to pursue. A computer genius and a derelict just don't hang in the same circles, and any possible single contact can be just a coincidence on a small island."

"They both spent time in lock up in your jail. Any chance they met as guests of HPD?" Brooke said.

"Why can't I get detectives on the force for ten years to think like that?" he lamented, then added, "And no, I checked for that. They were there on separate dates, years apart."

"How about secondary connections?"

'Wow. You were a fed, weren't you! No, we're not the FBI. And I certainly can't order up that kind of database search without probable cause during a duly authorized investigation, which, I may remind you, this isn't."

"So, the ransom had nothing to do with Kupalli's hacking?"

"It would appear so," Russell said.

"So then, why?" Brooke asked.

"Why is he hacking, or why was she kidnapped?" Russell asked.

Brooke used her hands on the tabletop to separate ideas as if she was bunching sand into a pile on her left. "Look, Kupalli was hacking, as far as we can tell, not for personal gain." She moved her hands. "We see no wealth amassed by Kupalli. No infusions of cash in his bank records." She made another "pile" to her right. "And certainly not regular withdrawals of six hundred per week." She had made three "piles."

"But if Lelani wasn't holding her for ransom, then why was he holding her?" Mush asked.

"Maybe the question isn't why, but for who?" Brooke said.

Russell was catching on. "His wife was being used as leverage by someone else?"

"He was forced to hack to keep her alive?" Chu said.

"I'm not even going to ask how you know any of this," Russell said wearily.

"How's Mrs. Kupalli?" Brooke said, happily changing the subject, but also reminding him of the good that had come from that which he did not want to ask.

"She's out of the woods, hydrated, on solid foods, getting her color back," Russell said.

"Is she in rehab for the drugs they were pumping into her?"

"The syringes? Actually, they were vitamins, keeping her almost alive."

That surprised Brooke, but it did make horrendous sense. "Does she confirm that it was Lelani that kidnapped her?"

"She confirmed he was the one who dropped off food and changed buckets once a week and took the pictures. But apparently she was snatched out of a strip mall parking lot, black hood put over her head. The only person she ever saw after that was Lelani."

"Did they find remnants of a computer in the fire at Lelani's?" Kronos asked as he came in to steal a cookie off the patio table.

"No, I don't remember that in the report. Why?" Russell said.

"'Cause without a computer, how did he send the proof-of-life pictures to the dark web?"

"Couldn't he use his phone, the library or a PC place? Hell, a Staples?" Russell said.

"The meta-data is from a smartphone camera; the path was from a hardwired device."

"What does that mean?"

"Means he'd have had to defeat a very serious firewall that all public computer places and libraries have to stop dark-web activity. It's possible, but extremely doubtful, that your indigent laborer would have that kind of digital muscle and programming knowledge and yet be too friggin' stupid not cash in mad skills like that at UniDynamics itself. Shit, he coulda pulled in a couple of hundred K a year," Kronos said as he brushed cookie crumbs from his shirt.

"So, Kronos, are you saying there had to be someone else involved in the kidnapping?"

"Unless this Lelani guy was a friggin' idiot savant, yeah!"

Brooke was pleased that her admonishments to Kronos to substitute "friggin'" for the other "F" word were taking hold. "So that brings us back to someone else pulling Kupalli's strings," she said.

"Has his death been ruled suspicious?' Mush asked.

"No, right now it's an accidental death. There's no evidence of a third party or foul play," Russell said.

"Of course, that doesn't rule out that he was murdered by someone with craft," Brooke added nonchalantly.

"Wet work? Here in Paradise?" Russell said as he harrumphed, referring to what the spies in his favorite thrillers called assassinations.

"Excuse me, but I don't see how any of this helps your case, Brooke," Chu said. "Whether he was the kidnapper or working for someone else, unless you can prove someone else killed Kupalli, you're still the number one suspect."

That bucket of cold water chilled the room for a few minutes.

CHAPTER 16

WALEED RETURNED to Penang triumphant. Both loose ends had been cut. Local Hawaiian news reports saw Lelani's demise as the accidental death of a junkie exactly how he had designed it to be. Thankfully, the "other" never made the papers, again a testimony to his skill and stealth.

f

In the backroom of a suite of offices, over a Chinese laundry that served as Waleed's cell's headquarters, five tables with five laptops each filled the space. Kupalli's codes were being loaded into these laptops. It took just under two hours to load a laptop and top off its battery and modify the GPS receiver. They were managing two hundred per day. At that rate they would be ready and fully deadly with a margin of safety of forty-eight hours prior to the operation's start.

The auto-executed programs were designed to lie dormant while the laptops were left in sleep mode. The sleep drain on the battery for this model of new laptop insured that the programs could self-activate anytime over a two-week period, more than double the time that was needed.

Then, at a certain time, they would all awaken in the cargo holds of one thousand planes inflight. Within thirty seconds after the machines woke up, each hacked plane would be put into a death dive from thousands of feet.

Then the true glory of the cause would be known by the infidels. The cost of the operation was around two million dollars, most of that in purchasing the laptops, fabricating and modifying the off-the-shelf Sat-tel USB devices, and shipping cases.

The Caravan part of the plan was free, in that a package, once in the pipeline and properly barcoded—with Kupalli's hacked account number—was shuttled around the world by the computer-controlled logistics system of Caravan. For their part, each airline that encountered a Sultan's Express-labeled shipping box immediately routed the parcel to the next plane out, secure in the knowledge that their scan of its barcode insured a "premium" payment in full, from what was now the world's largest company.

Of course, all that was the brilliance of the hack. False accounts, false shipping addresses and delivery dates each calculated by Kupalli's database-driven program to have all one thousand packages in the air at the same time.

All Waleed had to do was load them in his truck and, over three trips, just slip them into the system. Kupalli's hack was so complete, it erased any trace of itself as each laptop box was scanned. Because Caravan sold laptops on its site by the thousands, the company would never know of the relatively small number of one thousand additional laptops that were inserted into their system which traffics 1.8 million packages a day.

f

Upon walking into her dining room, which Kronos had commandeered, Brooke had to throttle back her attitude. She reminded herself that Kronos had volunteered to help. She was no longer an executive schedule 1 director of a federal agency and he didn't work for her, or the federal government, any longer ... and neither did she. So, she took a deep breath as she approached his massive set up of computers that used to be her dining room table as ... he played Flight Simulator.

His concentration was laser-like. She stood there for five minutes before she cleared her throat. As she did, the plane he was flying crashed into the ocean.

"Good thing you're only flying a game."

"Oh, hi Brooke. Didn't realize you were standing there."

"Is this a new game? It's pretty realistic."

"It should be. I've coupled actual flight control software to a Boeing 787 simulator used to train pilots."

"And you're playing or piloting it why?"

"Kupalli's code hacks were to get avionic control programs. At first I thought he was purloining them for a competitor. You know, so a company could save the tremendous costs of R & D on their own systems by plagiarizing the code. Saving them millions in development."

"And now, what are you thinking?"

"I'm thinking that I needed to know more about avionic software, so this lash up I created uses the same software flying in planes today."

"Fly by wire," Mush said as he entered the room in his daily service uniform. He had decided to go in this morning and help finish up deployment reports.

"Oh, hi Mush. Yes, exactly. As far as the avionic software on my computer is concerned, it thinks my computer is a real 787. Only of course, when it sends a signal to put the flaps at 5%, instead of the hydraulic system mechanically pushing the metal down into the airfoil, the simulator takes over and reports back to the software that the command, 'set flaps to 5%' is done. The simulator then acts like the flaps are adding lift, fooling the Boeing avionics software to believe it's controlling and getting input from an actual plane and its instruments."

"But it's really only talking with a program that's making believe it's an actual plane." Brooke caught on.

"Exactly, so my test of the avionics software is as real as real can get."

"So, what are you looking for, Kronos?" Mush asked.

"So far, I don't know, but I think the answer lies in the avionics package. I just haven't hit on it yet." He started his take-off roll once again, on what was a pretty decent graphic representation of runway 22 Left at New York's JFK International Airport.

"We had a Trident simulator when I was on gold and blue was out at sea on patrol. I used to keep sharp on updated systems and new software that was waiting for me on my next patrol." Mush was referring to the crew-sharing system by which two identical crews, one designated blue and the other gold, alternated tours on the same boat in two-month cycles, keeping the 5.6-billion-dollar nuclear weapons platform, SSBN, at sea for eight months out of the year. Then Mush had a thought. "Hey, Kronos, could you use a hand?"

"I kinda work alone."

"Yeah, I got that. But I'm going back to your description of a thousand yards of books. I had a D-5 missile tech on my last patrol who's a whiz at computers."

Kronos turned and looked at Mush. He was about to object when he realized that the admiral was right. There were millions of files, and one needle possibly in a haystack buried into a single line of code in any one of them.

"Sure."

"Great. He's on R & R for the next two weeks. Maybe I can snag him." He turned to Brooke. "Gotta go, hon." He kissed her on the cheek and left for his office.

CHAPTER 17

ADMIRAL GRAHAM HUBBELL came into Mush's office. "Brett, did you see the new deployment schedules that just came down?"

"I was just reviewing them now, Graham. You're concerned about the *Iowa*, right?" Mush said. His responsibility was to insure that there were always enough Trident missile subs out there, under the blue, to be an effective deterrent force against nuclear attack.

"She's scheduled for Virginia class upgrade, so we have to amend the deployment order. Either delay her upgrade or the deployment."

"I think the upgrade takes precedence over the deployment. We can cover the schedule by extending the *Massachusetts* patrol to cover the first four weeks. Then call up the *Oklahoma* thirty days early to relieve-on-station, and then we're covered in that quadrant," Mush said.

"Good plan."

"You want to notify Sec Nav's office, or should I?"

"I'll send an email."

"Thanks, Graham," Mush said.

"You look a little drag ass this morning. I'm pretty sure baby watch doesn't start for a few more months yet."

"Cholados Colombianos."

"Is that a new syndrome or something?"

"No, it's why I get up in the middle of the night on 'crave' watch!"

"What is it?"

"An icy fruit salad in a cup. She had it when she was stationed in Cartagena with the FBI. There's one Colombian joint over on the other side of the island. At first, I had him make a few, but they don't refrigerate well. So I bought all the ingredients and an ice crusher, and I cut up a batch when the crave alarm sounds."

"I got off easy, then. Denise just craved chocolate and peanut butter."

Mush thought for a second. "Hey wait, is that why you named your kid ..."

"Um hm, Reese!"

"Would Cholados be a boy's or girl's name?" Mush said.

Graham laughed and started to leave but stopped and turned back to Mush. "Hey, did you see the movie company on base?"

"I saw all the trucks and cars. What's going on?" Mush got up and walked over to his window. He could see the semitrailers, RV campers, special movie trucks and pristine quality 1940s Chevys and Fords on the backs of car carriers. On one trailer truck was a Grumman Hellcat fighter plane with folded wings. The plane was only painted on one side. It was obviously a prop.

"They're making a Pearl Harbor movie," Graham said.

"Don't tell me they're going to start blowing things up?"

"No, they specifically outlined that they're doing all that in CIG."

"I think the term is CGI," Mush said. Kronos was rubbing off on him, and he had heard him mention Computer Graphics Imagery once.

"Whatever, but the good news is, Susan Brock is starring."

"Whoa! She's a knockout!"

"Did you see her last film? She was almost naked for half the movie."

"I missed that one, but whenever her movies came up when I was deployed, half the crew of the Nebraska needed cold showers after."

"She is a fantasy walking. I'm dying to see her in person," Graham said.

"Why?" Mush asked as he went back to his desk.

"To see if it's all Hollywood fakery or if she really is a goddess."

Mush laughed, and said in an affected patrician tone, "Well, at least you have a postulate by which to proceed in your inquiry."

"Bullshit. I just want to see if those puppies are real!"

Mush looked at his office door and, satisfied it was closed, and nobody was listening, just laughed and shook his head.

f

On his way to lunch, Mush was distracted by a 1939 Ford. Its teardrop headlights and bird-beak-looking grill always fascinated him when he was growing up. He walked over to the movie guy who was spraying it with a dulling spray that took the shine off the pristine paint job. He did a double take as he looked at what he first thought was a dent, but realized it was just some shadows painted onto the sheet metal that appeared as a dent.

"Wow. That's good," he said, pointing to the faux blemish.

"Yeah, the director thought it was too clean. Wanted it to be more realistic as a car someone uses every day. The prop guys added this dark Streaks and Tip spray to mar the body, and I'm taking down the showroom shine with this stuff." He referred to the spray in his hand as he shook it and the ball inside rattled around the aerosol can.

"My dad inherited his father's '39 Deluxe Convertible. Just like this one, in cream color and dark-brown leather seats."

"Still got it?"

"Nah, Pop sold it in the early seventies"

"Too bad. These babies go for a pretty penny nowadays, even as junkers."

"I drove it a few times. He had to use hand signals because the car didn't have directional signal lights back —"

"Well, hello."

Mush was interrupted by a female voice. He turned to see Susan Brock. She was stunning, even in her vintage wool suit and clunky black shoes. Her hair was in a forties style, *A Gibson Tuck Roll.* He knew that because his mother always commented on the picture of his grandfather "Mush" Morton and his Grandmother Bryce. Grandma's hair was in that same hairdo, and his mother always commented on how "that woman was born for the Gibson Tuck Roll." In fact, this actress looked a little like his grandmother ... when she was younger, of course. It made him smile. "Hello, aren't you all gussied up? As my dad would say," Mush said.

"Thank you. Are you an extra on the film?"

Mush laughed. "No, no, this uniform is not from wardrobe. It's government issued. I'm stationed here at the base."

Her eyes lit up. She had just noticed his smile. It was refreshingly different than the usual jaw-drop, dry swallow, lecherous reactions that the Academy Award winning actress was used to getting. Her many R-rated movie roles and leaked sex tapes online further added to the mix.

She couldn't put her finger on it, but this sailor's reaction was more ... mature. Sweet even. Not a drop of fantasy or even desire, almost as if he thought she was someone else. She also noticed how handsome he was. "Well, hi, I'm Susan Brock. You know, you could be the leading man in this movie."

Mush blushed a little. "Well, thank you, but I'm happy with my role here. I'm Brett. Brett Morton. Nice to meet you."

"What is your role around here, Brett?"

"Well, Miss Brock, I work with the submarines. Kind of help with the scheduling and things like that."

"First, call me Susan, or, better yet, Sue." Her eyes scanned him from head to toe.

Mush took a deep breath and didn't want to hear what the "second" thing was, so he changed the subject. "Are you hot in that outfit. It looks heavy?"

"The director is a stickler for authenticity. This wool is all they had in 1941. We had to have the shoes made special." She deliberately lifted her skirt a little higher than needed to show her "new" old shoes. She pivoted one on her toe. Her perfectly shaped calf also in view, as she showed off her period-appropriate nylons, with the sexy seam running down the back.

Mush caught himself looking a little longer than necessary but broke off the contact as he returned his gaze to her face. He found it smiling, and her eyes were suddenly soft, and what one could only call, inviting. A nervous assistant dabbed the sweat that was forming on her forehead in the midday Hawaiian sun.

A seaman first-class approached and saluted.

Mush snapped a sharp salute in return.

"Admiral, CINCPAC wants to see you after lunch, sir."

"Thank you, sailor."

Susan Brock's body bristled when she heard him addressed as admiral. The only thing she could think to say was, "Is that the rapper, SyncPoc?"

Mush stifled a smile. "No, no musical ability there. He's my boss, commander in chief, Pacific Fleet. CINCPAC! Well, it was nice meeting you, Ms. Brock. Good luck with the movie."

He turned to leave, but she extended her hand, "It's Sue, Admiral. I hope to see you around. We're here for two weeks ... you know."

Mush shook her hand once then just nodded. He said goodbye to the guy with the car and walked to the officers' mess.

CHAPTER 18

GREGG RUSSELL was home. He was watching *Pawn Stars*. He loved history and questions like whether the cup the guy says George Washington kept his teeth in was real, or just a worthless antique that never touched the first president's choppers. His phone rang and he answered without looking. He quickly muted the TV when he recognized the voice on the phone. Suddenly he was actually *talking* to history.

"Mr. President. How are you?"

"Ah hell, Gregg, drop the Mr. President. It's just you and me on this call."

"No WHCA?" He doubted whether the White House Communications Agency allowed the commander in chief to place a truly personal call.

"I borrowed the phone. Besides, I got two days left, then the first lady and I are on the beach."

"You had a good two terms, Jim. Did a lot of good for this nation. I believe you have left office with a sterling legacy intact and bullet proof."

"So they tell me. You know this whole president thing was unexpected. I just thought I was running to build a case for four years later ... and now I'm looking at a presidential library and for a cause to champion like all of us in the ex-president's club."

"Very exclusive, that club. In fact, I'm thinking about how much money I'll be able to get for your old flight jacket in a couple of years."

"Wait till after I'm dead. You'll clean up."

"Hey, I'm older than you, Lieutenant," Russell said.

"Way older, Major. How's Missy?" POTUS said.

"Missy's good. She's counting the days too. Although the problem with living in Hawaii is there's no place better to retire too. She's going to be mad she missed your call."

"And how's your daughter?"

"Abigail's heading into her second trimester. So far so good."

"In a few months, let's get together ... Grandpa! You either come to me or Delores and I will head over. But let's make that happen."

"Hey, POTUS, like I'm free. Anytime."

"How's my girl Brooke holding up?"

"Oh, you heard?"

"Yeah, I can't say I was calling strictly for old time's sake. But now at least I know what happened to my leather jacket, you thief."

"I'll donate it to your presidential library. How's that?"

"Nah, keep it and cash in. We got enough junk to fill it ten times over. What's the latest on Brooke?"

"Jim, she's amazing. I see now why she's your favorite. Incredible instincts, measured, cool. Calm. She got a guy here who's working a computer like Liberace plays the piano."

"That would be Kronos. Yes, he's the best of the best. He and her and her whole team saved America at least twice. But it's all need-to-know, Major."

"Yes, sir. She's saved a woman's life, connected a kidnapper to the case, and stopped a young girl from getting abused, and it's only Thursday."

"I got two more days. Let me know if there's anything she needs. Including a pardon."

"Sweet, Jim, but these are state charges. You have no pardoning power in the 5-0."

"Crap. What good is being the most powerful man on earth if you can't help out someone who this nation owes so much."

"Jim, if it's any consolation, I believe her to be innocent. But the DA has means, motive and opportunity."

"So, if innocent is not a defense, any idea what Brooke's strategy is going to be?"

"She's trying to find the real killer."

"Why aren't the local LEOs doing that?"

"They got their collar: her! They aren't interested in continuing."

"I see. Well, keep this number. It's my body man's. He's always with me. Call me. Keep me in the loop."

"I will. Good luck with the transition to civilian."

"I'm serious about us getting together in a few months."

"Roger that, Lieutenant."

"Up yours, Major," the commander in chief said.

Gregg laughed as he hung up, then called his wife, who was out shopping for 'baby stuff' with his daughter, to fill her in on the call.

f

Mush introduced one tech wiz to the other. "Neal Kensington, I'd like you to meet Vincent DeMayo."

"Nice to meet you, Neal. Call me Kronos,"

"Then call me Crusher."

"No shit? Wait. Crusher688?" He snapped his fingers. "You racked up twenty-two million points in *Torpedo Run*." Kronos tapped the submariner's dolphins on the new guy's shirt. "Duh, of course. Wow." Kronos shook his hand again more energetically.

"Did you guys just bond?" Mush said.

"Crusher here is a legend, the all-time 'champeen' of a game called *Torpedo Run*. Of course. You're a friggin' submariner. Cool."

"I'd like to play that sometime," Mush said

The two tech-heads looked at the admiral and said, "Er, sure anytime, Mush."

"Yeah, any time, Skipper."

"Hey, you two, I played that game for real, remember."

"You got me there, Mush," Kronos said.

"So, what do you got lashed up here, Kronos?" Crusher said, changing the subject.

"I got two 12-core Pentium dual processors ..."

"I'll just leave you two ..." Mush tried to interject. But they weren't listening, as Crusher was oohing and ahhing over the horsepower Kronos had under his hood.

f

Mush met Brooke at the bottom of the stairs. "How did it go? Did Kronos kill him?"

"No, no, quite the opposite. Kronos was humble and laudatory."

"Wait. Are you sure you're talking about The Lone Ranger, FU, I-always-work-alone Kronos?"

"Yeah, apparently my missile tech had a secret life as the top scorer of a sub game on the internet. Kronos knew him by his game handle, Crusher. They bonded instantly."

Mush's expression was not lost on Brooke. "Look at you. You're all proud of yourself there, aren't you, buckeroo?"

"Well, I did overcome an immovable object with overwhelming force."

"So you did. Come upstairs. I want you to move something else," she said with *that look.*

"But what about the children?" Mush asked with faux sincerity.

"They'll be playing with their toys for hours."

"When you put it that way ..." He picked her up and carried her up the stairs. She covered her mouth as she giggled ... *because of the children.*

f

Going back to bed for some extracurricular activity this early in the morning was becoming a regular thing. They were really enjoying pregnant sex. No need for protection, no fumbling, just pure commencement to pleasure. They had gotten better and better at it, and they knew it. They looked for every opportunity to share themselves. Brooke was enjoying the new patterns and long, luxurious satisfying motion, allowing nature to decide when it was concluding. Not to mention her delight in discovering her new, hormone-fueled passion. Followed by the safety and warmth of holding each other until their breathing returned to normal. Brooke also took to the notion that the love they were expressing for each other was not lost on the baby she was carrying, and that they were creating a "cradle of love" for their child. Although she realized her breasts were starting to get a little sore. She'd have to ask Mush to be a little gentler.

f

"The successful mating of the two technosapiens still hasn't given birth to any further developments regarding Kupalli's true intentions," Brooke told her lawyer, Chu. She was astonished at how she was using maternity phraseology in her speech patterns lately.

"Well, we have to proceed under the worst-case scenario that they won't find anything exculpating. Now, the DA's case principally rests on your inability to prove your whereabouts between 7 and 9 p.m. on the night of the murder. If you were on base there would have been a record of your not having left, and witnesses. But you maintain you were on the beach at Ewa."

"It was a spectacular sunset."

"You drove there, leaving the base at 6:48 p.m. and returning 9:21, when you were observed by duty officer Lambert. Round trip to the murder scene, as I traveled it at that time of night, was twenty-two minutes. So, the state will maintain you had ample time to meet Kupalli, murder him and return to base."

"Hey wait. Kronos!" she yelled into the dining room.

"What's up?" He ran in.

She tossed her phone at him. "I took a picture of the sunset at Ewa. Can you secure the metadata in such a way as to preserve the chain of evidence?"

Chu was impressed that her law-enforcement ethics were in full force even at her own peril.

"Sure. Cinchy. Be right back."

She looked at Chu. "Maybe?"

"We'll see." He returned to his point. "Now, they still have to prove you did it."

"And all they have is the same kind of knife they say was used in the murder."

"About that. I called a forensic expert. He looked at the autopsy photos and said that even from the photos they were clearly wounds from a K-Bar."

"The most ubiquitous knife on an island where its standard equipment for most military personnel," Brooke said.

"We do have that in our favor."

"And the knife they took from here was clean," Brooke said.

"Not the get out jail card it seems. All they have to do is convince the jury that you cleaned it. Given your previous law-enforcement history, it's reasonable to assume you knew how to cover up a murder."

"I wish they shot him. I'd have passed a paraffin test."

"We have to prove there was a 'they' or convince the jury that state's evidence is circumstantial."

Kronos came back in and handed the phone back to Brooke. He printed out the sunset with the metadata in a box on the lower right. She showed it to Chu. "8:22 p.m."

"Not good. Even if it took you ten minutes to kill him, forty-four minutes there and back, you still had an extra eight minutes left before you returned to base."

"Yeah, I always take the scenic route home after slitting somebody's throat." Brooke looked off at the last lick of sun lapping at the Pacific. She turned back to Chu. "What about the van driver?"

"We got his deposition. Not great. He admits to stopping at the edge of the sand to smoke a joint and watch the sunset. But he couldn't pick you out of a photo lineup. He was a hundred yards away. The DA will jump all over that if we bring it in."

CHAPTER 19

ORAN, the armpit of Algeria. The great Albert Camus despised it so much that he set the main location of his novel *The Plague* in this second city of a country whose first wasn't worth writing about. The one saving grace was Rai music, a genre of melodies born in Oran. The esoteric rhythms were a favorite of the man known only as Mastieff. His sole reason for being in the steaming metropolis was to meet his one and only contact, financier and partner, Nasser. He arrived early and decided to stroll the Casbah, the other thing Oran was known for, mostly because of a misquoted attribution to actor, Charles Boyer, who actually never said, "Come with me to the Casbah." Also known because of a fifties cartoon in America where an animated skunk referenced it as he tried for the affections of a black-and-white alley cat which he mistook for the most beautiful skunk he'd ever seen. *Come with me to the Casbah*, became a line repeated in movies, jokes and literature from that point forward.

From a strategic point of view, Oran, Algeria, was the most neutral territory from which to launch the "package." Mastieff had spent years setting up, cajoling and guiding Nasser to be ready for this moment in history. It was very close at hand, within days.

Back at his hotel, Mastieff called Nasser from the lobby. "At the bench, in ten minutes." Mastieff was very cautious. Not about this specific project, but in general. The Algerian authorities had no qualms about bugging every room, whorehouse and hospital to gather information to be used as reason to expel or extort anyone. Either way, he didn't need any partners in what was about to unfold. If certain powers within the Algerian government caught wind of his plan, they would surely try to attach themselves to it for the glory of it all.

f

The "bench" was a five-minute walk from Mastieff's hotel. It was in what the locals called "Little Paris," although the palm-tree lined roadway and vista of the port made Mastieff think of it more like "Little Cannes." No matter, it was wide open, and the traffic noise and rustling palms made any long-distant acoustic surveillance difficult.

Nasser was his usual nervous self. Mastieff used his most calming demeanor and modulated voice to coax the information from Nasser with a minimum of hand wringing and stuttering.

"My dear Nasser, I trust you are well?"

"Yes, quite well. Glad that this will be over soon."

"Of course, and you have performed your tasks well, Nasser."

"Thank you. It's just that the duplicity of it all, it shudders my spine."

"All will be quelled when we make our move. Fear not, my friend."

"Still ..."

Changing the subject, Mastieff looked out at the ships coming into this port city as he spoke in a forced casual tone. "There was a small withdrawal from the account, nothing of consequence really, yet I like to know where our money goes."

"As you should. There was a loose end that needed to be cut. As you say, nothing of consequence. The matter was quickly disposed of. Actually, quite a bargain for a plane ticket and a hotel room."

"So, I'm not to assume that someone went surfing off Diamond Head on my money?"

"Our money ... and most assuredly not, Mastieff."

"Very well. And if, as you say, it was a necessary containment so much the better." He turned to him. "Do you have it?"

"Yes." Nasser unslung the laptop case from his arm and handed it over.

"This is the special one?"

"Checked it three times. Yes, this is the special one we spoke of ..."

"Then our business for today is concluded."

"I have to get back before I'm missed," Nasser said.

"You should consider a new line of work, Nasser. They keep too tight a hold on you."

"That's very funny, Mastieff. Oh, if I only could."

"Be well, my friend. The end is near."

They went separate ways.

Mastieff put his headphones in his ears and listened to the local radio's Rai station.

f

Nasser walked back to his security detail that he had ordered to stay half a kilometer away. Omar, his head of security, opened the door and spoke into his headset. "The minister is in transit to the plane."

It was an old G3. His cousin had the new, sleeker G6. Still, this other plane had Vitara, his personal cabin attendant, who was "newer" and sleeker than the cabin girl of his cousin, the Emir. That was because the Emir's wife had picked his cabin crew.

As the minister of the Interior for the House of Saud, and a member of the royal family, Nasser had great cachet with the true believers. The fanatics he personally enlisted into the great cause, shaheeds like Waleed, became the part of the machinery by which Mastieff's ultimate plan would run. Thinking about Mastieff, Nasser picked up the cabin interphone and spoke to the pilot. "I desire to go to Monaco instead. Please file a flight plan."

"Yes, Your Highness."

The Casino Monte-Carlo was notified of the impending arrival of the Saudi prince. They scrambled to change the schedule to accommodate his favorite "lucky" baccarat table. As always, the prince would be staying on the royal yacht.

f

Crusher had to do some stuff around his house, so he got to the admiral's late. He came into the dining room and went to place his computer bag down on the chair but missed. "Damn," he mumbled as it fell to the floor.

"Crush, you okay?" Kronos said.

"Yeah. You know who I just saw on the base?" Crusher was breathless.

"No friggin' clue," Kronos said.

"Friggin' Susan Brock! Right here! On Pearl."

"Geez, what a fox. Did you see the tape with her and that quarterback guy?" Kronos typed a few words into the search bar.

"How about that scene in the 'Angry Housewife' when she seduces that mailman. Can you imagine, having all that coming at you, just to get even with her husband."

"Why is she here?" Kronos said as the leaked sex tape came up on his screen.

"They're shooting a movie here."

"No shit. I gotta go check that out."

"Yeah, like when? You haven't left this room in days!"

"That reminds me, I need you to compile this code. I want to try this algorithm to weed through the files we pulled down yesterday."

Brooke, carrying a menu, and Mush came into the dining room. Both reacted to the naked woman and man having sex on the computer screen.

"Hey, guys! A little decorum here," Mush said.

"Sorry, Mush, Brooke. We was just checking out the babe that's on the base shooting a flick."

"What kind of film can she possibly be shooting here?" Brooke said.

"Some war picture."

"With a porno star?" Brooke said.

"No, babe, that's Susan Brock. She's the leading lady with that guy who was in that ransom movie," Mush said.

Brooke and the boys turned to Mush, all three surprised. She said, "How would you know that?"

"I met her yesterday or the day before. I forget."

"Sir, you met Susan Brock?" Crusher said like he was his new hero.

"On my way to lunch."

"To lunch," Brooke repeated.

"Yeah, there was this '39 For—"

"And you forgot," she interrupted.

Mush's sonar was pinging. "Er ... I was walking to the mess, and there was this '39 Ford, and she walked over and introduced herself."

"No shi—. I mean, wow, sir. She said hi to you?" The tone of incredulity was dripping from his words.

"Yeah, Admiral, she ... said hi ... to you?" Brooke now had her arms folded. "What did you two talk about?"

"How hot she was ..." Mush couldn't believe he just said that. "That came out wrong. She was in a wool costume for the movie, old clothes ... grandma clothes ... very heavy ... non-flattering wool, old lady shoes, nothing at all ..."

"Mush, stop talking," Brooke said.

Crusher and Kronos looked at each other with the same idea: *Sucks to be him right now!* They both jumped into their work to avoid the uncomfortable atmosphere that had suddenly descended on the room. "So, a reactive polynomial supplicant?" Kronos said.

"If I can get it to trigger in a nominal range."

"That's great. Don't forget negative values. There could be an inversion somewhere in algorithm."

Brooke knew better than to interrupt the two titans of tech as they spoke words of love. Kronos was working the big machines that he had brought with him, and Neal "The Crusher," Mush's missile tech, was working his personal laptop, which sat atop a big black box hooked up to it by a cable.

Mush left the room. Brooke saw her chance when the boys came up for air. "Hey, guys, we're sending out for pizza. What do you want on it?"

Crusher, who had been stationed at Pearl for the last three years, instinctively said, "Ham and pineapple."

Kronos, the hacker from Brooklyn, suddenly took umbrage. "What? Pineapple. On pizza? Dis-grazi-ata. What kind of communist, anti-American, freak-a-zoid, desecration of the noble, yet humble pizza is this? You could get shot in Bensonhurst for even thinking of ordering a slice of 'a-pizz' like that."

"Screw you. Like you should talk, when the best pizza joint in Brooklyn is called the Spumoni Gardens? Ice Cream! Not even pizza in the name?"

"Oh yeah! Hawaiian pizza was invented in friggin' Ontario, by a Greek no less, you strunz."

Brooke now remembered that nerds and pizza was a cult indivisible by modern reason and logic. In fact, it was the key to her boss Bill Hiccock's cracking the Eighth Day Affair. "Guys, guys, simple question. Focus. I'll get each of you a personal pizza, so you don't have to fight.

"Sausage, peperoni, mushrooms, extra sauce, thin crust. Aw crap." Kronos banged the table.

"I don't think crap is a topping," Brooke said.

"No, the simulator just crashed!"

"She lock up on you?" Crusher asked.

"No, not a program crash. I mean actual crash. Suddenly the controls all went to zero and we plunged down from 33,000 feet."

"I'll let you figure this out. Cokes and iced tea?" Brooke said.

"Run a processor error log. I'll bet it's an unassigned variable error, deep down in a loop," Crusher said.

"I had that once in a DOD hack. It was the seventh layer loop that triggered a crash code," Kronos said.

"Time bomb."

"Yeah, took me two weeks to find it."

They were lost in their world of zeros and ones, so Brooke just walked out, confirming to herself, "Coke and iced tea it is."

CHAPTER 20

DIANE PRICE had suffered professionally last year as the Washington anchor for MSMBC. She had dogged down an explosive story. She had the proof. She had corroborating witnesses. Within her grasp was a sensational headline and a much-deserved byline, but it was not to be.

She was derailed with less than five minutes to airtime. Her network, which ran a heavy schedule of promos touting the big story, was forced to eat crow, and she was summarily let go, without reason, cause or fanfare, lest the network suffer greater loss of status and possible libel lawsuits.

She was given a generous severance, once she signed away her right to sue, protest or claim discrimination.

Tonight, her thoughts returned to a colleague of hers, now in federal prison, Carly Simone. She was silenced by the Mitchel administration. Just for doing her job. She had another decade to serve out on the ridiculous charges of aiding and abetting a presidential assassination, illegal disclosure and wiretapping.

That was why she didn't reveal her history with the woman in the video, the woman on the bridge, the killer of that man on the tracks. She couldn't tell Cheryl or the legal baboon, Rod, that their paths had crossed before. The woman was, at minimum, a President Mitchell insider or his mistress, with the first lady's consent. The name Brooke Burrell-Morton was etched into her brain like the name of the girl in college, Lucinda Graves, who completely and totally ruined her life.

Lucinda, who always had designs on Diane's college boyfriend, Chad, recorded and released a sex tape with him just to get even with her. In the tape she coaxed, by teasing, Diane's Chad to say horrible things about her, or Lucinda wouldn't satisfy him. His words poisoned her life. She left Princeton in disgrace, changed her name to Diane Price, and made it into Wesleyan University. With the change in her hair color and some judicious plastic surgery, which made her facial features more appropriate for television, she was confident that most of the Princeton crowd would never remember her as the pitiful, unable to satisfy Chad without going "back door," Linda Watson. She shuddered again at the horrible things said and believed about her.

Her current dilemma was: Does she go up against this Brooke again? The video was incontrovertible proof that she was a ruthless, cold-blooded killer who should have never been within a mile of a federal agent's badge. The other consideration boding in favor of going forward was that Mitchell's administration was ending in two days. He would not be able to cover up this crime, *his mistress's crime*, any longer. *Could an ex-president be impeached for covering up a murder?* That notion created a tingle in Diane Price. She could visualize herself in the network's anchor chair once more.

f

Mush got to his office early the next morning. His mail was on his desk, and some folders with things he had to administer that day. On top of the mail pile was a small invitation envelope. It was addressed in a cursive script, ***Admiral Morton.*** He opened it up. It was a personal card, gold leafed and smelling of perfume. It read; "***Admiral, I would love to have a drink while I am here. I am staying at the Royal Hawaiian under the name Georgia Jones. Most nights I am free after 8. -Sue.***"

Mush was mildly shocked. He read it again. He sniffed the perfume. A smile came across his face. He placed the card on the edge of his blotter and dug into the morning mail and folders for the day.

Graham came in and said, "Hey, Brett, what's a good time for you to meet with logistic support today?"

"I'm good after two."

"Roger that." He turned to leave.

"Graham!" Mush called out. He held up the invite. "Here, I think I got this by mistake."

He read it. "Holy Shit! Is this ...?"

"Yeah, do me a favor. Put it the burn bag."

"Mush, this is a million ... check that, billion-to-one opportunity!"

"Gregg, then you go meet her. Tell her one admiral is as good as another."

Graham was in shock. "Mush, there are times that I wonder how you tolerate walking among us mere mortals down here on Earth."

"Hey, I already got my angel. See ya at two?"

"Affirmative."

CHAPTER 21

THE MUFFLED word "shit" followed by a thud sprung Brooke's drowsy eyes open. She wasn't sleeping anyway, but trying too. The alarm clock read 3:21 a.m. She turned and Mush was fast asleep. She touched his hair. Even being charged with murder, she was filled with joy. She was creating the human manifestation of their love for each other. She remembered a plaque she saw once at the home of a couple in their nineties, Cynthia and Rez, two wonderful people she met at one point in her life while on leave on the beach in Puerto Rico. The plaque on their wall read, "Family; because two people loved each other." Right before her at the time was living proof of that proclamation, the older couple's huge family, children, grandchildren and great grandchildren, all congregated at the same celebration she was attending with Peter Remo. He was a sweet older guy who was a friend of her White House boss, Bill Hiccock, and with whom she'd had a brief Parisian encounter a few years back.

She was starting *her* family because she loved the man next to her. Who knew, by the time she and Mush were retired and in their nineties, how many children, grands and greats would be celebrating life with them.

Another muffled expletive from the dining room rousted Brooke from her bed and her thoughts.

She went downstairs and entered the dining room. "Disobedient machine?"

"Aww, Brooke. No, it's actually working fine."

"Okay then, why aren't you working fine? And why are you still up?"

"I'm trying to recreate the crash, and this friggin' machine won't do it."

"Isn't that a good thing?"

"No. I mean yes, normally. But it shouldn't have crashed today. No reason, no condition that I can replicate."

"Want something? I'm going to the kitchen."

He looked at his cup. "Nah, I am going to call it a day soon, I just wish ..."

"Maybe with a little sleep your bio-processor will process better."

He threw the mouse down and pushed back from the table. "You're right. Sorry if I woke you."

"S'okay. Sleeping for two isn't all it's cracked up to be. I was just lying there, coveting sleep."

f

"Can I slit your throat?"

"Sure thing, honey."

"Okay so stand here." Brooke positioned herself behind Mush. "This won't hurt a bit," she said as she slid the back of her comb over Mush's throat. "No, that doesn't give the angle shown here in the medical examiner's drawing."

"So, the attack must have been from the front," Mush said.

Brooke came around and kissed his nose, then stepped back and sliced across his neck, freezing before the comb left his skin. "But this is at an up angle."

"How tall was Kupalli?" Mush said.

Brooke checked the report. "Five-nine."

Mush spread his legs a little to get down to about 5'9". She tried again.

Same result. Then Brooke lowered herself. The angle matched.

"You know I love how tall you are," Mush said. "Especially since it proves you didn't kill him."

"Proof? Hardly," Chu said. "State will find three experts to negate the height angle."

"But not from the front."

"True, but that doesn't help you either."

"I see what you're saying. From the front might indicate someone he knew. Which doesn't rule Brooke out," Mush said.

"But it does help us know that he knew his killer. Maybe we can find out who that was," Brooke said.

"How?" Chu said.

"Kronos, you busy?" Brooke called out.

They walked into the dining room. Kronos was at 36,000 feet in an MD-80 over the Atlantic. Everyone knew not to say anything, because this was actually work ... of some kind.

He switched on the auto-pilot and turned. "S'up?"

"Can you get into Kupalli's phone?"

Chen objected. "Whoa, that's hairy. Besides, the FBI couldn't crack a terrorist's smartphone, and they were kicking Apple's butt to release the code to unlock his phone."

"Forget that. Hand me his laptop. I'll tell you in ten seconds." Kronos opened the machine. In seconds, he turned it around. There were all Kupalli's messages.

"Holy shit? How many laws did you just break?" Chu asked.

"Just now? None. He had his messages linked to his MacBook Pro through his iCloud account."

"That's his laptop?"

"No, it's one of mine. I just loaded the image of his hard drive on it."

"So, it's a clone?"

"Zactly."

"Kronos, any messages prior to the murder?" Brooke asked.

"Let's see. 4:55 p.m. B3 830."

"That's it?"

"Hey guys, Admiral, Mrs. Morton, James." Crusher came in, took out his laptop and sat down to start work.

"Sounds like a map reference," Mush said.

"Yeah, but who's map?" Chu asked.

"Who's the message from?" Brooke said.

"It says, 'solicitation.' Meaning it says nothing," Crusher said, leaning over and looking at the message as he opened his laptop.

"Maybe there's something I can find ... Fuck!" Kronos said.

"Kronos!" Brooke admonished.

"Sorry, frig! The plane crashed again. Damn."

"Okay, look, see if you can figure out if this is a meet or just an order for vitamins. We'll leave you to swear at the machine now."

"Honey, I'm going online to see if where they found Kupalli has any kind of map ref or connection to B3," Mush said.

"Good thinking." She turned to Chu. "It's time we visited the murder scene, don't you think?"

CHAPTER 22

ALTHOUGH NO LONGER the anchor of the Washington based MSM-BC Evening News, Diane still had a few chits in the DC favor bank. Moreover, these were folks in government, media and law, with the right mindset. They formed the base of the anti-Mitchell administration undercurrent, those bureaucrats who were not fans of their current president. It took over twenty calls, but she finally talked to one person who gave her a lead to a disgruntled bureaucrat, an insider who made it quietly known to the person Diane reached out to that he had a powder keg of revelations that would bring the Mitchell administration to its knees. Her contact said that the subject matter was deemed to be so hot it was untouchable by anybody in town, meaning DC. But Diane was no longer in town, and this could be her ticket back. She asked the go-between to set up the meet.

When her person called back, the location the source wanted for the meet was off the beaten track, but that was par for the course. There was also a request for "expenses."

-f-

The chalk outline was still visible on the spot where Kupalli had died. Brooke squatted down and took in the sight lines, orienting herself the way the body fell to see what the victim saw. She looked at her watch. It was 8:25. There was a streetlight 150 feet away, a sodium vapor. "Where was the BMW parked?" she asked Chu.

"Three hundred feet east." A voice came from behind her.

Brooke turned to Russell.

"Mush said you were out this way," he said.

Brooke looked at her phone. She had missed Mush's text: "Russell looking for you."

"Nice to see you, Gregg."

"Communing with the scene of the crime?"

"First, just for the record, this is the first time I've ever been to this part of the island. Second, how did the killer get here?"

"This place was the perfect pick. No surveillance cameras. No one around at this time of night," Russell said.

"So let me play along. If I'm supposed to have killed Kupalli, how did I get him here? Did I text him?"

"Maybe. We can't get into his phone, and your lawyer there won't let us into yours."

"It's a national security matter, detective," Chu said.

"Okay then. Maybe you followed him here?"

"Okay, why was he here? Did he choose this perfect spot to be murdered in?"

"I'll admit the state's case is not great, which is why they're going to hang on to you till they get a conviction," Russell said.

"Look, I know he met his killer here."

"And you can prove this how?"

Chu looked at Brooke. His face said, *Don't do it!*

"Wanna know how I know?" she said, pointing a finger at herself.

Chu closed his eyes.

Seeing Chu's concern, Brooke made a last second decision not to share her "investigation" or the illegal measures employed to obtain the proof she had Kronos dig up. Instead, she went to stereotype. "Let's call it a lady cop's intuition, shall we?"

Chu breathed easier.

"Well, then all we got to do is get the judge to allow 'female intuition' into the body of evidence and we are all done here," Russell said.

"Very funny, Detective. But you have to admit, we are building reasonable doubt," Chu said.

"If ... he lets clairvoyance in," Russell said.

Brooke walked over to him. "Could you get me the ME's record of all the deaths on the island, a week before and a week after the Lelani murder?"

"What's your angle?"

"I want to see if Lelani maybe didn't work alone. Or, better yet, if he had an accomplice, who were they working for?"

"That's quite a jump in logic."

"Actually not."

"How so?" Russell said.

"Lelani didn't have the horsepower to pull off and hold a woman hostage for two years. If he was doing it for ransom, something more than a six-hundred-dollar a week deposit, he was either buying Fabergé eggs on the European market or giving it to charity, because he lived like a rat."

"Kupalli wasn't paying ransom. I think that's established," Chu added.

"So?" Russell said, palms up.

"So, somebody may have been running and paying Lelani."

"So why do you want the death list?"

"Maybe that somebody, also became a loose end, like Lelani? Brooke couldn't let on about the proof-of-life pictures that Kronos found on the dark-web side of Kupalli's life. And since Lelani didn't have a computer, it probably wasn't he who posted them.

"You're still a spook, aren't you?"

"A spook who's up for a murder she didn't commit."

f

On the drive back, Chu said, "I can make a motion to subpoena Kupalli's phone records and messages?"

"We sure can, but it will take the FBI to crack a Smartphone. I don't see the HPD pulling in that kind of juice."

"This is so frustrating, we know what's there, you've seen it! We just can't use it in a court of law," he said.

"Frustrating to the max." Brooke said. For a second she thought about reaching out to her old job, to tap a few favors at the Bureau, but in the end, Kupalli's texts were a very small piece of a larger puzzle getting larger every day.

After a few minutes Chu added, "I see where you were going asking for the ME's list. Do you think Russell will deliver it?"

"If he doesn't, I'm sure Kronos can get it. I just didn't want to take his, or Crusher's, eyes off the ball."

f

When they got back to the house, Kronos was smiling.

Brooke squinted and asked, "Okay, did you do something good?"

He nodded.

"Really good?"

He nodded more frenetically.

"Show me."

They walked into the dining room. "Of course, Kupalli didn't know what B3 was either. He had to look it up. So I went to his browser history, the dark one. And there it was: an annotated map. With seven locations penciled in."

"Tell me that B3 was where he was killed."

"Zactly!"

Brooke turned to Chu with a big smile, which dissolved when he said, "Fruit of the poisoned tree." Meaning all of Kronos's work was inadmissible because the hack was obtained illegally.

"Friggin' buzzkill." Kronos sneered at him and turned back to the dining room.

CHAPTER 23

GETTING TEN GRAND cash out of the station was not easy ... especially for what would be considered "checkbook journalism." But there was no other way to pierce the veil of secrecy surrounding Brooke Burrell. Her public profile only went up to the time she left the FBI. Those records clearly showed she was not an FBI agent when she executed that poor man on the subway tracks. Tonight, if $10,000 bought what it used to, she'd have the real story of who in the government Burrell was killing for.

f

In true clandestine manner, the man, who only identified himself as Doug, insisted on a diner up in Elmsford, New York. Specifically, after 11 a.m., well after the breakfast crowd and before the lunch rush. He was in a booth at the rear. No one around. He was nursing a coffee, and an uneaten bagel sat longing for attention next to a copy of *War and Peace*. He had gotten to the diner at ten, sat in the window overlooking the parking lot. He was watching to see if anyone came early to pre-position themselves to catch him in the act. He also made sure everyone who walked into the diner came from a vehicle in the lot.

f

As she approached, he watched her like he was looking for weapons, or, more likely, recording equipment.

His persona was trench coat and fedora, even though he was in a timberland jacket over a Ralph Lauren pocketless baby blue shirt with a Yankee's cap where the fedora should be.

"Thank you for meeting with me ..."

He got up, put his arms around her and whispered in her ear, "Play along." His hands traveled over her back as he said, "Oh Jenny, how long has it been? I missed you so much." His hands went everywhere an FBI tech would hide a transmitter or recording device.

Diane was in shock but understood he was being cautious. Until he said, "Open your blouse."

"Excuse me?"

He sat and motioned for her to sit as well. "Show me your wireless chest or I walk out in five seconds."

Go fuck yourself was on Diane's lips. But she found herself unbuttoning her blouse under her coat. She took a deep breath and flashed him. *Thank God I wore a good bra*, was the silly thought that entered her head. She had to give him this much: his eyes didn't land on her breasts. Instead he looked around the edges and down for any wire coming out of her pants.

"Give me your cellphone." He stuck out his hand.

She gave it to him. He opened the book on the table. It was hollowed out and had what looked like metal screen door material on both sides. He put her phone in the book's "RF cage" and closed it.

"Okay. Do you have my money?"

"Can we chat first?" Diane said as she buttoned her shirt.

"I'm out of here!" He threw down four dollars and slid out of the booth, headed for the door.

The waitress came over. "Anything else for you, hun?"

"Nothing, thank you." She left and caught up to him in the parking lot. "Okay half now, half if I think you're giving me what I want."

"Look, I'm in violation of at least nine federal statutes and an oath I took. I could spend the rest of my life in Club Fed just for meeting with you without filing a contact report."

"How do I know you even knew Burrell?"

"Burrell? She's small change. What she was a part of, that's the story! That's the Pulitzer. What the Mitchell administration did in our name. And not known to this day."

Diane Price handed over the cash-filled envelope. They headed back across the parking lot to the diner.

Before they entered, Doug asked her to show him her ears. She did.

"Turn," he said. Not seeing any earwigs or buds, he went over the ground rules. "This is our one and only meeting. You may never contact me again. There are no cameras or surveillance in this diner. You may only take notes, no recording. No voice prints. I will tell you everything you need to do your job, which is to dig. I will show you where to put the shovel, but that's as far as I go. Do I make myself clear?"

"I agree to everything unless you're planning to write a book. Are you planning to write a book?"

"What?"

"Look, I'm not going to agree to anything if you're going to turn around and scoop me. Or talk to anyone else. This is an exclusive, and I reserve all rights to the story."

"Yeah, sure, whatever ..."

"No, agree or give me back the envelope."

"Okay, you're exclusive. Agreed."

"Good. I could use a cup of coffee." She opened the door and went back to the rear booth.

She reached into her jacket pocket and took out a threefold letter. "Read this and sign it."

"What? Why?"

"It says you're not an agent or in law enforcement; you're not engaging in entrapment, and you are giving this information in the public good."

"I'm not signing any ..."

"I don't care if you put an X, just date it."

He looked at her and then grabbed the paper and scrawled "Doug" and the date.

"Give me back my phone. I'm just going to shoot a picture of this for the metadata. Then you can put it back in your book."

"No, take your picture and put it in your jacket pocket, and hang it over there on the coat rack far away."

"Fair enough." She got up and placed her jacket on the hook by the booth twenty feet away. As she walked back, Doug put out his arm. She stopped. He patted her pockets.

"Excuse me! You don't get to keep touching me."

"And you don't get to fuck me over. Now sit or go. I got my money. I'm good."

Diane remembered her father's words: "You lie down with dogs, you get up with fleas." But what did she expect? She was dealing with a whistleblower. No, strike that, a traitor, as far as the oath he took to keep the government's secrets, secret. No matter. The truth was all that mattered, and if what he was saying was anywhere near the truth, this was a monumental story. Historic!

f

While she was out on bail, Brooke was persona-non-grata at Pearl Harbor High School. Everyone was very polite, but obviously, being on bail for murder, murder of the father of one of your students, made all sides agree it would be better for the school and the students if Brooke stayed away from PHHS. Lisa Barnes took over Brooke's coaching duties with the girls' soccer team. She came over to Brooke's house to go over her line up and strategies for the upcoming semi-finals. When they were finished, Brooke asked, "How's Jenny?"

"She has stayed home with her mom."

"I guess that's good. They have a lot of time to make up for."

"Imagine thinking your mother is dead for almost two years and then she shows up one day—a kidnapping victim."

"It's got to be a rollercoaster for the poor kid."

"Brooke, there's a rumor ..."

"What rumor?"

"That you had something to do with her mom being found?"

"Lisa, sometimes rumors are true and sometimes not. But I believe my interfering in any way with the Kupalli family would violate the terms of my bail."

"I think I understand."

"Hey, thanks for running the lineups by me. Remember, keep Mary G. in reserve. She's great in the final minutes. Moanalua High won't know what hit them."

"Good luck with your case. I never believed it for a minute, Brooke."

"Thanks, Lisa, you're a good friend."

CHAPTER 24

BROOKE CHIDED HERSELF. With everything going on in her life, she forgot to get a maternity dress, something that would be somewhat formal, yet let out a little to accommodate her ever-expanding waistline. Instead, she was testing the sanity of wearing her larger size LBD. It was snug, but this was just a reception for a new head surgeon at the base hospital. It would maybe last an hour or so. She decided she could put up with the tight fit for that long. She wanted to go to this social event because she needed to show the people on the base that she wasn't guilty of murder and she wasn't hiding.

f

At the reception Brooke had found a cluster of navy wives who had previously welcomed her to the base. She cautiously approached, ready to defend herself or be gracious, depending on what their opening salvo was. She was relieved when each expressed disbelief at the charges against her.

"Thank you. Thank you so much for those encouraging words. The day you all took me in and made me feel right at home was one of the reasons I decided I could actually live here, in paradise, with good people like you."

One of the wives was not so charitable. "Brooke, I want you to know that, although I believe everyone has the right to be considered innocent until proven guilty, I don't like the aspersions that your ... situation, let's just say, has cast upon us all. Do you know they're actually talking about a TV show called 'The Admiral's Wives?'"

Another wife jumped in. "Well, Penelope, I heard that rumor six months ago. I doubt Brooke's current troubles created that."

Brooke spoke up. "Yes, and thank you, Judy, but there's no denying that my case makes it more sensational a sales job or 'Pitch,' as they call it at the networks. So, to that end I'm so sorry that I'm being used to give momentum to that bad idea."

"Brooke, that young good-looking lawyer, the one that's always on TV defending you ... Is he married? My niece ..."

Brooke had stopped listening to the women because her eyes fell on Mush as a stunning woman in a dress that was just under the legal limit for "too revealing" walked up to him. *This has to be the porn star,* she thought. She looked down at her frock, her bulging middle, her swollen feet hurting from standing in heels. She suddenly felt ... matronly—for the first time in her life. She shook it off, blaming hormones once again.

⸗f⸗

"Admiral, how nice to see you here."

"Ms. Brock."

"It's Sue, and did you get my note?"

Mush took a deep breath. "Yes, I did. Thank you. It was very considerate of you to invite me for drinks, but Ms. Brock ..."

"Sue ..."

"Ms. Brock, I already have my leading lady."

Her head went back. This was new to her. No man, a CEO, senator, athlete or plumber, had ever said no to her. It intrigued her more. "So, no supporting actress role?"

"No." At that second, he spotted Graham at the bar. "Have you met Admiral Graham Hubbell? He's single."

Brock looked over at the bar. She gave it a few seconds and turned back to Mush. "He's not really my type."

"Probably just as well. He wouldn't know who Sync Poc is either."

She looked at him. She had never realized how rejection could be an aphrodisiac. "You know, I have my own jet, and LA is just three and change away. If you're ever casting for the role."

"Not going to happen ... Sue."

"Darling, introduce me to Sue."

Mush felt the splash of cold water on his back as he heard Brooke's sugary sweet voice, that he knew was fueled by vinegar, come from behind him. "Oh, hi babe. Mrs. Brooke Burrell-Morton, I'd like to introduce you to Susan Brock. She's on base shooting a movie."

"Pleased to meet you, Miss Brock," Brooke said with a slight emphasis on the "Miss."

"Nice to meet you too."

"What were you too talking about? Don't let me interrupt."

"Well, actually—" Mush started to speak.

Brock jumped in. "We were talking about my plane. I just got it, a new jet. It's baby blue and I redid the interior in a soft, kid-glove leather, yellow."

"Sounds kitschy. But anything to relieve the boredom of long flights, I guess."

"What do you do, Mrs. Morton?"

"That's Mrs. Burrell-Morton, and I was coaching girls' soccer here on the island ..."

"Was?"

"Yes, now I'm up for murder in the first degree! You know, assault with a deadly weapon?"

"Oh boy ..." Mush said under his breath.

Brooke continued, "Slicing a man's throat clear through from ear to ear."

Susan didn't know how to respond, so she did the actress thing. "In *Sobriety Sisters*, I played Janice Wheatly. You know, the alcoholic who killed off all the folks from her support groups?"

"No, I don't believe I saw that one? Did it go straight to video?"

Mush took a deep breath. He longed for Global Thermal Nuclear War to break out so that he could excuse himself from this awkward encounter.

"No. Actually, it was my first nomination for best supporting actress. That was before I took best for *Harlot*."

"Well, good for you, Ms. Brock. So nice to meet you." She turned to Mush. "Darling, don't be too long. The doctor's wife is just dying to meet you ... too."

Mush quickly exited. "Well, excuse me. Good luck with the movie." Mush followed Brooke to the gaggle of wives.

To his relief, nothing more was said about the "encounter." He hoped it wasn't just lurking below the surface like a depth charge waiting to explode.

f

The drive home was silent. Mush wondered whether or not he should just ask the driver to drop her off and take him directly to the doghouse.

When they were up in the bedroom, Brooke came out of the bathroom. She brushed her hair at the vanity before putting it up. She burped. "Excuse me," she said.

"Honey, it's all part of the pregnancy. I get it."

"Do you think I'm still pretty?"

Mush knew this was dangerous waters. Navigating this course could determine his sleeping quarters for the duration. "No, I think you are stunningly gorgeous. Every time I see you, I want to kiss you."

She turned and burped again. "Even now?"

Mush came over and adjusted the scrunchie. "You are my everything. I'm second in command to your every whim. I married you because you were the part of me that I had been looking for all my life. Brooke, I never thought I'd find my soulmate. And then you came sloshing and thrashing onto my boat. From that moment on, we were destined to be here, right here, right now—burps, flatulence, pee, and hormonals and all. I love every second of it, and I love you ... love you more with each passing day."

Brooke grabbed his hand and stroked it. "That's almost the most romantic thing I've ever heard; next time leave out the bodily functions." She kissed him. He kissed her back.

They found their way to the bed and made love. Sweet and tender. They held each other until they fell off. They awoke in each other's arms when Brooke needed to go to the bathroom.

Mush was lying on his back, his hands under his head.

She came back in and straddled him. Even though they had just made love, looking up at her—her fuller than usual breasts, more protruding nipples, just visible behind the sheer of her nightie—had an effect on him.

She felt it and wiggled her butt a little. "Oh, I see someone didn't get enough."

"I got plenty. Just something in the way you sat on me makes me want more."

She felt a little sore after the previous love making but didn't want to deny him. So she inched up a little towards his stomach and reached around behind her. As she paid attention to him, she said, "You know, little Susie there ... She was all over you."

"Yes, well, she did offer me a part in her movie."

"Oh really? Do tell."

Mush felt her grip get tighter.

"She thought I was an extra, you know, being in uniform and all."

"Extra what?"

"Extracurricular activity. But I shut down her engines. What you saw was her trying to restart the propulsion."

"And did she? Did she restart your propulsion, Admiral?"

Now Brooke was more forceful, and he had to adjust his position a little.

"Nah, she was out of fuel, and you were really funny. I thought she'd bust out crying. You really laced into her. Especially with the, the ... murder rap."

It was getting harder ... for him to talk.

He breathed in deep. He was confused. He didn't understand how being interrogated by her didn't stop him from reacting to being stimulated by her at the same time.

"So, you weren't tempted?" she asked in a sly voice.

"Not for a second."

"C'mon, I had brothers. She's right in there." Her smile was meant to coax a small admission.

"She's a kid. And she's got nothing on you. You, my wife, are the real one in a billion."

"Keep talking," she said, her own breathing starting to change.

"She's all Hollywood fakery. A movie poster, nothing real, nothing to ever desire or want. Brooke, you're all I ever wanted ... all, all I ever want now ... and all I will ever want."

She could feel him getting close. "You told her she was hot?"

"No, I asked her *if* she was." He was now struggling just to talk.

"What was she wearing when you met her?"

"Gibson."

"What?"

"A Gibson curl, what my grandmother wore. She looked like my grandmother. In the old picture in my house. She was dressed for the scene in 1941." He moaned. "All I saw was Nana Bryce—and her Gibson Tuck Rolls."

Brooke was very active now. "Wait, you're telling me that you met Miss Sex Tape, Miss Sobriety Sister, little Miss 'I have my own plane,' and all you saw was your grandmother?"

"And I saw you, my woman, your beautiful face, your incredible body, your eyes. Oh, baby. I love your eyes ..."

"And these?" She lifted her nightie with her free hand.

He reached up and grabbed those luscious, full breasts, as he reached the moment.

"Good, good, my big boy." A few seconds later, he pulled her down on top of him and kissed her deeply, grabbing a hand full of her hair as he pulled her in close as they kissed. They kissed and kissed until they once again fell off into a deep slumber.

CHAPTER 25

"MORTON," Mush said as he answered the house phone.

"Mush, it's Bill Hiccock."

"Bill, how the heck are you?"

"I'm good."

"Got to be a crazy time for you, handing over the reins and all," Mush said.

"The transition is going well, actually."

"Have you met your replacement yet?"

"Yeah, good woman. Lots of grit."

"Got a name?"

"Lieutenant General Melissa Bryant."

"I know the name. She's distinguished. Good choice, but she was a chopper pilot in Iraq. She going to run SCIAD?" Mush was referring to the top-secret group of SCIentists in America's Defense. It was Hiccock's brainchild when he headed up the clandestine "Quarterback Operations Group," an ultra-secret operations cluster operating out of President Mitchell's White House. The moniker "SCIAD" was a double-entendre of sorts, also meaning science advisor to the president in White House shorthand.

Brooke was his number one operator, and Bill's SCIAD network helped them defeat America's deadliest enemies. Although Bryant was a decorated hero, and more than capable of running missions, Mush was questioning whether she was the proper head for SCIAD.

"In fact, we're in discussions now to make it a separate part of the Intel community that I would head up. Because everything in Washington doesn't exist until it has an acronym, they're throwing around SCINT."

"Scientific Intelligence! Good luck, it's a smart move," Mush said, decoding the intel community shorthand.

"How's Brooke doing?"

"You heard?"

"Kronos told me."

"So then, you know what he found."

"Yes. Fooling around with avionic software could have serious national security implications," Bill said.

"So far, he only suspects plagiarizing, presumably corporate espionage."

"Tell Brooke if she needs anything, we're still a team. How goes the baby making?"

"So far so good. We're both enjoying it, maybe me a little more than her."

Bill laughed. He remembered the nice things that arose at the beginning when his Janice was pregnant with Richie. "I hope the bliss period holds, Admiral. Enjoy it while you can."

"Roger that, SCIAD. Hold on, I'll get Brooke for you."

Mush found Brooke on the couch.

"It's Bill." He handed her the phone.

"Hey, boss. So nice to hear from you."

"I just wanted you to know that Janice and I are ready to fly out there if you need anything."

"That's so sweet, thank you so much. But we're pretty good here. In fact, miracle of miracles, Kronos is actually working well with someone."

"That is truly amazing."

"About your offer to help. Right now I need to find the real killer. We have no leads as yet, but if something pops up, I could use some federal access: FAA, Passports and the like," Brooke said.

"If it happens in the next twenty-four hours, easy! If it takes longer, then I'll have to see how far my juice goes. By the way, we're going to spin off SCIAD to the intel community."

"With you at the helm?"

"Yes."

"Don't settle for anything less than an Executive Schedule 1. That director title is pretty sweet. It's what I had at CinFen."

"We're hashing that out right now, whether I will be SES or appointed."

"Would Pearson appoint a Mitchell man?"

"Mitchell has pushed for it. We'll see where it comes out in the wash."

"Good luck, Bill. Love to Janice and Richie, and thanks for calling."

f

Chu came to the door. Mush saw him. "C'mon in, James."

"I'm here to meet Russell."

"Is he coming here?" Brooke asked.

"Yes. I need to take custody of the ME's death records and the autopsy report as an officer of the court."

"Nice move. Russell can't be considered doing anything below the radar as long as you requisitioned it, in your role as my co-counsel."

"Only because the judge gave us a little wider scope."

Russell walked in through the open door.

"Admiral, Brooke, James. Here you go." He handed the file over.

"Glad there was a way to do this that didn't have you looking the other way," Brooke said to him.

"I still think you're literally chasing ghosts here. But you nailed the kidnapping and a few other tidbits. So, we pulled the report. And the autopsy finding's in there, too."

"Have you read it?" she asked Russell.

"The autopsy? Yes."

"Anything in the toxicology?"

"Nothing illegal."

"Look for the legal. I just saw a documentary on TV on drug-induced rage. And it looked just like what I was facing when I confronted Kupalli."

"A documentary?"

"Yes. In color."

"Did the TV show say what I might be looking for?"

"They did mention something about Hydrocodone."

"It's amazing what one can learn from TV these days ..."

"Ain't it though. Thank you, Gregg. Want anything?"

"No thanks. I have a robbery at an auto repair shop to check out. I'll let you know if I turn up anything."

"Thanks."

She handed the list to Kronos.

"I will OCR scan the list, create a relational database, then use it as a comparator for a criteria search," he said.

"The only part of that I think I got was Optical Character Reader. That turns words on a paper into a digital file. But however you do it, look for someone killed alone, or under suspicious circumstances. Better include natural causes too, in case we're dealing with a high level of craft."

"So now we're back to everybody. There's 238 names here for the two weeks," Kronos said.

"Eliminate the infirmed, the hospitalized, the nursing home residents. Oh, and prisoners. We'll hold off on them unless we don't find anything on who's left," Brooke said.

"Okay, so what's the next thing?" Kronos said.

"Run their bank recs. We're looking for regular withdrawals of six hundred cash, plus access to the dark web and, if we're lucky, who they talked to."

"I'll get Crusher on this right now."

"How you holding up? You haven't gone surfing or been out of the house in five days."

"Plenty of time for that later, but thanks for asking."

CHAPTER 26

"GEORGE STOVER? Diane Price, Metropolitan Broadcast News. Do you have a minute to chat?"

"On or off the record?"

"Let's start with off and see how it goes," Diane said.

The woman on the phone had mentioned Warren Kass, his old boss. That got her call through the switchboard. "How do you know the former secretary of the Treasury again?" George wanted to make sure this wasn't a set up.

"He was a subject of a story I was doing before he got ill. His admin assistant gave me your number."

"How's Francesca doing?"

From the trap he just set, Diane knew this guy was good. "Sally, Sally McMahon."

That was the right name, so George continued, "What do you want to know?"

"Did you work with a Brooke Burrell?"

"Yes, on a financial fraud case through CinFen."

"Was she at that time working for the White House as well?"

"What is the nature of your interest in Ms. Burrell?"

"It's Mrs. Burrell-Morton, actually. I'm trying to get background for a story we may decide to air. But I'm double checking all my sources."

"I suggest you direct any further inquiries to the White House."

"Were you involved as part of a team that carried out a mission in Grenada last year?"

"No comment. And I think we're finished here. Have a good day."

George hung up the phone and wondered how this newswoman knew about the impromptu midnight raid and rescue of the Prescott family from their ISIS captors? That was close held, need-to-know mission data. He thought for a few seconds then picked up the phone and dialed a number he never thought he would dial again.

⸗f⸗

Diane Price walked her Shih Tzu, Pinky, down the tree-lined 10th Street in the East Village section of New York. Poop bag in hand, she let Pinky sniff the same places she always sniffed, no doubt checking her "pee mail" on every walk. Diane figured she'd go at the last tree on the block, as was her usual preference. The neighborhood association put up low, garden border fencing around the tress to protect them from being targeted by animals. Pinky was content to just be near the tree, so it all worked out well.

She didn't notice the man across the street, who followed her to the end of the block. Nor did she notice that, as she was walking back to her brownstone, he had crossed the street to be behind her.

Pinky turned and tugged Diane as she went up to the man, tongue and tail wagging.

He bent down, scruffed her neck. "Hey, little one. What cha doing?"

"Sorry, she's very friendly," Diane said.

"So she is." Pinky was now enjoying a little scratch behind her ear. "That's okay. I am too."

He was a big man, yet he was gentle with the little pocket-purse dog. "Do you live around here?" Diane asked.

"No. Just visiting."

Figures. Too nice to be a New Yorker, was Diane's thought.

He gave Pinky one last scruff and stood up. "Diane, isn't it?"

"Yes." She was, after all, on TV. Then it hit her. She was on local TV. How would a visitor know her?

"Here's a little advice. Whoever your source is, they're leaking top-secret information covered under twenty-seven federal statutes and punishable by up to seventy-five years in Leavenworth. As you know, the first amendment, and freedom of the press, doesn't cover treason. They'll keep your bones there in Leavenworth prison cemetery, under a headstone with a five-digit number on it, until your 112th birthday." He looked around the tawny New York City block. "And you don't want to die in Kansas, Diane—not after this."

He turned and walked away.

Diane froze.

f

"Did he physically threaten you or indicate harm to your person?" Rod Weinstein, corporate lawyer for MBN, asked.

"No, he just threatened me with jail."

"What do you think, Rod?" Cheryl, Diane's boss, said.

"I don't think there's a harassment case here. It was on a public street. He knew your name, but you're a public figure. And what he told you about the law is true. He didn't touch you, and from your words he was nice to your dog. So there's no real smoking gun here."

"But it was intimidation, pure and simple," Cheryl said.

"But couched as a warning of potential litigation. Like a street sign that says: Fine for Parking Here."

"That's a rather blasé attitude. I was scared," Diane said.

"What I'm interested in is what is he talking about?" Rod dug in while leaning into the question.

Diane was suddenly aware that she was talking to the corporate lawyer. Even though Cheryl had given her the money to loosen up a source on "background," she never told her that it was a disgruntled member of the intel community. Realizing it was her butt out on a limb now, she suddenly wished she had her own lawyer.

Rod opened a folder and took out a check request. He slid it across to her. "Ten grand. Is this what he was talking about?"

Cheryl jumped in. "Rod, Diane came to me and said she had a source. And that he wanted 10K on background."

"An anonymous source?"

"Is there any other kind?" Diane said. "He was given to me by someone who I spoke with who didn't want to go on the record but suggested that this fellow would."

"Is he a current employee of the government?"

"I didn't ask, and he didn't tell."

"How did you know he was not lying to you?"

"I've been checking into his allegations and, so far, no outright denials but lots of flak."

"We think the man on the street who accosted, er, confronted Diane, was tipped off or directed by one of the calls she made to ascertain the source's validity."

"I don't like it. I don't like it one bit. If your man on the street is active intelligence community personnel, then the government knows what you're doing," Rod said.

"But Rod, if that were true, wouldn't we have gotten a cease and desist?" Cheryl said.

"It could be waiting for me on my desk."

"But if it isn't, doesn't that indicate this warning was not official? In fact, why warn her at all if the justice department is on the case? Why not just serve the writ?"

"All good points, Cheryl. How about we cool it for a couple of days until the government either files or doesn't," Rod concluded.

"If they don't, then we'll know that these are unofficial attempts to cover up wrongdoing in the system," Diane said.

"Either way, I want a security detail around Diane, 24/7."

"Why, Cheryl?" Diane said.

"Because the government will kill you first and *never* ask questions later," Cheryl said.

"Thanks. Now I feel all warm and cozy." Diane stared at a spot on the table for a small eternity.

CHAPTER 27

Fort Hamilton sits in the shadow of the Brooklyn side of the Verrazano Narrows Bridge. An active military post in NYC, it was where Sergeant Major Richard Bridgestone preferred to live, his on-again, off-again service to America fully recognized as a sergeant in the Army Rangers. He was jogging down by the seawall when his cell rang.

"Bridgestone."

"Hey, Bridge, it's George. How did it go?"

"I informed the woman of the legal liabilities of the course of inquiry she was on."

"Do you think she learned anything?"

"I seriously doubt it. But she can't say she wasn't warned."

"Thanks for doing that."

"No need to thank me, George. Brooke saved my life. Hell, she saved New York City!"

"Someone is feeding her hot intel," George Stover, who had received Diane Price's call, said.

"I guess we'll never know who."

"What if she's just using Brooke as the way in?"

"Then she's going after Mitchell. And smelling the blood in the water."

"What do we do then?'

"*We* can't do anything else. She's a US citizen, subject to the laws of Uncle Sam. So, the next move would be the Justice Department."

"You think President-Elect Pearson would protect President Mitchell?"

"The unit Brooke, Bill, Kronos, Remo and I worked for is still operational. He could call it up if he needs to. With or without us."

"What good is the Quarterback Operation's Group without the Quarterback, Bill Hiccock, calling the plays?"

"It's Washington, and in Washington, the bureaucracy outlives the individual players."

"Good point."

"George, let me know if anything further pops with this."

"Will do, Bridge."

f

Back in Brooke's dining room she and Mush were getting a lesson in digital forensics from Kronos. "I took a shot and only dug into deaths within a twenty-four-hour spread of Lelani's. That gave me thirty-eight. I eliminated thirty-two of these as either not having regular withdrawals, or out of the technical footprint."

Mush interrupted him. "Footprint?"

"Oh yeah, anybody with limited bandwidth service, simple Facebook-only grandparents, and anybody who's online activity never got near the dark web."

"Makes sense," Brooke said. "So any hits on the six that were left?"

"Yes. Only one had metadata that conformed with the sent timestamps on the proof of life pictures," Kronos said.

"Over how long a time?" Mush asked.

"Every single one!"

Brooke smiled at Mush. He was a sharp cookie, and Brooke loved his mind. "So, this is our guy!"

"It seems so."

"His bank rec shows six-hundred-dollar hits?"

"Yes, irregularly. Some 800 some 650, most 600. But all one week apart," Kronos said.

"Who is he?"

"A dishwasher."

"Brooke, why aren't you doing the happy monkey dance?" Mush said.

"Because all this proves is that Lelani had a partner, or a handler. Not who killed this dishwasher, or killed Lelani, or Kupalli, for that matter." Brooke turned back to Kronos. "What's his name?"

"Two names. Edward Malo. But his Facebook and other emails are under Al Rashid Benlavi."

"Convert?" Mush said.

"It would appear so, although I can't find any court records of a legal change of name. So, all his business was under his old name."

"Could this mean there might be a bigger connection here?"

"A convert could be working for an international group."

"An international group with interest in hacking Caravan and airplane manufacturers," Mush said. "All of a sudden, I don't feel good about this."

"Cause of death?"

"Cardiac arrest brought on by accidental overdose of medication," Kronos said.

"Easy enough to do to eliminate someone," Mush said.

Kronos turned from his screens. "Brooke, I think we need to do what we did with Kupalli."

"Another B & E to get his computer?"

"If we're lucky, we might find who he was working for."

"And we can't go to the cops because all of this is from your initial data dump from Kupalli's machine," Mush said.

"Done without benefit of warrant," Brooke said. "What's his address?"

f

As they drove up, Brooke was impressed. "A dishwasher?" She couldn't believe the sweet little house surrounded by Polynesian floral beauty could be obtained on a dishwasher's salary.

"There's a reason they call this paradise," Mush said.

"His dishes must be really squeaky clean," Kronos said.

"But not his intentions," Brooke said. "This might be easy." Brooke got out and walked up to a woman putting a yard sign down on the lawn. As she approached and saw the words "For Sale" she changed her opinion. This might not be easy. "Hi, are you the agent for this property?"

"Yes."

"Are Mr. Malo's belongings still on the premises?"

"No, the family removed them."

"May ask if you can direct me to a member of the family?"

"He was my uncle. I'm also a licensed real-estate agent."

"I'm sorry for your loss."

"Thank you. What are you looking for?"

"I was told that your uncle bought a piece of art that I was very interested in. When I went to ask for his contact, the seller informed me of his passing."

"Artwork? Like what?"

"If you don't mind, I'd like to have that discussion with the rightful owner of the piece. Was he married?"

"No, he was a bachelor."

"Who has custody of his things?"

"We put everything in storage. Until we could figure out who gets what."

"May I have a card?" Brooke held out her hand.

"Certainly." She reached into her bag and handed over a card.

"If you don't mind, I'd like to call you in a few days."

"No, that's fine."

"Good luck with the sale. I'm sure you'll have no trouble. It's a darling house and the grounds are splendid."

"Thanks. I've gotten three offers already and I just listed it this morning."

Brooke got back in the car. She handed Kronos the card. "Find me a storage locker somewhere on the island under the family name or her last name. We have work to do tonight."

CHAPTER 28

BROOKE WAS at Oahu Lock and Store at 8 a.m. when the office opened. She paid $99 for the first month's introductory offer for an 8-by-10-foot unit. She bought a fourteen-dollar lock. The clerk said, "Sign here, Miss Burrell."

She hesitated. "May I ask a favor?"

"Anything," the clerk said with a dreamy smile.

"Are you into numerology?"

"Er, no."

"Well, I hope this doesn't sound funny, but is there anything on the second floor with the numbers either 2, 3 or 5 or 6 but not the number 4. That's not a good number while Taurus is in retrograde."

The clerk had no idea that numerology and astrology didn't mix, but it had the desired effect. "Let me check," he said.

"Thanks, sweetie." Brooke had fun turning it on while this kid couldn't keep his eyes off her chest. Kronos had hacked into the storage company's records and found the rental agreement for a locker in the last name of Malo's niece, rented last week. It was unit 234.

"How's 232?"

"Perfect. You're so sweet to help me. How late can I access the unit?"

"24/7. Your keycard will get you through the main gate, and the only lock on your unit is yours, unless there's a hold put on the unit for lack of payment. Your first payment is due the eighteenth of February. And, uh, if you need anything else, my name is Olson." He handed her his card.

"Thanks, Olson, I will." She smiled and walked off.

He watched her walk away. His smile disappeared when he looked down at her signature, *Mrs. Brooke Burrell-Morton.*

f

At midnight, Kronos and Brooke pulled up to the Lock and Store and removed a suitcase and an old table lamp from the back seat before heading to the building, so to anyone watching, they were a couple finally getting stuff out of their place and into the storage unit. Brooke swiped her keycard at the front door and once again to call the elevator. They took it to the second floor.

The units were arranged with odd numbers on one side and even numbers on the other. 232 was right next to Malo's unit 234. This was going to be easy. Brooke took out her pick and tension bar. The round hasp lock was no match for the lock-picking skills she learned while training for the FBI at Quantico. They found Malo's laptop. It was charged, which meant this was going to be a single trip. While Kronos put his cloning device on the IBM Think Pad, Brooke searched for any other computer devices. She found his iPhone. She held it up.

Kronos turned it on and was immediately presented with a password screen. "We'll have to take it."

There went the single trip.

f

Malo's un-passworded laptop was child's play for Kronos. His phone, however, was a little trickier. But Crusher was able to rifle through the laptop and find possible passwords for the phone. He had it unlocked in five hours.

On the day of his death, Malo received a text message asking him to "*pick me up 2:30 HNL Arrivals.*" The ominous part of the message was, "*as usual, please be alone.*"

Brooke read the message and reasoned out, "Malo died the day before Lelani. Did Malo pick up his, and Lelani's murderer at Inouye International?"

Her suspicions were confirmed by the first part of the message. "*Just flew in, new orders, more money for you.*"

"Kronos, can you crack the TSA?" Brooke said.

"I got a better idea." He took out his phone and called Bill Hiccock, their old boss.

"Yo, Hick, Kronos here...yeah, I'm with her now. We're getting somewhere here. Look, can you get me TSA records for Hawaii for this last week. I need the total records, you know, with port of embarkation and passport scans so that I can backtrack legs and equipment changes."

f

Back in Washington, Doctor William Hiccock looked at his watch. He had thirty-two hours left to his presidential appointment as one of the most powerful men in the US government. "What are you looking for, Kronos?"

"There's a good chance the murderer who killed the man, who they say Brooke killed, flew into Oahu on the day of the first murder."

"Wait. First murder?"

"We're peeling back the onion here, Hick."

"I'll get on it. Am I sending it to the same drop box, Kronos?"

"Yup. Thanks. Say, 'Hi' to Janice and Richie."

"Will do."

CHAPTER 29

DETECTIVE GREGORY RUSSELL had a dilemma. Brooke calling him at the discovery of Mrs. Kupalli, kidnaped and near death, thrust him into the middle of the case, which he would have been all too happy to hold at arm's length. Now he stood by Mrs. Kupalli's bedside. She was demanding justice.

"What's happening with the trial of this horrible woman who killed my husband?" she said.

Russell wanted to tell her that this "horrible woman" had saved her life. But he couldn't say that because he couldn't reveal that he knew Brooke, and that she was working outside the legal system ... and being more effective than HPD. "Mrs. Kupalli, please understand, I would caution you against false hope. The woman is not guilty until proven so and then convicted in court. As you may be aware, her claim is that the prosecutor's case is purely circumstantial."

"What does that mean?"

"The DA may have charged the wrong person."

"Wait, why hasn't anybody else told me this?"

"I can't speak for others. I've got thirty years in as a cop, and I'm just telling you not to get your hopes up. This woman could be found innocent at the end of the day."

"Oh my God. That would be horrible."

"Not if she didn't kill your husband. In that case it's justice."

"What happens if she's found innocent? What happens to my husband's killer if it isn't her?"

"Unfortunately, if it wasn't her, then all the attention and focus on her may have given the real killer time to cover their tracks or leave the island."

"But why would they indict her if they weren't sure, and allow the killer to go free?"

"Again, she may indeed be guilty. But the DA is a political position. Sometimes that overrides law-enforcement norms."

"Do you think she killed my husband?"

"Ma'am, I'm not on the case. I don't know the evidence or lack thereof. I'm here because of an anonymous tip that led me to where you were being held."

"Sorry, I'm grateful for your finding me and saving my life. Yet my husband was killed days before. Is there a connection?"

"I can't say for sure. The main thing is that you're safe and getting well. And that your daughter isn't an orphan. That's a blessing in anybody's book." Russell was in mental anguish over having to hold a line that was tugging at him to be let go. "Mrs. Kupalli, if I may, you have been through a horrendous experience. I can't begin to imagine what terrors you went through, but I know this: deep wounds make deep scars, especially mental ones. Please don't obsess on things outside your own recovery, and please accept counseling. I've seen it do wonders for other victims who were held for much shorter periods of time than you."

"Thank you, Detective, I will try."

"One more thing. Do you know if your husband had cancer?"

"Yes, he was in remission. Last time I saw him. Do you know if it came back?"

"No. I was wondering because we found some medicine in his cabinet and I was just curious. My brother is going through pancreatic, and I was wondering if that medicine was good in helping ease the pain."

"I don't know, but he wasn't on anything two years ago. It may have come back."

"As I said, I was just curious. Rest up. I'll check in on you in a few days." He turned and left the room.

Once outside he breathed a huge sigh of relief. He feared her retort to his statement, "I couldn't say for sure." Because if she had picked up on it, she might have challenged him with, "You can't say for sure, or you won't say for sure?" A direct question like that coming from a victim would have put him in a real pickle. He'd have had to lie, or expose the whole Brooke digging around episode, in which case he would surely lose his pension and possibly gain a cellmate!

On the other hand, Kupalli's rage under the influence could be the kind of exoneration Brooke's defense needed.

f

"Bingo." Kronos came out to the lanai.

Mush and Brooke were paying bills on the patio table. "Got a hit?" she asked.

"The files Bill got me were full data scope. The day of Malo's death, a Waleed Farouq arrived on a Malaysia Air flight 378, wheels down at 2:18 p.m. Carry on, no checked baggage. He had come from Singapore but started his trip in Penang. He flew out the next night, the night of the Lelani killing. He paid for a room for three nights at the Kuhio Grand Suites. I called them. They say he checked out after one night. He didn't ask for a credit. He went back to Singapore on the 10:30 flight out that night, same carrier."

"Fits the time frame. Do we call in Russell, see if HPD can track his movements on the island?" Brooke said.

"Want to know the really interesting part?" Kronos beamed like a little kid. "I called our old buddy at CinFen, George Stover. I asked him to run the credit card on the room."

"Not the plane ticket?" she said.

"He paid for his tickets cash. It should have set off flags, and now I know why it didn't."

"Okay, why?" Brooke said with a tinge of exasperation. But she respected Kronos's methodology. He spoke like he thought: this bit connects to this bit and then this part was connected here, and so on.

"George traced it through a series of shell corporations and cut outs to the Royal Bank of Saud."

Brooke was genuinely stunned. "Whoa! Kronos, is he sure?"

"Brooke, he was your best hand-picked agent at Treasury, but yeah I asked him to double check. Seems some or all of the funding for the murders, and possibly the hacking, is coming from Saudi Arabia. Although I haven't connected it that far yet."

"I don't want to be a party pooper here, but you assume this Waleed guy was the killer. How sure are you? I mean, isn't this all circumstantial?" Mush said.

"Out of the three thousand arrivals in the forty-eight-hour period, his movements are the only ones that come close to the times of death. And the 'pick me up' message from Malo's phone gives us half the matrix."

"Again, since we don't know the identity of the texter, how do we know that Malo wasn't just picking up a friend or business associate—who didn't kill him."

"Two compelling facts, Mush." Kronos counted on his fingers. "One, the message was the only one between Malo and an unrecognized number. And two, there was no, 'Can't wait to see you, honey pumpkin.' Or nothing like, 'The deal is imminent.'"

Brooke recognized the pattern. "Just a single, terse, tradecraft-styled message." She looked up and squinted at Kronos. "Honey pumpkin?"

"Hey, I guess hanging with you guys has had an effect on me."

Mush spoke up. "Brooke, honey ... pumpkin ... this is getting big. You may have uncovered an international conspiracy to murder and maybe to commit industrial espionage. Shouldn't you hand this over to the State Department or the FBI ... pumpkin?"

Brooke thought about it for a moment. "We're really exposed here. Bringing any of this forward invites a whole bunch of Inspector General and Justice Department questions. I'd personally take the risk, but Kronos is volunteering. I won't put him back in El Mira prison for helping me."

"Oh, that's right. I remember you telling me how Bill Hiccock got you a presidential pardon after they put you away for hacking for the mob," Mush said to Vincent "Kronos" DeMayo.

"Billy really came through for me. One minute, I'm being blackmailed by prison screws to fix their kids' computers, and the next I'm in the Oval Office explaining AI to the friggin' prez of the US. I got to tell ya, Billy boy was good like that. He didn't take all the credit. He let his people get the cred. Face to face with the fuc—"

Mush short-circuited Kronos, mid-obscenity. "Hey, how about we give George the credit?"

Brooke lit up. "That's a great idea. George is the only one of us that is still a federal agent. Kronos, can you give George an anonymous tip into all this? An 'untraceable' anonymous tip? And then George can call in the cavalry!" She put her arms around Mush and planted a big one on his cheek. "Perfect, my big strong admiral guy ..."

"Honey pumpkin, not in front of the guys. Geez." Everybody laughed.

CHAPTER 30

DIGIEARTH'S Geospatial Amassed Data Platform was the culmination of over fifty low-orbit satellites, all feeding imagery and topological mapping to its clients around the world. The data was essential for natural resource management, forestation control, environmental impact studies and a host of other geo-data points to aid businesses and governments.

The deal struck with the Saudi Arabian government insured that the natural resources, and, more importantly, new oil fields and deposits could be better identified from space and exploited.

As minister of the Interior, Nasser successfully lobbied for, and obtained, sole official jurisdiction over the arrangement. He was DigiEarth's point person in the kingdom.

For the greater good of the House of Saud, the satellites brought much improvement in resource management. But Nasser's "other" interest was the uplink feature. Or, more specifically, the ability to "bounce" data off an orbiting satellite.

DigiEarth employee and satellite communications tech, Rashad Farouk, was a key employee and held a critical position in the company. He was also a true believer.

Nasser had identified and recruited him to the "great cause" with relative ease. First, because Rashad was in awe of the Saudi Prince who took an interest in him. But, more importantly, because he was ecstatic to learn the Saudi minister of the Interior was not a stooge for the west, like many in the royal family. Rashad had grown to hate the nonbelievers and dreamed of teaching them "immutable" lessons.

It was Nasser who convinced, by hardball negotiations, the DigiEarth Company to assign Rashad to the Saudi satellite data center as a condition to signing the multi-tens-of-million-dollar contract for the Saudis. The move brought no scrutiny from the Saudi government because, as per Nasser's prowess in negotiation, Rashad remained on the company's payroll while on post in Saudi Arabia.

When the time came, Rashad would literally be the final link in the great blow struck against the nonbelievers.

Nasser had the memory stick that held the last work of Kupalli in his safe. The final module. That memory stick would be handed to Rashad on the day.

f

George Stover smiled when his in-box blew up. Thirty-seven emails came in from an address that was only a long number. He immediately knew it was Kronos, and he also knew that no one, other than the master geek of geeks, could swing an email dump into the US Treasury Department. And he also knew, no one here would ever know or get to within a country mile of suspecting it.

Following protocol, he called Treasury Department IT. Their security protocols would effectively quarantine these emails, until they did their analysis and they found they contained no spyware or viruses. Normally that would have happened before the emails appeared in his in-box, but Kronos wrote the government protocols every department used. So he knew how to get by them to make sure George saw them first and then requested them cleared, before they were preemptively trashed by the cyber snoops at Treasury, thus never getting to George.

An hour later, the emails came back from the .gov address at the IT department. These were the disinfected copies of the emails that were now safe to open. Although George knew that they were always safe, it made all this official.

This is hot stuff. George could see that the requests and leads before him in the email were all related to his own digging into the credit card of one Waleed Farouq. George forwarded various relevant emails to his counterparts at State and Justice. He asked for a Sec-Conf at 11 a.m.

f

The secure conference started late. George's emails quickly elevated to high-concern areas. Assistant directors were now on the video conference call. Anything that touched the Saudis was an attention getter within the halls of the American government. Each one asked George the same question as to how he came across this intel. And every time he answered, "Anonymously."

They decided to make the FBI the lead agency on this, with State running diplo support.

f

After the secure confab, George decided to call Brooke. He took a walk down 15th Street and, looking at the White House, used his personal phone. His phone which used VoIP together with his own personal VPN. That meant, as he was encoding his speech using Voice Over the Internet Protocol and then connecting to the internet over a Virtual Private Network, there was less chance of anyone, like the NSA, listening in.

"Well, you certainly got things moving here in DC," George said to Brooke.

"Let's hope it's just a nasty case of corporate espionage gone wild, and nothing more."

"There was a reporter nosing around here the other day."

"I guess the news traveled all the way back east, huh?"

"What news?"

"What are you talking about, George?"

"The woman reporter, asking about you and your team at the White House."

"Hold on. George, did you know I'm going on trial for murder?"

"What? That's impossible."

"It's all circumstantial, but that's how we stumbled on what we sent you."

"Who were you supposed to have killed?"

"The father of one of my students, but, George, we think he was into some nasty shit, the hackings and God knows what else."

"Got a good lawyer?"

"I'm defending myself."

"Whoa, hold on. You're going *pro se* in a murder trial? Brooke, I got friends over at justice. I can make a call ..."

"That's sweet of you, George. I have a co-counsel, a Pub Def, but he's sincere and got some game, and I got a good rolodex too."

"What's a rolodex?"

Brooke laughed. "Old world ... contacts page."

"Oh. Tell Kronos his submarining his own firewall worked like a charm. Take care. Call if you need anything."

"I just need you to put some muscle into this Waleed guy *et. al.*"

"In progress."

f

Kronos was clicking away on the keys like he was in a speed-typing competition as Brooke came up behind him. "George says you submarined the firewall real good!" Brooke said trying to "Bronx-ize" the compliment.

"Zactly."

"What's got you all typey on the keyboard?"

"I found a whole 'nother cache of Kupalli's files. Only these are web pages, URLs and videos. This guy had to be working for a major aerospace/aeronautic company."

"Why?"

"He's reading up— No, check that. He's studying satellites, sat comms, Ultra High Frequency radio transmissions, in addition to the airplane flight control systems and the Caravan hack."

"The satellites. That's new, isn't it?"

"Yeah, I just found a whole shit load of documents, some classified, in his stash."

"Any idea what he was baking with all these ingredients?"

"So far there's a ton of possibilities. Too many to narrow down."

CHAPTER 31

A year ago: Africa

IN THE MIDDLE of a pitch-black, moonless African night, a cadre of mercenaries surrounded a walled-off compound. Their leader, Mustafa Mastieff, known to them only as the "Big Dog," had painstakingly planned and drilled his men in every tick of the assault. "Amir, take your men and circle around. Wait for my signal, then lay down a pattern. Vegas, that will be your signal to open up. I'll be in the lead tank. We'll go right through the front gate."

Mastieff nodded, and the men dispersed. He picked up the night-vision binoculars. The compound he was about to breach was dark. Dwali, the owner and warlord who was their target, was not a foolish man. Therefore, Mastieff knew there had to be sentries. Maybe not awake, but that would change with the first salvo.

However, his employer, Roberto Mangonoti, an Ethiopian warlord of Italian descent, and the one who owed him three month's salary, was intent on smashing his rival, Dwali, and taking his drug, slave, and ivory business. Tonight that would be accomplished by overwhelming force and split-second timing.

In an odd twist of the soldier of fortune's "fortunes," Dwali had once hired Mastieff to protect a shipment coming in from Ukraine. Therefore Mastieff was familiar with Dwali's defenses and what lay in the compound beyond the gate. This special knowledge, or intel, allowed him to demand double his usual pay, which, so far, was not in his pocket.

Looking right and left, confirming his men were in position, Mastieff fired a flare gun, signaling his men to attack. Amir's men opened up with gunfire from the left flank. Vegas's men rushed from the right. "Go, go, go," Mastieff said to the tank driver as he lowered himself down and closed the hatch on his Russian T55 tank. The driver started up the noisy tank and rolled it off the back of the tank-carrier trailer truck that had quietly delivered the beast to Dwali's front gate. He yelled, "Fire!" The main gun belched a round right into the metal gates of the compound. The tank could have just as easily broken through the wall to breach the compound, but this was a grander entrance.

Bullets from small-arms fire pinged off the outside of the tank as it drove right up to the steps of the opulent main house. "Reload. Fire!"

The exhaust flame that erupted out of the tank's 100-mm cannon's barrel singed the doors a millisecond before the armor-piercing shell annihilated them, as its red-hot, razor-sharp shrapnel mushroomed out, tearing men and furniture to shreds and impaling the back wall of the main structure. He opened the hatch. He thrust his MP5 out first and rose slowly. The defensive fire quieted down. He jumped down from the turret and hung off the warm barrel with his left hand as he jumped onto the steps. He was in the main building in a flash. A stream of bullets tracing a path across his twelve o'clock, he dove right and returned fire to the upstairs balcony. The groans told him he had eliminated the threat. He advanced into the main part of the complex, towards Dwali's office. The man was frequently in there at this time of the morning connecting to contacts, vendors, suppliers and customers from time zones across the globe.

As he was advancing down the hallway, two loyal guards fired at him, but he had heard them rack their weapons a split second before and he took cover and returned fire. Vegas's men advanced into the corridor, and one of them threw a grenade further down the hall where the guards were. The exploding grenade fragments tore into their backs, killing them instantly as they turned to run from the smoking pineapple.

Mastieff rose and waved his men onward. He machine-gunned the lock on the two carved and ornate mahogany doors of the office. The wood began splintering outward as whoever was in there fired through the doors in an attempt to kill anyone on the other side. One of Vegas's men went down in a plume of blood as a bullet from the door ripped his jaw from his face.

Mastieff looked to Vegas who had made it to the opposite side of the door from him. He pointed to Vegas's webbing and the grenades dangling from it. He held up two fingers, then made a tossing motion, then a second motion. Vegas understood. He pulled the pin on one grenade and gently rolled it up against the door. He took cover. Mastieff also took cover, yelling, "Fire in the hole!" The concussion blew the doors open. Vegas already had the pin out of the second grenade and tossed it into the room before the reverberation of the first died down. As the second explosion echoed off the walls, more of his men rushed into the room. There was sporadic gunfire, mostly from his men shooting the downed bodies to make sure they were dead and not a threat. Mastieff made it to the other side of Dwali's desk. The man lay on the floor, his right arm gone. Blood was pouring from his shoulder. With dying eyes, he looked up at Mastieff.

Mastieff saw the recognition in his eyes. A small smile escaped the warlord's contorted face as he spasmed in pain. Mastieff removed his .45 from his holster. He pointed it at Dwali's head. The dum-dum slug went in neat but blew the back of Dwali's skull off. Mastieff took out his iPhone and took a picture of the bloody mess. That "proof of death" picture was his invoice for this job.

f

All the men had left the room now, to plunder what they could find, except one. This one in particular caught Mastieff's eye. All the others were ransacking, looking for things to steal or checking to see that none of Dwali's men were alive. But this one, Sendi, was tracking Mastieff. Like a hunter. Mastieff had gotten him this job, so he was surprised when Sendi raised his weapon and pulled the trigger.

Mastieff's arm was already coming up when the shock registered on Sendi's face as he pulled the trigger again. His weapon had jammed. Mastieff adjusted his aim from center mass and hit Sendi in the shoulder, sending him spinning towards the floor. He approached Sendi writhing on the floor. The .45-cal. slug shredded and separated a huge amount of flesh and muscle from where it should have been, inside Sendi.

Using the side of his boot, Mastieff turned him over. Sendi looked up in agony.

"How much?"

Sendi closed his eyes.

Mastieff stepped on his shoulder. There was bone showing. Sendi screamed. "How much did that bastard son of a goat offer to pay you?"

"Half your back pay."

"Not enough." He shot Sendi in the face.

f

Mastieff and his men returned to their employer's camp. They had lost six of the original thirty they started out with. Mastieff went to Mangonoti's tent to report.

Mastieff saw Mangonoti squelch his shock and surprise at seeing him alive instead of Sendi standing there, reporting that he was dead. Mangonoti turned down the Puccini opera playing on a surround-sound audio system. He covered his astonishment well. "How did it go?"

"Mission accomplished. Dwali is dead; his men are dead. His empire is now yours for the taking."

Mangonoti held out the palm of his hand and wiggled his fingers.

Mastieff opened his phone to the bloody "POD" picture and placed it in his hands.

Mangonoti smiled. "Well done. Bravo."

Mastieff wasn't interested in his false praise. "My money?"

"I don't suppose you'd take a check?" Mangonoti smiled. "No, I suppose not." He walked around to a footlocker and pulled out an envelope and handed it to Mastieff.

Mastieff grabbed the envelope and stuck it in his tunic, and then, just to see the man wince, Mastieff brushed his hand by his sidearm. He saw the fat man's eyes widen, half expecting Mastieff to assassinate him on the spot.

Instead, Mastieff turned to walk out, not knowing who among the guards were loyal to the warlord. This was not the place or time.

Mangonoti just had to ask, calling out to his back. "Your man Sendi? Did he make it?"

Mastieff stopped, turned and looked at him for an uncomfortable amount of time.

Mangonoti tensed.

"No. We lost six. He was one of them." He turned and walked out.

f

With his hand shaking, Mangonoti turned up the opera. It was his one concession to his Italian roots. Being half white, the son of Italian settlers to the Ethiopian colony back in the thirties, Dwali labeled him the "half breed." Mangonoti considered Dwali a savage. There was truly a blood feud between them. One that Mangonoti had won tonight. He was alive because Mastieff was unaware of his plot to have him eliminated on the raid. Sendi had obviously been killed before he could rid him of this arrogant mujahedeen.

With that thought, Roberto's hand calmed as it floated like an orchestral conductor on the fortissimo forte section of the aria.

Current Day:

Mastieff was a force of nature. Always the warrior, he grew tired of mercenary life. Making a few thousand each time for risking his life. The endless parade of good- and evil-intentioned clients, considering him expendable because they paid him for his time, skills and talent but, to his mind, not his life. His need to make one big score and get out of the mercenary game came from his last assignment in Africa, a year ago. The very man that he talked and urged his employer, the African drug lord, Mangonoti, into hiring, was offered a bonus by Mangonoti to kill him. Freeing the fat bastard of paying Mastieff the three months back wages owed him.

He thought about this new mission, which was days away, the enormity of it, the preplanning, all the moving parts, the shock on the faces of the world governments as they faced a nightmare from which there was no waking up. Mastieff's anticipation of what he would accomplish in a few days from now humbled him. For he would have achieved what no man had ever accomplished before. Including Osama Bin Laden ... in a capitalist way of thinking.

That grandiose thought faded as, from across the strata, he watched the fat bastard get into the back of his Rolls Royce. The rotund man settled in the soft camel-colored leather of his royal-blue Silver Cloud while his personal security men loaded into their cars.

Mastieff reached for the remote in his pocket. The Rolls was pulling away from the Opera House, boxed between the lead and follow black Mercedes security cars. Mastieff was feeling especially charitable this night, so he waited till the Rolls was a good distance away from the young couple in a kissing embrace at the curb, then he pressed the button in his pocket.

The Rolls exploded and went ten feet into the air in a fire ball. The follow car also exploded as it was engulfed in the flame.

"Good night, Mr. Mangonoti," Mastieff said.

As he walked away from the inferno that was melting the asphalt of Via Giuseppe Verdi, the street alongside Milan's Teatro alla Scala, his cell rang. "Yes."

"This is Rashad. I'm starting to have doubts. I can't sleep. I have headaches."

Mastieff immediately weighed the strategic over the tactical. If there were a backup satellite tech, Rashad would be dead before morning prayers.

But, alas, he had to play the game. "Rashy, Rashy. What is it? Am I not paying you enough? How much more do you require? I like you, Rashy. There's no need to stress. God's will, will be done. We are merely his unworthy hands here on earth."

"I know, I know. But my job, my position ..."

"If you do exactly as we discussed, no one will ever know of your contribution. And you'll be $25,000 richer!"

"I know I know, it's just that ..."

"How would an extra $5,000 make you feel?"

"That is very generous. I'll try to be brave, as you say."

"Good, good. Then we shall hear no more of this?"

"Yes."

CHAPTER 32

THEY CALL IT Foggy Bottom, an homage to the swamp land the US State Department was built upon in Washington DC, way back when.

George Stover's disclosure of Saudi Arabia financing two murders on US soil was shunted to the undersecretary for middle eastern affairs. He dutifully sent a secure memo to the charge d'affairs of the US embassy in Riyadh.

That foreign service officer alerted the chief of station (the CIA resident) and the ambassador. In a rare case of ambassadorial prerogative, his excellency the ambassador himself decided to forget all the cloak-and-dagger skullduggery and present the evidence that George Stover had uncovered to the House of Saud directly.

The impromptu high-level meeting had aides scrambling on both sides.

f

Nasser's intercom beeped. The words that followed shot a voltage of apprehension throughout his body. He usually received a heads-up well in advance whenever his uncle, the king, was going to ask him to his office. It rankled him that the caller, the king's secretary, used the term, "immediately."

Nasser's palm suddenly sweated. His breathing grew sharp. He was just days away from reconstituting the shortfall in the account. He considered feigning sudden illness, maybe pay off a doctor to remove an appendix. He could double over in pain right now. They'd call the ambulance. By the time he was well enough to see the king, he would receive his cut, and the royal coffers would be replenished.

His aide walked through the door with a file and handed it across the desk. "For your meeting with the king."

Somewhat confused, Nasser immediately assumed the king, or his secretary, must have called his personal aide directly to prepare the paperwork. Nasser's worst fears were confirmed when he glanced briefly at the cover sheet. It was from the Royal Bank. Not that his life passed before his eyes; it was more his death—by decapitation. He shook off the image and remembered he was ninth in line to the throne and should act accordingly. He stood, adjusted his suit jacket, fixed his keffiyeh so it sat right on his head, picked up the file and marched out of his office through the halls of the palace to the king's office.

The king was signing some decrees. He was being handed leather-bound documents which he signed and returned, not reading them. When his task was finished, he nodded to his staff to leave the room.

When it was just the two of them in the palatial office, he said, "The Americans are snooping around our finances, Nasser. Are you aware?"

"Sire, they have been doing that since 1931."

"This is a matter of more recent concern." He nodded to the file in Nasser's lap.

"I was handed this on my way here. What, may I ask, is the matter?"

"There's been activity in your ministry's account that is indeed troubling."

Nasser could hear the blade slicing through the air prior to slicing through his neck. "Sire, I can explain—"

"You can? I'm impressed. But it's not the amount, it's the criminality."

"What can I do, Uncle?"

"Start by explaining how nine thousand dollars from a 7.8-billion-dollar account found its way to a murder in Hawaii. The American's suspect a Waleed Farouq. Ever hear of him?"

Nasser suddenly found life. The room actually became brighter. His Harvard educated brain kicked in and was already in damage control before he knew that he was going to speak. "Sire, I'm very close to a full explanation and bringing the guilty to justice. However, I would ask that you give me another twenty-four hours to make sure my suspicions and discoveries are accurate."

"So be it." He waved his hand. "I just want to be able to get this American gnat buzzing around my African oil initiative out of my way. Twenty-four hours, Nasser."

"Yes, sire." With that, Nasser stood and bowed and backed away from the desk for ten feet, then turned and left the room.

Nasser walked down the hall. The release of his nerves had his body reacting like he was in subzero weather. Chills and shakes attacked him, the result of tension and guilt leaving his body.

Back in his office, he headed for the liquor cabinet. He opened the Hardy Le Printemps cognac and just chugged it from the $9,000 ornate Lalique cut-crystal bottle. His hand shook so much as he placed it down on the edge of the cabinet that it teetered and crashed to the highly polished marble floor. His intercom beeped. "Sir, are you okay?"

"Yes. I dropped a bottle. Call building maintenance. They'll need a mop."

"Do you need me?"

"No, no. I'm fine."

He sat at his desk as the smell of the spilled $600-an-ounce brandy permeated the room. He had learned two things from the king. The first, and most important, was that the two million dollars he paid the bank president to cover up such things was still having the desired effect. He knew that because the king referred to it as a 7.8-billion-dollar account, which meant his bribed bank officer was dutifully masking the 3.2-billion-dollar shortfall. Second, his offering to supply the banking for the operation to Mastieff was not the best idea. Nor was giving Mastieff the password to watch the account activity. But Mastieff would not have agreed to the whole operation without that observer status. He was, after all, a mercenary.

Nasser had a day to find, convict and execute someone who he could find guilty of financing the Oahu murders. He started mentally listing those he liked least who worked for him, and whom he could plant the evidence on to achieve summary execution. He also had to make Waleed disappear ... electronically, for now.

CHAPTER 33

"I CAN'T BELIEVE I'm back here again," Russell said as he stood in the front doorway of Brooke's home.

"It's nice to see you, too. Please come in." She closed the door behind him. "To what do I owe the pleasure?"

"I assume you already know this, but of course, officially, I can't know that you do, so here's me, officially informing you that we got a call from the FBI. Seems they are thinking that Lelani and some guy named Malo, a dishwasher, were murdered by an international conspiracy of some kind." He stopped to see if she was going to acknowledge this.

"Go on," Brooke urged, pokerfaced.

"So, as the FBI has it, person of interest number one flies in, kills Malo and Lelani, then flies out. He rents a hotel room, but never goes there. And doesn't rent a car," Russell said.

"Intriguing. Is that all?"

"Brooke, I'm still a cop, and I know you're behind all this somehow, but what I can't fathom is: How does any of this help your case?"

"We know Lelani had a motorbike. Did Malo have a car?"

Russell smiled. *This girl is good,* he thought. "Actually, that's one thing I can tell you that I'm sure you didn't already know. Malo's car was found at the airport."

"So, what could that mean?" her open-eyed expression more leading the witness than a question.

"Why don't you tell me?" he said in a grandfatherly tone.

"Well, of course, as you know, I can only guess." She placed her hand over her chest like her dear sweet aunt would do when she shared gossip or feigned insult.

"I'm sure," he said, the sly grin all too evident.

"Well, and I am just spit-balling here, but ... It could mean that Malo got a text to pick up Waleed at the airport, so he didn't need a rental. Waleed then killed them both and stayed at Malo's house, so he didn't need the hotel room that he booked in advance, and then took Malo's car to the airport and just left it."

"Why the hotel then?"

"Maybe he didn't know Malo's address and needed a local address to fill out on the custom's card on the plane."

"But you are just spit balling here?"

"Totally."

"How did you know the name Waleed?"

She held her hands wide. "Big, big spit ball."

He laughed. It was her first slip up. But he had to let it pass because none of this was on the record anyway. "Again I ask, how does any of this help you?"

"Don't know if it does, but it does satisfy the oath I took ... five times in my life."

"You know, we usually only get heroes here once a year, on December 7th."

"And those Pearl Harbor vets are the real heroes. The rest of us owe them so much."

"Amen, Brooke. See ya around," he said.

"You too, Russell, and thanks."

He turned and saluted.

Brooke snapped back a crisp return.

f

Brooke had no sooner got to the lanai and lain out on the chaise when the doorbell rang again. She got up with a grunt and walked back to the door with her hand applying pressure to her back, which had started nagging her more and more. She opened it and was surprised to see Susan Brock standing there. She was wrapped in two year's worth of Brooke's highest salary. "Ms. Brock, what a surprise. To what do I owe this visit?"

"Two things I'd like to say."

"Would you like to come in?" She stepped aside and waved her arm.

"No, thank you, this won't take long. I wanted to say that I think you're very lucky having such a loyal man for a husband. I'm not used to *not* getting my way, but he's really proved something to me that I never knew existed."

"What's that?"

"That there is a love, the kind of love we play at in movies but never believed existed. That a total commitment to someone was real and actually does exists. And now, suddenly my life is upside down. Everything I believed, and the way I lived my life, is now somehow a lie."

"I'm sorry that you feel that way."

"No, please don't be sorry! Maybe for the first time in my life, I have hope that a love, a real love, a love like yours really does exists."

"Well, thank you. I guess I'm glad that something good for you came out of this." Brooke wanted to say, *You meant to steal my husband. Instead he rocked your world without ever touching you. That's my guy, bitch.* But instead, she just smiled like a mom in a sitcom.

"There's one more thing. I read up a little about you. From what I know you are one ass-kicking bitch. And I just want to say that if the rights to your life story ever become available, there's no amount I wouldn't spend to secure those rights and have the honor of playing you in the movie."

"Wow. That's one I never thought of."

"Really? You never thought that you are a modern American female hero?"

"Kind of busy lately."

"Yes, defending yourself for the murder of a child abuser! But it seems you were always busy, a graduate of Harvard Law, Navy lawyer, former head of a federal agency. The top cop running the FBI's New York office. Being blown out of building in New York, and a zillion other things that I'm hearing through the grapevine, like working in the White House. That's a story to be told—must be told and must be known."

"Well, thank you. That's very kind of you to say."

She looked down at Brooke's belly.

"I didn't realize you were expecting. How far along are you?"

Even in my matron's dress? she thought before she said, "Thirteen weeks."

"Well, good luck. It isn't every day that an egotistical Hollywood diva gets to meet her new hero."

That softened Brooke's mood. "Well, it isn't every day a movie star knocks on my door. Good luck."

But she wasn't finished. "Even if it's against me, hold out for ten million for the rights, minimum."

"Good tip, thanks." At that moment, Brooke had a conscious revelation. "Susan, are you really looking for a good man, a real man?"

"Yes, I want that now, even more than an Oscar."

"Hold on ..." She turned and called out, "Crusher! Crusher come here. I want to introduce you to someone."

As Crusher approached the doorway, his eyes bulged out of his head, but he quickly recovered.

"Susan Brock, it's my extreme pleasure to introduce you to Lieutenant Neal Kensington, an officer and a gentleman."

She held out her hand. "Pleasure to meet you, Neal."

"The pleasure is all mine, Ms. Brock."

Susan thought, *There it is, that mature, sweet look in his eye ... just like ...* "Please, call me Sue."

They stood there looking at one another, smiles on their faces.

Brooke couldn't take it any longer. She crouched down and said with urgency, "Why don't you two go have a lemonade out on the lanai. I really have to go to the bathroom."

"I'd like that," Susan said as she walked with Neal through the house.

Brook shut the door, smiled, and trotted to the bathroom.

f

As his driver pulled up to his home, Mush looked up from a briefing paper he was reading in the back seat and noticed a large dark SUV in his driveway. The plates were local Hawaiian and not the white US government tags. He got out and approached the two men in the front seat. "Hello there. Who are you guys?"

"Personal security, sir."

"Personal security for who?"

"Is this your house?"

"Yes."

"Well, Miss Susan Brock."

"She's here? In my house?" Mush looked toward his front door, imagining it opening and firing a torpedo that was heading right for his boat.

"Yes," the security man said.

"Oh boy ..." He took a deep breath and turned to go inside.

f

He came in the front door and saw the back of Ms. Brock sitting out on the lanai. He heard laughter. "Thank God," he said as he exhaled.

"Thank God for what, hon?"

He pivoted. "Oh, you're here. Then who's out there with her?"

"Let's just say, I too overcame an immovable object with overwhelming force."

Mush still didn't get it.

"I introduced Miss Hollywood to Neal. So far it's working." Just then a squeal came from the lanai followed by laughter. "Pretty well I'd say."

"Now who's all happy with herself?"

CHAPTER 34

THERE ARE NOT a lot of birds in the desert, but as he jaunted down the hall to the king's office with a spring in his step, Nasser swore he heard them.

"Your Majesty, it is with great satisfaction that I inform you that my investigation into this financial irregularity has borne fruit. The guilty party is Saba Jalal, a staffer in the mapping department. It seems he was in gambling debt to two unsavory characters in the United State of Hawaii. Transmissions found on his personal computer show his treachery in siphoning off royal funds to eliminate these men and also his $432,000 debt. I recommend we write off his expenditure, because the assassin he hired, the man named Waleed Farouq, who was traveling under a forged Saudi passport, is reported dead in Malaysia, an unsavory man meeting an unsavory end, no doubt."

The king grunted in agreement.

Nasser continued, "All records of that discovered passport and any record of him in our country has been erased, so that no further inquiry will exacerbate US-Saudi relations. My suggestion, Your Majesty, is to let this dog lie."

"I agree, Nasser. The quicker resolved, the better. We cannot allow transgressions against the family to go unavenged. When is the execution?"

"At 3 p.m. By your order, which I forwarded in your name."

"Very well." He waved his hand.

"Thank you, sire. I would like to apologize for this lapse in my oversight."

"Run a tighter ship, my nephew." He admonished Nasser with a pointed finger as if he had failed to clean his room.

"Yes." He bowed, back stepped and left. Outside he breathed a sigh of relief that comes from knowing his head would remain on his shoulders.

As for Saba's head, he had defied Nasser's edicts and managerial structure once too often, even having the audacity to suggest that staffers should unionize!

f

At 2:59 Nasser's aide peeked his head into the office. "Sir, it's nearly three."

"Thank you." Nasser opened his browser and went to the live execution site. They had switched to HD cameras last year. The quality was vivid and crystal clear. The constable read the charges against Saba. He couldn't protest or do much of anything. Nasser had told the doctor to sedate Saba so that he would not embarrass the royal family. Although, wailing from his family could be heard in the background. Nasser was amazed they were allowed to get that close. Or even be there at all. He'd send a memo restricting this in the future. An imam said a perfunctory prayer and then, with a skillful swipe of the blade, Saba's head was cleanly separated from his body, which twitched for a few seconds. There was much blood.

Nasser shut off the video feed and went back to his report page as he breathed out a slow sigh. But a larger issue now loomed. Somehow the American FBI had caught wind of Waleed's adventure. He himself had recruited Waleed, who had become a key, non-replaceable part of the operation. He had all records of Waleed erased. Now he had to inform Waleed of his new identity.

CHAPTER 35

NASSER HAD ARRANGED to get the name of the American that informed the king of the missing money. The key to finding out was his brother-in-law, Sumni. A few years ago, Sumni was found with pornographic material in a very compromising manner. Because he was married to Nasser's sister, he covered for him, and thus no "fifty lashes in the public square," but Sumni had to pledge undying loyalty to Nasser, even above the king!

Nasser's reasoning at the time was: Sumni, who was educated and graduated from NYU in New York City, had valuable insights into American culture and speech patterns. So much so that his familiar, colloquial, east-coast blabber would disarm any American that Nasser ordered him to get close to. Sumni's fondness for the Yankees American Baseball Club was a constant irritant to Nasser but a breaker of ice, as the saying goes, with most westerners.

As it worked out, Nasser was able to place him in a trusted position at the US embassy a few years back. There he acted surreptitiously as Nasser's personal eyes and ears, inside the building.

As a local Saudi hire, however, Sumni was never allowed into any of the core rooms or secure areas. However, being looked upon by the embassy staff as a trusted liaison to the Saudi government meant he could glean much from the comings and goings and, more importantly, the internal traffic, even if he could not be close to top-secret materials or areas.

Those data points that Sumni reported on, when mixed with other Saudi Intelligence observations, gave Nasser a pretty accurate picture of what their "ally," America, was up to in the kingdom. The whole situation became a bonus for Nasser because it gave him the aura of having a "unique intelligence insight" which was held in high esteem by the king and the ministers.

Nasser met Sumni on a long stretch of desert highway by a small farm stand that served fruits and figs to travelers on this long, dusty road.

"You understand, we never had this conversation?" Nasser looked away because his Luis Vuitton 1.1 Millionaires Sunglasses were reflecting the sun into Sumni's eyes, making him blink.

"Yes, Your Highness."

"Good. Now, do you have the name?"

"Yes. A US government Treasury agent named George Stover."

"Is this reliable?"

"Yes, sahib. There's this girl who works in communications. She loves figs. I buy them here for her and make a present of them from time to time. She sometimes lets down her guard and doesn't cover the papers on her desk when she grants me entry to the radio shack. The figs I gave her that day were extra good. She hurried to put them in her lunch bag in the refrigerator in the break room, and I had a minute to see the file. The US ambassador was following a request by Stover to look into a murder, and some financial irregularities."

Nasser shook his head. "Figs."

"Have you tried them? Khalid has a green thumb," he said, motioning to the Bedouin merchant farmer behind the ramshackle roadside stand.

Nasser walked away without so much as a thank you, not to mention any critique of Khalid Wasser's figs.

f

Nasser was amazed at how good he was getting at manipulating people for his own ends. His power had always been applied for the good of the royal family, but now he was seeing how valuable that power truly was. He could ask of people things that weren't necessarily in the interest of the House of Saud. To his amazement people did what he asked, without question or delay. He was enjoying this feeling of omnipotence. By simply asking his cousin in the bureau of records to delete all the files of Waleed, and to do this before he met with the king, was a masterstroke. While Nasser was at it, and to give his request more gravitas, he also included

Saba Jalal, using his recent execution as the rationale. "To avoid embarrassment."

Nasser then flew to Penang to warn Waleed that he was the target of the Americans and hand him a new Saudi identity kit.

"But I cannot change my Caravan employment," Waleed said.

"Just don't use any credit card, phone, license or identity as Waleed until the day of the attack. Then on that day, and that day only, hang your Waleed ID around your neck. But the trail of Waleed Farouq ends today, this minute. Do you understand?" He handed him $50,000 dollars. "Don't return to your apartment. Rent a new place. Buy all new clothes, shoes, everything. Get another car. There's a Saudi license in the package. You must have absolutely no connection with the past."

"What about my mother?"

"You can call her after we have struck the blow and tell her of your new identity. But for the sacred undertaking we chose, you are no longer Waleed Farouq. He has to be dead." Nasser placed his hand on Waleed's shoulder. "Or you will be."

Waleed froze. He looked at the hand of a royal on his shoulder.

"In fact, it was reported to the king that you were killed in a foreign country. So, Waleed can no longer walk the earth. Do you fully comprehend? There's no margin for error. The FBI is looking for you, and the Malaysian police will be putting a price on your head, dead or alive."

There was fear in Waleed's eyes.

"Much will be sacrificed by others in our cause. Yours is mercifully simple. Just assume this identity and you will live to eat your mother's lamb stew once again."

Waleed looked down at his new name on the Saudi passport and back to Nasser and nodded.

CHAPTER 36

"HOW IN THE HELL could this have happened?" George said.

"George, I'm sorry. The ambassador decided to go straight to the Saudis," Owens from the State Department reported over the phone.

"What a dumb-ass move. He tipped them off! Has he always been this much of a schmuck?"

"He's new, a Pearson guy. He's got like four days on the job!"

"Political appointee then."

"Yes."

"God help us." He hung up. He picked up the phone again. Brooke wasn't going to like this. He was right.

f

"What the...?" Brooke stamped her foot.

"The trail's gone cold. No records of Waleed. Like he never existed," George said over the phone.

"I thought this was contained." Brooke's frustration tore at her composure.

"New ambassador trying to show a newer, more open relationship."

"Dipshit!"

"Amen."

There was silence. Brooke couldn't think of anything more to say so she just said, "Thanks, George. I guess we're back to square one."

"Sorry, Brooke. Good luck. I'm here if anything else pops up."

"Thanks. "

Kronos ended the secure conference video call.

CHAPTER 37

THE PIZZA was cold in the middle of the table. Everyone was quiet. The ticking of Mush's family's grandfather clock was the only sound. The search for Kupalli's killer had reached a dead end.

Brooke picked sausage off her slice, demurring from the crust. Mush sipped his beer. Crusher and Kronos were tapping on their phones.

"You gonna finish that?" Kronos said, pointing at the last slice.

"All yours," Mush said.

After a few minutes more of only tick tock, Brooke broke the silence. "Okay, look. We gave it a shot. Kronos, Crusher, I can't thank you guys enough. But I think it's time to put my fate in the hands of the courts."

"You can't do that. We got gigabytes of evidence: criminal mischief, blackmail, kidnapping and hacking," Kronos said.

"All illegally obtained without warrants or a badge. I could just take the hit on procedure and walk it in myself. Coming clean might count for something."

"Then they'll add wiretapping, criminal hacking of governmental systems, interference with a murder investigation and ten other things to the murder charge," Mush said.

"Yo, ten thousand emails will go out to ten thousand cops, FBI, DAs and newspapers before I let that happen, Brooke," Kronos said.

"Not one of those emails will have any more evidentiary value than me walking it in. It's time to plea bargain," she said, looking off.

"Hold it, honey. Let's review where we are," Mush said.

"You think we may have missed something, sir?" Crusher said.

"Possibly. Before we throw in the towel, let's use the brain power around this table to see if there's a clue we missed," Mush commanded.

An hour later, they had circled back to nothing. The pieces were just so incongruous. The three murders were all connected, but only two could be credited to Waleed.

"Hey, wait a minute! Kronos, what would it take to see if Waleed was also on the island when Kupalli was killed?" Mush said.

"Duh." He bolted up from his chair and headed to the dining room.

f

The eleven o'clock news was starting when Kronos came into the living room.

"Anything?" Brooke said.

"It's not Waleed. But I believe the same account he used was used to bring in a Mustapha Sendi that morning. It tracks back to the same account Stover uncovered tracking Waleed."

"That's great news, Kronos!" Mush said.

"Maybe not. He left the next day and flew to Oran."

"Algeria?"

"Come with me to the casbah," Kronos said in his best Pepé Le Pew cartoon voice.

f

The next morning, Kronos set up a secure video conference with George at Treasury.

Twenty-five minutes later, as the session was ending, George summarized. "Okay, so we'll look for this new guy, the Sendi fellow," George said.

Brooke sensed something with George. "What is it, George? Are you having second thoughts about getting involved with all this?"

"No, Brooke. What you did for this country, what you stopped—and that was just the one time I worked with you. God knows what else is blacked out in your file. That buys you my loyalty up to and including, ready, aim, fire."

Brooke felt a tear coming on. *Damn hormones.*

George continued, "No, what's bugging me is these guys are really lax. I mean, it doesn't seem like they were too worried about exposure."

Mush spoke up. "I have a theory about that, George. None of this gets to within a thousand miles of the radar scope if Brooke wasn't accused of killing Kupalli, and she just happens to have Kronos and Crusher and you on her six."

Brooke was about to add, "and you, too" to her husband's list, but he was on a roll and she decided not to interrupt him.

"There's no way any other defendant could bring these resources to bear. Two of the three murders would have never even been ruled a homicide. In fact, they were actually already in the books as natural causes, until the team here dug in. In a strange way, if this does turn out to be some international thing, some horrible master plan, the good news indeed is that Brooke was accused of the murder! Otherwise, these guys stay in the shadows. Again, it's weird, but she and you guys are the only ones who could have followed these leads. The cops wouldn't have had a clue!"

"Good point, Mush. I'll get back to you about Sendi." The image clicked off.

"I'm going upstairs to lie down," Brooke said.

When she was gone Mush said, "I meant that, you guys. Without you, all this never comes to the surface. Good job both of you."

"No probs, Mush-man," Kronos said to the admiral.

"My pleasure, sir," the active-duty sailor said to his old sub skipper.

CHAPTER 38

"WHAT DO YOU want first, the good news or the bad news?"

"Good. I'm feeling lucky today, George," Brooke said over the secure chat with the Treasury agent.

"We found Sendi. He's a known mercenary. Formally trained by the Republican Guards in Iraq. He landed in Oran from Oahu right after the Kupalli murder. And the best part ... drum roll please ... he was traveling under Saudi passport."

Brooke looked at her guys. "The Saudis again."

There were smiles all around. This certainly tied out the notion that all three of the killings on the island were related.

The joy was short lived however as Brooke's brain stumbled on one fact. "Hold on, an Iraqi Republican Guard under Saudi passport?"

"Yeah," George said on the screen. "Which two of these things don't belong? I went to dig further but he disappeared. Just faded into the city. No trail or further use of the card, no hotels or rentals, no manifests or rent. He just stopped existing."

"Maybe these guys aren't as lax as we thought," Mush said.

"Wait, so Sendi disappearing was the bad news?" Kronos asked.

"Noooo." George rolled out the long vowel across the eight thousand miles from the secure conference room at the Treasury Department in DC to Brooke's Pearl Harbor dining room. "Not by a long shot."

"Oh dear," Brooke said.

"I have another report here from my DIA guy. Mustapha Sendi died last year in Africa. He was under the employ of a Robert Mangonoti, a local warlord who did a very hostile takeover of his competition. A bloody affair."

"This might sound crazy, but is it possible to maybe get this Mangonoti on the phone, see what he knows about Sendi?" Mush apologetically couched the suggestion because it was too simple to be possible, but sometimes stuff like that actually worked.

"Yeah, that may have been a good idea last week, but here's the front page of the Corriere Della Sera." He held up an Italian newspaper to the camera. "It seems that when you blow up a guy in his Rolls in front of the big Milan opera house, it makes the evening paper."

George slid the front page under the document camera and shared the feed. The burnt-out hulk of the Rolls Royce dominated the picture in front of the classic façade of La Scala, the prized opera house.

"I guess the fat lady sang for Mangonoti, that night!" Kronos said.

Brooke rolled her eyes. "Kronos! That's highly inappropriate ... but very funny!"

"Not such a big future in war lording, I guess," Crusher said.

"So, are we at another dead end?" Mush asked.

"Maybe not. I'll get State to rock the Saudis on how a dead mercenary gets a passport from their ministry of travel. Maybe something will shake loose from there."

"George, we got burned last time by State. Is there another way?"

"Good point. I got a buddy at CIA. I'll make a call."

f

Two hours later, George called back over the vid-con. "My CIA guy got his buddy at the NSA to dig. You're not going to like what they found out."

Brooke sighed. "Go ahead."

"This Sendi guy? The term the NSA geek used was 'erased.' Somebody wanted it to appear that he never existed!"

"Well, that seems par for the course for this whole affair," Mush said.

"Sorry, Brooke, I know you liked him for the Kupalli murder. But this is a dead end from here," Stover said.

Brooke opened her mouth like she was going to say something, but she was out of options. So instead, she nodded and said, "Thanks, George, you've been a real friend through—" She stopped and snapped her fingers. "Wait. The Saudi Sendi is erased? Can you try to find the Iraqi Sendi?"

"He's dead."

"Yes, I know. I meant dig and see who knew him well enough, maybe well enough to assume his identity?"

"You mean, if this wasn't just a case of a random stolen ID?"

Brooke hadn't considered that, the alternate explanation that Sendi reappeared because somebody just temporarily assumed the identity of a dead merc. Then came here and killed Kupalli. The more she thought about it, the more likely it seemed that was the case. And yet ... "You're right, George. The pattern and probability suggest strongly that it's a random identity snatch, but, and I know it's thin, it's all we got."

George concurred with both parts of her argument. And even though it was probably a wild goose chase, he acquiesced. "You got it, Brooke. We'll leave no stone unturned."

"And George ..."

"Yes."

"This time, do keep the politicians out of it!" she said.

George laughed and ended the call.

CHAPTER 39

LATER THAT DAY, Brooke had an inkling of what James Chu wanted to discuss as she walked out with him to the lanai. She looked out at the harbor as a nuclear sub, not unlike Mush's old command, was traversing the horizon with cascades of white foamy water accenting her prow. She seemed to remember they called it making a moustache or something like that. She looked up. Birds were circling the beach, looking for slow-moving food. And she was feeling a little lightheaded. She lay out on the chaise, rather than sit at the patio table, and put her feet up, waiting for the iron pills she just took to kick in. Chu sat upright on the cushion of the chaise next to her. She patted the back of the cushion. "C'mon, James, sit back. It's good if you're pregnant or a little tense, like you seem to be."

"I prefer to sit up." Chu was serious.

Brooke was respectful. "What is it?"

"To be honest, I don't like all the deep digging, *illegal* deep digging, that you and your team are doing."

Brooke saw the contents of the leather portfolio he just opened. She recognized the form of it immediately. The reason for his guilt was the exculpatory evidence handed him by the prosecutor during this morning's pre-trial conference. "Is that what's got you second guessing? *Brady*?" Referring to the *Brady* doctrine, where a prosecutor is duty bound to share evidence even if it exonerates the target of their prosecution.

"They are playing by the rules Brooke, and ..."

"And you think we're not?" She turned full body to him. "James, a *Brady* disclosure is mandatory. Hell, I wound up doing the defendant's work for them half the time, and then had to hand it over, under *Brady*," Brooke said.

"Yes, but Brooke, that's exactly my point. Same thing. They've handed me so much here that I know we could vacate the charges against you. It's all right here." He tapped the folio. "Brooke, we can win this, without you risking imprisonment by hacking and tapping private citizens."

Chu's passion was contagious, but she remained skeptical. "Like what? What do they have?" She scrunched over to read the documents as he read out loud.

"Well, for one thing, they admit that no forensic evidence was found at the crime scene, no fibers, hair or skin samples of yours were evident."

"What about the knife?"

"All they can do is make a circumstantial case; the knife was clean. All they can do is allege that you cleaned it after the killing. But they can't prove that. No bloody rags in the garbage, no trace of blood in your drains."

"I could have cleaned it in a gas station bathroom."

"They'd have to provide some evidence of that." He flipped the pages. "And it's not in here. You see what I am saying? You're out of this case. Their own investigation proves it."

"And yet, with all that, they haven't dropped the charges," Brooke said as she pushed away from the table and arched her back, relieving some of the strain.

"As I said, the DA is a political position, and they need a scalp."

"Well, they certainly are risking the votes of admirals' wives all across America in that case."

Chu wasn't in the mood to laugh. "It's obvious they're playing for a confession. Or slip up by you or me." Chu sighed. "Brooke, as you know, I'm only a public defender. I have a year of experience, but I know enough to know that my three times in court may lead to me screwing up. They know it too, and that's got to be part of their strategy, me making a rookie mistake and you being rusty and paying for it with your life."

"How could you possibly screw up? John, you've been very good so far." Brooke knew there were a million ways he could screw her pooch, but wanted to show her confidence in him. Brooke hoped that settled his concerns, but she could read the look on his face. "James, you don't look convinced."

His hesitation told her this was the true reason for his gingerly approach. "You say you understand, you know how this works. Then you had to know they had nothing on you. Yet you're digging and violating statutes with abandon every day. With no regard for the consequences."

"Oh, that ..." Brooke nodded.

"If the DA gets wind of your little side endeavor here and he asks me, well, Brooke, I'm an officer of the court. I can obfuscate a little, claim attorney/client, a little, but if I have knowledge of a process crime that isn't covered under the charges that I'm specifically representing you on."

"The crime-fraud exception of *Clark v. US*?"

"As Kronos would say: Zactly!" Chu said.

Brooke stiffened. Her voice dropped. Sweetness and her cajoling lilt were eradicated. Brooke, the leader of men and woman, replaced it with both barrels. "James, five times I took an oath to defend this country from all enemies, foreign and domestic. That didn't and doesn't end with my government service. With all that digging, we may be on to something that could harm this nation. That's bigger than me, bigger than this case."

"But don't you see? Brooke, I took an oath too, to faithfully represent the interests of those who put their life in my hands, legally. And your extracurricular activities may force me to violate that oath."

"No, James. As you noted in *Clark*, what's troubling you is outside the scope of attorney/client privacy protections. You're good and still good to your oath. And I got no bitch if you're forced to reveal any of this. It's outside your obligation to me and justice."

"But ... it's not fair."

"What's not?"

"That, in you, I have the best client a lawyer could ever have at the start of their career. It's all going to be downhill from here." He shook his head.

Brooke smiled at him and his long-way-around compliment, then said, "Then you're going to hate this."

And Chu didn't like it, but Brooke had asked him not to contact her for two days.

CHAPTER 40

MUSH WASN'T crazy about her plan either. But he got her onto the tarmac of the Marine Corps Air Station at Kaneohe Bay. Five minutes later, the two-star fender flags of Mush's official car fluttered as the government C37A turned and parked. The hydraulic stairs folded out. The pilot kept the outboard engine going as the one on their side revved down. Brook kissed Mush goodbye and jogged up the steps. The steps retracted as the plane started to roll to take off again.

George Stover greeted her in the cabin. He introduced her to Kevin Harley, undersecretary of State for African affairs, as she strapped in.

"State?" She shot George a questioning look. She specifically asked him to keep politicians out of this.

He held up his hands. "I know, but Kevin is a professional foreign service officer, not an appointee. In fact, Kev here greased the skids for us last year.

Kevin extended his hand. "Great to finally meet you, Stiletto."

Kevin addressing her with her code name during last year's operation proved he had been a behind-the-scenes part of her team, and that quelled any concerns Brooke may have had.

"Or should I say, Ms. Burrell?" Kevin handed Brooke a US passport in her maiden name.

Her immediate thought was, *This guy is good.* True to the nature of spy craft, it wasn't a new document, straight out of the printing office crisp and stiff. It was worn, "broken-in," so as not to tip off a customs inspector that it was newly issued yet had six-year-old POE stamps within. She studied it. Her "new" home address, and the port of entry stamps of the places she supposedly traveled in the last six years. If challenged, she needed to know how much she liked the Seychelles Islands and the ten other ports of call her passport now indicated.

Mush watched the plane as it taxied to the other end of the runway to turn and start its takeoff roll into the wind. When the wheels lifted off the Hawaiian runway right in front of him, Mush realized, at that instant, that his wife was now technically in violation of her parole. She was off the island.

f

It was a five-hour flight to Samoa. George had discovered a retired mercenary, Francisco Vegas, who lived there. George's contact at the Defense Intelligence Agency had high confidence that Vegas was a merc on the same raid as Sendi, both on the same side, working for Mangonoti.

At one point during the flight, George was regaling Kevin with Brooke's and his exploits on their last case. "So, she gets the president to suspend Posse Comitatus. Meanwhile Kronos puts every snapshot and iPhone video in the tristate area on a slow boat to the internet, so the bad guys can't see our forward operating bases or troop movements in real time."

"This is the guy working with you now?" Kevin said.

"He's part computer, part juvenile delinquent," Brooke said, a warm smile betraying her affection for him.

"Hey, what I want to know is about that little excursion to Grenada that I papered you on, George."

Brooke looked at George. "So this is the guy who made the diplomatic BS disappear?" She turned to Kevin. "Thanks for being there at a moment's notice."

"Glad I could help. I hate diplo-shit too. So, can you share?" Kevin said as he actually rubbed his hands together, awaiting the juicy details.

George took the lead. "We jump down to Grenada an hour after getting proof of life confirmation to rescue a hedge-fund guy's family being held hostage to pressure him to play ball with the bad guys. Our drone op out of MacDill never shows, mechanical problems. So our VC-25A pilot volunteers."

Brooke put her arm on George to interject. "He flew a Radio Shack toy drone with his kids."

George turned to Brooke. "That's right, I forgot that! He laughed and continued. "Anyway, we get there, take out some bad guys, we rescue the family, and as we're leaving ... Can I tell him this part?" He looked to Brooke for a nod. "As we're leaving, we find out that one of the captors, a real disgusting dirt bag, raped the wife and the nine-year-old daughter. I wasn't there, but ..." He looked at Brooke stifling a laugh. "But somehow, this human garbage tripped going down the stairs and broke his spine. The son of a bitch is paralyzed from the neck down for the rest of his life."

"I guess there is a God," Kevin said.

"No, there's a Brooke!" George said as he stuck out his leg and made a pushing motion as if to trip someone.

"Okay, I'm going to try to catch some shut-eye," Brooke said to end the war stories. She turned away and reclined her seat.

George curved his hand over his stomach in an arc that indicated a pregnant belly and hitched a thumb over at Brooke.

Kevin nodded and smiled.

CHAPTER 41

ON SAMOA they were met by a US State Department car out of the embassy in the capital city of Apia. The State Department employee, Jess, who was their guide, had a problem. He couldn't find the man they flew down to see. The best he could locate was possibly his sister or other female relative, Francesca Vega. He apologized. But after all, this Vegas was a low-level player on the international mercenary market. The intel on him wasn't as vetted as it was with the bigger players.

Brooke sighed, and hoped that his sister, mother, or whoever she was, could shed light on his whereabouts.

f

The name above the front of the establishment, Lass Vegas Tavern, was a dead giveaway that they had found Francesco's sister or wife, or mom for all they knew. From outside it had the all the charm of a Tex-Mex border taverna.

As they approached, the front saloon-type doors flung open, and a woman manhandled an obviously inebriated man onto the street. When he turned to take a swing at her, she ducked, went in low and judo flipped the drunk to the ground like a tenth degree "judan" black belt. The woman then said something in a Samoan dialectic that had the note of finality to its tone and went back inside.

They looked at one another. George adjusted his holster on his belt. They stepped around the groaning man.

They entered the not-too-shabby dive bar. Looking around, Brooke thought of it as "kitschy." She could see her and Mush having a beer here. That thought reminded her she was pregnant and strictly following the rules she and her husband had agreed on, given her age and their desire to have "just the healthiest baby ever."

Immediately upon seeing the woman behind the bar, who had bodily escorted the former patron to the street, Brooke understood. She approached Francesca. "I get the 'Lass' part now, Vega. When did you get reassigned?"

"Post op, six months now ... tomorrow," she said, doing the math in her head.

"Love your eye shadow," Brooke said.

"Thanks. Maybelline, can you believe it?"

George and Kevin just watched as the two girls bonded.

"I got to revisit that. I'm off into some brand that's getting harder and harder to find," Brooke said.

"But it's a good match to your skin tone, though."

"Thanks. Do you have a minute to chat?"

"About what?"

"About when you were a merc."

"Who are you?"

"I'm someone being accused of murder, and a SOF you worked with last year may be able to get me off." Using the abbreviation of their preferred term, soldier of fortune, paid a form of respect to "his" former craft.

"Who are those guys?" Vegas nodded to George and Kevin.

"Them? They're leaving." Brooke turned to them and gave them a hitch of her head towards the door. They left. Brooke extended her hand. "Hi, Francesca, I'm Brooke. I almost went PMC after Spec Ops School, but I stayed in and just retired to start a family. Now, I'm up for murder."

Vegas shook her hand. "That sucks. Want a drink?"

Brooke patted her belly. "Club soda."

Vegas looked down at her bump. "Good for you!"

She ran a glass through the ice bin, hit the gun and filled the glass with non-alcoholic bubbly and placed it on a coaster. "Who are you looking for?"

"Sendi. You worked with him for Mangonoti, about a year ago?"

"How do you know all this? You sure you weren't a merc?"

"No, instead of private military contractor, I went the federal way: benefits, pension and medical. I tapped some favors. I'm fighting for my life here."

"How far along are you?"

"I'm awaiting a court date."

"No, I mean, what's your due date?"

"Oh, I'm just shy of four months in." A natural smile appeared on Brooke's face.

"Medical huh? That would have come in handy," the post-op female said. "Sendi was killed in the raid."

"Do you know anything about him?"

"He was one of the last-minute hires. The main contractor on the job personally convinced Mangonoti to hire him when we learned that Dwali—that was the rival warlord that Mangonoti hired us to eradicate—had beefed up his security." She wiped off a wet spot on the bar with a rag. "Sendi was quiet. Kind of aloof. But I had no bitch with him. His shit was wired tight."

"How did he die?"

"That's the funny thing. It was already all over. We took some casualties, but Dwali was dead and we had control of the compound, then something happened in Dwali's office. I was outside when Sendi and Big Dog got into it. Then Sendi was dead. I always thought that Big Dog, the guy who hired him, must have killed him."

"How do you know that?"

"Everyone else was already dead. We made sure before we left Dwali's office and went to collect the stuff on Mangonoti's list." She made a pistol with her fingers, pointing at the floor and "pulling" the trigger a few times, indicating they administered a coup d'état to every enemy down.

"Who's Big Dog?"

"Can't tell you his name. He was just Big Dog. Even in his ads."

"Merc ads?"

"I'd seen it next to mine sometimes. But that was the first time I ever worked with him. For him, actually."

"You wouldn't have a picture, would you?"

"Nah. He was very tight about his own shit." Vegas snapped her fingers. "Try Mangonoti. He's a big deal now!"

"He's tits up!"

"No shit, when?"

"Yesterday, Milan. Messy."

"Professional hit?"

"Message. Too big for practical purposes. This was literally a message sent on a grand stage."

"Or someone wanted it to look that way."

Brooke was stopped by that notion. "You mean look like a warlord hit. When it might have been personal?"

"Just sayin'." Vegas jutted her chin at Brooke's chest. "Did you have those done?"

Brooke looked down. "No, I didn't have boobs till nineteen. Tomboy. Then I got 'em good. With the pregnancy, they're getting in the way more and more. Yours look great."

Vegas squeezed her arms together, accentuating the fine work. "Spent $10,000 on these. I love 'em."

Brooke looked around the tavern. "Nice place, by the way. I like the vibe. Good luck."

"Thanks. Good luck with the kid. I hope I helped."

"Going to go find myself a big dog."

CHAPTER 42

BACK IN the dining room/computer room, Kronos was laughing his ass off. "Hold it. Wait! Some blood-and-guts soldier for hire is now a woman? You can't make this shit up!"

"Hey, Kronos, you'd have to push your tongue back in your pie hole if you saw her," Brooke said.

"Not me, Brooke, I'm OEM all the way."

"OEM?" she cautiously asked.

"Original Equipment Manufacture only!"

"Geek! So, can you help me find Big Dog?"

"I'm going to ask Crusher. I'm still trying to get the flight-control mystery out of my head," Kronos said.

Crusher was running a processor intensive routine on his personal laptop, so he opened the clone of Kupalli's Mac Book Pro. "So, Brooke, did he say where he saw the ad?"

"He is now a she! And no, *she* didn't"

"I'll start with *Soldier of Fortune* magazine and see where that goes."

"Check the classified ads in the back. That's the motherload of that mag," she said.

"Aww fuh ... frig!"

They both turned to Kronos.

"I crashed again. Shit!"

Brooke turned back to Crusher. "Let me know if you find anything." She turned to leave and remembered something else. "Hey, guys, we're thinking sushi. You good with that?"

"Great," said Crusher.

Kronos didn't answer as he was buried in the virtual burning wreckage of another Boeing 787.

CHAPTER 43

GEORGE STOVER rubbed his eyes to relieve the strain. He had been at his office computer most of the day, stopping only for lunch and one sit-rep meeting, on the fraud case he had been working for three weeks. With luck, tomorrow he'd get his warrants and Bengal Partners SA would be served, and all incriminating financial records seized. Then he'd hand it off to the Treasury Department legal team and they'd get DOJ to prosecute. He uploaded his last case profile and then saw it was half past six. He thought about a roast-beef sandwich at Fitzpatrick's but decided to go straight home, nuke something and hit the rack.

Although he did the drive every day, he opened Waze on his cell and popped it into the holder on the dash. He liked that it told him what was ahead and where the obstructions or cops were, especially—this being DC—if the president was on the move.

When asked how far he lived from work, George would say, "One 'Hey Jude,'" based on the fact that one Sunday morning, when the traffic was light, he started up his car and the measured piano chords of the start of the Beatles song "Hey Jude" came on the radio. The song ended exactly as he pulled into his spot at Treasury. But an evening rush hour in DC could easily make it "Two Judes," sometimes three! Tonight's drive was blessedly fast, under the seven-minute-eleven-second length of the mega hit. At six and a half minutes, it made George think that maybe he should leave later every day.

He parked in his spot in the garage, took his iPhone 12, closed the Waze app and slid it into his jacket's breast pocket. He was walking through the "deep throat" garage. That was the way he thought about the dark eerie structure featured in the movie, *All the President's Men*. Although the actual garage where the source known as "deep throat" clandestinely met the reporters was over on Wilson Boulevard, it was all about the break-in at the Watergate complex, where he now lived, and this garage was just as eerie and dark, hence the "deep throat garage," in his mind. A shadow coming up behind him caught his eye. At that exact second, a car horn beeped, and parking lights blinked as someone hit their remote. He turned just as the muzzle from the silenced gun flashed five feet from him.

f

Susan Bickers was walking to her car that she just clicked open from her key chain when she saw a shape on the floor. As she neared, she saw it was a person, a body. She came upon the man from the fifth floor, *Gary or George or something.* A pool of blood was rapidly spreading as it soaked through his white shirt, under his jacket, from the hole in his chest. She gasped and took out her phone to call 911.

f

Tyrone Weeks walked out of the Watergate garage and dropped the twenty-two-caliber pistol without the silencer in the corner mailbox. He removed his rubber gloves and held them in his hand until he stuffed them between the seats of the DC Circulator bus he hopped on, which was headed to Union Station. By midnight, he'd be in Atlanta, and the second half of the $20,000 would be waiting for him in the same place he got the gun, picture and address of the target, and the first stack of one hundred hundred-dollar bills. He had no idea who the target was, why someone had paid him to kill the man, or even who paid him for that matter. It was all done on the dark web, by a man whose screen name was Fig. But the money and gun were where he said it would be, and the reference he gave was Big Dog, a merc he had worked under back in the day.

f

DC Metro Police arrived at the garage four minutes after Susan called. She waited at the entrance and swiped her resident fob to let the cop car in, saying, "Level 3 by the red BMW, my car."

One cop got out to take her name and statement. The other officer drove up the ramp to the body. The first thing the officer did was check for a pulse. Even though the woman said the man was dead, he felt a faint pulse. He radioed in to stop the meat wagon and get a "bus" here *forthwith*.

Dispatch responded, confirming the ambulance, or bus as they called it, was on its way.

Out by the garage entrance his partner was getting her name and what she witnessed.

She was shaking.

"What happened, ma'am?"

"I was going to my car and saw this man, this man on the floor. So much blood. So much blood on the floor."

"Ma'am, ma'am, did you see anyone else? Is there anyone else up there?"

"No, no, I didn't see anyone, just so much blood. So red ..."

"Ma'am ..."

"He must be dead, all that blood ..."

"Ms. Bickers! Do you know the man? Is he from the building?"

"I think he lives on the fifth floor. His name starts with a 'G'. I've only seen him in the elevator, really."

Sirens were approaching. "May I have your key card please?"

"Of course."

He held it on the sensor. The gate went up just as two more cop cars roared up the ramp followed by an ambulance.

f

In the E.R., when they stripped the jacket off George, his perforated iPhone hit the floor. An orderly bent over to pick it up and, seeing it was destroyed, was about to toss it in the trash when the attending physician said, "Harold, hold that. It could be evidence for the cops."

Looking for something to put it in, Harold grabbed a surgical glove from the dispenser and slid the cracked and crumbling phone into it.

f

As he inspected the chest wound, the doctor figured out what happened. He stuck the blunt end of a scalpel into the bullet hole and found it shallower than he expected. They were about to take an X-ray when he said, "Harold, that cellphone might have just saved this guy's life." He observed a black-and-blue bruise in the shape of a rectangle on the skin right under his breast plate. It was apparent that the concussive force of the bullet hitting the cell phone had made the geometric trauma as it was slammed into the man's chest by the slug's velocity. Much of the shot's energy must have been spent by the resistance of the cell phone. Consequently, the lead projectile hadn't gone that deep and a vital organ was spared and not perforated, or he'd have expired at the scene. Transfusion and oxygen were starting to bring his vitals back into the zone of near stable. *This guy might make it.*

CHAPTER 44

CRUSHER DID a smart thing. He checked the classifieds in the various merc mags as far back as three months before the African drug-lord raid. *Soldier of Fortune* was no longer published, but a website called *Paladin* seemed to be the biggest marketplace to find warriors for hire. He learned that among SOFs it was called "The Circuit." Although that seemed to refer to word of mouth recs from other men. The same kind of recommendation that Sendi was supposed to have gotten from Big Dog to get the Africa job.

He found a few ads that referenced the Big Dog. The copy said,

RUN WITH THE BIG DOG
PMCs needed, SSA, NGO,
Hi Pay/Risk. 1 mo/min,
+5-years VBC, PFG kit fee.

The reply address to which to send the CV was that of a known third-party broker, who was the "cutout" between credible professional soldiers for hire and wannabes. Crusher had figured out most of the ad, but asked Brooke for her opinion.

She translated. "It's pretty obvious. Private military contractors needed in South Saharan Africa, non-governmental operation, one month pay minimum. Send your resume with minimum five-years verified battle credentials. Bring your own personal fighting gear and get a kit allowance. Definitely sounds like the job Vegas and Sendi were on.'

"How do you know all this?"

"I was headhunted to do this out of the FBI. Pretty good money, ten to fifteen grand a month. More if you got special skills, and usually a flat one-thousand-dollar kit fee for bringing your own webbing etc."

"Sounds like a good deal, a lot of money."

"It is, but there's only one flaw."

"What's that?"

"You have to live to spend it. Have you tried to locate Big Dog or the broker?"

"As near as I can tell, the broker placed and paid for the ad. I'm running a profile search now for the broker's online records or banking info."

"Do you think it will be that simple?" Brooke said.

"No, but it's the only place to start."

"Maybe not," Brooke said as she dialed her phone, trying George to see if his DIA buddies could shed some light on the broker or Big Dog. It went straight to voicemail. She left a message.

CHAPTER 45

In the after-hours offices of MBN News, two women sat and tried to be as frank as possible with each other. One was the employee who, years before, gave a sorority sister a second chance. The other was that sister, now her grateful boss, happy to have returned that college favor.

Cheryl and Diane sat with a bottle of bourbon between them on the small table in Cheryl's office. Old habits die hard, but back in the day it was Mateus and a much longer lift to a higher altitude. The level of candor rose as the level of booze in the bottle lowered.

"He had a small dick anyway," Cheryl admitted.

They both laughed.

Cheryl got serious. "Really, though, you saved me from a fate worse than—"

Diane raised her hand. "We're even. You gave me this job, no questions asked, so let's not talk about who saved who, okay."

She raised her glass. Cheryl met it and they did two clinks, which for some reason was the current standard.

"You don't have to share," Cheryl said, "but I'd be less than honest if I didn't tell you I have heard rumors from people in the industry. I'm good with you, Di, but if and when you're ready ... Well, I didn't major in journalism because I wasn't rabidly curious," she said as her mouth circled the tumbler.

Diane took a deep breath. She poured another glass and topped off Cheryl's. "Okay, here goes. Last year, the then secretary of the Treasury ..."

"Warren Cass."

"Yes, Cass. He took me into his confidence and pointed me in the direction of an affair in the Oval Office."

"Wait, Mitchell? Ewwww. Who would fuck that ...?"

"I know, right? And let me tell you that was my first problem with what he was telling me. But he showed me Secret Service logs, visitor logs actually. And this woman, the same one who summarily executed that man on the bridge, was the one who was in the residence no less than three times with Mitchell. And once at Camp David."

Cheryl was totally shocked. She downed the remainder of her glass. "Holy shit. Diane, you had the story of the century there."

"I know, right?"

Cheryl egged her on. "So, come on, don't bury the lead here."

"Well, I forgot that a president and his wife are a political force. And I guess she considered herself a political partner first and not a wife until sometime after their term was up. She went to bat for the schmuck. Threatened me. Probably demanded my firing by the owner of the network. Or at least that was her threat to me. Well, our legal department—"

"Hold on, the fucking first lady of the United States threatened you, a member of the press, personally! That, all by itself, is a Pulitzer."

"Up till that moment, I believed in what we do. That exposing corruption, greed and malfeasance was our sacred duty and that no force on earth could deny us our first-amendment privilege. But that bitch turned all that on its head."

"Why didn't Cass defend you?"

"He got 'sick.'" She made air quotes with her fingers. "I'm sure his diagnosis came right from the Oval Office, and he resigned and essentially disappeared."

"I heard a rumor he was in rehab for addiction to pharmaceuticals," Cheryl added.

"He never returned my calls. They must have put the fear of God into him."

"I'm so glad that goody-two-shoes faker, that tyrant in the White House and his witch of an anti-Roe v. Wade, *Handmaid's Tale* wife are out at twelve noon today. Good riddance." She went to toast the demise of the Mitchell administration, but her glass was empty. She nudged it toward Diane. She topped them both off, and Cheryl said, "So long, you mother fucker."

Two "tinks" and that was the end of a very expensive bottle of Oak Barrel bourbon.

With a devilish grin, Cheryl said, "Do you still have the Secret Service logs?"

CHAPTER 46

THEME MUSIC up: Announce: "This is MBN Newsnight with Shannon Greene."

Take camera 1, Cue Shannon. "Good evening. An MBN exclusive tonight as recently surfaced bombshell video has emerged with shocking events in the final minutes of the most devastating attack on New York since 911. Here with the story is national affairs correspondent, Diane Price."

And take camera 3—roll insert—cue Diane. "Shannon, the shocking video of a summary execution of an alleged terrorist is too graphic and too disturbing to show in full here on broadcast television. We have blurred out the truly egregious parts here. But our experts have confirmed that this event happened in the final hours of the Con Edison attack last year."

They looped six seconds of the chopper video showing Brooke raising her gun and firing, and then the video cutting out as the train enters the frame as a blur. It repeated over and over again in a small screen inserted over Diane's shoulder.

She continued, "What you are seeing is a premeditated, cold-blooded execution of what is, at best, a person of interest in the attack. Although the identity of the victim is unknown, what is known is that his civil rights, his right to a trial—to be judged by a jury of his peers and to be sentenced by the judicial system—was erased with a fusillade of gunshots from the full magazine of a rogue federal agent's weapon. We have identified the gun-happy shooter as one Brooke Burrell-Morton. As far as we can tell, she was last assigned to CinFen, a little-known government agency."

The scene in the box over her shoulder switched and briefly showed a long shot of a burning midtown office building and a woman dangling from a flagpole as FDNY officers reached out to her with a long pole.

"Viewers may remember her as the woman rescued by FDNY after a midtown office gas explosion days before last year's terrorist attack. Although then identified only as a federal agent, she was not made available to the press at that time."

Next the image returned to the loop of the bridge execution which began endlessly repeating again. Then she turned to Camera 2 as the image behind her changed to a blurry image of Brooke and President Mitchell, which was lifted from an official White House reception photo. First lady, Mrs. Mitchell, was somehow cropped out of the image. Brooke and the president were highlighted, and the rest of the image was darker.

Diane's tone became deadly serious. "But what this self-styled judge, jury and executioner couldn't escape was a charge that she had an illicit affair with now former President James Mitchell, which may explain the lack of transparency over this unwarranted execution. I spoke ..."

Roll Tape 1, pot up:

"... with retired FBI agent, Hank Ines: 'This is a murder, an execution, pure and simple. There is no procedure that I can see being followed by the arresting officer here.'"

Roll Tape 2, Mitchell Package, pot up Diane's mic, cue her VO.

With her camera now off-air, Diane read from her teleprompter as a video package with scenes from the Mitchell inauguration and file footage of him as president rolled to the home viewers. She read: "Mitchell ascended to power after a controversial election where he was anointed president after what many have called the most crooked election in US history. He went on to ..."

CHAPTER 47

THE KNOCKING on the door became louder. Brooke rolled over and checked the clock: 6:00 a.m. Her alarm was set for 6:15. Mush rolled over. "What the hell?" He jumped up and grabbed his robe.

He came downstairs and opened the front door.

"Good morning, Admiral."

"Lieutenant, what's up?"

"Sir, it's about your wife, sir."

"My wife?"

Brooke came down the stairs. "Brett, what is it?"

"Mrs. Morton, the fleet public information officer has asked you come to her office at once."

Brooke looked at Mush and shrugged. "Okay, just give me a minute to get dressed."

f

Forty minutes later, Brooke and Mush were sitting in front of Commander Jennifer Jeffries, public information officer for the Pacific fleet. She was all business. And not just because she stood and crisply saluted Rear Admiral Brett "Mush" Morton, but because she never relaxed her ramrod-straight shoulders while she delivered some really bad news.

She didn't sugar coat anything as she said, "One of the smaller news outlets out of New York City has moved a story that you summarily executed an innocent man on the Manhattan Bridge last year."

Mush shot up, sat forward and was about to say something, when Brooke waved him off. "Go on, Commander."

"The story further asserts the whole incident was covered up and never investigated because you were having an affair with the president of the United States at the time."

Mush was as red as a tomato. Brooke calmly asked, "Is that all?"

"The reporter claims that prior to release of this story, they were pressured and intimidated by a government operative, trying to suppress the story."

"Thank you for relaying that information."

Mush had had it. "Commander, are you aware you're talking to my wife?"

"Yes, sir."

Brooke turned to him. "Dear, don't get involved. She's just the messenger."

Jeffries countered. "Well, I'm afraid the admiral is involved. You see ..."

Brooke's experience as a former JAG officer, had her finishing her sentence. "Yes, as my husband is a flag officer, if I'm accused and convicted of a crime it may reflect badly on his record."

"You are not navy, and this is a personal issue for you, but the admiral is under the Uniformed Code of Military Justice. It is possible this could trigger a board of inquiry. To that end, Admiral, I have alerted the JAG core and an attorney is waiting for you outside. Do either of you have any questions?"

"Was the reporter Diane Price?"

She looked down at her notes. "Yes."

Brooke looked at Mush and nodded knowingly. They stood.

Jennifer shot up and saluted.

Mush returned it. They turned and left.

Outside the public information officer's door, JAG officer, Lieutenant Commander Peter Kesselman, snapped a salute. "Sir, I have been assigned by the chief of Naval Operations to advise you of your options and remedies."

"Where are you out of, Commander?"

"Pentagon, sir."

"You just happened to be in the neighborhood, LC?"

"I was as of oh-five-hundred this morning."

"Get any shut eye on the plane?"

"Caught some, sir. I have secured a room. Would you follow me?"

They reached the door to a nondescript small meeting room in the main building. Kesselman looked towards Brooke who was walking in with Mush. "Sir, I'm here for you. Your wife is not covered by my authority."

"She goes where I go. I waive any privacy or procedural issues."

"Very well. Would either of you like anything? Water, coffee?"

"No thank you."

They entered and took their seats.

A young seaman entered and put a thick loose-leaf in front of the JAG officer.

He nodded towards the heavy tome. "I read most of this on the plane overnight."

"Commander, why are you here?"

"Admiral, you are still enrolled in the Nuclear Reliability Program. You are literally the face of America's nuclear retaliatory strike capability. As such, your judgment has to be beyond reproach and your personal ethics beyond reproach."

"Affirmative, but again, why are you here?"

"I am to be your spokesperson. Any interaction with the press has to go through me. I talk to them. You are ordered by the Department of the Navy to stand mute, until further notice."

"You! Are going to speak for me? They're actually expecting me to stand by and watch my wife be dragged through the mud?"

Brooke interceded, patting her belly. "Dear, we're going to need that pension."

Mush was torn. The only way to be able to speak up for his wife was to resign. And he'd do it in a second, except Brooke was reminding him that he wasn't vetted yet as a flag officer in terms of pension. In a few more months it would almost double. Brook didn't want to jeopardize that.

"You and the chiefs have put me in a difficult situation. But I will agree to this under protest. I'll take it up with them."

"Admiral, do you know what's going on at the front gate?"

"No, we came right here."

"One hundred reporters trying to get in. That's why PIO Jeffries was your first stop. She will direct any press inquiries to me."

"Well, that's the first thing this morning that I guess I should be thankful for."

The lawyer opened the book and flipped through. “I’m pretty up to speed on this but there was one thing I couldn’t find in any of this. How did the two of you meet?”

They both answered in unison, “That’s classified.”

Kesselman was impressed with the instant echo from both of them. “Okay. Mrs. Burrell-Morton, did you indeed execute a man on the bridge?”

Again, they both simultaneously said, “That’s classified.”

Kesselman sat back and shook his head. “This is going to be interesting ...”

CHAPTER 48

THE MOON hung low over the Pacific, reflecting in the water like a road leading right to her bedroom window. Brooke was lulled by the serenity of Hawaii and was still up at 3 a.m. trying to get some sleep. She had her hand on Mush's hip as he was turned away from her, sleeping on his side while she watched the dappled light on the water, hoping to have it hypnotize her into a deep slumber. The gentle breeze coming in from the ocean and the distant sounds of waves kissing the shore were interrupted by a crash from downstairs. Brooke reached over and placed her thumb on the square on the door of her gun safe.

Mush, now awake as well, rolled over and grabbed the gun from her and said, "You stay here."

She grabbed the gun back and said, "You shoot missiles, Skippy. I shoot guns, remember? Call the cops."

Out in the hall, Kronos came out with a blindfold up on his forehead and wearing a pajama shirt. She motioned for him to stay. She crouched and swung around, gun first, pointing it down the stairs. She padded down the steps. There were sounds of muffled grunts and scuffling on the floor.

She whipped around to the living room, and there on the floor were two men wrestling, one with his hand over the other's mouth. She hit the lights, and started laughing ...

Mush flew down the stairs and landed next to her. "What?"

Brooke trained the gun at the men. One was a big, grisly, hard-bodied Army Ranger, the other a puny, geeky string bean. She said, "Let 'im go Bridge. I got him."

"Evening, Admiral, Brooke," Sergeant Major Richard Bridgestone said from the floor, with one knee on the intruder's chest and his hand on the guy's face.

"Who you got there, Bridge?" Mush asked.

"I don't know. I was trying to keep him quiet not to wake you." He took his hand away from the man's mouth.

He gasped, "Get off me, you gorilla. I'm Wallace Jenkins NBC 4 news."

"ID," Brooke said, still not letting the gun down.

He went to reach under his jacket.

Brooke jutted her gun forward. "Uh, uh, uh," she said, waving her gun. "Bridge, would you please do the honors."

Bridge retrieved the ID and confirmed he was press.

"Well, Jenkins, the first amendment doesn't cover breaking and entering."

"I did neither. The lanai door was open. This is federal property and as such public land."

"And yet you couldn't do this at the White House. Get out of here, and I'm keeping these creds and handing them to the PIO and having your press pass rescinded," Brooke said.

He was about to object when Bridge placed a clamp-like grip on his shoulder that made him grimace and complain, "Ow. Ow. Ow. Hey," as he turned him towards the door.

"Nice to see you, Bridge. What the hell are you doing here at 3 a.m.? Not to mention, in Hawaii?" Brooke picked up the phone table by the door that had been knocked over in the struggle.

"I was wheels down at 1:30 a.m. and didn't want to wake you, so I sat in my rental outside. That's when I saw that character sneaking around."

"Well, thanks for the perimeter security," Mush said.

"Da nada."

"Want a cup of tea? I am dying to know what brings you to paradise," Brooke said.

Mush put the kettle on the stove, grabbed some Jameson's from the liquor cabinet and parked it on the table. "Better than sugar," he said with a wink.

"Perfect," Bridge said.

"Okay so ..."

"There was a story about what we did on our summer vacation on the news. They're being pretty rough on you. But the operative word there is YOU. Your cover has been blown and, well, I figured, since I was in LA, I could use a little diversion." Bridge looked up. "Nooo shit!" Bridge said as Kronos came into the kitchen. He got up and the two men bro hugged. Bridge's slaps on Kronos's back made him wince.

"Great to see you, Bridge."

"How the hell are you, Vincent?"

"Good, good. I actually got in a day of surfing."

Mush looked at Brooke and mouthed the word, "Vincent?"

Brooke smiled. "Bridge is the only one he allows not to call him Kronos." She shrugged.

"Can we get back to you being here? Because this is a secured naval base and I do have a gun," Brooke said.

"So did George."

"George? George Stover? What happened?" The snarky smile washed from her face as concern took over.

"He was shot going to his car. It looks like a pro hit."

"Oh my God! That's why he hasn't answered my calls. Where, when?"

"Yesterday, his garage at the Watergate. He's in critical. Lucky bastard's cell phone took the brunt of the hit, but he's touch and go."

"And you think that has something to do with me?" Brooke said.

"He called me a few days ago, when I was at Fort Hamilton. He had me recite some friendly religion to this reporter ..."

"Diane Price?"

"Yeah, good looking dish, cute dog. Anyway, she called George the day before asking about you and QUOG. She must have someone inside the government who can't stand us beating the bad guys."

"What hospital?"

"Washington General, gunshot unit."

"Figures a Washington DC hospital would have a special wing for gunshot victims. There's more gang bangers per square block there than there was in Chicago during the prohibition. And those guys had Tommy Guns," Kronos said.

"Well, aside from that little history lesson, I guess he's in the best possible place. I'll call him." Brooke looked down at Bridge's duffel bags. "Grab your gear. We have the nursery in waiting. Still has a queen-size bed—because the admiral hasn't gotten around to moving it out yet." She turned to him as she raised the volume of the last part.

"I'm going back to sea duty ..." Mush said as he brought the kettle to the table.

"Trivet?" Brooke reminded him.

"Yes dear ..." Bridge watched Mush grab the little round disk that protects the table from a hot pot. "Definitely anchors away at dawn."

Brooke laughed. "At least he'll be good in the galley now."

Bridge just shook his head.

CHAPTER 49

Please Don't Tell My Mother I Work Here,
She Thinks I Am A Piano Player in A Whorehouse.

THOSE WERE the words on the self-deprecating plaque that graced most newsrooms across America. It was hardly noticed by the FBI agents as they blew by it, as a nervous receptionist was trying to stop them ...

"Ma'am, please step aside. This is official government business," one of them said, holding up his creds.

They barged into Diane Price's office at MBN followed by Rod, the network's attorney. "Gentlemen, do you have a warrant?"

"We don't need a warrant."

"Then this is harassment of the press. I'm the in-house counsel for the network and, without a warrant, I'm afraid I'm going to have ask you gentlemen to leave. This is private property."

The lead agent said, "What's your name?"

"Rod Weinstein."

"Well, Counselor, we're not here to retrieve evidence."

"Then why are you here?"

Diane Price spoke up. "You can't arrest me for doing my job. He's not the president any longer. He's open to the same level of scrutiny as any average citizen."

"Diane, please say no more," Rod said.

Cheryl ran in, adding to the cacophony. "The government cannot intimidate us; we stand by our story and our reporter."

The lead agent put two fingers in his mouth and whistled like he was hailing a cab in Times Square. Diane covered her ears. Cheryl shuddered.

"Please, stop," he said.

"Ms. Price, you are a person of interest in a case the Washington DC office of the FBI is investigating, and we are here to ask you a few questions that might help us solve this case."

"Gentlemen, I'm going on record, as an officer of the court, that you have indicated that Ms. Price is not a suspect or suspected of having committed any crime or malfeasance."

"Yes, sir. And would you please turn that off," the FBI guy said as he turned to answer and saw Rod holding up his iPhone with the recorder graphic showing the sound waves it was recording.

He complied then asked, "Ms. Price has been named a person of interest in what matter?"

"I'm going to ask you all to clear the room."

"As counsel, I represent Ms. Price."

"Is that true, Ms. Price. Is he your personal attorney as well?"

She hesitated. "Er ..."

"She is my pro bono client, aren't you, Diane?"

"Er ... Yes. Yes, I am." It was news to her.

A crowd had gathered in her office and outside.

"Very well. Everyone but Ms. Price and her counsel please leave the room."

They all left.

He sat across from her, the two other agents on the couch at the side of her desk. "Ms. Price, as previously stated, you are not a suspect. You are someone who we want to talk to in order to form a timeline. Do you understand?"

Rod jumped in, "Yes, we do."

"Is that the way you want this to go, Ms., that he answers for you?"

"Isn't that what lawyers do?" she said.

"Very well. Thursday last, you called Federal Agent George Stover. At that time, you had a conversation with him. What was the nature and content of that conversation?"

It was obvious that Rod had no knowledge of that. He nodded to Diane.

"I was doing background on the story we moved yesterday, on the Con Ed attack last year."

"I'm sorry, I don't understand. Stover is Treasury. What would he know about the attack?"

"I had reason to believe he was on the team that thwarted the attack."

"And was he?"

"Unclear. He was evasive."

"On what specifically was he evasive?" he asked.

"On whether or not he worked with a certain female agent on that day?"

As he made notes, he asked, "And why did you want to know that?"

"Again, on background. That's all."

"What was this female agent's name?"

"Brooke Burrell."

The agent had a poker face. He did not react when he heard the name of the former SAC of the New York FBI office. But he knew that the once Special Agent in Charge of FBI NYC field office had headed up the counterattack on the bad guys that day.

"Did agent Stover indicate to you at that time that anyone else was also making inquiries?"

"No. No, he didn't mention that."

"How many times did you speak to Agent Stover?"

"Just that once."

"Are you sure? Are you sure it was only one time?"

That caused Diane to pause. "Yes, yes of course. As I said, he was mostly evasive and not sharing."

"In the course of your story, uh, doing background, did you speak with any members of ISIS, Al Qaeda or any terrorist group with or without connection to the attack?"

Rod stepped in. "Don't answer that, Diane." He addressed the agent. "You have to disclose if you have any proof that she did, otherwise this is reversible error."

"That's only in a court room, but nice try, Counselor." The misquote told the FBI agent that her counsel was a corporate litigation lawyer all the way and had never been in a criminal court.

"Then I'll have to ask, what is the basis for this question?"

"What is the basis for not answering?" the FBI agent quickly said.

"Ms. Price is a reporter, and it is not outside the realm of possibility that she, in the course of her work, will occasionally, from time to time, speak with people known or unknown to her as freedom fighters, terrorists or radicals. So once again I ask, what is the basis for this line of questioning?"

"George Stover was shot. Attempted assassination. It could have been done by the very same people, *those freedom fighters*, who Ms. Price spoke to in her"—he looked down at his notes—"'background.' So, I ask again, did you speak to anyone who would have wanted to retaliate against the team that foiled the attack?"

"Again, I'm going to direct Ms. Price to not answer that until I have had a chance to review those facts with her, and we will respond in the proper time."

The agent tapped his pencil. He could see this was all he was going to get. He stood up and the other two agents followed his lead. He turned to leave, but not before saying, "Make the proper time sooner rather than later, Counselor. I would hate to have ISIS think Ms. Price here may have been privy to whatever they shot Agent Stover to hide."

He turned to her.

"Thank you for your cooperation. We ask that you notify us if you are planning to leave town." He handed her his card and was walking out.

"Wait," Diane said.

"Diane!" Rod said.

She ignored him. "Are you saying my life may be in danger from an ISIS hit squad?"

"You tell me?"

"Diane, I'm ordering you to speak no further! We'll discuss this in the appropriate setting."

"Good luck, Ms. Price. Counselor." He nodded to him and they left.

Diane was rattled. "They weren't here as government lackies, to shut me down. Somebody tried to kill that agent I spoke to. And they think I may be next!"

Cheryl came back in. "Next for what?'

"Assassination!"

"Wait, start at the beginning? They weren't here to harass us over the story?"

CHAPTER 50

THERE WAS a certain cachet to the scar. It made women curious and men fearful, yet Hamad would trade all that for the face he had a year before; before he was injured by the explosion. He still couldn't figure out how they knew. The plan had been perfection, as if God himself had ordained it. He commanded the northern group. He was the only one to escape. Everyone else was killed by the helicopter gunships that came out of nowhere. As soon as the attack started it seemed to be over. The Americans counterattacked his team at the reservoir with superior force and numbers while his team was blowing up the water tunnels that led to, and fed, Manhattan.

As he ran for his life, everything around him was exploding or on fire. The wreckage of one of the two busses they used to get to the target gave him temporary cover as he looked for an opening or a chance to get away. He slipped out from under the wreckage of the second bus and escaped a hail of gunfire as the infidels' thirst for blood was not satiated with that of thirty of his team who went to surrender but were machine gunned with their hands up. Or so he had been told by other followers of the truth. He was too busy running away to actually see the atrocity. He remembered that the gunfire from both sides was tremendous. But the Americans were out for blood and wanted everyone to die.

In a way, he understood the American warriors' ire. A perfectly planned attack on their jewel of a city was nearly accomplished, one that would have killed millions of infidels and made New York City a pile of burnt-out rubble for decades. Dequa, the leader of the attack, and the man he answered to, was valiant to the end as legend had it, as he was killed with his hand inches from the switch which would have decimated the city.

As for Hamad himself, Allah was with him that night. After escaping the slaughter of the American ambush, he found refuge in a horse trailer at the nearby racetrack. In the morning, he confronted a groom who had arrived early to tend to the horses. Brandishing his sidearm, he convinced the scared man to drive him to the safe house. Well, close to it. He had planned on killing him to not leave a trace, but the man was a devote Muslim, a good man. He even gave Hamad bandages and veterinary medicine to ease the pain of his wounds. So, to spare the good Samaritan, he had the man drop him off blocks from the safe house and left him with enough disinformation to send any authorities in the opposite direction.

He spent two months in the safe house then flew out of JFK back to his home, back to Syria. His ISIS commanders treated him as a returning hero, even though he felt the sharp sting of failing the great cause. They knew his team had mostly succeeded in knocking out one of the two water tunnels and they would have destroyed both if the gunships hadn't showed up. He still couldn't figure out how the Americans knew. Their intel said the American military was not permitted to operate within the borders of the US. And yet ...

Today, as he watched the video being shown on CNN International, he recognized the man being executed on the train tracks of the bridge as Paul. Aside from Dequa, he was the only other member of the six isolated cells that he had met. Met him twice, actually, because Dequa also brought him along when they scouted the reservoir and the bomb test in a stone quarry in upstate New York.

But this woman, firing on the bridge, displaying the same anger and same bloodlust as the soldiers who assassinated his men, was someone within whom the fire of the infidel burned bright. Later in the report, the talking head of news said that she was the architect of the response to Hamad's and his warriors' attack. She was shot in the exchange, but the newswoman kept talking about her as if she were alive. Hamad had an inspiration at that moment. A possible way to avenge the death of his men and their glorious mission. He rewound the tape to study the woman more closely.

f

Bridgestone stood looking out at the USS *Arizona* Memorial as the morning colors were played. At every base he was stationed at, over his career, this ritual was as ubiquitous as boots and jeeps. But here, at Joint Base Pearl Harbor-Hickam, it took on a soulful remembrance. While the "Star-Spangled Banner" played, Bridge stood at full salute, facing the flagpole atop the pristine white structure that marked the watery grave of hundreds of men. Bridge caught sight of Brooke, in her track suit, standing with her hand over her heart. She must have run down here right before Bridge left for his morning run.

Here they were, the two people who were instrumental in stopping an attack which would have been more catastrophic than 20,000 Pearl Harbors. That notion made him stand even taller. He wondered what history would be if Kronos and Brooke were on the case back in '41? Would the attack on this base have been thwarted the same way the intended "Pearl Harbor" against New York City was last year?

Today the Royal Canadian Frigate, HMCS *Calgary*, was in port, so the Canadian National Anthem played over the base-wide siren system right after the US National Anthem. Bridge and Brooke maintained their salutes out of respect. After the carry-on bugle played its notes of release allowing movement to return to the base, Bridge walked over to Brooke.

Brooke took a deep breath. "As many times as I have been here, it never ceases to get me."

"If it weren't for you and the team, there could very well have been one of these in New York every morning."

"I seem to remember you were a very big part of that."

Then they both said the same thing at the same time to one another. "You saved my life."

Both smiled.

"Okay, since it's your base, which way do we run from here?"

"Want hard and strenuous or scenic and flat?" she said, starting to run in place.

"Show me what you got, Director."

"Not a director anymore. Now it's just coach. Wait for ya at the top of the hill, Sergeant."

"It's Sergeant Major, and I'll be waiting for you, mommy-to-be."

They took off.

CHAPTER 51

CHERYL WAS really pissed off. They had an exclusive on the Burrell story but now every news outlet was piggybacking off their reporting. Across the networks a new 'hook' was being adopted, they were referring to this unknown woman as, "The Blonde Bridge Killer." Upon first hearing this, Cheryl admitted, "Damn that's good, wish we had thought of it!"

Now, the only good part about it was the MBN logo bug was burnt into the story that they were all rebroadcasting. So even viewers of CNN International were being exposed to their news logo. The boardroom was very happy with that. They too had dreams of a worldwide expansion. Even though each news operation made sure to mention that it was a copyrighted story by MBN, they did this not out of charity or friendly comradery, but to avoid any litigation from MBN or libel suits from the actual Blonde Bridge Killer, because they were not taking credit for the content, while gaining the viewership.

But today, once again, we will scoop the world, Cheryl thought as she leaned with her butt against the top edge of the anchor desk on the now "half-light" set and read the large type of Diane's teleprompter copy three minutes before airtime:

WE START TONIGHT WITH AN MBN EXCLUSIVE. DURING THE INVESTIGATION OF THIS STORY, THERE WAS AN ATTEMPT ON THE LIFE OF ONE OF OUR SOURCES. [<CAMERA 2] THIS MAN, FEDERAL AGENT GEORGE STOVER, WAS GUNNED DOWN IN A WASHINGTON DC GARAGE AFTER HE SPOKE OFF THE RECORD WITH ME ABOUT BROOKE BURRELL-MORTON - WHO WE EXPOSED LAST NIGHT IN AN MBN INVESTIGATIONS EXCLUSIVE – AS HAVING MURDERED AN INNOCENT MAN ON THE SUBWAY

TRACKS OF THE MANHATTAN BRIDGE. WE'LL HAVE A LIVE REPORT ON AGENT STOVER'S CONDITION COMING UP. BUT THIS HEINOUS ATTACK WAS NOT THE ONLY ATTEMPT TO BLOCK THIS STORY. [CAMERA 1>] IN FACT, THIS REPORTER WAS RECENTLY APPROACHED AND WARNED OFF THE STORY - IN A SLIGHTLY LESS LETHAL WAY - BY AN INTIMIDATING FIGURE WITH MILITARY BEARING, POSSIBLY REPRESENTING ROGUE ELEMENTS WITHIN OUR OWN GOVERNMENT. [<CAMERA 2] IN A STATEMENT FROM MBN NEWS CEO CHERYL ADDISON RELEASED TONIGHT SHE AFFIRMS, AND I QUOTE, NO AMOUNT OF GOVERNMENT SUPPRESSION OR THREATS WILL SWAY THE MBN NETWORK FROM ITS MISSION TO INFORM THE PUBLIC OF ANY AND ALL MALFEASANCE AND DISHONESTY OF THEIR GOVERNMENT'S OFFICIALS.

"Uh, Harold, change dishonesty to corruption," she said to the prompter operator in the control room. She watched the words change under the cursor.

THE MBN NETWORK FROM ITS MISSION TO INFORM THE PUBLIC OF MALFEASANCE AND CORRUPTION OF THEIR GOVERNMENT'S OFFICIALS.

f

"... for more on this story let's go to Brad Davies at George Washington hospital for an update on the federal agent's condition," Diane Price said as Brooke, Kronos, Mush and Bridgestone watched the streaming video on Kronos's computer. The picture switched to a reporter outside the hospital.

"Good evening, Diane. At this hour, doctors at George Washington Hospital's Gunshot Unit are reporting that Federal Agent Stover is labeled as in critical condition, and doctors say the next twenty-four hours will be crucial. He was admitted here ..."

Kronos stopped the feed they were all watching from Brooke's dining room. "Got Hank Walters Skyping in."

Soon they were looking at Agent Walters, the third member of the team that Brooke and Stover cowboy'd into Grenada with that night to rescue a family being brutally held as hostages. He was calling in on his iPhone from Stover's hospital room.

"Good to see you, Hank. How's our boy doing?" Brooke said to the camera atop Kronos's middle screen.

"Brooke, Kronos, Admiral, Bridge. This is unbelievable. The bullet was stopped by his cell phone. But it's the cell phone that might kill him."

"What? Explain," Brooke said.

"Well, it seems the cell phone has all kinds of rare earths and nasty materials in it, like phosphorus, arsenic, boron, indium, and gallium. All stuff that doesn't mix well with blood."

"So, the bullet impact carried those chemicals into George's body?" Bridge said.

"Yes. The actual bullet damage is very survivable, but the poisoning to his system is what could kill him now."

"Yes, but if it wasn't for the cell phone, he'd have been dead on the scene," Kronos said.

"Ain't that the bitch," Walters said.

"Thanks, Walters, stay with him, okay? Let us know if anything changes," Brooke said.

"I'll be here. I'm on hospital security detail. We don't want to give whoever did this a second shot."

"Do we have any leads?" Brooke said.

"Nothing. It was a professional hit, and it was clean. FBI forensics can't find a thing. Two security cameras were disabled. The other's pointed the wrong way. Whoever this guy was, he was good."

"Not that good," Kronos said. "He left Georgie alive."

"We have a theory about that. One of the residents of George's building stumbled on the hit, and the guy ran off before he could double-check his work."

"You mean double tap," Kronos said, pointing his finger at his own temple like a gun and "firing" it twice.

"Hank, the TV is saying that George was hit because he talked to a reporter about me and the attack last year. Was there anything else that George was working on, where somebody could have ordered a hit?"

"First place we looked, Brooke. Of the three cases he was working, two are in the preliminary mode, and the targets of his investigations aren't even aware. The other case was set to go to grand jury next week. Again, all held tight. Very doubtful that this attempted murder could have been a move to derail an investigation, which it wouldn't have anyway, as you know."

"So, could the TV reporter be right? This happened because he talked to her?" Mush said.

"Yeah, it's possible, but who gains? Besides, he didn't tell her anything. We got the transcript from NSA. As soon as she mentioned Brooke and something called QUOG, George shut it down. Filed a contact report to the DNI."

Bridge jumped in, saying, "And then George called me and asked me to remind this Price woman that she was playing in a need-to-know sandbox."

"I didn't know that. So, you're the military-bearing male? How cool is that?" Hank said.

"Not cool at all, Hank. Not cool at all," Bridge, the operator whose very life depended on stealth and anonymity, stated.

"Be safe, Hank," Brooke said, as Kronos waved bye and cut the connection.

Brooke sighed. "So what do we think?"

"Bad break for Georgie. I guess him being shot could have something to do with us," Kronos said.

"Yes, but how? Why?" Brooke said.

"All he did was look into Sendi for us," Mush said.

She snapped her fingers. "Actually, all he did was alert the embassy in Saudi Arabia."

"You think there was a leak?" Bridge asked.

"We know the ambassador stupidly tipped off the Saudis."

"So maybe the idiot revealed Stover's name?"

"Yeah, but hold it. Then you're saying this was a state-ordered hit by a friendly power against a US federal agent on American soil. That's tantamount to a declaration of war," Mush said.

"Unless it wasn't sanctioned," Brooke said as she turned to Kronos.

"Gotcha, Brooke. Checking now." His fingers started dancing on the keyboard.

Bridge looked to Brooke and she explained. "This whole thing started when Kronos traced blood money to the dark web, and, through cutouts, George traced it back to the Saudi regime."

"So, let me guess, with you guys out of the government, you asked Stover to dig officially?" Bridge said.

"We had reached the end of what we could do, Bridge. Handing it over seemed the best way to at least get justice for the two, then three, murders that happened here on the island," Brooke said.

"The first one being the one they are trying to hang on you?"

"There's that too." She shrugged her shoulders.

"Oh, this is sweet. Yes," Kronos said as his fingers dug deeper into the keyboard.

Brooke looked at Bridge. "Mail's in." They walked over and stood behind Kronos and looked at the monitor."

"Same account as before; two ten-grand withdrawals. Cross-checking with the dark web and ... Bingo. Check this out. It's a dark-web email out of the same account where we found the map coordinates."

Brooke read it aloud. "'Big Dog says, Hi. Matter needs attention in DC. Pic enclosed, lives Watergate complex. As soon as possible. Gear and first half in usual spot. Balance upon POD. And its signed, Fig."

"Here's the attached jpeg," Kronos said as it opened to a picture of George.

"Oh, dear God!" Brooke said. "We did get George shot!"

"How can you be sure?" Mush said.

"Big Dog is the name that Vegas gave me. That means the hit man was probably also a former merc."

"Kind of obvious ain't it. Dog of War," Bridge said.

"That's right. I'd forgotten that. Dogs of War, another name for a mercenary."

"Any idea on location?" Bridge said.

"Not on the hitter. But lookie what else I found in his in-box," Kronos said.

Brooke leaned in. "It's another order for a hit in Jersey City. Not from our Big Dog or the Fig guy, though."

"But now we know where our hitter's going to be in two days and who he'll be following."

"If he lives that long," Mush said.

Brooke and Bridge turned to him.

Mush explained. "I'm assuming POD means proof of death. Well, he doesn't have any POD because George wasn't DOA. So not only is he SOL, because he ain't going to get the balance of his pay COD, but he might find himself terminated, PDQ."

"I like what you did there, babe, and you're right!" Brooke said, then turned to Kronos. "Kronos, keep checking and see how pissed off this guy, Fig, gets. Let us know if he orders a hit on the hitman."

"Meanwhile, we have advanced knowledge of an impending murder. Do we call the Jersey City cops ... anonymously?" Mush said.

Bridge interjected. "Or, alternatively, I can go. Break up the little party and maybe get our friend to talk."

"So, no cops?" Mush said.

"Maybe after I have my chat?"

"So, you intend to use this Jersey City guy, his target, as bait?" Mush said.

Bridge held up his finger, turned to the geek. "Vincent, has he opened that email yet?"

"No. It's waiting in his in-box, unread," Kronos replied.

Bridge took out his phone, opened the camera and handed it to Brooke. "Catch my good side."

CHAPTER 52

TYRONE WEEKS was pissed off. That DC guy wasn't dead. And, worse, the TV said he was a Treasury agent. Weeks knew he had covered his ass, leaving nothing for the cops or feds. But he was concerned that Fig, whoever the fuck that was, might take his failure to complete the job personally, and come after him for either the ten grand that he got up front, or just to take him out on principle.

This was going to be a pain in the ass. He had to remove himself from his internet storefront. Close shop and digitally move to another "town." It was a shame. Tyrone had spent five years at his current online address on the dark web as "Typo." He loved his tag: "erase your mistakes." His clients knew how to reach him there. But now, all that had to go.

Now he'd have to erase everything and start fresh; because all Fig, or anybody for that matter, knew about him was his dark-web email.

He went to the same Atlanta hotel lobby as he always did, sat behind the courtesy computers off to the side of the elevators. Instead of swiping a room key, that he did not have, through the reader, he put three dollars cash into the money slot and bought one half hour of machine time. Once on the web, he would shut down his site, erase all metadata, and vanish into thin digi-bits.

He was about to delete everything when he saw he had a new message in his in-box. He considered if this email could contain some kind of tracking software that Fig sent to locate him. Although he would never use this hotel again, he paused. Curiosity getting the better of him, he clicked on his in-box. He was relieved to see it was from another client, Bakerman, with whom he had a long profitable history. He could be in Jersey City the day after tomorrow. He sent the email to his phone, right before he hit "Delete All (Y/N)." Ten seconds later, Tyrone Weeks, gun for hire, known as "Typo," no longer existed—erased.

f

Brooke and Bridge were in the middle of an argument.

"Will you stop it!" he said.

"Will you stop being so thickheaded," she said.

"Me? You won't take no for an answer!"

"I got you into this. Let me at least pay for the goddamn ticket!"

"No. Go away."

"Look, Bridge, a last minute booking is nearly twelve hundred dollars. I can't ask you to shell that out!" she reasoned out of frustration.

"You're right! So don't ask me. I'm just doing it."

Kronos walked in and laid a boarding pass on the table. "Here ya go, Bridge."

Bridge looked down. "Son of a bitch. United Flight 218 HNL to EWR 7 p.m. tonight. Wait. Who's paying for this, Vincent? Better not be her or I'll kill you."

"Relax, it's a dead account of an old mob guy I used to do work for. He and I were the only ones who knew it existed. Got a couple of mil' in there. He died by multiple lead poisonings before I had a chance to give him the password. I would think he'd be touched to know his money was going for a good cause."

"Hold it just a minute, mister. You told me you hacked your ticket to come here," Brooke said, in the tone of a mom who found out he didn't clean his room as he promised.

Kronos shrugged. "A guy's gotta keep up appearances, Brooke."

"Vincent, you 'appear' amazing. And first class!"

"Now don't go overboard, Bridge. He'll get a big head," Brooke said with her arms folded.

"No not him. I actually mean, first class; as in, he got me a first-class round trip, Honolulu to Newark, seat 1A! This is like 3400 bucks here. Nice."

Brooke couldn't decide if the cop in her was happy Vincent DeMayo didn't steal the tickets, or if the fan-girl crush she had on Kronos's hacker-extraordinaire skillset was somehow lessened.

CHAPTER 53

HERE ON Sandy Hook the tactical situation was good. It was a remote stretch of beach with dwellings separated nicely from one another. Number 83 was set a little more forward towards the water line. That bulge put the back of the house in the shadow of streetlights. The buildings were old, and brick. If he hit him inside, he could probably get away without a silencer, but his .25 cal. with suppression was whisper quiet. "You could pop a guy in church and the next pew over wouldn't hear a thing." Actually not true, but that's what the mob guy who sold Tyrone Weeks the piece claimed.

The only downside was one road in and out. But if he struck fast, silent and accurate, he'd be out of there before morning. With his POD this time!

He opened his cell phone and took another look at the "job." He was a bruiser. Looked like the scumbags who ran the show when he was in the army. This was going to be personally very satisfying.

He rented a bicycle. Lots of folks biked here during the day, die-hards, bundled up against the January cold. It was a great spot: ocean waves, and the New York City skyline a few miles off.

The license plates in the nearest public parking lot were from New York, Connecticut, Pennsylvania; even one from Ohio. He imagined in warm weather the lot would be packed. As it was, during today's chilly scout, it was at least twenty-five percent full. Still surprising. But by nightfall, they were all gone. The place was a ghost town.

Many houses were dark. The place was definitely a summer community. Only one out of five or so houses showed any signs of life tonight. But the only one he cared about was number eighty-three. That's where he spotted his over-six-foot target, bringing in groceries from his SUV late in the afternoon. He hadn't left since. At 1 a.m., the lights were still burning in eighty-three. He'd have preferred to hit him in his sleep. Neater, cleaner that way. But the setup in front of him was as perfect as perfect can get.

Through a small window there he was, "Bruiser." This was how he thought of this nameless target. Bruiser was asleep in a big ole chair, a table lamp behind his head lighting the room and outlining his head perfectly. From his cover it was a twenty-foot shot. Even with a silencer, he was center-mass accurate from fifty feet out. The next nearest lit house was four houses away. They'd never hear the muffled shots. *Three ought to do it,* Weeks thought. Just in case there was any drift or deflection from the glass, which would be gone with the first shot. That noise was the only kink in the plan. But, again, the set up was so good. The chair would keep Bruiser upright even if he slumped.

He drew a bead on Bruiser's head. He felt no wind, so no need to adjust.

He squeezed the trigger. The first shot seemed to hit him in the head, go right through and take out the lamp too. The muzzle flash took away his night vision for a second. He fired six more into the darkness in a slight right to left sweep, not knowing which way Bruiser slumped.

He strained to listen for any sign that someone was alerted. After fifteen seconds of dead silence, he approached the house to take his POD picture. He screwed off the silencer and blew through it to cool it before sliding it into his pocket. Then he took out his iPhone to snap the kill shot. He checked that the flash was on and rested his arms on the windowsill and jutted the phone through the broken window into the pitch-black room. He wouldn't even have to enter the house. He raised the phone and leaned in his head to take the picture, when the barrel of a 9-mm automatic pressed into the top of his head. A voice said, "Freeze."

He froze, unable to look up.

There was a sound like a clap, and the lights in the room went on.

The voice continued, "You're in the sights of an entire assault team. If you want to test that, just move. You'll be dead before you hit the floor. Rickles, show the man."

Weeks watched a laser targeting dot, coming through the window from behind him, dance on the floor and far wall.

"Keep your hands through the window, and you'll live. And you'll want to live. Because we ain't the cops. So, you walk."

Weeks thought quick. He put both hands further through the window and a nylon restraint zipped around them, cinched so tight that he dropped his phone.

The man with the gun came around from the side of the window and faced Weeks. He was shocked to see that it was Bruiser. Then he saw the shattered mirror. The large kind used in bedrooms. It was at a forty-five-degree angle to the window. The chair, lamp and Bruiser were sitting safely behind the brick wall a few feet from the window. Weeks had shot at the reflection.

Bruiser talked in his sleeve. "Rickles, you and your men hold your positions in case he has backup." Then he jutted the gun at Weeks. "I'm coming around to get you. If you try to run, you'll be perforated by at least fifty rounds of 7.62. Do you understand?"

Weeks just nodded. And froze.

A few seconds later, Bruiser hustled over to him along the side of the house and looped another nylon restraint through his pants belt loop and through the one on his wrists. When he was secure, Bridgestone said, "What a jerk." Then he talked into his sleeve again. "Rickles, show the man."

Then Bruiser took out a pocket laser and shone it on a mirror propped up on the house across the way. The reflected dot danced all over both of them.

"No team?" Weeks said.

"Just a cat toy."

"But I shot out the light!"

"Ever hear of the clapper? You know, 'clap on,' glass shatter—off."

All Weeks could say was, "Shee-it."

f

In the living room, Bridgestone had Weeks in the chair. His feet were now also hogtied.

"I don't suppose you want to share your real name?" Bridge said.

"If you ain't 5-0, who are you? Who you workin' for then?" Weeks said.

"The Big Dog."

The shock on Week's face was all too plain to see.

Bridge continued, "He wanted me to say hello." Bridgestone put the gun to Weeks's temple.

Weeks squeezed his eyes tight.

"Then goodbye."

The sweat was pouring off Weeks's bald head as he waited to be shot. He opened his eyes when Bruiser lowered his gun and said, "But he literally ain't the boss of me."

Weeks was confused and cautiously relieved.

Bruiser continued, "So, I figured he had it in for you, like it was personal. So, then I think, maybe it really is personal, like as in maybe you two guys know each other. And that, my friend, is why your brain matter ain't splattered all over who's ever nice rug this is."

"Dis ain't your house?"

"Nope. I ain't even your original target, sweetheart. Oh, by the way, one of your client's is going to be very pissed. I'd consider Argentina."

"Why you asking about the Big Dog? If he sent you."

"You see, me and the Big Dog, we are only pen pals. So, when Big Dog tells me that you blew a contract down in DC, I figure, here's my chance to use a little leverage on you and find out who the Big Dog is."

Weeks's mind raced. He knew that only two people knew of that DC hit, Big Dog and himself. That meant this guy was telling him true shit.

Bruiser continued, "That's why this contract was from Bakerman, 'cause you would know it was a set up if he used Big Dog or his buddy, Fig."

Weeks's head snapped up. "How'd you know 'bout Bakerman?"

"We've both done jobs for him, and he once threatened to give a contract to you because I was too expensive ... Typo. Told me how you erase mistakes for chump change."

Weeks realized this guy had him dead-to-rights. "Why you want to know about Big Dog?"

"You see, Big Dog had my partner killed. I let Big Dog think I was okay with him putting out the job on my partner. You know, I treated it as just business. As you also know, sometimes screwups happen in this game. But after all the jobs we did for him, the ungrateful prick, he had some mook put three in the pumpkin of a guy who always had my six for years, the same way like he ordered you dead, Typo. So, I just want to find him and repay the kindness."

Weeks hesitated.

Bridgestone said, "Dog's giving me that ten grand back end you were supposed to get for the Watergate hit you blew, as a bonus just to whack you. Plus twenty more for your prom picture."

That last bit about the ten grand hit Tyrone solid. This guy really was looking to fuck up Big Dog.

"Look, man, I don't got no beef with you, Typo. And I don't give a shit about the money. Fuck Dog. Fuck him and the horse he rode in on. All I want is for the hump to be dead for what he did to Ross. And now, because he sent me here to mess you up, you should want him dead too ... and I ain't even going to charge you. So, once again, you were a merc. Who is Big Dog?"

"Okay, but if I tell you, I walk, right?"

"Right out that door. Call it professional courtesy."

"Can you loosen these?" He tugged at his restraints.

"Talk first."

"His name is Mastieff,"

"First or last?"

"Last. His first is Mustafa or Mahmood or some Muslim tag."

"Really?"

"Yeah, he was big mujahedeen back when they was kicking Russian ass out of Afghanistan. Then he went private. He's sometimes the contractor but always a head PMC."

"Big Dog is?"

"Exactly."

"Where is he now?"

"Now? Couldn't tell ya. But he used to base out of Oran. Might still be. He digs the culture or some shit."

"You wouldn't have a phone number?"

Weeks just looked at him.

"Hey, it was worth a shot. It would have been so easy. Anything else before I let you go?"

"Nah, 'cept 'sa shame, man. Big Dog, Bakerman, theys were good money."

"Yeah, but you get to live, Holmes. Fair trade?"

Weeks nodded.

"Okay, you know the drill. Get up, turn around, spread your feet and lean your head against the wall."

Bridgestone patted him down, then took out a handkerchief and pulled Weeks's piece from his waist band and snapped open his very own illegal stiletto. He cut the restraints. "Go."

Weeks rubbed his wrists, looked down at his gun in Bruiser's handkerchief. "Why you taking my ...?"

"Shut up and go," Bridge said as he put his own gun in Weeks's face.

Weeks shrugged it off and walked out the front door.

f

Bridgestone turned, looked down and sighed. He loved that mirror. How many times had he had to wear full dress uniforms, and it was perfect for seeing the full look. Right about now, he figured the Sandy Hook police would be stopping his gunman on the road. The DC detectives would come by shortly. He doubted the piece in his hand was the same gun he used on George, but at least the guy's prints were on it. He went for the broom.

He heard the distant whoop-whoop of the police car and saw the reflections of blue and red lights blooming on the buildings down the street. True to his word, he told the man he could walk, and walk he did—right into the waiting police net.

On cue the DC detectives knocked on the front door.

"Come in. It's open."

"Sergeant Major Bridgestone?"

"Yes. Excuse the mess."

They flashed their DC detective IDs. "I'm Rickles and this is Demarcy. Anything further you can tell us?"

He handed over the gun in his hankie. "This is his. Probably a virgin piece, but it might be dirty somewhere back when."

Rickles looked around and chuckled. "You pulled this all off by yourself? Took down a gun for hire?"

"It's kind-a what I do."

"And what exactly is that?"

"I am a bigger gun for hire. Only my client is Uncle Sam."

"Nice place. You live here on Sandy Hook all year long?" Demarcy said.

"This is my summer place, compliments of the Pentagon. I'm technically billeted over at Fort Hamilton in Brooklyn. I just got lucky one year when the secretary of the Interior lost a bet to the army chief of staff, who owed me big time. So, it came down to: if I could fix it, I could have it. It was an old officers' quarters, dilapidated, abandoned since the fifties when they used to have Nike missile batteries based here. The porch was crooked and falling apart. I put a year into it while I was in rehab from a nasty bit of shrapnel. No taxes, federal land. Now everyone on this little stretch of the Hook is armed forces on R & R or holdover."

"My mother had a mirror like that. Shame it's all busted up," Demarcy said.

"Yeah, mine did too," Bridge said, looking at the broken mirror.

f

The next day, Bridge got off the phone with "Avy the Glazier," an old guy out of the Bronx who could put a "new," old silvered glass in the mirror. Luckily the bullets didn't mar the frame. He was about to dial another number when he saw Weeks's original target pull into a space at the Jersey City Morris Canal boat basin, opposite where the man's forty-foot Chris Craft classic cabin cruiser was docked. He swiped to the pictures screen of his phone.

He got out of his car and walked over to the man he had a picture of from Weeks's original email assignment. "Your boat?"

"Yup."

"Great name," Bridge said, looking at the stern art. 'Never Again II'

"The two best days ..." the man said.

"When you buy it ..." Bridge said.

"And when you sell it." He completed the adage.

"Rich Haber..." Bridge said, extending his hand.

"Tony Cherubini. Nice to meet ya. Are you docked here?"

"No, actually I came to speak to you."

He was a little surprised. "Really? How did ...?"

"Look, Tony, I'm here as a friend. And I can't tell you how I know this, but someone is very angry at you."

"What the fuck? Who the fuck are you?"

"Tony, listen, I'm really trying to help you here, no shit."

"You got thirty seconds."

"I'll take twenty. Somebody, I don't know who, put a hit out on you. I intercepted the contract, for my own reasons, but if I were you, I'd take that boat to Mexico with whatever money you took from whoever it was that was willing to pay the guy that I just clipped twenty large." Bridge put his hands up palms out. "That's it. I'm out of here. You do what you want. But I just thought you should know that you pissed in somebody's linguine—big time!"

With that, Bridge got into his rental car and headed for Newark Airport and a first-class seat back to Hawaii.

f

Tony called his girlfriend. "Babe, grab the grey lock box in the closet and come down to the boat now. Dress warm."

Then he called Fat Frankie.

"Genaro's baked goods. Who's this?"

The surprise in Frankie's voice at hearing him alive told him all he needed to know. He hung up and jogged over to his boat.

CHAPTER 54

"MASTIEFF OR MASTIFF?" Brooke said.

"The way he said it was like in, thief: Mastieff," Bridge said.

"Oh, because a Mastiff, as in stiff, is the largest breed of canine on earth."

"Hmmm, Big Dog! I didn't think of that?"

"Okay, so whichever way we spell it we got a name," Brooke said. "By the way, George is out of the woods. There's some residual damage to his central nervous system because of all the crap in the cell phone, but they're treating that with heavy fluids to counteract the poisons that were blasted into his body." Brooke sighed with relief. "And Bridge, that was real sleek the way you single-handedly trapped Weeks, the hitman."

"Thank Vincent. It was his being able to change the hit's location to my quarters on Sandy Hook and being able to put my picture in the contract that did the trick. In fact, he suggested my Sandy Hook place. He's more tactically aware then we give him credit for."

"That reminds me ... Kronos."

Brooke walked into her former dining room which was now "Oahu Computer Central." "Kronos, is Crusher here?"

"No, he had to get his car inspected. Wha' cha need, Brooke?"

"I wanted to look at the ad he found for Big Dog one more time."

"I can do that. It's in his browser history here." Kronos turned from the flight control he was running on the big machine and grabbed the laptop on the card table Crusher used as a desk. The laptop was shut down. He started it up. "What are we looking for?"

"We have a name, Mastiff. I wanted to see if there were any other references we could confirm ..." A beeping noise from the simulator announced Kronos's flight had crashed, again.

"Fuh ... frig. Holy mother of ..."

"Vincent, my lad, I see you are cleaning up your language." Bridge stopped because Kronos had wide-opened eyes. His jaw dropped with a look on his face that could only be read as WTF? Or, in accordance with house rules, "What The Frig?"

"What is it, Kronos?" Brooke had never seen him like this.

"Holy Frig! I can't believe it." His fingers were banging on the keys at superspeed on the laptop.

"Is there something wrong with Crusher's laptop?"

"This isn't Crusher's. He takes that with him every night. This is Kupalli's clone. Holy frig. Holy Mother friggin' frig."

"Okay, I am starting to regret my edict. Kronos, what is it?"

"This machine is sending out signals that are crashing my flight control software."

"So, this laptop is crashing your computer?"

Kronos switched back to his main computer. "No, not the computer ..." He rapidly entered keystrokes. Then stopped. He pushed back from the table in shock. Speechless.

"Kronos, you're freaking me out. What is it?"

Just then Mush came into the room. "Honey, you need to see this."

Torn, she looked at a frozen Kronos and relented to Mush's request. They went into the living room where the local news was on the TV. A reporter was standing in front of the courthouse in Honolulu. Then the picture switched to the video shot from the helicopter of Brooke shooting Paul Grundig on the Manhattan Bridge.

The reporter's voice was heard under the images. "... the district attorney, citing the recent revelations that the suspect in the Kupalli murder has been exposed as the Blonde Bridge Killer, shows, and I quote, 'predisposition to violence' and has asked for an immediate hearing before Judge Pilipo to remand the thirty-seven-year-old Admiral's wife, currently out on quarter-of-a-million-dollar bail, to county custody while she awaits trial. Legal sources say ..."

Mush killed the audio because Brooke's cell phone rang.

"James. Yes, we are watching. Can she do this?"

Mush leaned over to try and hear what James, her lawyer, was saying.

"Hold it, James, let me put you on speaker. Go ahead, repeat what you just said."

"This is a grandstand play. The DA is just hitching her public profile to a national news story to get more screen time. I think we can vacate her move by claiming prejudicial bias among a potential jury pool. If fact, we may even be able to call a mistrial if we go to court and should lose."

"So, you're saying this a political move, but could form the basis of reversible error?"

"'Could' is the operative word there. Or, at minimum, we could claim that her public pronouncements have tainted the jury pool, and then we can appeal for a change of venue."

"So, what do we do?" Mush said.

"Nothing till I get served a notice to appear, which I'll probably get in the next few minutes. I think I can fight—we can fight—the remand order on prejudicial grounds, since no new evidence or revelations have been made or attached to the initial cause of action and the case before the court."

For a second, Mush just marveled at what she just said. "Wow, I keep forgetting you were a lawyer. So, why are they doing this?"

"I can answer that," James said on the phone. "The DA knows she's going to lose, and this is the most she can milk out of the case."

Brooke jumped in. "Sure. When I get acquitted, it will be a one-paragraph story in ten-point type on page thirty. With this move she's getting a one-hundred-point frontpage headline."

"As your geek guy says: Zactly!" James said over the speaker phone.

"That phrase is starting to catch on," Brooke said. "Which reminds me. James, we got to get back to Kronos. Let me know when we have to go to court."

"Will do."

She hung up, and they walked back into the living room.

Kronos was standing like a statue, arms crossed, staring at the screen.

Brooke approached slowly. "Kronos ... are you ... okay?"

"Kupalli wasn't just good, he was a fucking genius!"

Brooke wasn't going to go there on the language police, but was amazed that Mr. "I am the best there ever was" was now humbled.

"Wanna talk about it?" She put her hand on his shoulder.

"He wrote software that turns hardware into a weapon!"

"You mean, the laptop?" Mush said.

"Zactly."

"Okay, slow up. What are you saying, Kronos?" she said.

"Now that I think about it, every time my flight simulator crashed, Crusher had opened Kupalli's laptop."

"So, you're saying this machine, *his* machine, crashed your computer?" Brooke said.

"No, dear, he means that laptop crashed the plane," Mush said.

"That's right, Mush. I wasn't running a game, I was running a manufacturer's Flight Control Software. As if I had a 757 parked right here in the dining room."

"Okay, why? Why build a machine whose very presence can disable a plane?"

"Corporate espionage?"

Kronos grabbed a soft-roll tool kit which, as he unrolled it, displayed multiple sets of color-coded screw drivers and pliers. He grabbed a red-handled tool, flipped over the laptop and started opening it up.

"What do you mean, Mush?"

"Well, if a plane manufacturer is testing or rolling out a new plane, and you get this on that plane, then they have a disaster of a coming-out party for a billion-dollar plane design."

"What are you doing, Kronos?"

"About to find out if this is a specially rigged machine or standard production model."

"And ..."

"And I'd rather not say what I'm thinking. Give me a few minutes."

CHAPTER 55

BECAUSE BROOKE lived on a naval base, press access was problematic, but this story was too good to not sell toothpaste, cars or pharmaceuticals. The ratings were so good that whenever the news media mentioned the "Blonde Bridge Killer," the numbers went through the roof. Ergo, network assignment editors spent thousands of dollars a day to send over reporters, crews and equipment, including the cost of expensive satellite time.

The problem was there was nothing to shoot.

Brooke stayed on the base. The PIO of the base wasn't handing out press passes. So, the two major background visuals for their reporters doing "Stand Uppers" were the front gate of the Pearl Harbor naval base or the high school from which the Blonde Bridge Killer was on temporary leave.

Even though there wasn't much to shoot or report, spending tens of thousands to send reporters, producers and technicians to paradise was still a good investment for the networks. It gave them a reason to go "live" from the Honolulu courthouse, where the Blonde Bridge Killer was up for murder, every half hour. During the day in the east, when Hawaii was still asleep, the on-scene producers were still pressured to keep reports coming, since any connection to the Blonde Bridge Killer was pure ratings gold.

They even collared the school janitor one night to get his "experiences" with the Blonde Bridge Killer whose classroom he cleaned. Although hoping for a bombshell angle like, "She's a slob," or "She doesn't separate recyclables," or the revelation that they all secretly hoped for, "I found body parts in her wastepaper basket," they were dismayed that the best the kindly old janitor could relay was that "she was always nice to me."

The New York office then got three "talking head" psychologists to diagnose this blatant case of sociopathic double personality with the lower-third chyron graphic, "Blonde Bridge Killer—Nice?" for the full hour!

f

A reporter from NBC was interviewing a parent who just dropped off a student. "How do you feel knowing your son goes to the same school as the Blonde Bridge Killer, a despicable woman who could do such a horrible thing?"

"Well, I'm concerned. I mean, what was the school board thinking, hiring her? She's an animal. And to put our kids at risk like this ... I just don't have the words."

Gladys had stopped on her way into the building, overhearing what the woman was saying. When the interview was over, the reporter started looking for someone else to talk too. At first, Gladys was turning to go to work, but her hackles were up, so she turned and made eye contact with the reporter.

The woman reporter took the bait. "Do you have a minute to talk with us?"

"Sure," Gladys said.

"Stand here please." Jenny, the reporter, checked that her shoulder was in the corner of the shot. And that the mic flag was turned to show that the square box on the neck of the microphone displayed the peacock network logo.

"Roll, Jim. In 3, 2, 1 ... Please say your name and spell it for us."

Gladys did.

"Are you a teacher at the school?"

"Guidance counselor, actually."

"Did you know the Blonde Bridge Killer?"

"Who?"

"Brooke Burrell-Morton."

"Oh yes, our wonderful girls' soccer coach. Yes, she's a friend of mine."

"You know her?"

"Yes."

"Would you like to comment on the fact that she is currently awaiting trial for killing the father of a student at this school?"

"As I understand it, there's no actual proof that she had anything to do with Mr. Kupalli's death."

"Wasn't the student on her soccer team?"

"I'm really not comfortable talking about our students. I'm sure you understand they have a right to privacy."

"Are you concerned you were friends with someone who executed an innocent man on a bridge in New York last year?"

"Look, here's all I know. Brooke loved the girls on her team. She cared about those girls as much off the field as on. She has a wonderful heart and has done many good things for those girls. Next to her husband, the girls were the most important thing in her life. She dedicated herself not only to winning games but helping them win in life. In fact ..."

"Okay, thank you."

"Can I say one more thing?"

"No. You've said enough. We got what we needed."

"But?"

"Please, I have an air deadline and I need at least three more people, or my editor will kill me."

Gladys walked away with the feeling that they weren't here to broadcast anything good about Brooke. They probably wouldn't use what she just told them on the air. No matter, at least she got to set that reporter straight.

f

"Yes, sir. Yes, sir, of course, er ... Jim. Yes, sir, er Jim. She's right here." Mush handed Brooke her phone she left on the bed stand while she was soaking in a hot bath.

She looked at him a little annoyed. This bath was her "uninterrupted time."

He jutted the phone to her with a strain on his face. She lifted her soapy hand and pointed to a towel.

Mush dried her hand with the towel and handed her the phone.

"Hello? Mr. President! What a surprise sir, er Jim. Is the first lady with you?"

Brooke hit the speaker phone so Mush could hear what they said.

"Yes, Brooke I'm here, but it's just Jim and Delores now," she said.

"How's your pregnancy going?" the former first lady asked.

"Very well. A little anemic but I'm taking supplements. Thank you for asking, Delores."

"Brooke, I've spoken to Jack Darcy from Darcy, McMahon and White. He's ready to fly out there and represent you in this absurd murder case," James Mitchell said.

"I appreciate that, Mr. ... Jim, but their entire case is circumstantial. Right now the DA is milking it for every political drop of votes. But ..."

"Brooke, they have a video ..."

"A video? How can that be ...?"

"It's all over TV..." Delores said.

Brooke's mind raced. *A video of me confronting Kupalli in the parking lot?* Then she caught on. "Oh wait, you're talking about the bridge?" Brooke said.

"Yes. I know all about the DA. Russell tells me they've got nothing. I'm talking about this horrible breach of operational security on the attack," Mitchell said.

"Sir, I know. This is a national security nightmare. But don't worry about me. I was on the clock, sir. Er ... Jim. I'm shielded by at least ten federal statutes covering agents in the field and three conventions of the War Powers Act."

"Brooke, I have no doubt about any legal liability, but I'm concerned that you have been exposed, which makes you a target. Not to mention, it eliminates you from any future undercover work."

"I have a little person inside me who already eliminated me from UC duty."

"Of course, but that still leaves you and your little player to be named a target, Brooke."

"Oh, and that's not even considering what those horrible people in the news will do to you, dear," Delores, a former reporter herself, added.

She took a deep breath. "Well, Jim, one way to fight that would be to declassify my part and let me tell my side." Brooke floated the idea as she had been thinking about it for a few days now. She realized she was handcuffed by her oath of secrecy from defending herself against these one-sided accusations that had made her infamous across the nation.

"We're a few days too late on my being able to declassify anything. And Pearson, he isn't the biggest fan of government muscle," Jim Mitchell said.

"That's because, as of yet, he hasn't faced what you had to face, Jim. And for the sake of our country, let's hope he never has too."

"Amen, but I'm sorry to say, only the US president has changed. Sadly the world remains the same."

CHAPTER 56

"BROOKE, MUSH, I need to show you something," Kronos said.

"Is it about your crashes?" Brooke said.

He didn't answer.

They followed him into the dining room. They were amazed he didn't sit behind the computer. He flopped down on the loveseat that Brooke had Mush move into the room.

His hand came down hard on the armrest. "I just can't see the whole picture here. I feel like I'm looking at the bottom of a shredder. I see tendrils of digital code, some legible, some tantalizingly seductive as to their purpose. Then there's hack code, program modules and telemetry data all mixed up. The dates of creation and the similar style of Kupalli's coding tells me they're all related ... maybe. Ya see, I don't even friggin' know what I know anymore." He banged the arm again.

Mush and Brooke looked at each other.

Brooke trod lightly. "Kronos, when was the last time you slept?"

"I catch cat naps while I'm compiling."

Mush spoke up. "You need five hours minimum to take a combat station. How can you expect to see anything clearly?"

He banged the couch arm again. Brooke winced. It was a good piece of furniture. She had snagged the last one, a floor model, from the furniture store in Hilo.

"Hey, when was the last time you went surfing?" Mush said.

"Second day I came here."

"Look, grab some rack time. Tomorrow we'll paddle out and catch a few, off Diamond Head."

"You surf?"

"I've hung ten with some of the champions living on this rock."

"Okay ... Okay. Sounds good. I'll catch some zees and we'll hit the beach tomorrow." He stood up, started to walk out of the room. "Yeah, good idea. Just what I need. Yup ..."

He hesitated. Brooke watched what he was doing. He stopped, turned around and headed for the computer. "Right after I run this cleaner program."

Both Brooke and Mush jumped up. "Oh no you don't, mister," she said.

"In the rack now!" Mush ordered. They both grabbed an arm and walked him out the room to the foot of the staircase.

"Lights out in ten, mister!" Brooke said, emulating Mush's command voice.

They watched Kronos reluctantly go up the stairs.

Mush looked at her. "That was good. This is good training for us for when junior arrives." He patted her belly.

ᶠfᶠ

The next morning, they had learned two things, one being that Kronos snored. Two was that you couldn't watch local, national or cable news without hearing about the "Blonde Bridge Killer."

One network even ran a story about a college professor of woman's studies who protested the network's identifying of this woman by the color of her hair, thus objectifying women everywhere. Unfortunately, when asked what this "murderess" should be called, the teacher mangled Brooke's name. "Simply Brooke Mortons-Burnell."

ᶠfᶠ

Brooke got Mush and Kronos out of the house at just past seven. She couldn't remember the last time she was home alone. She looked around. *What to do?* She was tempted to go into her dining room and finally straighten up in there. Both Kronos and Crusher were like frat boys. The place could definitely use some freshening up, maybe even some Febreze.

She cautiously approached the inner sanctum. Her first thought was, *Did I buy all those Oreos?* The wrappers were everywhere.

Her phone rang. She had left it in the kitchen. Not to waste the trip, she grabbed as many wrappers and soda cans as she could carry. She caught it after five rings.

"Brooke, am I interrupting?" It was Bill Hiccock.

"No, Bill, I was just straightening up. What's going on?"

"Well, one of the people I worked with at the White House was a legislative affairs guy. He called me just now to tell me that this afternoon some senator is going to hold a press conference. He's going to demand a senatorial investigation into the attack last year and how the Mitchell administration handled it."

Brooke's breath shortened. "Got to be a closed hearing ... right?"

"There actually already was one with a gang of eight on the hill last year. This guy is pissed because in that hearing, your take down of Grundig was only listed as 'killed in the attack.' Now he feels we were hiding all the bullshit that's out there now about you and the take down."

"So, he wants to go public?"

"That's his first stop. Then he's got to get the Pearson Administration to declassify. The DNI might resist, but for how long?"

There was silence. Bill waited. And waited. "Brooke are you there?"

"Bill, this is just what I wanted."

"Wait, you want this to be out there?"

"I asked Mitchell to declassify just my part so I could clear my record, but he's not the commander in chief anymore."

"Gee, I have to tell you, Brooke, I didn't expect that reaction."

"Bill, it's out there anyway. My cover is blown. And besides, I'm retired. I'm proud of my service. And as far as popping that human debris on the bridge ... Well, it was a gun battle. If you remember, he shot me first. Shit, it still hurts when it rains."

"I see your point."

"Were you just calling me to let me know, or did you have a plan?"

"I don't know. You remember I tapped a lot of my SCIAD group to triangulate these guys. Exposing them could put their lives and all of SCIAD in jeopardy."

"And it's not Pearson's idea, so it's unlikely you'll get full throated support from him," Brooke said, then remembered. "Oh, that reminds me, Bill, not to change the subject ..."

"But you are ..."

"Yes." Bill's snarky reaction, and the words, *"but you are,"* triggered a realization at that exact moment which caused her to blurt out, "You know, I never realized how much you and Mush had in common."

"Believe me, it's just a common male reaction to common female stimuli."

"I think you just scientifically dissed women everywhere."

"No, just an objective observation about Janice and you. I never knew *you two* had so much in comm—"

"Okay, truce. I digressed. Speaking of SCIAD, Kronos could use some help."

"Before risking none of my computers ever working again, I have to ask, did Mr. Ego ask for help or are you assuming?"

"No, no, Bill. Mister Infallible is genuinely stumped. He needs some perspective on what he's uncovered. Can I tell him you'll take the lead on this?"

"Is this about the thing on the bridge or your murder charge?"

"Neither. We may have stumbled on to what is, at best, corporate espionage and, at worse, something hideous. But that's the point. He doesn't know. He's just swimming in all kinds of digital contradictions and bits and pieces of a whole picture."

"Okay, put him on."

"He's out with Mush right now. Poor guy's been working nonstop for over two weeks. Hardly sleeping. He was fried. Mush took him surfing."

"That usually clears his head."

"I hope so."

f

When the boys got back from surfing, Brooke had lunch set up for them on the lanai. "How was it?"

"Some great sets."

"Yeah, your husband here got mad skills."

"Really, do tell." Brooke had the grin of a proud mom.

Mush shrugged it off. "Nothing to tell. Just lucky today."

"Don't believe him. Everyone was wiping out and he practically stepped off the board and onto the beach every time."

Mush looked at Brooke and winked. "Keeping my center of gravity low ..."

"Okay, then. Eat, and Kronos in twenty minutes Bill is calling. He's going to put SCIAD on your puzzle," Brooke said.

"That's great! How did he ...?"

"He called me, and we got to talking."

"Solid. Let's eat."

f

After lunch, they all got around the video call with Bill. Kronos had uploaded his evidence and his suppositions to the private, ultra-secured network of Scientist in America's Defense. Soon the best and most brilliant minds in the country and beyond would generate their ideas about what possible threat these shards of data might portend.

"I'll put it up on the rings and see what we get?" Bill was referring to his multilayered structure of SCIAD organized like the rings of electrons surrounding the nucleus of the atom. The close rings were top secret cleared, further out less so, so what they saw was redacted of any top secret or sensitive information.

"How long, Bill?" Brooke said.

"These guys are pretty quick to respond. I think we'll see something in a few hours."

"Cool," Kronos said.

CHAPTER 57

HAMAD'S BIGGEST tactical challenge was that this female from hell was hiding on a US naval base. There was no way to reach her without a Pearl Harbor-sized attack on ... Pearl Harbor. He had to find a way for a much smaller force to deliver righteous vengeance and right this wrong as an attempt to atone to God for the interruption of His grand plan to destroy the infidels in New York City.

The other choke points on the island had their own tactical limitations. Because of all the press, there was extra security and police presence at the court. A bomb could do it, but there were no local bomb makers loyal to the jihad on Oahu.

On the display of his laptop was a screengrab of Brooke from one of the many news reports he had accumulated off the internet in the past few days. Pinned to the tent material to his right were photographic maps of Pearl Harbor. Big blow-ups of the residences in "officers' country" and community centers were tacked up along another flap. Pictures lifted from the videos were enlarged and dispersed everywhere. There were even a few pictures of Admiral Brett Morton, the husband of the blonde she-devil who killed many of his comrades and disrupted God's retribution against the great Satan.

At that point he turned back to the large flat-screen TV, so out of place in this Bedouin tent. But not as out of place as the satellite truck parked outside on the desert sand. He rolled the latest report which he received this morning. A schoolmarm was speaking glowingly about this bitch from hell. He was about to fast forward when she said, "... all I know. Brooke loved the girls on her team. She cared about those girls as much off the field as on. She has a wonderful heart and has done many good things for those girls. Next to her husband, the girls were the most important thing in her life. She dedicated herself not only to winning games but helping them win in life."

He rewound and hit play again: "...those girls. Next to her husband, the girls were the most important thing in her life. She dedicated herself ..." He hit stop. He tapped the bottom of his chin with the top of the remote, deep in thought.

Inadvertently his chin pressed the remote's "Play" key. An inane story about a Hollywood star shooting a motion picture on the island ran next. Suddenly, he could see how this might work.

CHAPTER 58

WALEED OPENED his computer and started up Kupalli's Caravan hack program. This would be the last module. It was number "4" in the main menu. He entered that number and hit return. A progress line started across the screen.

While the line crept forward, Waleed knew what was happening: the fictitious "Sultan's Express" account which had already, by a previous hack, been established in the Caravan customer database was being addressed. For now, it used the internal billing code APD232145 under the Caravan Promotions Department. That guaranteed not raising any eyebrows for the one minute or so that it would exist. The routine, written into the current running module, was ordering the pickup of one thousand pre-labeled boxes. Within minutes, a pick-up order was dispatched by digital connection to the screen in the cab of a Caravan truck the size of a moving van.

The boxes were waiting, already stacked on twenty palettes of fifty, each wrapped in cellophane wrap. In six hours, they would be sent out from a Caravan distribution center to one thousand commercial airliners under the Caravan "next plane out" blanket agreement it had with over twenty worldwide, national, and regional airlines. The second part of the module would wait patiently while monitoring the entire Caravan network, waiting for each one of the one thousand bogus barcoded labels to be scanned. Then the program would manipulate the sorting and routing machines to hold back or let pass certain barcoded boxes over a four-hour interval in order to get the boxes on the pre-targeted "next plane out" flights.

The efficiency of the huge internet retailer's automation, which handled nearly two million packages a day, also insured that no human being would come in contact with any of the boxes until the baggage handlers loaded it into the cargo holds of the one thousand flights. The program's algorithm timed it so that at exactly 1327 hours and 32 seconds Greenwich Mean Time, or forty-seven minutes after the last laptop was loaded on the last flight, every plane with a laptop on it would be in the air. But then, thirty seconds later ...

f

An hour after module "4" was activated, Waleed backed his Caravan truck into the loading dock at the warehouse his cell rented through many cut-out corporations, rented for just this last part of the plan alone. Waleed laid down a diamond-plate bridge, spanning the two-inch differential between the truck's bed and the dock's height, and the three-inch gap. Then he operated a powered pallet jack, a small hand-controlled mini-forklift type device, and loaded the twenty skids on the truck in twenty minutes.

At the receiving end there was a forklift with a driver who would unload it. Waleed was also proud, because he had recently lobbied for the bigger truck over his assigned van. His friendship with Mo, the dispatcher, made his task easier than him having to drive his smaller Caravan van three times to the back door of the Caravan distribution center himself. Once the boxes were in the center and mixed in with the thousands of other packages, their distribution to their appointed planes was guaranteed with Caravan's artificial-intelligence-guided, automated distribution.

CHAPTER 59

As usual, the bullet went in small and came out messy. Luckily none of Rashad's brains splattered on the keyboard. Mastieff rolled the body away from the control panel in the chair it was sitting in.

In a way, he thought of it as a mercy killing. If Rashy saw what was about to happen over the next four hours, he would have killed himself or, worse, stuck a knife into Mastieff's throat.

Rashad had bounced Mastieff's computer control codes off a dozen internet nodes across the world. Virtually untraceable, given the short burst of code and something Rashy referred to as a self-replicating polynomial which worked randomly to spray the instructions across the twelve nodes. It was explained to him that it was like sending a letter (the control codes) by tearing it up into one hundred pieces, then putting each piece in an envelope along with fifty other pieces of letters from the garbage pail (inserted into a meaningless string of gibberish code) and addressing each (the self-replicator) to a different post office (internet node), where someone (another replicator) in that post office would send it to another post office, where someone else would send it to another. Somewhere along the line, one "postal worker" would send it to a final destination, where all the torn pieces could be assembled into the letter, but only by extracting each useful code from the mishmash of garbage code. Randomly, it could take a path of up to twelve nodes, or "post offices," all over the World Wide Web, before any torn segment might get to the final address where it was joined back together with the original intended code. Of course, this kinetic activity, not dissimilar to a "break" at the start of a pool game—when the cue ball scatters every ball all over the table—all happened in milliseconds.

Mastieff took the "special" laptop out of his leather briefcase. He plugged in the modified USB GPS satellite receiver made in a Kenosha Wisconsin electronic fabricators facility, under private "prototype" contract. The company, Zeus Systems, Inc., worked up the units from the design specs of Kupalli. These devices were re-tuned to a satellite frequency of the NOAA satellite channel. Ostensibly, as far as Zeus Systems knew, the 1001 modified USB units were for a third-party contractor who was anticipating a large government contract with the agency that tells all of us the weather.

Piggybacking his signal stream on the UH-10 National Oceanic and Atmospheric Agency satellites was pure genius. Their broad-signal reach from geosynchronous orbits insured that every laptop on every plane could be sent signals from right where Mastieff was sitting.

That's why Rashy had to die. Not because he held up the Big Dog for more money, but because, for the true believers like him, the death of 350,000 infidels in one thousand planes was a fate unstoppable once the laptop's internal clocks reached 13:47 GMT.

Only Mastieff and Nasser knew that it was never the plan.

CHAPTER 60

American High Schools. Hamad watched with disdain as these pampered children of infidels drove their own cars, expensive cars, to school. Or, worse, were chauffeured by their parents in luxury autos. From the online events calendar on the school's website, he learned the girls' soccer practice was always before class. He watched from the parking lot through the chain-link fence as the girls drilled and stretched. For Americans, he was amazed that a few of them were very good at ball control and shooting. There was no soccer team at the madrassa he attended. Just endless hours of reading the Koran and prayers.

He read in the papers that these kids were actually forbidden from even mentioning God in their schools. *Infidels.*

He was amazed that here, right outside a naval base, security was light. In fact, the school safety officer wasn't scheduled to arrive on duty till classes began. Not that one policeman with a gun amounted to anything more than a nuisance. Still, it was nice to count on no resistance.

The girls left the field and entered the school. He noted the time. He walked off to his rental car. His next task was to set up a safe house where his cell would reside as they started flying in. There was a motel four miles away that seemed perfect and took cash in advance. No questions asked. Many whores brought their tourist customers to the roadside motel. He also needed to meet with a "friend of the cause" to secure the weapons and equipment that they would need.

Each new arrival would come with US$9,900 to add to the $9,900 he was legally allowed to bring into the country.

He calculated that he and his cell would be ready to exact retribution in a few days.

f

Brooke, Kronos, Mush and Bridgestone stood around the video screens to see what Bill's SCIAD network had come up with. The opinions and supporting data from the scientists, engineers and programmers who were part of the super-secret network were tabulated by Hiccock himself, who held three degrees, one in statistical analysis. He found that there were three different ways to read the tea leaves that were combined in Kronos's "shredder pile."

"There is a 92% certainty that the avionic hack was industrial espionage. A 72% probability that the Caravan hack was a stand-alone endeavor, possibly by organized crime to use the giant retailer's distribution system to distribute drugs." Hiccock went on, "There was very low confidence, 33%, that the satellite signal data had any purpose other than a possible commercial application to deliver weather information through some kind of direct subscription channel, touting satellite weather up to the second. Several programmers added that this could be in anticipation of the release of a new smartphone app."

Kronos was scratching down notes. "So, Hick, we just have normal criminal endeavors here, corporate shenanigans and the mob?"

"It seems so. In fact, only one respondent, 0.3%, a Professor Nichols from Innsbruck Institute, posited a radically different concept."

Kronos thought to himself, *Of course, that one outlier of an idea caught the attention of Hick, whose whole career was based on "outside the box" thinking. That's how I got here.*

Hiccock continued, "Nichols pointed out that, given certain RF supplemental equipment, a radio frequency could interfere with a plane in flight. But in order to send a strong enough signal to an airplane in flight, you would require at least thirty thousand watts to penetrate the aluminum skin of the airplane's fuselage. And then only in direct line of sight."

"Bill, what does all that mean?" Brooke said.

"That's what I wanted to know so I wrote back to the professor. We concluded that we were speculating about something like a directional antenna, being fed by a transmitter the size of a couple of refrigerators, with an ample power source nearby. And then all of that under a flight path that he calculated would have to be no higher than 10,000 feet."

"So that could be runway approaches or take offs," Mush said to the room and to Bill on his computer back in Washington over the video call.

"I'll send an advisory to the FAA and TSA to be on the lookout for strong radio frequency emissions," Hiccock said.

"Good luck with the EMF cloud around an airport!" Kronos said, referring to the "cloud" of radio energy surrounding any airport.

"It's worth a shot," Bill said.

Kronos shrugged.

Mush asked, "Bill, what if this is industrial espionage intended to bring down a prototype or roll out of an airplane? Can you check and see if any commercial or military rollouts are scheduled? That could be a good place to— Bill?"

Brooke noticed he was not listening to Mush. He must have been distracted by something on his monitor. "Bill what is it?"

"Wait. Let me put this up on the screen," he said.

On the big screen appeared a fragment of the code that Kronos had forwarded to be uploaded to the assembled scientific geniuses on Bill's web. Kronos looked at the room and shrugged again.

"One of my etiologist's just sent me this. Thinks these bits of data on this shred are RFID codes."

"Etiologist? Bill, how does a disease specialist know from RFID codes?" Kronos said.

Brooke was impressed that Kronos knew what one of those was.

"She had a summer job at a warehouse and did computer inventory while she was paying her way through college."

"I like this woman," Brooke said. "What do these RDIF codes mean. Er ... RFID?"

Kronos jumped in. "Radio Frequency Identification codes, R, F, ID. It's how warehouses can find the needle you want to buy in a building full of haystacks."

"They are usually chips, stuck to, sewn in or attached to a product which can be uniquely identified down to the individual piece."

"Who uses these, Bill?" Mush said.

"Practically anyone who stores, ships or sells anything. You know, manufacturers, big stores, military parts and logistics."

"Fuck! Like Caravan!" Kronos said.

"Kronos!" Brooke admonished.

"The friggin' Caravan hack, Brooke!"

"Sure, Caravan is the world leader in RFID inventory control," Bill said.

"Hacking into Caravan now ..." Kronos said as if he was looking up a ball score.

"I'm going to make believe I didn't hear that. Connection must be bad," Bill said.

Brooke laughed and look over Kronos's shoulder.

Kronos looked up and down and up and down as he typed. Brooke read off those numbers on the data fragment on Bill's screen to help him.

Brooke leaned in to see the small type: "CDE784 FFF347 AAB875 CDA342 ..." She continued until Kronos erupted. "Holy shit! These are laptops! Hundreds of friggin' laptops."

"So, somebody went shopping on Caravan for a school or college?" Brooke said.

"Or company?" Mush said.

"But that doesn't sound like anything scary. Certainly nothing worth killing Kupalli and two others for," Brooke said.

"Yeah, this sounds like a dead end," Bridgestone said.

"No wait, guys. These IDs are off of the one thousand shipping labels that were hacked into Caravan. Holy FUCK!

"Kronos ..." Brooke was getting tired of this.

Kronos's face turned white, even with the new surfer's tan.

"What is it?" Brooke said, worry suddenly modulating her voice.

CHAPTER 61

JFK BAGGAGE handler Joseph DeFino was thinking about whether or not to have the Parma ham or the meatball sub for lunch as he was loading the last flight before his break. As usual, the last things to go into the hold of this United 757 was the gate-checked baggage. So that it would be first off in order for deplaning passengers to retrieve them right outside the aircraft. They were about to lock the compartment when he saw his supervisor approaching driving a tug tractor at top speed, which for a machine designed to pull a 400,000-pound airframe from a gate was around 20 mph.

"Hey, Joe, one more ..." he said as he took the box next to him and handed over the 20 x 14 x 5-inch package to him.

Joe saw it had a Caravan, Sultan's Express— Next Plane Out sticker on it. It was a check through to Budapest, Hungary. This plane was going to LHR in London. There the package would be routed to whichever the next plane from Heathrow to Hungary was. Figuring it was a computer or iPad, he wedged it between the checked bags and the end of a luggage container.

"Hey Joe, come see me when you're back from lunch. I got to change the schedule for next week. Derick's wife's gonna pop any minute. I can't count on him for next week."

Joe locked and safety'd the cargo door mechanism and signaled the tug driver that the bird was ready to push back.

"Okay, Pete. Want me to bring you a sangwich?"

"What cha getting?"

"Don't know yet,"

"Yeah, surprise me," he said as he turned the wheel many times and putt-putt-ed back to the tarmac's edge.

Joe did his usual double tap of his hand on the fuselage. A kind of "be safe" gesture to the plane he just sealed against rapid, explosive decompression.

CHAPTER 62

"OH FUCK!" Brooke said, disregarding her own ban on foul language in her home, as Kronos was piecing together what was happening in real time as all his fragments were forming a terrifying picture. "How many planes?"

"I'm trying to rebuild his database now."

Brooke was on hold for Bill, and when he came on she didn't mince words. "Bill, we have an imminent attack ... could be happening now. Kronos is trying to find out how many, but it looks like there are bombs or something being put on hundreds of planes all at once. We have to alert FAA, TSA, NORAD, FBI and the State Department.

f

Bill called out to his head of the department, Cheryl, and told her to alert the NCA. The National Command Authority was the top of the food chain on immediate action alerts.

"Line one, it's a General Hanks," Cheryl said.

Bill picked up. "General, this is science advisor to the president, my authorization code is Bravo Xray Bravo Oscar Yankee 256. I'm ordering a full aviation alert."

It took a second for the general's terminal in front of him to return Bill's authentication.

"Passcode?"

"Quarterback."

"Is this an exercise or real world?"

"Real world."

As Hanks brought up the emergency action screen and applied his thumb print to the sensor, he asked, "Hijacking?"

"No. Hi-*hacking*, sir," Bill said, coining forever a new phrase on the threat board.

"Hihacking? What the hell?" The general pressed a record button. "Proceed."

"I'm ordering a full alert status; attack is imminent to immediate. We have a condition red, general aviation threat. Up to one thousand planes currently in flight are carrying in their cargo holds active devices that can cause the plane to lose control and crash. Further asking for a worldwide ground stop effective immediately."

"The general typed General Aviation Threat into his threat matrix screen. A preprogrammed contact routine was loaded. This method was installed in the aftermath of 911 where valuable minutes were lost as information trickled all too slowly through the massive federal system. With this new protocol, automatically, TSA, FAA, FBI, CIA, Dep State, DIA, US Customs and Border, Air Marshall Service and DOD were put on line. Within those organizations, over seven hundred individual desks and personnel were immediately notified. For example, the Department of State emergency action desk would notify the UN, Interpol, Scotland Yard and other international police organizations to the threat. The FAA would immediately reach every airline, to alert their planes and all ground control, ATC and tower personnel throughout the worldwide air traffic system.

Bill took a deep breath, and then made the call he should have probably made first. "This is Quarterback for POTUS. I have a level-one national-security threat."

The White House interconnect in the office of communications connected him to the Oval.

The chief of staff answered. "Gates."

"David, it's Bill Hiccock. We got an emergency."

"Terrorism?"

"Undetermined at this time. But confidence is one hundred percent that one thousand planes are going to crash in the next hour and thirteen minutes."

"Dear God. Hold on." The COS interrupted the president mid-sentence in his conversation with the prime minister of Canada. "Sir, we have a situation."

President Pearson, four days on the job, turned to his former campaign manager. His mind immediately went to the Carter administration. How they were tested in the early days by terrorist events that would later cast a dark shadow on their legacy. "What is it, David?"

"Sir, Hiccock is saying there's a threat to aviation."

"A hijacking?"

"No, sir, bombs or devices on one thousand planes."

"Dear God. When?"

"Right now, sir."

"How could ...?"

"Sir, that's for later. Hiccock has called for a ground stop and he's initiated a threat-matrix protocol."

"Get the cabinet. I want whoever knows anything about this on the phone or in the house now."

The Secret Service entered the room. "Sir, come with us."

"Are you crashing the house?" the COS said.

"We have a general aviation threat. We're heading to the PEOC."

"Please escort the prime minister as well," the president said.

The Secret Service agent looked to the president. Only the president and the individuals they drilled with were on his list. "Sir, the prime minister is not on my list."

"It's okay. He'll be able to call his government from downstairs."

He being the president and all, the agent had but one response. "Yes, sir."

CHAPTER 63

Air Traffic Control is a worldwide radio, radar and data network which establishes the virtual highways crisscrossing the earth that planes use to go from A to B. The ATC's job is keeping hundred-ton objects hurtling at just under the speed of sound in their "lanes" and preventing them from bumping into one another at 550 mph.

An EMERGENCY ACTION MESSAGE from NORAD, the North American Aerospace Defense Command in Colorado Springs, goes right to the controllers and they open the direct line to all planes in flight and on the ground. The message was live from the four-star general who headed up the command.

"This is an emergency action notification from North American Aerospace Defense Command. To all aircraft, confidence is extremely high that avionic interference devices have been placed in the cargo holds of currently in-flight aircra—"

Mastieff was monitoring aircraft radio frequencies as a way of gauging the impact of his attack. He didn't expect what he heard. Somehow, the FAA in the United States had found out about his plot. They started a warning message to all planes in the air. He immediately turned off the radios in the one-thousand planes he controlled, stopping the message mid-sentence. But he listened to the whole thing as it continued:

"... an immediate global ground stop is hereby ordered. All aircraft are immediately directed to land at the nearest practical landing strip. This is not a drill. One thousand aircraft, all types, are carrying this device. Please isolate all flight control from fly-by-wire if mechanically possible for your type. Repeat, please isolate all flight control from fly-by-wire if mechanically possible for your type. This message will now repeat."

"Go ahead, repeat," he said to the message. "No one can hear you." He was not bothered that they were on to him, because all was already set in motion. There was little, if anything, they could do. He and every pilot and every ATC controller knew that there were only a few planes nowadays that could disconnect from their computer-controlled flight operation systems. He had his thousand planes under his control. He had them all where he wanted them above 10,000 feet. "Now for a little demonstration," he said to the dead Rashy.

f

The cockpit crew of United Flight 837, at 33,000 feet over the north Atlantic, only heard half the message when their radio cut out. In fact, none of the one thousand planes heard the complete message. Copilots and flight engineers started toggling circuit breakers, checking settings. They were unaware that a laptop in their luggage compartments had just shut down their radios.

CHAPTER 64

"KRONOS, do something," Brooke said.

"It's preprogrammed. There's no stopping it!"

"There has to be a way," Brooke said.

"Yeah, take a hammer, go into every plane and smash the fucking laptop to bits."

"Hold it. Let's think about this, Kronos. What was the satellite connection? What was it ... the NOAA birds?" Mush said.

Kronos snapped his fingers. "Mush, maybe."

"What's that?" Bridgestone asked.

"Kronos found some data strings and code that seemed aimed at geosynchronous satellites. All of the scientists on Bill's network dismissed that it could potentially tie to any attack ... all except one. And to me that guy made the most sense," Mush said.

The video conference program rang.

It was Bill. "Guys, this was just posted on YouTube LIVE and a link sent to every news organization on earth. We're trying to trace it now."

The screen switched to black with white letters in English being read by a text-to-voice computer-generated voice. "Attention United Nations. We control one thousand planes currently in flight. To prove to you that we do, please track United Airlines Flight 837. In thirty seconds, it will rapidly descend from its current flight level of angels 33. I will give you further instructions one minute from now."

f

As the flight engineer of the United 837 was opening a circuit access panel to try to fix the busted radio, the plane suddenly went into a steep dive, throwing him forward. In the cabin, the passengers' dinners and drinks slammed against the backs of the seats in front of them. Screams and cries filled the cabin. Flight attendants were grasping at seat legs as they were suddenly down and sliding forward. The sound outside the plane was a roaring hurricane-like howl as the wings were suddenly stressed to their design maximums.

The pilot and copilot pulled back on the yoke, but the plane didn't respond. No matter how hard they pulled or pushed, their yokes had ceased controlling the plane. They were now nothing more than passengers along for what would surely be a very short ride to eternity.

f

Flight controllers watched the United plane's rapid descent in horror. Many grabbed their desk, sympathetically turning away as if they themselves were in the cock pit watching the ocean rapidly fill their windshield. At 9000 feet, the blip that represented United 837 and the 354 souls on board the aircraft disappeared from radar. In more than a few flight-control centers, people crossed themselves. Still others frantically tried to hail other aircraft, but there was no response. The transponders of the 2037 aircraft that were in the air, all around the world at that moment, were all on and sending data to the system. But there was no way to contact half of the planes.

f

The four-star general in charge of NORAD was feeding the radar screen image of that portion of the Atlantic to PEOC under the White House. He narrated over the secure line to the president. "Sir, as you can see by the flight-level data received from the plane's transponder, it is descending at a very rapid rate, and now it has disappeared. Presumably crashing in the next few seconds. May God have mercy on their souls, sir."

The president sat stunned for a few seconds. The Canadian prime minister murmured something in French. The funereal quiet was shattered by the YouTube audio continuing. "As you have been shown, we control your planes. One thousand to be exact.

Our demands are simple. In exactly ten minutes an online address will appear on this screen. At that instant one hundred billion in Bitcoin must be transferred to that address. That portal will close exactly one minute later. Trust us, it is untraceable. If in eleven minutes there is not one hundred billion dollars credited to that account, in Bitcoin, all the planes we now control will plummet to the earth. And unlike the plane you just witnessed, many are over land and populated areas. You now have nine minutes thirty-five seconds to comply. As a show of good faith, watch your screens."

f

Confusion reigned in the cockpit of United 837. The plane leveled off at 2,000 ft above death. All by itself. The copilot's bowels had loosed. The captain thought he felt the mechanical feedback from the yoke. He pulled on it slightly. The plane responded. "Harris, you son of a bitch, you fixed it. How did you ..." he called out to the flight engineer.

"Sir, I didn't do anything. I was pinned against the bulkhead."

"Well, we have stick. Bruce, try to raise ATC. Let's get to a safe lane. Harris, I need your eyes up here. Keep a sharp eye out for aircraft. I'm going to give us some altitude and take us right up to the ten-thousand-foot ceiling. Turn on the landing lights. I want to give anyone above us a chance to see us coming up until we have flight-level clearance from ATC."

The captain reasoned that, out over the ocean, no commercial airliner would be below the ATC controlled air lanes for pressurized airframes, which start at 10,000 ft, and there would be very sparse traffic under the public aviation's 10,000 foot ceiling. If the controls went out again, he wanted some breathing room.

The copilot keyed his radio. "United 837 heavy to Gander. Declaring an emergency."

He was relieved when he heard, "United 837 heavy, state your emergency."

"Gander, we have lost altitude but have regained control. We are too close to the deck. Requesting angels 33."

"Gander to United 837. Hold current flight level. Traffic above you being cleared."

The pilot looked at the copilot and breathed a sigh of relief, then immediately caught a whiff of what was permeating the small, enclosed cockpit. He donned his oxygen mask.

f

Cheers erupted in the main room of NORAD as United 837 ascended back on the radar screen, which meant it had achieved at least 10,000 ft. It was under pilot control again.

f

There was palpable relief in the PEOC as the general reported the plane had not crashed and was seeking safe flight level. The open mic in the room caught the president saying. "General, is this real or are we being duped, some kind of hack of your screens?"

"Hiccock here, sir. I'm bringing in our computer expert, Vincent DeMayo, who discovered all this and alerted me. Vincent ..."

"Er ... Mr. President. I have all the programs and algorithms that are currently being executed. I can assure you that the avionics software of at least eight major aircraft manufacturers has been compromised and a laptop has been placed on at least one thousand planes currently at altitude. A similar laptop loaded with this software has been crashing my simulated planes for two weeks now, although we just figured it out thirty-five minutes ago. This is no deception, sir. This is the best friggin' hack code I have ever encountered. We are under a well-planned, very sophisticated attack, sir."

Just then the chief of staff interrupted. "Sir, the secretary general of the UN on the line."

"Very well." He waggled his fingers in a give-it-to-me gesture. He picked up. "Mr. Secretary, my people tell me this is a real threat. As far as we know, and confidence is very high, he does indeed control the planes. Yes, sir, I'm just getting that now." A handwritten note with numbers worked up was handed to him. "Roughly 354,000 passengers on one thousand planes." He listened. "Yes, one hundred billion. My Treasury is working on that now. How much do you have in your discretionary fund?" The president motioned to his COS and mouthed the words, *Get Treasury on it.*

The president listened. He put his hand over the handset and spoke to the conference call on the speaker phone. "Hey, computer guy. Vincent, is it?"

"Yes, sir!"

"Can we do this? How do we Bitcoin this son of a bitch?"

"Your SWIFT guys can handle that. I'm too busy trying to block his friggin' control system."

Mush interrupted and identified himself. "Sir, this is Rear Admiral Morton, COMSUBPAC. We think he's using a satellite link to communicate with the laptops. Krono ... er, Mr. DeMayo here is trying to sever that link."

The president just assumed some admiral, somewhere, was on the call. He had no idea that this admiral was in his own house and the whole plot was discovered in his dining room. "Very well. I'll get somebody here to set up the payment, but admiral ..."

"Yes, sir?"

"If he figures that out in the next eight minutes, I'm ordering you to stop me from making this one-way transfer."

"Yes, sir."

CHAPTER 65

Nasser left his briefcase at the safe house. He did not go back to get it, nor would anyone find it. The five men in that house were the five cell leaders who had literally gotten the "Planes" project off the ground. Each was the only contact he had to their respective cells. With the exception of Waleed, Nasser never met with anybody except these five, and they would carry out his instructions—actually Mastieff's directives—to the one hundred or so cell members that he assumed they needed to accomplish these critical tasks in exacting order. As he left them, with apologies for pressing business that would take him away from this glorious moment when the planes would fall from the skies, he praised God on "the beginning of the great revenge that would cripple the infidels and reestablish the cause as the true fate of history by which others would find their calling in the great struggle." *Blah blah blah,* he added in his mind.

He crossed the street in this poor village in Syria that smelled of human waste and burning tires that the peasants cooked food over. His driver opened his door, just as the building exploded. His driver/bodyguard shielded his protectee with his body. Nasser didn't even look back. Five out of the only six links to him had been eliminated in that celebration to honor God at the conclusion of their mission. *Well, they can honor him personally now*, he thought. He got into his armored Rolls and headed to a "conveniently timed" meeting at the Syrian Ministry of Defense.

f

Mastieff watched the video as it was being watched in all the capitals in the world at that same instant. As the on-screen timer clock clicked down, he readied the Bitcoin retrieval program to be executed with a single keystroke. Because he disabled the radios of all the aircraft as soon as he heard the Emergency Action Message, all the world's governments were desperately trying to reach their flight crews. It was another way they knew he had control of their planes and the lives of the passengers. They would not play games. To the west's way of thinking, one hundred billion in international finances was a small price to pay for 350,000 lives and the security of the world's leading infrastructure, air travel. He looked at Raffy's fingers starting to curl from rigor. He assumed that by now Nasser had dispatched the five others who could connect them to the plot. The world governments would never know it was he, or the Saudi prince, who were behind the attack. But the true believers, like Raffy here, the sixth, who put their faith and trust in him because of some allegiance to God, they would become rabid, leaving no stone unturned to find out who betrayed them and their God. And it was those religious zealots that he feared most.

f

"Crusher, can you reverse-track the NOAA satellite up feed?" Brooke said.

"You think they're connected?" Bridgestone asked.

"Kronos taught me about logical if/then statements."

"Huh?"

"IF this happens THEN he can do that. He has to have a control point ..." Brooke said. "It's pretty clear this isn't just a terror attack. If it was, the planes would have crashed first, then they would have taken credit—after the fact. So, in order for him to threaten us for ransom, this can't be on a preprogrammed, unchangeable timetable. He needs to be able to control the terror."

Mush was on her wavelength. "She's right. They brought that one plane back up to altitude. That proves that they have control. This isn't a one-way, one-end proposition."

"Unless the diving of the airliner was also preplanned to make it look like they were controlling it?" Kronos said as his eyes never left the screen or his fingers the keyboard.

"Well, if that's the case then there's nothing we can do about it. But on the off chance they didn't plan that well, I'm going to request we proceed as if they have a command-and-control point," Mush said.

"Okay, why?" Kronos said.

"Because he wants money not glory. Let's say that if we were to blow the deadline and the planes crashed, then he would have no bargaining power," Brooke said.

"So, he needs to be able to respond ... adapt," Bridgestone said.

Mush jumped in, "And a satellite could signal a plane at 30,000 feet."

"How? I thought you needed 30,000 watts. You can't get that from a satellite," Bridgestone said.

"That's true, but that's only to blast through the fuselage from down on earth. Atop every plane is a satellite receiver. Works on flea power, the microscopically weak signals emanating from satellites all around the earth. The laptops must be tapping into those receivers as part of the hack." Crusher said.

"That was the friggin' weather satellite data Kupalli was screwing with. He's piggybacking his command and control off geosynchronous birds," Kronos said.

Mush turned to Crusher. "Can you do it? Can you find the location of the satellite uplink?"

"I'm on it!" Crusher said, diving in.

Mush looked at Brooke. "Logical if/then statement?"

"You don't think I listen when the children talk?"

f

The president was shaking his fist as he watched the seconds tick down to a precious few. "Somebody tell me what's happening with the funds transfer?"

'Sir, the UN has not deposited their twenty billion into our account, as yet."

"Get me the secretary general now!"

It took thirty seconds. The president knew this because he watched each second tick down on the video's clock.

"On 2, sir,"

The president picked up. "Mr. Secretary, what's the delay? We're running out of time!"

"China is objecting to the payment. They say it's blackmail and they don't pay terrorists."

"Can you move them? What do they want? Mr. Secretary, they're negotiating with you. Ask them directly what they want, and for God's sake, do it fast! I'll hold on the line."

As the video counted down, a message appeared at the one-minute mark. "The deposit link is now open for sixty seconds."

The president was wringing his hands. "Anything from Cyber Command?"

"Sir, they still can't find the source of the video."

f

Crusher looked up the signal frequency for the NOAA satellite, while Brooke had Bill get them a direct line to the NSA.

Bill said, "Crusher, this is the watch commander at NSA. Go."

"Sir, can I monitor ground-listening posts, Timberland, Moonpenny and Ironsand. At 14.6 gigahertz."

"That's a weather band uplink freq," the commander said.

"Yes, sir. We believe there's an unauthorized uplink to the NOAA bird and we need a triangulated fix."

"Hell. Son, I can do that from here."

"Great."

There was a few second pause then he reported, "Okay, nothing so far."

"Please keep watching. It's probably going to be short bursts."

"Rolling data tapes now."

f

As the final seconds ticked down, the president called out over the open connection to the UN, "Mr. Secretary ... Mr. Secretary."

A sheepish voice came back. "I apologize, Mr. President, but the UN is a deliberative body. I'm afraid we're not designed to respond to immediate emergencies."

Political correctness hit a new low as the president watched the counter hit zero. "Ah, shit." He cut the connection to the UN and barked, "Get Treasury on the phone. We need to make up for the UN shortfall. NOW!"

The screen went black.

"Now what?"

Suddenly the flight path of an airliner came on. It was from a commercially available flight-tracking system. The transponder information next to the blip identified it as DAL 631 Heavy. Someone, somewhere on the line, which was patched to no less than eight government agencies all watching the same video, broke in with, "That's Delta flight 631 nonstop service Orlando to New York. Currently at 23,000, eighteen miles south of Philadelphia."

"Oh my God!" was all the president could say.

f

"Got a short burst on the 14.6 gig band."

"What's the source?"

"Triangulating now."

Kronos shouted, "Fuckin' A."

"What is it?" Bridgestone asked.

"Crusher ask the NSA guy for a link to the uplink. I think I have rebuilt his command-and-control program," Kronos said.

"The link is parked in your assembly folder, Kronos," Crusher called out.

"Okay, let's see if this friggin' code works."

f

At an altitude of 22,236 miles, in geosynchronous orbit over the equator, NOAA satellite KH-709 repeated the command string from Kronos. Unlike the last command, this one ordered all planes to remain at flight level.

f

The cockpit crew of Delta flight 631 were fighting for their lives. Forty-two years of flying between the captain and first officer, and they had never experienced a "dead stick." Nothing they did, no emergency procedure, had any effect. They were in a wing-tearing dive, nose first into the center of Philadelphia. The co-pilot, purely from training, opened the announce key and broadcast to the cabin, "Brace, brace, brace."

As he said it, he realized the cabin attendants were most likely plastered to the bulkheads, the passengers were probably screaming at the tops of their lungs, and you cannot brace against a 400,000-pound plane hurtling to the ground at five hundred miles per hour. He then flashed on the fact that they would all be totally vaporized—braced or not. The thought froze him.

"Fred! Fred! Kill all the circuit breakers. Trip them then restart the systems," the captain ordered as he fought a battle with a control yoke that was no longer controlling his plane.

"Fred! Snap out of ..."

Suddenly the plane started to level off. It groaned as the ship tried to achieve level flight all by itself.

"What did you do?" Fred asked, suddenly out of his momentary freeze.

"I didn't do anything. This plane has got a mind of its own."

f

The display of the flight track on the screen at the White House started showing a constant altitude.

"What's happening, people?" the president asked.

"Sir, the plane has stopped diving."

Bill Hiccock spoke up on the network. There were yells and cheers in the background coming over his channel. "Sir, my people in Hawaii have interrupted the control signals to the plane. They now control it." *Fuck yeah! Great job. Yes!* The exuberance in the dining room was heard by all on the network.

"Bill, what the hell?"

"Later, sir. Let's see if there's a countermove."

f

Mastieff looked over to Raffy. He, being dead, couldn't help him figure out what just went wrong. He muttered a Pashtun curse as he typed the dive command again ..."

f

Delta flight 631 suddenly lurched down again. "Son of a bitch..." the captain said. They were dropping through 2,500 feet. At 500 mph that gave them seventeen seconds to death.

f

"Oh yeah, take that you friggin' bastard," Kronos said as he once again not only counteracted Mastieff's command, but wrote a new line of code locking him out. "Suck on that, you strunz-a-menz. Now you can't fly the friggin' plane!"

f

"Okay, okay, I got her back. Thank Jesus. I got her back," the captain said, out of breath, as his yoke once again responded.

f

"Kronos, have you stopped him?"

"Yes. Well, just with this Boeing version avionics package."

"So, this is not over?" Bridgestone said.

"I have seven other manufacturers and two release version of Boeing to go."

"How long?" Mush said.

"It's going to take time, Mush."

"Time? Time is what the hundreds of thousands of passengers don't have."

Brooke and Bridgestone just watched as Kronos dug in and Mush was now caught in deep thought.

Mush asked Crusher, "Do you have a geo fix on the uplink?"

"Just getting that now from NSA."

Mush turned to the screen Bill was on. "Bill, the source is in Penang, Malaysia. We've got the coordinates."

The president was on the line. "What's that mean? This is the admiral speaking, right?"

"Yes, sir. Morton, sir. Mr. President, I'm asking for your authority to launch a Tomahawk strike on the site of the uplink and stop this guy. We have a sub that's three and a half minutes out flight time from that location. My boys can spin up a Tommy and deliver the message in four minutes from receipt of the EAM. We drill for this every day, sir.

"Attack a sovereign country?" the Secretary of State, who was on the call, asked.

"What about collateral damage, Admiral?" POTUS said.

"Sir, there are, by all estimates, 350,000 souls who are in this guy's crosshairs. That's not to mention the casualties on the ground when they come down over land. We could be talking a half a million dead in the next five minutes. We can stop all of this in four."

"Sir, we need to notify the Malaysians," Sec State said.

The president suddenly remembered his history. Truman was asked to drop the first atomic bombs to save a half million US troops and countless more Japanese in order to prevent an invasion of the Japanese homeland to end World War Two. History now chose him to make this same terrible decision, a small amount of murder to stop mass murder. "Admiral, is this a conventional weapon?"

"Yes, sir. I'll order up a TLAM-C with only one thousand pounds of explosives. It will do the job but without a bigger boom."

"Admiral, is there any other option?"

"Like what, sir?"

"I don't know. Some electronic jamming. A hack or something."

"Any ECM countermeasure would take at least thirty minutes, sir. The Tomahawk flies just under Mach 1. Awaiting your order, sir." Mush looked at Brooke. She nodded. She knew her husband was right. She also understood that asking POTUS to attack a friendly power was tantamount to an act of war. She held his hand. With his other hand he took out his cell. "Franks, this is not a drill, repeat, this is not a drill. Fleet Action Message the *Tiger Shark*. Have them prepare a Mark 4 Tommy for immediate launch. Target data coming to you now," he said as he copied the coordinates from Crusher's screen to his text. "But hold fire until presidential release by EAM. This is not a drill; this is real world. Thus, I hereby order as Rear Admiral Brett Morton, COMSUBPAC. Be ready to fire immediately. Standby for presidential authority." That last part he said for the benefit of the tape, which would no doubt be scrutinized for the next one hundred years.

f

In an amazing display of the command-and-control machinery, the military attaché to the president took out a red phone from a drawer in the PEOC, broke the seal holding the receiver to the 1960s-style device. He put it to his own ear. "Standby for the president." He handed the phone to the commander in chief and said, "Secretary of Defense, awaiting your order, sir."

The phone smelled of Lysol. He wondered when it was last used. *The Bin Laden raid? Desert Storm?*

The SecDef was already on the network, but the red phone was the actual verifiable link. Everything up to now could be misunderstanding, or, worse, subterfuge. But the red phone was the undeniable link that the president was giving a direct order to the military.

"Mr. Secretary, I authorize this attack. May God have mercy on the innocents who may be killed, and shed that mercy on us."

"Yes, sir."

f

In the conning tower of the *Tiger Shark*, the captain of the boat watched the Emergency Action Message indicator above his head. It flashed. From the radio shack he heard, "Sir, incoming EAM."

"Mr. Holmes, bring the *Shark* to the roof," he said as he read the EAM. "Give me 1MC."

His mic was switched to the communications channel for the entire boat. "Men, we have been ordered by the president to launch. Battle stations missile. This is not an exercise..

Thirty seconds later, the skipper watched the feed from the camera on the conning tower sail, as the forward hatch on missile tube 7 opened.

"Weaps, weapons free. Fire tube 7 at will."

There was a huge plume of smoke and flame gushing out from the vertical launch tube as twenty-five million dollars' worth of Tomahawk cruise missile started its ascent. At fifty feet the wings sprouted, and the rocket leveled off into a ground-hugging, radar-evading short trip, 36 nautical miles east. At 550 mph, it would take just under 210 seconds, with the nosecone camera recording the flight all the way to detonation.

In the intervening minutes, before the launch, they were able to see, on the military version of Google Earth, that the target coordinates landed on an oil refinery which appeared deserted. The nearest structure was one thousand feet away. There was no sign of an uplink dish, but this was an archived view, probably updated once a year. You could set up a ground uplink in minutes. The video from the Tommy showed it crossing the coastline at tremendous speed.

"Sir, tube 8 spun up and standing by."

"Very well," was his response to the procedural prep of a second Tomahawk in case the first suffered a malfunction or was shot down. There were 12 Mark 4 Tommy's on the *Tiger Shark,* and each one would be thrown at the target until the mission was accomplished and the target destroyed.

f

Mastieff was shocked. Somehow, his commands were being countermanded, and now he was locked out. There was no time to switch to another satellite, even if Raffy were alive. His survival instinct kicked in. Without control, his whole plan was rendered impotent. Somehow, they were on to him. He wasn't an electronics expert, but he knew enough to infer that the same path that he used to get to a satellite was the same path someone else could track back to get to him.

f

It's amazing, the president thought as he was now tuned into the nosecone of the hurtling missile. The screen showed the terrain disappearing under the missile at a super high speed. Suddenly there was a building off in the distance which rapidly filled the screen. A target graticule appeared right before the camera showed the blur of the wall of the building, then static snow of a video interrupted.

f

"It looked like an isolated building, thank God," Brooke said.

"I think we got lucky," Mush said. "Crusher, let us know if the NSA hears anymore uplink chatter."

"Kronos, how did you figure out the control codes so quickly?"

"I've been living inside Kupalli's code so long, I was friggin' starting to think like him. Also, I got lucky."

"Luck, you? I thought everything was freakin' YOU all the time," Brooke said, in an affected Brooklyn accent that came from the heart.

"True. But so happens the Delta plane was a 757, and that was the flight control software I've been fooling with since the beginning. But it was Crusher here that got the job done."

"Yeah, I'd say a field promotion is in order," Admiral Mush Morton said.

"Thank you, sir. It was really the NSA."

"Stow it, sailor, you accomplished a mission with undefined parameters, you innovated and overcame. That's a set of bars in my book."

"When you put it that way, sir ..."

"Helloooo. Hey guys, you know the president's still on the line," Bill said.

"Who is this you got in Hawaii, Professor Hiccock?"

"Sir, my pleasure to introduce you to my friends and true American heroes, Brooke Burrell and her husband Admiral Brett Morton, Sergeant Major Richard Bridgestone, and Vincent DeMayo, computer whiz extraordinaire; and I'm sorry, but I don't believe I know ... Crusher?"

"He's Lieutenant Junior Grade Neal Kensington, my missile tech from when I commanded the SS *Nebraska*, sir," Mush said.

"Well, I'll make this all formal later, but today you served not only your country but the world. To the extent any of this can be known, I'll see you get all due credit. But from me, personally, I want to say thank you for a job well done. Who do you work for? I can definitely see a unit citation is appropriate here."

"Well, sir, we used to all work for you," Brooke said.

"I'm sorry ..." the president said.

"Sir," Bill interjected, "these people, with the exception of Lieutenant Kensington, were on my Quarterback operations team."

There was palpable silence. The noises and static from the network line rose up, filling the gap. Everyone in Brooke's dining room looked at each other.

"Where's your team working from now?" President Pearson asked.

"Er, my dining room, sir," Brooke said with a slight hesitation.

"Well, I'll be damned ... Hiccock, tomorrow be in the Oval at eight. Let's revisit this whole operations group initiative."

"Yes, sir," Bill said.

"Again, folks, I'm extremely grateful that you saved all those lives, and my administration from an embarrassing defeat. I expect to meet all of you soon, at the residence. I'll have my staff make the arrangements."

Then scores of clicks and beeps filled the line as the president and half the government hung up, leaving just Bill and them on the circuit.

"Like he said, great job, guys. I assume they'll want an after-action report. Let's talk about it tomorrow, okay?"

"Bill, you neglected to point out that you ... that you ... Ah hell, I'm going to say it, that you quarterbacked the whole operation," Brooke said.

"I'm just glad we stopped these guys."

"Do you think the boss was serious about dinner at the White House, Bill?" Mush said.

"Definitely. You saved him one hundred billion dollars. Why?"

"Because my wife is under court order not to leave the island."

CHAPTER 66

NASSER WAS in shock. He managed to put himself in the Syrian Ministry of Defense a few minutes before the attack was scheduled. Therefore, he could passively monitor the events without having to inquire. He sat in the main room with his jaw dropped. *It was over! No transfer of funds. The attack must have been thwarted. Not one plane was crashed. What was Mastieff thinking? He wasn't strong enough with the Americans. And what was that business over the American city of Philadelphia?* His thoughts were interrupted by a conversation at the front of the room. He got up and wandered over.

"... not much ancillary damage," one man said.

"And we are sure it was the Americans?" a major asked.

"Yes. They just put out a statement claiming they stopped a treacherous attack on the world. They're saying they're grateful to the Malaysian government for their unprecedented cooperation in this matter."

"What matter?" Nasser asked.

"Sahib, the Americans have struck a facility in the Malaysian oil fields where they claim the airline attack emanated."

"Where in Malaysia?"

"Penang, sahib."

The words stabbed at his heart. He suddenly felt ill. He walked away and found a room with a couch. *How?* was all he could think. *Security was tight. The cells insulated. How could anyone figure out the total plan? It had to be a traitor, someone inside. But who?* Then his mind settled on two simultaneous realities. One was that it no longer mattered because his connection to this whole affair had been severed. Especially with Mastieff killed by the US missile strike. But the second unnerving thought was that without the ransom this scheme would have generated, his shortfall in the Royal Bank would soon be discovered.

That was the whole reason for all this in the first place. To keep his head on his shoulders and replenish the royal account. The promised payoff to the head of the bank was also now impossible. He'd have to eliminate him. This was getting sloppy. Or should Nasser just disappear? Take the five million in "mad money" from his safe and change his identity and live in relative obscurity as a commoner in some place with a good climate and a not-too-inquisitive government.

Still his mind returned to, how? It was such a layered plan. No one, only he and Mastieff, knew all the pieces. No one else. How? Then a second thought emerged. Good that Mastieff was assassinated, otherwise he would ask the same question and deduce that it was only the two of them who could have possibly sabotaged the plot. And Mastieff wouldn't hesitate to kill him just on that probability alone.

f

The president went live to the nation in an Oval Office address at 8 p.m. He told the American people and the world of the attempted attack. How it was thwarted by American intelligence, working closely with Malaysian authorities and the secretary general of the United Nations. To his credit, he handled that bit of political subterfuge with the oral skill and convincing air of a con man, but, after all, he was a polished politician. He reasserted his efforts to keep America and the world vigilant against such further attacks, but assured the citizens of the planet that air travel was still the safest form of transportation in the world today. He concluded his remarks with the de rigueur invocation ...

f

"... and may God bless the United States of America."

In safe house cells and hookah bars across the earth, certain individuals sat in shock as the US president ended his speech. Their belief system shattered; their faith eroded. Their great blow against the infidels had failed. Worse, their plan to take down the west had turned into a victory for those godless souls who lived in what they referred to as Dar. Some vowed to double efforts, maybe take up a personal jihad, become martyrs and don explosive vests; others just walked away, not sure of what they so righteously believed seconds before. Not one of them was aware or suspected that they had been deceived from the start and it was an elaborate extortion plot. Just a criminal enterprise.

CHAPTER 67

JAMES CAME OUT onto the lanai and was amused by what he saw. Brooke and Mush were dancing to an old disco tune. Crusher was downing a beer, Bridgestone was puffing away at a fat cigar and the Kronos character was dunking Oreos in milk, some of which dribbled down his chin. "Celebration?" he said with a smile.

Brooke looked at Mush. He gave a nod. "Yes, James, grab a drink. There's pizza coming."

"So, you heard?" James said, a little shocked.

"Heard? James, we did it!" Mush said, doing his best straight white-guy dance, the arms never rising above the shoulder.

"*You* did it? But I just got the order from the judge."

"Wait, what are you talking about, James?" Brooke said.

"Hold it, what are you celebrating here, then?" James said.

"We stopped the airplanes attack," Brooke said.

"Wait, you mean the thing on the news? You? Him?" He pointed to Kronos. "You did that?"

"Yo, Jimmy boy, what's so hard to believe? We stumbled on this weeks ago. We just had some trouble putting all the pieces together until right before they were going to kill all those people," Kronos said.

"That's what you guys have been working on?" James said, finally getting it. "Not the case?"

"The case uncovered the plot. Kupalli wrote all the programs for the terrorists," Brooke said, handing him a beer from the ice bucket without missing a step. "What are you talking about, James?"

"I just got the judge to consider dropping the proceedings, pending an evidentiary hearing tomorrow."

"What? That's fantastic!" Brooke grabbed James and planted one on his cheek!

Mush grabbed him and gave him a bear hug. "That's great, man. Couldn't have come at a better time."

Kronos held up an Oreo and said, "This one's for you, James."

Bridge said, "Way to go, James."

He was still incredulous. "You guys stopped a terrorist attack from here?"

"No big whoop," Kronos said.

"With computers you can be anywhere," Crusher said.

Mush stopped dancing and walked up to James. "Do you know what this means, James?"

"Thousands of people are safe?"

"Yeah, well that too, but also now Brooke can go to the White House with us to be personally thanked by the president." He continued dancing with his wife.

"Wow," James said as he took a long pull from his beer.

CHAPTER 68

MALAYSIAN POLICE had found a body—well, what was left of one—in the debris of the pumping station building that was destroyed by the American cruise missile. Also among the wreckage of the building was the remains of a satellite uplink dish, the portable kind that you could tow behind a car.

Forty yards away, they found a crushed Range Rover. From all appearances, the sole occupant was caught up in the fireball and shockwave that came from the exploding building as he drove by on the road alongside the facility. The SUV itself was blown into a retaining wall that surrounded a fuel storage tank. It was so badly crushed that it took the fire brigade several minutes to extract the man with their jaws-of-life tool. He was in critical condition at the hospital in Penang.

The local cops, acceding to the request from the national government, didn't touch much, in anticipation of the arrival of the FBI "Go Team" already wheels down at Penang International Airport and heading to the scene. The Americans were here to look for any forensic evidence to determine who was behind this attack.

CHAPTER 69

BILL WAS outside the Oval at 7:55. In his hand was a folder with everything he had on the attack, if it should come up. The rest of what the meeting was about was in his head. After all, he was the designer of QUOG, the Quarterback Operations Group, and could speak extemporaneously about it at the drop of a dime.

Twenty-five minutes later, the president was asking the kinds of questions one would ask if he were buying into a concept. "So, your group answers only to me?"

"Yes, sir."

"I don't know if I like the part where you are the titular head of all the intelligence agencies."

"It streamlines the flow of information and protects you, Mr. President, from, let's say, disgruntled employees in the federal government."

"Bill, you're going to have me looking over my shoulder with a comment like that."

"Sir, your predecessor didn't enjoy the respect of many in the intelligence community."

"But he was a no-party president. I got thirty-eight years of the party behind me."

"Democrat or Republican, sir, the intelligence agencies have carved out their own niches. In order to be effective and nimble, my team sometimes have to go around them, or right through them. Either way, you'll know where you stand and what you'll get with me, sir."

"I'll consider that point and reconsider bringing your group back online."

"Will that be all, sir?"

"Yes."

Bill got up to leave.

The president then snapped his fingers.

Bill turned and stood by his chair. "Yes, sir."

"Actually, there is one more thing. My wife recognized the name of Brooke Burrell last night when I told her about this whole attack. From what she tells me, the woman is getting a pretty good going over in the press, I take it?"

"That's an understatement, sir."

"I had them send the after-action report of last year's attack up to the residence last night."

"Did you read it?"

"Like a thriller novel. God, they came so close. I had no idea. Our briefings over in the Senate last year left most of that stuff out."

"Held close by Mitchell's orders, sir."

"Last year, I would have screamed like a stuck pig at those redactions, but now that I'm behind this desk, I get his point. But none of that changes the fact that this woman is a fierce warrior."

"Then you know what a crock of ... rocks the press is printing."

"Well, let's see if I can spend a little of my press honeymoon credits on this."

"Yes, sir. But not just the press. There's a senator you served with. He was on the gang of eight with you. He's smelling electoral votes in the water on this as well. He's going to ride this news story to national fame."

"That's quite an astute political analysis from a man of science."

"I learned a few things about *political* science in my years here as well, sir."

"So, I should quiet Paxton down?"

"Actually, sir, Brooke wanted him to go forward, only in a public hearing, but that would require you to declassify much of what you read last night."

"That's a tall order, Bill."

"Maybe just her part, then. She'd like her day in the court of public opinion. Right now, she's being called a murderer, a judge, jury, executioner and Mitchell's hit woman. As you read last night, sir, nothing could be further from the truth."

"That video from the bridge, it's very damning. She's shooting an unarmed man."

Bill took out his phone and swiped a few times. He moved to the president's side and showed him a video. "Sir, here's a close up from that hi-def video from one of my forensic scientists."

The video was zoomed in to Paul on the tracks. A puff of smoke can be seen coming out from under him. It replayed.

"You can't see it from the high angle of this helicopter shot, but he fired at Brooke from his right hip while he was down but propping himself up from his right side, his body blocking the gun from the chopper's camera above. But in this close-up, you can see the gun smoke just before the train enters the picture. That's the shot that severed Brooke's femoral artery."

The president looked up at Bill, convinced. "I can pardon her."

"Sir, with all due respect, a pardon would just be an admission that she is, in fact, guilty, and all you'll be saying is that she can't be tried for her crimes."

"I see your point." He paused. "And what's this business in Hawaii? My chief of staff says she's on trial for murder?"

"And that, sir, is the blessing you and I should get down on our knees and thank God for."

That odd statement got a screwy look from the president. "Fill me in, Bill, and make it quick. I got a whole cabinet cooling their heels in the Map Room."

"Brooke didn't kill anybody, but the cop in her knew someone did! Even if the DA was only focused on her. It was Brooke digging in to find the real murderer of her student's father that allowed her to unravel the planes attack."

"How's that?"

"The person that she was accused of murdering ... Well, he wrote all the code that was used to hack the planes. He was killed by whoever launched this attack, probably to leave no loose ends. Brooke was circumstantially connected to the murder. No evidence, no murder weapon, just supposition. Her team, my old team, trying to give her a good legal defense on their own time, stumbled on the plot. They even saved the life of the victim's wife who was kidnapped to insure he'd keep writing their code, then abandoned and left to die when they killed her husband, the hacker."

"That's incredible, Bill."

"It will all be in the after-action report, sir. We're going to start putting it together right after this meeting."

"I can't wait to read it." For the second time Bill turned to go.

But the president asked, "Bill. Also, this Bridgestone that I read about last night. He's as grit as grit gets."

"You should have met his partner, Ross. I named my kid after them both."

CHAPTER 70

Diane Price wrangled a ticket to the reception for the prime minister of Barbados. Not the hardest ticket to get. With the exception of the necessary dignitaries from Department of State and other government parts, very few senators or congressmen had a reason to attend, except for Senator Paxton, who had a vacation home in the Bajan capital. So, he was the highest-ranking elected official there, giving the whole affair a bit more legitimacy than the George Washington High School prom.

Getting to Senator Paxton and getting him to be her source was a sure ticket to a week-long series on the wrongdoing of the previous administration. Diane's boss, Cheryl, had let it be known that getting the latest news from inside Paxton's investigative committee was the oxygen needed to keep Diane's story, and her career, alive.

"Ms. Price, what a surprise seeing you here."

"Senator." She extended her hand. She saw his momentary glance off to his left. And then, right on cue five seconds later, his chief of staff appeared and ushered him away to meet some dignitary or other. A sudden frigid chill reverberated under the flare of Diane's Valentino short crepe couture dress. *He doesn't want to talk to me. Surely he must know we're on the same side, wanting the same thing.*

"Politics is like shifting sand, Ms. Price."

She turned and was shocked to see President Pearson's chief of staff standing there.

"Mr. Walsh, are you here representing the president?"

"Yes, most definitely."

"And what would be the administration's interest in Barbados?" she said, splaying her hands to the room and the reception.

"I'm sorry, are you here on a press pass?"

There obviously wasn't one around her neck. "No, just socializing."

"Nice dress. A word of social advice then?"

"What's that?"

"The president has declassified portions of last year's attack and the government's response. Especially the part relating to then CinFen Director, Brooke Burrell-Morton."

"Why would he do that?"

"To take the shackles off Ms. Burrell. Allow her 'her day in court,' so to speak. Which will be Monday, by the way, when she appears as Paxton's opening witness."

Diane's mind raced.

"Ms. Price, the playing field is now level. Good luck, fight clean. Oh, and try to snag a bacon-wrapped date from a passing tray. They put an almond inside, salty, sweet and crunchy. Very good." With that, he marched right to the door.

Through the window of the Georgetown Brownstone, she watched him get into an SUV with red and blue lights flashing and pull away.

Diane immediately realized that he had come to this event to deliver a message directly to her—directly from the president. The new president that had no love lost for the old one. The one she thought was on the same side as her. And yet, by him declassifying top secret documents, he was essentially taking away her scoop, sending it out to every news organization and blogger in the known universe. It instantly made Diane's blockbuster story "old news."

The woman from the State Department who had checked Diane in at the table near the front door came through the crowd. "I'm sorry, Ms. Price is it?"

Diane was a little thrown. She had registered as Diane Masters to not be corralled into the press pool. She knew what was coming next. "I'm afraid there's been an oversight. I mistook you for a Diane Masters, who is on our guest list. As a class-four security event, we have to follow the rules of entry. Please come with me."

"Are you throwing me out?"

"Actually, I'm allowing you to leave before the Diplomatic Security Service has a minute to ask you far too many questions. I'm sure you'd agree."

"I'll need to get my wrap."

"It's waiting for you at the door. Thank you for coming, and please excuse our oversight."

She took one last look into the main room. She saw Paxton. Their eyes met. His were cold, indifferent, unresponsive, as if he was looking right through her. He had been reached by the administration, or ambushed by the declassification. Either way, he didn't need her anymore. He was, in the end, a feral politician.

CHAPTER 71

NORMALLY ONE court reporter from the local paper would attend a routine hearing, but only if it were interesting and somehow decisive to a case before the court. And only then if their editor also deemed it newsworthy.

Somehow the rapidly scheduled evidentiary hearing on the State of Hawaii versus Burrell-Morton leaked, so the normally lonely court reporter doing yeoman's duty was practically shut out of the entire building as satellite trucks, news vans and reporters from all over the world crammed onto Alakea Street across from the Honolulu Criminal Court House.

Sherriff deputies approached Brooke, Mush and James as they were heading for the building entrance through the media mob out front.

"Would you follow us please?"

They led them towards the back entrance, prisoner door, secluded from the public. They entered the courtroom from the rear.

The bailiff was having a hard time keeping the pandemonium in the court room to a loud roar.

"All rise." He tried again: "All rise!" Then he put two fingers in his mouth and let out an ear-shattering whistle so loud cabs in Manhattan pulled over. "All rise."

The room settled and the judge entered. He nodded to the court clerk.

"Hearing to determine continuance, docket number 101901, State versus Burrell-Morton. Counselors approach the bench."

James and the ADA approached.

"Okay, let's make this short and sweet. Does the state object to the defendant's motion to dismiss charges?"

"No objection, Your Honor."

"So be it." She banged the gavel. "Step back, please." The judge collected her thoughts and then announced, for the purposes of the court reporter, "In the matter of the State of Hawaii versus Burrell-Morton, a motion for dismissal of any and all charges in this case has been granted and, thus having been agreed to by both parties, I hereby so order that the docket number 101901 is hereby closed by mutual agreement of both parties and in the interest of justice. The state having failed to provide any evidence of any crime, the defendant is now free to go, without guilt, prejudice or stigma. That being the only matter before the court this morning, the court is now adjourned." She banged the gavel, got up and walked off to her chambers.

"That's it?" Brooke said to James.

"Done. You're no longer a suspect, defendant or under house arrest."

"James, thank you. You were great," Brooke said.

James looked at her. "Brooke, it helps when your client has more legal experience than her lawyer."

"Honey, let's catch a plane," Mush said.

The reporters in the room rushed the defendant's table as court officers linked arms to fend off the hoard. A cacophony of questions pelted Brooke. All of them about the shooting on the bridge. James took the lead, as Mush and Brooke were escorted out the side door that led to the judge's chamber by sheriff deputies.

"I will only answer questions about this case," Chu said.

They all quieted down. Everyone looked at each other. No one had a question about this case.

"Okay, then. Aloha, and have a good day." James closed his briefcase and waded through the throng.

f

Brooke caught on first that the deputies weren't taking them the same way as they came in. They made a left when the rear door was straight ahead. "Hey, where are you taking us?"

"Just follow us, ma'am." Brooke hated being called ma'am, but her senses were starting to tingle. She looked at Mush. He noticed they were taking a detour too. She was just about to confront the armed deputies. Both had their service weapons. The one on her right had his hold-down snap strap open. That would be the one to grab. She mentally went through what would go down. She would grab the gun, push Mush away and hold the gun on the other guard.

They walked and made another turn down a hallway with no exit. *This is it!* she thought.

She could be wrong, but that was better than being dead.

She went to reach for the dangling gun ... when Russell popped out of a doorway.

"Thanks, fellas"

"No problem, Detective," one of the guards said as they stepped aside.

"Russell? What's going on?" Brooke said, her heart returning to a normal BPM.

"I figured you needed this, and I owed it to you." He stepped aside. Standing by the window of the lawyer's prep room was Jenny's mom.

Brooke put a light hand on Russell's arm and mouthed the words, "Thank you." She took a deep breath and entered the room. She stood a few feet away from the woman who had put on some much-needed weight and got her color back. Brooke was happy to see she had gotten her hair done. There was no trace of the emaciated, near-death, bedraggled body they'd rescued from that dank, awful-smelling bunker.

"Mrs. Kupalli, I'm so sorry for all you've been through."

"No, Mrs. Burrell-Morton, it is I who owe you an apology, and a debt I can never repay for saving my life."

"Call me Brooke, but how do you know ...?"

"Detective Russell told me everything this morning. He brought me here to say what I needed to say to you."

"There's no need ..." Brooke said.

"Please, this will be hard enough for me to get through ..."

Brooke smiled and came closer to her.

The woman had tears in her eyes and her speech faltered. "Mrs. ... um, Brooke, I said and held some very awful things about you in my heart. I never connected my kidnapping with my husband. They never told me why I was in that awful place. They never said a word to me."

She started to shake. Brooke cautiously placed her hand on the woman's forearm. "There's no need to bring up bad memories, Mrs. Kupalli."

She sniffled her nose into an already drenched tissue crumpled in her shaking hand. "No, I can do this. You saved my life. Everyone literally left me for dead, and you didn't. And I also understand now that you were looking out for my Jenny when you got involved in all this. I owe you my life and my family."

"You don't owe me anything. Just overcome this terrible wrong that's been done to you and work on healing for both you and Jenny."

"Oh, where is she? She left for practice this morning. I tried to call her, but I guess no cellphones on the field."

"Yeah, sorry about that. It's my rules. I try to be a good example to the students of disconnecting from the phone, otherwise they'd be on them all day."

"I guess that's a good thing." She looked up at Brooke. "God bless you."

"And may God bless you."

They hugged.

Russell came back in the room. "Brooke, your husband says you have a plane to catch."

Brooke looked at Mrs. Kupalli. "When I get back, what do you say we all have dinner at our place?"

She dabbed her eyes. "Yes, that would be nice. Jenny really loved you before all this. Wait till I tell her. Practice ended an hour ago."

"Well then she's back in class."

"Oh, I wish I could get her on the phone right now to say hello."

"No rush, there'll be time."

"Yes, thanks to you, we now have time. All the time in the world."

Brooke wrapped her hand over the woman's hand and gently squeezed it. "I see where Jenny gets her strength, and that tells me you are both going to be okay."

"Yes. Yes, we will. Have a safe flight."

With that, Detective Russell walked Brooke and Mush to the rear entrance where the admiral's car was waiting. Before they got in, he turned to Brooke and held up a religious medal. "My wife gave one of these to my daughter. It's Gerard, the patron saint of pregnant women. She says he protects the unborn. Anyway, I figured you should have one, too."

Brooke smiled, "Oh, thank you, that's very sweet. And thank your wife, it's a lovely gift." She leaned in and planted a kiss on his cheek.

"Safe travels." He said.

Mush shook his hand as their car pulled up.

f

Hamad's men watched from across the way as the dark SUV pulled up. It was time.

f

Already packed, and having a change of travel clothes in their carry-ons, they headed right to the airport. Tonight, they'd check into the Washington Marriot, and tomorrow night dinner at the White House.

In the car, Brook put the chain of the medal over her head and snuggled up against Mush's shoulder. A deep exhale let out all the tension and brought her body into the realization that the trial ordeal was finally over. Making peace with Mrs. Kupalli settled in like warm honey in her soul.

Many police cars, lights flashing and sirens blaring, were passing their car as they made their way to the airport. At one point Mush turned as five shot past and watched them through the rear window. He turned to his driver. "Barnes, any idea what's going on?"

"I don't know but it must be something big"

f

At the Hawaiian Hilton the reports of shots fired came in four minutes before the first arriving units. Patrol officers were cordoning off the area and the dark SUV with the bullet holes in it.

A radio reporter ran out of his car, microphone and transmitter in his hand. He knew the sergeant. "Hey, Malo, what's going on?"

"Don't know, Kyle. We got people down. And there's a movie star in there. I heard she was being held."

"How many injured?"

"I have no idea. No information is available at this time as to casualties. Look, Kyle, can you get over there behind the police line."

"Sure, Malo." As he walked away, he phoned his editor. "Shots fired at Hilton. Get me on the air right now. I'm here."

Kyle threw the switch to transmit and put the earwig in. "Hello, Jim, are you receiving me?"

"Yes, you go live in five seconds," then Jim cut in the return audio minus Kyle. Kyle heard the anchor man throw it to him. "Once again, if you're just joining us, a band of armed men have taken over the Hawaiian Hilton. Here now is reporter Kyle Parker."

"Bob, it's just all-out pandemonium here at the Hilton. Practically every police car on the island is here or on the way. It all started some fifteen minutes ago when ... Hold on, I'm just getting something now." Kyle held the mic away from the conversation so as not to spook the sergeant. "Yes, thank you ... I just received word that two security men accompanying the actress Susan Brock were shot as they were escorting Ms. Brock to her vehicle. I'm overhearing that the gunmen are holed up in the restaurant in the hotel's lobby and are demanding the release of the prisoners from Guantanamo Bay. Although not confirmed by the authorities as yet, this certainly seems like a terrorist event."

Just then the anchor from the studio cut in. "The only two people confirmed shot are Ms. Brock's security men, but, Bob, I expect that number will change very soon."

f

Brooke was resting her head on Mush's shoulder and telling herself she could hold out a little longer—being pregnant made her a constant bathroom visitor—when her cell phone rang. She looked down. It was Gladys from the school, no doubt calling to congratulate her on the dismissal.

"I should take this." She righted herself in the back seat. "Gladys, how nice of you ..."

Mush saw her body stiffen. He leaned in with a questioning look on his face.

Brooke's expression went to immediate stone. Her whole demeanor hardened. "Yes. I understand. I'll be there. No, I won't. I'm coming. There's no need for any violence." A sharp noise emanated from the phone as she winced and pulled it from her ear.

"What is it, Brooke?" Mush said, concern coursing through his voice.

Brooke's eyes darted around. She breathed in deeply. "Mush, I want you to remain calm." She leaned forward, her hand on the back of the front seat. "Driver, please head to the road to the Haiku Stairs. I need to get there as fast as I can."

"Brooke ..."

"Mush, that was Gladys, my friend from the high school. She and some of the girls from the soccer team are being held hostage. The man on the phone, he wants to trade them for me."

"No fucking way, Brooke. Call the police."

"No, they have video surveillance and say they're monitoring the police frequencies."

"I'm not letting you ..."

"Mush, there's no other way."

"Have Kronos trace the cell," Mush offered.

"The last thing they did was crush the phone. Almost blew out my ear."

"Honey, I can't let you do this."

She picked up her phone, dialed. "Give me a moment to think."

As she waited for the person to pick up, she had a chill imagining the horror those poor girls and Gladys were going through. *Oh my God, was Jenny there too? Is that why her mom couldn't reach her?* were her thoughts as she spoke into the phone. "Bridge, I need you."

f

One mile out from the Haiku Stairs, Bridge rolled up with an unexpected passenger.

"Kronos, what are you doing here?" Brooke said.

"Fuck these guys," he said as he unloaded a scoped rifle from the back of the car. He handed Bridgestone the M24 Remington sniper rifle. He grabbed the spotting scope.

Bridge handed Brooke an earbud. "Here. It's blue tooth, so stay within a few hundred feet. Give us a three-minute head start to get into position." He flicked her blonde hair down over her shoulder to hide the earpiece.

Kronos showed her his phone. "According to Google Earth there's one structure, an abandoned home with a walled off garden, where they told you to go."

"The cops may not be coming, Brooke. There's a hostage situation on the other side of the island."

"Hey, guys. What about me?" Mush said.

Kronos opened the trunk. He pulled out a controller and a buzzing noise started. A drone rose out of the open trunk. "Can you fly this sucker?"

"I drove a nuke sub. Can't be harder than that."

"Good, stick with us. Keep your eye on the screen and tell us what you see."

Kronos started in with the specs. "Over five hundred feet and you're really quiet. The camera is 4K and has zoom, tilt and pan, so ..."

"Enough, Vincent. Let's move out," Bridge said as he handed Brooke a vest. "Here, this is the perfect accessory for your Channel suit."

It was JC Penny, but the point was made. She opened her suit jacket, donned the vest and buttoned up the high neck collar. It smushed her already sore breasts, but she knew it would hurt less than a slug.

Mush hugged her. "You don't have to do this."

"Yes, I do. Hey, I love you. And ..."

"I love you more. And we're both going to spoil our kid."

They kissed a long, desperate kiss. Then he held her by the shoulders. "Don't do anything stupid."

He gave her one last kiss, turned and hustled off to catch up to the others. She went over to the car and swapped her heels for the sneakers in the carry-on bag.

The driver walked over. "What's going on? What's with the guns? Who are those guys?"

She looked at her watch. "In exactly ten minutes, call the cops. Tell them there's a hostage situation in an abandoned house, one mile down this road. Silent approach. The bad guys are monitoring the tac frequencies. Got that?"

"Silent approach, bad guys are monitoring the track frequencies. Got it."

"No not track, tac, as in, tactical frequencies. The cops need to switch to encrypted."

"Tack frequencies. Encrypted only. Got it. But ..."

"No buts. Call them in ten minutes. Gotta go."

Something Brooke never thought of was how being pregnant was a pain in the ass on a mission. Before she went into battle, she found a spot in the bushes a little further down the road and quickly relieved herself. *Thank God I wore the dress suit*, she thought.

Brooke had executed "little" or "no prep" ops before. They relied mostly on the experience and situational awareness of the individual operators as to how smoothly, or otherwise, the mission went. There was no one better to spearhead this than Bridgestone. Kronos and her husband were no slouches, either.

Everything depended on how the bad guys played this. They seemed well planned so far. Remote location. Gladys. Police channel monitoring.

Brooke's training from the hostage-rescue courses she took at Quantico, when she joined the FBI, kicked in. Getting them talking was key. Proof of life was mandatory. She needed them to actually release the girls and Gladys before offering herself up for what was certainly her execution.

Her hand went to her stomach. "Kiddo, I wish I didn't have to take you with me. But somebody else's babies are in there, and, somehow, it's because of me. If we don't meet in this life, I'll be there to nurse you in heaven, my little one."

She shook off the hormones that had brought a lump to her throat and a sinking sadness to her belly. She felt as if her very soul was being sucked out of her at the thought of losing her baby and herself. Brooke knew evolutionary biology was making her want to run into a cave and wait a few months to deliver her baby. She stiffened her resolve and picked up her pace. She adjusted the Glock snugged into the waistband in the small of her back. She tucked the hem of the jacket behind the butt of the gun, so she could get to it quickly.

As she approached the structure, she yanked the medal from under her vest, rolled her fingers over it as it dangled over her suit jacket from her neck, "Gerard, if you're not too busy..."

Her impromptu plea was interrupted by Bridge's voice in the ear bud. "Brooke, if you can hear me, scratch your head."

Bridge had her in his sniper scope. She looked up at a small silent dot in the sky. It was the drone that Mush was piloting. She raised her arm nonchalantly and scratched her head.

"The drone shows us the girls are outside behind a garden wall of sorts on the side of the building. We count three bad guys. No idea if there are any in the building. They are heavy, two with automatic rifles, the other has a handgun," Bridge reported to her. "How are you going to play this, Brooke?"

She kept her lips stiff and talked like a ventriloquist so as not to let on she was in contact with anybody, in case the bad guys were scoping her. "Carefully ..."

At two hundred yards away from the house, she sought cover behind a rock. She spotted the next three places of cover she could advance to. She looked hard for any signs of someone pointing a weapon at her. "Can you see in the windows of the building, Bridge?"

"No one in the window I can see."

"Anyone pointing a gun at me?"

"Not so far. I don't think they see you yet."

"Let me know. I'm going to move in closer."

"I gotcha back."

As she scrambled to the next cover, she thought that "I gotcha back" from Bridge was the best guarantee you could hope for in a situation like this. He was the best of the best, and maybe God put him there to be her "other" Guardian Angel ... *With an M24 air-cooled, recoilless rifle.*

From her second cover about fifty yards out, she took a deep breath. "I'm going to try to get them talking."

"Hey. I'm here!" she yelled.

Bridge saw them all react on the drone's monitor screen that Mush was holding. The girls and a woman were all tied together by their hands with what looked like one rope. "You got their attention," he told Brooke over her earbud.

Brooke waited for them to call out. And waited. She knew they were waiting to see if there was any police chatter from their scanner. She looked at her watch. Five minutes till the driver called in the cavalry.

Then one of them shouted out, “Come slowly to here. Approach building.”

“So you can shoot me? I’m not stupid. Send out the hostages. I need to see that they’re alive and well. Then I’ll walk into the gate.”

“Hold it, Brooke,” Bridge said. “I got one in the bushes off to your right. He’s ready to ambush you.”

“Roger, that.”

Bridge ripped of his shirt. Pulled a water bottle out of his bag. He wrapped the shirt around the rifle barrel and opened the plastic water bottle and slid it over the barrel. He pointed to Kronos in the direction of the lone man on the side of the road twenty yards ahead of Brooke. Kronos read off the distance and the wind speed.

f

The man positioned in the bushes took a bead on the woman as she approached, placing the crosshairs of his scope on the shiny piece of metal hanging over her heart. A glint of sunlight off of it temporarily caused him to blink.

f

Bridge adjusted his scope and fired one round. The shirt and the “Ghetto” silencer did much to stifle the rifle’s report. It wasn’t totally suppressed but would have to do. The guy’s chest exploded. He went down.

Brooke heard a mild thud followed a split second later by a sonic snap of the bullet off to her right. There was a slight groan.

Bridge watched the drone screen. The bad guys didn’t react. The sound hadn’t made it that far. “One down.” He grabbed another water bottle.

Brooke called out to the captors, “I’m not coming out until the girls and Gladys are a safe distance from you.”

Hamad yelled over the wall, "We will kill them if you don't come out!"

"Then you'll kill them anyway! So why should I play?"

There was hesitation.

"Bridge, what are they doing?"

"They are having a discussion, it looks like."

"I'm going to up the stakes. Cover me. Let me know if any of those bastards takes a bead on me."

"Roger that."

Brooke took a deep breath and sprinted to a burnt-out car fifty feet from the structure. She slid in, scraped her knee and tore her panty hose.

"They caught the last ten feet of your run. They got their guns trained on your location."

"How many girls?"

"Five and the woman. I'm going to reposition to higher ground to your left. Stall 'em."

Brooke looked left and saw a rise in the terrain. From there Bridge could get off a limited shot into the compound. "Hey, genius! Send out the girls. Or I'm out of here."

"We will kill them unless you come out." From her closer vantage point Brooke could hear the girls whimper at the threat to their lives.

"Hey, girls! It's me, coach! Don't worry. These guys couldn't beat Maui school district one. It will all be over soon."

"Quiet. You may not speak to the girls," Hamad said.

"You want me, send them out. Send them all out."

"You are in no position to make demands; we make the demands."

"Look, genius, you're not giving me any hope that you'll keep up your end of the bargain, so you can go to hell. By the way, your man in the bushes fell asleep. I can hear him snoring from here."

As Mush and Bridge and Kronos scuttled through the bramble to reach their higher position, Mush kept one eye on the drone screen. He saw the guys react. The leader lifted his radio and talked into it.

Mush nudged Bridge to take a look. He whispered over the phone because they were now closer. "Brooke, looks like they're sending out a guy to check on their man."

"Do you have a shot?"

"I will."

She called out to the captors, "Why are you doing this, genius? You'll never get away with this. They must be looking for the girls by now."

"That is not your concern. You come out and they live."

"Bullshit! You're not giving me any reason to believe you."

This time Brooke heard the pop of the water bottle and the bullet crack over her head. She heard the squishy impact on the man they sent to check on the other. It sounded like a head shot.

"That's two down, two to go," Bridge said.

"And anyone who's in the building," Brooke added.

She covered her earpiece so as not to yell in Bridge's ear over the bluetooth. "Look, genius, what's your name?"

"Does not matter. You have one minute, or we start killing your precious girls."

"Bridge?" she whispered, "I think he means it."

"I got one in my sights, but I can't see the one that's close in. He's blocked by the edge of the house's roof. Oh, and Brooke, I'm out of suppression. This next one's going to be loud."

Brooke pulled the gun from her back. She hazarded a look over the hood of the wreck she was using as cover. She could see one of them, the close in one, to her right, the one that Bridge couldn't see. The man was aiming his rifle at her.

"Bridge, I can see the one you can't see. We got one shot at this."

"On your count."

"Okay." She took a deep breath and gently patted her stomach.

She raised her voice. "Okay, to show good faith, I'm coming out. I'm coming out." She clasped her hands behind her head and got up and walked towards the structure.

Bridge's shot rang out. She could see a plume of pink fly up over the five-foot wall. Hamad, the one that was left, opened up. She dropped down as bullets spit by her. She brought the Glock around from behind her head and fired at the face of the man firing back at her. She was emptying her magazine and had no reloads. His cover was too good. His head too low. Suddenly, out of nowhere, the drone came down, aimed at his head. He looked up and raised his gun to fire at the buzzing machine just as Brooke's last bullet caught him under the chin. Hamad's hand spasmed and the gun let out a burst as he flew back, dead.

Brooke rolled over, grabbing at her chest. Mush, Kronos, and Bridge ran down from the rise off to the right. Mush ran right to Brooke. Bridge kicked in the door of the small house. Kronos ran through the archway of the walled off garden to check on the girls.

"Brooke. Brooke, are you okay," Mush said as he slid to a stop on his knees right beside her.

"No ..." she said with a groaning strain. "I caught one in the chest going down."

"Where?" He started to search her. He opened her jacket. Saw the vest. And the slug embedded in it.

"Hurts like a bitch," Brooke said. "Help me sit up. Your little drone stunt saved my life."

Bridge helped Kronos lead the girls out of the garden and cut their ropes. Gladys was a nervous wreck. The girls were whimpering.

From the ground, being propped up by Mush and holding her ribs, Brooke said, "It's okay. It's okay. We're all safe now. I know it was horrible, but it's all over." She winced; a rib was broken. "Come, come here girls, Gladys, Jenny, Susan, all of you. It's over."

Police cars silently rolled up. Bridge and Kronos put down their weapons and put their hands up. The cops ran to them.

Bridgestone said in a calm, professional, cool voice, "Officers, four bad guys down. None of the hostages hurt or injured, but our lady there needs medical attention." He jutted his chin towards Brooke who was in Mush's arms, with the girls and Gladys surrounding them.

"Who are you?" the HPD sergeant said.

"That's classified, sir."

f

The police found a note which they handed over to the FBI, who took jurisdiction as soon as the nationality of the dead kidnappers was established. It explained that Brooke, as the public face of the counterattack that foiled the assault on NYC twelve months earlier, was their target.

The note was written in bad English but said that the Brotherhood of Jihad had successfully exacted retribution for the killing of those heroes who lost their lives in the glorious struggle against the Great Satan last year. It went on to say that this action was proof that The Cause was strong, and its soldiers could attack America at will and as it wished.

"Pbbbbt," was the fart sound Brooke made when they read her that statement.

CHAPTER 72

Hospital Pulau Pinang was a busy place. Nasser had to wait in line, like a commoner. But it was necessary. He needed not to be noticed while he was here.

In very bad English he was asked, "Who here are you to see?"

"Mr. Mastieff."

The desk person looked down a list of patients. "Room 715."

"Would that be a private room?"

"No, two."

"Is his son in the bed next to him?" Nasser randomly asked.

"No, other bed empty."

"Thank you."

Nasser found Mastieff in heavy traction. It appeared his legs were broken. His right shoulder was at an odd angle with a metal rod propping it up. His jaw was wired. His head seemed immobilized. Nasser shut the door behind him and locked it. As he approached, Mastieff's eyes found him. Through a wired jaw he said, "We failed."

You failed, Nasser thought. "What happened to you?"

"I was leaving when the building exploded."

"Yes, the Americans sent a cruise missile. They also managed to save all the planes. I checked the account. The Bitcoin never arrived."

"We were betrayed!" His anger forced his face to contort and aggravate his fractured jaw.

"Most certainly," Nasser said as he pulled out a syringe from his pocket. He stuck it into the PICC line on the IV drip. The potassium chloride flowed into the tubing and directly into Mastieff.

"What are you doing?"

"Tidying up loose ends, as you would say."

"No! Why?" his voice rose to a gurgling rasp, as he couldn't move his jaw.

"Simple. As soon as you were well, you would blame me, so I am simply eliminating the need to look over my shoulder for the rest of my life. Which, thanks to your incompetence, will be spent as a commoner, never to return to my kingdom again."

Mastieff started to convulse. Nasser pulled out the plug to the heart monitor just before it started acting wildly, and, without emotion, watched him die. He put his two fingers on Mastieff's neck to make sure there was no pulse and that he had expired.

He wiped down everything he had touched and left.

f

The FBI noted in its report that the critically injured driver who was caught up in the explosion had died. Officially, it was due to cardiac arrest. It listed the man as Mustafa Mastieff.

Kronos had set up a search algorithm for any web traffic concerning the words Mastieff and Mastiff, but excluding any reference to words like breed, pedigree etc. He did leave in Big Dog. There were a few hits on gmails that had things like, "Wow, that's a big dog." Or "Who walks who with a big dog like that?" But the FBI report that mentioned Mastiff went right to the top of his relevancy score.

He found the URL for Lass Vega's Tavern in Samoa and sent the FBI picture of the deceased to Francesca Vega's email listed on her site.

"That's dog!" was the positive response that told Brooke and everyone else that this was indeed over! Mush's missile had nailed the mastermind as he was fleeing.

f

Reluctantly, Diane Price accepted an assignment as the host of a local New York City Sunday morning, 6 a.m., public affairs program called "Newsmaker Sunday." Doing such in-depth interviews of people like: the assistant deputy commissioner of sanitation on this year's efforts on snow removal. It was the purgatory her boss, Cheryl Addison, sentenced her to, so she could still keep a paycheck.

f

Susan Brock spent three hours as a captive of the same terrorist team that attempted to kill Brooke. Their selection of the hotel's restaurant to hold the hostage in was flawed, due to the fact that it was originally built to be a casino. Large, two-way-mirrored "pit boss" perches surrounded the entire ceiling. SWAT Team sharpshooters simply ended the drama, and the gunmen's lives, with precision accuracy from above. The seven people who were shot in the diversion all recovered, including Brock's two security men.

She and her Lieutenant Kensington took a few days and got lost in the rainforest of Kuai.

CHAPTER 73

WITH LIFE finally settling down to normal, Brooke and Mush cocooned themselves into each other. He went to work every day, and she to her reinstated job as the coach. They nested at night, content to be each other's best friend, lover and spooning partner in bed, without the benefit of an international crisis or people shooting at them.

Their one exception to their nestled lifestyle was Friday. That was their "date night." Something they religiously made time for every week but had let lapse during the recent ordeal. There was a wonderful Polynesian place, Mama's. Mama was a big, local island woman, who had a belly laugh and presence that filled the restaurant. She was as much a reason to come to her tiki-torch-lit, grass-shack, beach-front restaurant as the incredible food.

Having not seen the "admiral and the coach" for a while, she came over and welcomed them both back. "Where you two been?"

"We were busy but couldn't wait to get back here," Mush said.

She looked down at Brooke. "I can see the kind of busy you been!" she said with a big toothy smile. "How far along are ya, child?"

"Almost five months."

"Only five?"

"Yes. Why did you say it like that?" Brooke said.

"'Cause I'm thinking, you got yourself twins there."

Brooke and Mush looked at each other...

"Twins?"

f

POSTSCRIPT:

My literary tag line is "It's only fiction 'til it happens!" Here now, at the end of my tale you may ask, "Can this really happen?" Let me assure you that there are folks, much smarter than I, (a very large constituency) who apply their true genius to prevent these kinds of things from interrupting our lives. In this book, I took away from them the redundant safeguards that would have killed the story in the opening graph. Thanks for coming along on this journey and allowing me the selective suspension of reality.

ABOUT THE AUTHOR:

Tom Avitabile is a creative consultant, writer, director and producer. He has a background in high-tech, Washington D.C., and the media. He is also a "book coach" to authors who occasionally need their work tuned-up. You can find him hitting the skins and playing jazz most weekends in various spots in and around the New York area.

ACKNOWLEDGMENTS

Authoring a novel is a solitary endeavor in the main, but at some point, I need to check my facts, structure, and sanity. Enter the valiant individuals who volunteer their time and their brain power to my manuscript. They are an author's blessings and without them, my work would not be as accurate or as rich. Any errors or maligning of reality are solely mine, as in some places, I didn't let their facts get in the way of my story.

George Cannistraro who lends his excellent story sense to first and second draft nonsensical errors.

Colonel Michael T. Miklos, US Army Retired, my "go to" guy for all things military, patriotic and *esprit de corps*.

Charles "Chuck" Parkin, whose insights into how things work, in the Navy and in life, made my book that much better.

Hon. John J. Kelly, a very busy man who nonetheless was generous with his time as he guided me through legal procedures and proper court decorum.

Chris Zizzo, a constant source of intellect wrapped in humor. A casual conversation with Chris delivers more education than a college lecture, without the professorial fog.

Lisa Davis Engel, who was there for me throughout my protagonist's pregnancy and a mid-wife to the emotional arc of this story.

Lou Aronica, my publisher who does the truly hard work, behind the scenes, that result in you being able to read this book. Lou is a literary impresario who nurtures and compels authors to their best performances.

Finally, you, the reader, because without you, I am writing to myself. To those who have read my previous work, I hope this book keeps you in the club. If you are new, welcome, and I hope you'll read more of my work.

—Tom Avitabile
Tom@auhtor.nyc